"*If you read it you must stop where the Nigger
Jim is stolen from the boys. That is the real end.*"

The true adventures of Huckleberry Finn

as told by JOHN SEELYE

A CLARION BOOK

Published by Simon and Schuster

A Clarion Book
Published by Simon and Schuster
Rockefeller Center, 630 Fifth Avenue
New York, New York 10020

First Clarion paperback printing 1971
SBN 671-20951-5 Clarion paperback edition
Manufactured in the United States of America

INTRODUCTION
"De ole true Huck"

S ome years ago, it don't matter how many, Mr
Mark Twain took down some adventures of
mine and put them in a book called *Huckleberry Finn* — which is my name. When the book come
out I read through it and I seen right away that he
didn't tell it the way it was. Most of the time he told
the truth, but he told a number of stretchers too, and
some of them was really whoppers. Well, that ain't
nothing. I never seen anybody but lied one time or
another. But I was curious why he done it that way,
and I asked him. He told me it was a book for children, and some of the things I done and said warn't
fit for boys and girls my age to read about. Well, I
couldn't argue with that, so I didn't say nothing more
about it. He made a pile of money with that book, so
I guess he knowed his business, which was children.
They liked it fine.

But the grownups give him trouble from the start.
When the book first come out the liberians didn't
like it because it was trashy, and they hadn't but just

got used to it being trash when somebody found out there was considerable "niggers" in it, which was organized by then. Well, the liberians didn't want no trouble, so they took it off the shelves again. And the crickits was bothered by the book too. At first they agreed with the liberians that the book was trash, but about the time the liberians had got used to the trashiness, the crickits decided the book warn't trashy enough, and then when the liberians got in a sweat about the word "nigger," the crickits come out and said there warn't anything wrong with that word, that it was just the sort of word a stupid, no-account, white-trash lunkhead would use—meaning me, I suppose, not Mr Mark Twain. They said it suited the book's style. Well, the liberians and the crickits ain't spoke to each other since.

There was a crickit named Mr Van Wyck Brooks who was particular hard on Mark Twain. He said that Mark Twain was the victim of women, mostly his mother and his wife, and his friend, Mr William Dean Howells, who had crossed out all the rough words in his books—including mine. He thought it was too bad that Mark Twain was brung up where he was, in Hannibal, Missouri, which was just a ramshackly river town, and he thought it was even worse that he had got married and went to Hartford, Connecticut, where he got mixed up with the quality, mostly preachers and such. He said if it warn't for Christianity, women, and Hartford, Connecticut, Mr Mark Twain might a come to something.

Well, Mr Bernard DeVoto put Mr Brooks straight on that score. He showed where Hannibal warn't at fault at all, nor religion, nor women, nor even Hartford. He said that Mark Twain *asked* to have all them rough words cut out, and that it was his own doing, and nobody else's. He said it was because he wanted to sell his books.

Mr Van Wyck Brooks, now, even though he said some ornery things about Mark Twain, he kinder liked my book. He said it was the only *honest* thing Mark Twain ever wrote. But Mr DeVoto come down pretty damn hard on it. It warn't that he didn't enjoy it, because he did—some parts of it, anyway—but he couldn't help pointing out where Mark Twain went wrong. He could see all the little lies and the short cuts and the foolishness that was in it, and he wrote considerable about them in two books of his own. He was especially hard on the ending Mark Twain had thought up, and said it actually give him a *chill*.

It warn't that Mr DeVoto didn't like Mark Twain, because he did. He even called him "Mark" most of the time. But he could see where he had his faults, and he didn't hang back none in telling about them. Like *sex*, which Mark Twain couldn't ever bring himself to write about. Mr DeVoto said it was silly having a fourteen-year-old boy like me not thinking about sex *some* of the time. He didn't say what kind of sex. He left that up to Mr Leslie Fiedler.

Mr DeVoto was tolerable lengthy, but he didn't settle the matter. The next thing you know Mr T.S. Eliot and Mr Lionel Trilling come right out and said they *admired* the book. Well, that was foolish enough, but then they went on to say that the ending seemed all right to them, and that was suicide. Mr Eliot let on that Tom Sawyer's pranks and foolishness was on the tiresome side, and Mr Trilling admitted that the ending warn't exactly up to the rest of the story, but they didn't stop there, and that's how the trouble started. Mr Eliot allowed that *he* didn't know of any ending that was better than Mark Twain's ending, and Mr Trilling said it was fit that I should finish up where I started out, only a thousand miles south. Which was interesting, but a trifle tough.

Well, there was this crickit named Mr Henry Seidel Canby, and he got hopping mad. He said that there warn't no ending *worse* than that ending, and that Mark Twain ought to be shot for writing it, but he had died anyway, so nobody took him up on it. Then along comes Mr Leo Marx, and give both Mr Eliot and Mr Trilling hell. 'Cording to him, that ending warn't *moral*, and it was all because Mark Twain couldn't face up to his own story — by which he meant mine. He said that Mark Twain couldn't measure up to the nat'ral ending his book deserved, that he just plain lost his nerve and had to cheat by tacking on a faint-hearted, immoral ending.

Mr Marx said that Mr Eliot and Mr Trilling warn't no better than Mark Twain. He said they was immoral too, and done nobody any favors by making out that ending was worth more than shucks. He said maybe Mr Eliot couldn't think of a better ending, but *he* knowed of one, and though he warn't up to messing around with Mark Twain's ending, because that warn't very moral either, he didn't think there would be any harm in *suggesting* how the story *should* a come out, which he done. He said the book ought to end so as to make something out of our escape down the Mississippi. He knowed that Jim couldn't ever a found his freedom down river in no moral way, so that was out, and whatever other ending you chose would just disappoint everybody. But he said that was the *point*, and the only honest way to end the book was to leave me and Jim no better off than we ever was, but still more or less trying to get clear. He claimed this ending was more moral than Mark Twain's, and it certainly would a been disappointing.

Well, Mr Eliot and Mr Trilling was squshed flat, and never did answer up to Mr Marx, but Mr James Cox did. He said that maybe the ending warn't as good as Mr Eliot and Mr Trilling claimed it was, but nuther was it as bad as Mr Marx had let on. He said it warn't perfect, but it was *explainable*, and that was the important thing. He explained all about death and reborning and nitiation, and how it was fit that Jim and I should a come back from the river, because the free and easy life on the raft was a lie. He said what was wrong with the ending was Tom Sawyer, because Tom's *style* was all wrong. That made Tom biling mad, but before he had a chance to say anything about Mr Cox's explanation, a whole passel of crickits jumped in with theirs, and there was a power of explaining and arguments and reasons the like of which I never heard before unless it was at the coroner's jury where the remainders had been pisoned, stabbed, shot, and hung, and they was trying to figure out what had killed him.

Right in the middle of all this powwow the door opened up, so to speak, and in walked Mr William Van O'Connor. He give all those other crickits a sad kind of smile, like he felt sorry for them poor ingoramuses, and then he let rip with a damn stunner. He didn't mess around with the ending. He said he was only interested in that ending because everybody seemed to think it was the only thing wrong with the book. He said he reckoned they was modest in their estimate, and then he got right to work, down in the innards of the book, and showed how sloppy it was put together. He would tear a part out and show how loose it had been wired in, and then he would reach down and tear out another part. It was bloody, but grand. The floor was simply covered with poor transitors, and claptrappy episodes, and meler-dramas, and minstrel shows, and sentimentering. Mr Van O'Connor said they warn't nothing, though. He said the worse thing about the book was its *inner-scents*, which was wickeder than the sloppy work by far. He said if you took out the innerscents, you'd have something, by which he meant the book's skin I reckon, because that's all there was left.

Nobody said a word for quite a spell, and it did seem there warn't nothing left *to* say, like at the end of a six-hour funeral, where the dear departed has begun to stink a bit and the windows is stuck shut because of the rain. But if there's one thing a crickit can't stand, it's stillness, and after a time they begun to creep around in the wreck, seeing if there warn't anything worth salvage. Mr Henry Nash Smith, f'rinstance, give it a try. He said the important thing was the way Mark Twain *told* my story, that's what saved it and made it great, never mind how it was hung together. And he said you couldn't take out the innerscents without making the rest go bust, that it was needle and thread for the whole pair of britches. He wouldn't a had it no other way, because it was the innerscents that made the wickedness all the worse. If quality and style counted, he said, it was just about the best damned innerscents on the market. Mr Smith allowed the ending was slack on innerscents, but he seemed to figure the book had stocked up a whole wood-yard of it by then, and could go the rest of the way on credit. Chapter XXXI all by itself had enough innerscents to keep a saint in good supply for a year, with enough left over for a hard-shell Baptist or two.

Well, that seemed to keep the other crickits satisfied for a while, but then along came Mr Richard Poirier, and after he got through, what Mr Van O'Connor done seemed like a Sunday-school picnic.

Mr Poirier said the trouble with the book was it warn't innerscent *enough*, and not just the ending nuther. He said if you chopped off the end you still had too much snake, that you had to keep chopping back and chopping back till you got to Chapter XV or thereabouts, which warn't much farther south than the neck. All that come after it just ain't the true Huck, he said, and some parts above it ain't all that long on innerscents either, having too much society or Tom Sawyer or something else bothersome and contrary in them. He let on that finding the bits worth saving was harder than getting a meal off an owl, and he give it up for a bad job all round. He said it was all because of Miss Jane Austin, a tolerable slim old maid which Mark Twain didn't much cotton to on account of she was always harping on marriage.

After that, it did look like the kindest thing you could do for the book was scrape it up and bury it. People still read *Huckleberry Finn*, but the ones that see what Mr O'Connor and Mr Poirier done to it say it just ain't the same afterwards. They can't forget the sight of all them damn parts laying around, and it makes them uneasy.

Well, it was kinder sad, in a way, with everything scattered about and people saying it was a good book they guessed, but it had terrible weaknesses, and nobody really able to enjoy it any more except children. So I thought to myself, if the book which Mr Mark Twain wrote warn't up to what these men wanted from a book, why not pick up the parts — the good ones — and put together one they *would* like? So I done it, the best I could anyways, only this time I told the story like it really happened, leaving in all the cuss words and the sex and the sadness.

Everything went just dandy till I got to the end. I nailed her down easy enough, but then it hit me that maybe the crickits wouldn't like this one any better than they liked Mr Mark Twain's. Well, after I had sweat over that thought considerable, it come to me that there ain't nothing a body can do except what is in him *to* do, and since there just warn't no other ending besides that one in me, I said what the hell, and let her ride. All the same, I didn't want no trouble from the crickits if I could help it, so I left in a spare page, where anybody that wants to can write in his own ending if he don't care for mine. I suppose the liberians ain't a-going to like this book much either, but maybe now the crickits will be a little less ornery.

And I want you to understand that this is a different book from the one Mr Mark Twain wrote. It may look like *The Adventures of Huckleberry Finn* at first sight, but that don't mean a thing. Most of the parts was good ones, and I could use them. But Mark Twain's book is for children and such, whilst this one here is for crickits. And now that they've got *their* book, maybe they'll leave the other one alone.

Contents

I

I discover Moses and the bulrushers

I suppose I ought to begin where Mr Mark Twain left off in *The Adventures of Tom Sawyer*. There's a bit of overlap, as you might say, but I ain't taking so much that there won't be plenty left of the other. It's like borrowing eggs. Pap says you don't never clean out a nest, only take your share of what there is, and nobody'll ever mind. So if I take an egg or two from Mr Mark Twain, I guess he won't miss them none.

Now the way that book winds up is this: Tom and me found the treasure that the robbers hid in the cave, and it made us filthy rich. We got damn near six thousand dollars apiece — all gold. It was an awful sight of money when it was piled up. There was considerable brass in there, but they was all black and easy to tell, so we just put them to one side, thinking maybe they'd come in handy some day. And Judge Thatcher he took the gold and put it out at interest, and it fetched us a dollar a day apiece all the year round — more than a body could tell what to do with. The Widow Douglas she took me for her son, and allowed she would sivilize me; but it was rough living in the house all the time, considering how dismal and decent the widow was in all her ways. She washed and combed hell out of me, and it warn't long before I couldn't stand it no more. I lit out for my old hogshead and got into my old rags again, and was free and satisfied. But Tom Sawyer he hunted me up and said he was going to start a band of robbers, and I couldn't join if I didn't go back to the widow and be respectable. So I went back.

The widow she cried over me and called me a poor lost lamb, and she called me a lot of other names, too, but she never meant no harm by it. She put me in them starchy new clothes again, and I couldn't do nothing but sweat like hell and feel all cramped up. Well, then, the same derned old thing started in again. The widow rung a bell for supper, and you had to come to time. When you got to the table you couldn't go right to eating, but you had to wait for the widow to tuck down her head and cuss a little over the victuals, though there warn't really anything the matter with them—that is, nothing only everything was cooked by itself. In a barrel of odds and ends it is different; things get mixed up, and the juice kinds of swaps around, and the things go better.

After supper she got out her book and learned me about Moses and the Bulrushers, and I was in a blue sweat to find out all about him; but by and by she let it out that Moses had been dead a considerable long time; so then I didn't care no more about him, because I don't take no stock in dead people.

Pretty soon I wanted to smoke, and asked the widow to let me. But she wouldn't. She said it was a mean practice and warn't clean, and I must try to not do it any more. That is just the way with some people. They get down on a thing when they don't know nothing about it. Here she was a-bothering about Moses, which was no kin to her, and no dang use to anybody, being gone, you see, yet finding a power of fault with me for doing a thing that had some good in it. And she took snuff, too; of course that was all right, because she done it herself.

Her sister, Miss Watson, a tolerable slim old maid, with goggles on, had just come to live with her, and took a set at me now with a spelling-book. She worked me middling hard for about an hour, and then the widow made her ease up. I couldn't a stood it much longer. Then for an hour it was deadly dull, and I was fidgety. Miss Watson would say, "Don't put your feet up like that, Huckleberry—set up straight"; and pretty soon she would say, "Don't gap and stretch like that, Huckleberry—why don't you try to behave?" Then she told me all about Hell and I said I wished I was there. She got mad then, but I didn't mean no harm. All I wanted was to go somewheres; all I wanted was a change. I warn't particular. She said it was wicked to say what I said; said she wouldn't say it for the whole world; *she* was going to live so as to go to Heaven. Well, I couldn't see no advantage in going where she was going, so I made up my mind I wouldn't try for it. But I never said so, because it would only make trouble, and wouldn't do no good.

Now she had got a start, and she went on and told me all about Heaven. She said all a body would have to do there was to go around all day with a harp and sing, forever and ever. So I didn't think much of it.

But I never said so. I asked her if she reckoned Tom
Sawyer would go there, and she said not by a considerable sight. I was glad about that, because I
wanted him and me to be together.

Miss Watson she kept pecking at me, and it got
dern tiresome and lonesome. By and by they fetched
the niggers in and had prayers, and then everybody
was off to bed. I went up to my room with a piece of
candle, and put it on the table. Then I set down in a
chair by the window and tried to think of something
cheerful, but it warn't no use. I felt so godamighty
lonesome I most wished I was dead. The stars were
shining, and the leaves rustled in the woods ever so
mournful; and I heard an owl, away off, who-whooing
about somebody that was going to die; and the wind
was trying to whisper something to me, and I couldn't
make out what it was, and so it made the cold shivers
run over me. Then away out in the woods I heard the
kind of a sound that a ghost makes when it wants to
tell about something that's on its mind and can't
make itself understood, and so can't rest easy in its
grave, and has to go about that way every night
grieving.

I got so damn downhearted and scared I did wish
I had some company. Pretty soon a spider went
crawling up my shoulder, and I flipped it off and it
lit in the candle; and before I could budge it was all
shriveled up. I didn't need anybody to tell me that
that was an awful bad sign and would fetch me some
bad luck, so I got scared as hell and most shook the
clothes off me. I got up and turned around in my
tracks three times and crossed by breast every time;
and then I tied up a little lock of my hair with a thread
to keep witches away. But I hadn't no confidence.

You do that when you've lost a horseshoe that you've found, instead of nailing it up over the door, but I hadn't ever heard anybody say it was any way to keep off bad luck when you'd killed a spider.

I couldn't help wondering what kind of bad luck was meant for me, and figured most likely it was to do with pap. He hadn't been seen for more than a year, and that was comfortable for me; I didn't want to see him no more. He used to always whale hell out of me when he was sober and could get his hands on me; though I used to take to the woods most of the time when he was around. Well, about this time he was found in the river drownded, about twelve mile above town, so people said. They judged it was him, anyway; said this drownded man was just his size, and was ragged, and had uncommon long hair, which was all like pap; but they couldn't make nothing out of the face, because it had been in the water so long it warn't much like a face at all, just a damn mess of pulp—what the fishes had left leastwise. They said he was floating on his back in the water. They took him and buried him on the bank. But I warn't comfortable long, because I happened to think of something. I knowed damned well that a drownded man don't float on his back, but on his face. So I knowed then that this warn't pap, but a woman dressed up in a man's clothes. So I was uncomfortable again. I judged the old man would turn up, by and by, and here was this dead spider nailing it down.

Well, there warn't no sleep for me after that, so I got out my pipe for a smoke, my danged hand a-shaking like fury. I set by the window so the room wouldn't smell none, and after a long time I heard the clock away off in the town go boom—boom—

boom — twelve licks; and all was still again — stiller than ever. It warn't a good stillness at all, it was a dead quiet, like what you can find deep in Tom Sawyer's cave, rotten heavy, and so weighed down you can't hardly breathe, like drownding. No damn good ever come of that kind of stillness, and I didn't go back to bed until I heard a rooster call, and knowed bad luck had passed me by *that* night.

Nitiation night, and the morning after

Well, Tom Sawyer he kept talking about how he was going to form up this pirate gang of his and ambuscade Spaniards and A-rabs, and got me and Joe Harper and Ben Rogers and the rest in a goddamn sweat for them ingots and julery, but all that ever come of it was a meeting we held in the cave one night. There warn't no reason why we couldn't a held it in the daytime, far as I could see, but no, Tom Sawyer said pirate meetings was held at night, and showed me where it was writ in a book, which made it true, I guess. So one night I snuck down the shed roof and met Tom and then we went down the hill to the old tanyard, where the rest of the gang was hid. We unhitched a skiff and pulled down the river nearly three miles, to the big scar on the hillside that showed where the secret entrance was, only now a path was wore up the hill by people that come to see where Tom and Becky Thatcher had got out. There was talk of boarding it up, same as at the other end, but the Judge said only a dern fool would crawl into a dark hole like that, and I guess he was right. It give me the fantods just thinking about it, and if Tom hadn't crept in first and lit a candle, I don't reckon any of us would have gone in there that night.

We went about two hundred yards on our hands and knees, and then the cave opened up. Tom poked about amongst the passages, and pretty soon ducked under a wall where you wouldn't a noticed that there was a hole. We went along a narrow place and got into a kind of room, all damp and sweaty and cold, and there we stopped. Tom says: "Now we'll start this band of robbers and call it Tom Sawyer's Gang, and anybody that doesn't want to swear a bloody oath to eternal secrecy had better leave now or forever hold his peace." Well, nobody was of a mind to crawl back out of that cave by himself, so we all stayed. The meeting lasted forever, it seemed, and was mostly swearing bloody oaths and getting nitiated into secrets Tom had thought up, which didn't amount to shucks, and we was all getting a trifle riled, not being able to see how all this was getting us one damn inch closer to them ingots and julery, when Tom brung out our weapons—swords and guns he called them.

But they was only pieces of wood nailed together, and Ben Rogers said so, and when Tom said they warn't, why we seen how it was going to be with them gold ingots, too. Then it was Tom Sawyer's turn to be nitiated. We pulled off his britches and give it to him tolerable heavy with the swords, and then we kind of rolled him around in the wet part of the room, where it was all clayey muck, and then we give it to him even heavier with the swords again. He begun to cry and carry on, saying he warn't ever going to tell us no secrets anymore, so we all made fun of him, and called him crybaby, and then we took all them damned wooden swords and guns of his and tossed them down a deep hole and went home. And that was the end of Tom Sawyer's Robber Gang.

You see, Tom never could get a holt of something without he didn't have to stretch it till it busted. Too much book-reading had done that to him. Like that same night, when Tom and me was sneaking away from the widow's, he said we had to take the path that run amongst the trees back towards the end of the widow's garden. It was the hard way, being close to the house and all, and under branches loaded with wet leaves, but Tom said bandits and pirates did a heap of prowling around peoples' houses at night and that we should give it a try as long as we had such a bully chance. Well, I said I didn't see why we couldn't give it a try somewheres else, and Tom called me a numskull and a flathead. He said if I warn't so ignorant, but had read a book called *Don Quixote*, I would know why such things was always done the hard way. Well, I didn't want to stand there and argue all night so I give in and followed him along the path, stooping low so the branches wouldn't dump too much water down my neck.

Then, just as we was passing by the kitchen, I had to go fall over a root and make a noise. We scrouched down and laid still. Miss Watson's Jim was setting in the kitchen door; we could see him pretty clear, because there was a light behind him. He got up and stretched his neck out about a minute, listening. Then he says:

"Who dah?"

He listened some more; then he came tiptoeing down and stood right between us; we could a dang near touched him. Well, likely it was minutes and minutes that there warn't a sound but for the danged skeeters and we all there so close together I couldn't budge. A skeeter raised a bump on my ankle that got to itching, but I dasn't scratch it; and then one got to my ear, and that began to burn like hellfire; and next my back, right between my shoulders. Seemed like I'd die if I couldn't scratch, say nothing of slapping at them damn skeeters. Pretty soon Jim says:

"Say, who is you? Whar is you? Dog my cats ef I didn't hear sumf'n. Well, I know what I's gwyne to do: I's gwyne to set down here and listen tell I hears it ag'in."

So he set down on the ground betwixt me and Tom. He leaned his back up against a tree, and stretched his legs out till one of them most touched one of mine. He didn't make a sound, only now and then a whack at a skeeter, and we knew he was busting an ear, listening. How I envied that nigger, being able to smash them skeeters, whilst I was laying there next to him, itching all over. I didn't know how I was going to set still. This miserableness went on as much as six or seven minutes; but it seemed a damn sight longer than that. I was itching in eleven different places now, both inside and out. I reckoned I couldn't stand it more'n a minute longer, but I set my teeth hard and got ready to try. Just then Jim begun to breathe heavy; next he begun to snore — and then I was able to scratch all them bites and was pretty soon comfortable again.

Tom he made a sign to me — kind of a little whistle

with his mouth—and we went creeping away on our hands and knees. When we was ten foot off Tom whispered to me, and wanted to tie Jim to the tree for fun. But I said no; he might wake and raise hell, and then they'd find out I warn't in. Then Tom said he hadn't got candles enough, and he would slip in the kitchen and get some more. I didn't want him to try. I said Jim might wake up and come. But Tom wanted to resk it; so we slid in there and got three candles, and Tom laid five cents on the table for pay. Then we got out, and I was in a sweat to get the hell away, but nothing would do Tom but he must crawl to where Jim was, on his hands and knees, and play something on him. I waited, and it seemed a God-damned age, everything was so still and lonesome and skeetery.

As soon as Tom was back we cut along the path, around the garden fence, and by and by fetched up on the steep top of the hill the other side of the house. There was a little hollow there, and Tom he had to pull me down and tell me all about the bully trick he had played on that poor nigger. He said he slipped Jim's hat off his head and stuck it on a limb right over him, and Jim stirred a little, but he didn't wake. Tom was like to hug himself he was so monstrous proud of that joke, but I said it didn't seem too gaudy to me, as jokes went.

He says:

"Why Huck, don't you see? When that nigger wakes up and sees his hat up there on the limb, he'll just naturally think that *witches* done it. That's the way with niggers, every time. And then he'll probably make up some wild story about how the witches put him in a trance, and rode him all over

the state, and then put him down under the trees
again, and hung his hat on the limb to show who done
it. And next time Jim tells it, why he'll most likely
have them riding him all the way down to New Orleans. Wait and see. Every time he tells it he'll
stretch it more and more, till by and by he'll be saying how they rode him all over the world, and tired
him most to death, and his backside was all over
saddle-boils."

I says:

"Maybe he'll just think he hung his own hat up and
forgot about it."

"Huck, you ain't nothing but a goldarned *ingo-
ramus*! What about that five-center piece? I s'pose
he's going to think he put *that* there and forgot
about it."

Well, Tom had me up a stump on that one, and I
said so.

"Of course he ain't. He's going to lay that to
witches' work, too, you can bet. He'll most likely
keep that five-center piece round his neck on a string,
and say it was a charm the devil give to him with his
own hands, and told him he could cure anybody with
it and fetch witches whenever he wanted to just by
saying something to it; only he forgot what it was he's
supposed to say. That's *always* the way with niggers,
to work up any little witch thing into some monstrous
story. Why, other niggers'll probably come from
miles around and give Jim anything they've got,
just for a sight of that ole five-center piece."

Then he pulled out a little bit of wood on the end
of a string which he said was his watch and looked
at it, holding it up to the starlight so as to see better.
"We got to get going," he says, hopping up. "You

watch, Huck. Jim'll be most ruined for a servant, on
account of being stuck up over seeing the devil and
being rode by witches. Most likely they'll have to
give him such a hiding that what those witches done
to him will seem mighty pleasant next to it."

Well, nothing ever come of it that I heard of, and
if Jim thought he had been rode by witches he never
let on to anybody that he had. I warn't much surprised. Tom could spread himself like that for hours,
getting everybody in a lather over something that was
bound to happen, which any fool could plainly see,
and then that would be the last of it. It warn't no
good calling his bluff. The best thing to do was just
let him have his say and then pay it no heed. Like
Pap says, there ain't nothing you can do with a bag
of crap except bury it.

It was most daybreak when we got back to town,
and the roosters was crowing to each other. On the
way home, I stopped when I got to the top of the hill,
and looked back down at the village. I could see
three or four lights twinkling, where there was sick
folks maybe; and the stars was beginning to soften,
with the dawn light making a yellowish streak off to
the east; and down by the village was the river, a
whole mile broad, and awful still and grand. I wanted
to stay and see the sun coming up and all, like I
used to whenever I wanted, before the widow took
me over, but I had to go on over the hill to her house,
and as it was the birds had already begun calling
before I clumb up the shed and crept into my
window.

It was dusky in the room, and the first thing I seen
was somebody standing there, all greased up and
clayey, like he had just come back from a watery

grave, and I almost let out a yip, thinking it was pap's spirit a-laying for me, but it was just myself in the mirror, my new clothes all mucked up. I was so damn dog-tired that I didn't even take them off, but just rolled up in one of the widow's hook rugs and went to sleep on the floor.

Well, I got a good raking over in the morning from old Miss Watson on account of my clothes and what they done to the hook rug, neither of which was hers; but the widow she didn't scold, but only cleaned off the grease and clay, and looked so sorry that I thought I would behave awhile if I could. Then Miss Watson she took me in the closet and prayed, but nothing come of it. She told me to pray every day, and whatever I asked for I would get it. But it warn't so. I tried it. Once I got a fish-line, but no hooks. It warn't no dang good to me without hooks. I tried for the hooks three or four times, but somehow I couldn't make it work. By and by, one day, I asked Miss Watson to try for me, but she said I was a fool. She never told me why, and I couldn't make it out no way.

I set down one time back in the privy, and had a long think about it. I says to myself, if a body can get any dern thing they pray for, why don't the widow get back her silver snuff-box that was stole? Why can't Miss Watson fat up? No, says I to myself, there ain't nothing in it. I went and told the widow about it, and she said the thing a body could get by praying for it was "spiritual gifts." This was too danged many for me, but she told me what she meant—I must help other people, and do everything I could for other people, and look out for them all the time, and never think about myself. This was including Miss Watson, as I took it. I went back to the privy and turned it over in my mind a long time, but I was damned if I could see any advantage about it — except for the other people; so at last I reckoned I wouldn't worry about it any more, but just let it go. Sometimes the widow would take me to one side and talk about Providence in a way to make a body's mouth water; but maybe next day Miss Watson would take hold and knock it all to hell again. I judged I could see that there was two Providences, and a poor bastard like me might stand considerable show with the widow's Providence, but if Miss Watson's got him, there warn't no help for him any more.

Well, Tom Sawyer's bandit gang had turned out to be just another of his damn fool notions, so there warn't no more reason for me to stick around the widow's. But winter was coming on, and a sugar-hogshead ain't much of a show for warmth that time of year, so I thought it all out, and reckoned I would make a stab at belonging to the widow's Providence if He wanted me, though I couldn't make out how He was a-going to be any better off than what He was before, on account of I was so ignorant, and so kind of low-down and ornery. But that was His look-out, and even if it didn't amount to anything, I couldn't see how I would lose.

The hair-ball oracle

Three or four months run along, and it was well into the winter now. I had been to school most all the time and could spell and read and write just a little, and could say my tables up to six times seven is thirty-five, and I don't reckon I could ever get any further than that if I was to live forever. Them eights and nines was ornery and snakey, and besides, I don't take no stock in rithmetic, anyhow.

At first I hated the school, but by and by I got so I could stand it. Whenever I got uncommon tired I played hookey, and the hiding I got next day done me good and cheered me up. So the longer I went to school the easier it got to be. I was getting sort of used to the widow's ways, too, and they warn't so raspy on me. Living in a house and sleeping in a bed pulled on me pretty tight mostly, but before the cold weather I used to slide out and sleep in the woods sometimes, and so that was a rest to me. I liked the old ways best, but I was getting so I liked the new ones, too, a little bit. The widow said I was coming along slow but sure, and doing very satisfactory. She said she warn't ashamed of me.

There was good times, beside, taffy-pulls and sleigh rides when the winter come, or just sitting round the fire roasting apples and telling ghost-stories. There was this girl named Sarah Ann Winchell, and she and I used to do all them things together, and I give her a ring made out'n a barn nail. It seemed like everybody had a girl that year, but Sarah warn't like most of the rest, mimsey-wimsey and just too good or scairt for anything. She was reglar, and *bully*, with lots of sand. Not a tomboy, like old Hellfire Hotchkiss, which used to train with the boys and try to beat them at all the games, but with plenty of grit just the same.

It was so blame cold that year that the river froze solid, and we went skating together with the others, and Sarah warn't scared to go way out where the ice was thin, and where a boy had fell through that very same year and damn near drownded, but they pulled him out, and then he come down sick with scarlet fever and nearly died, only they filled him up like a jug with castor oil and molasses. He was deef and dumb as a stone after that, and Miss Watson said it was Providence. She said that's what wicked boys got for skating far out on the river where they shouldn't be, instead of at home attending prayer meetings.

I says:

"How about Tom Sawyer? He was out there with him."

Well, she had an answer for that one. She most nearly *always* did.

"It wasn't necessary, Huckleberry. Providence judged that Tom Sawyer would profit by the other child's example."

"But it was Tom teased him into it. It was *his* idea. How come Providence didn't let *him* through the ice, and profit Willy?"

"Oh, *I* don't know. I only know it was for a good and wise and merciful reason. He does nothing that isn't right and wise and merciful. You can't understand these things now, Huckleberry, but when you are grown up you will understand them, and then you will see that they are wise and just."

"But Tom went out there all the time, and Willy only that once. It don't seem fair somehow."

"Huckleberry!" she says. "Don't be blastfamous!" which she always done when I was about to pull out and pass her, and then she stuck a track into my hands and made me spend the rest of the afternoon studying it, which was a Sunday. Well, I read it but there warn't a word in it about ice-skating, so Sarah and me kept at it.

Skating was the grandest at night, when it was so dark you couldn't see the ice under you, only hear the *snick*, *snick* of your blades. We would go way out and then stand there and look back at the fire, where the rest of the people was, and nothing in between but darkness and the light on the ice shimmering toward you, only never reaching you quite, not even when you skated back towards it. So far out like that, you felt kind of lonesome, and the cold wind would come a-swooshing across from the Illinois side. I wouldn't a done it all alone, but Sarah would skate close to me, and I'd put my arm around her, and then it was all right. It was lovely out there, with the stars so sharp and clear you could almost touch them, and I said I reckoned I could reach up and pick out the North Star if she wanted it, but she said no, the niggers needed that when they run away to Canada.

Well, that damn near threw me. I says:

"Why, Sarah Ann, where did you get an idea like that?"

She answered up pert, but there was a little shake to her voice, like she knew she had said something wrong, but warn't sure what.

She says:

"Oh, now, everybody knows that, Huckleberry."

"I mean the part about *leaving* it up there. You ain't *wantin'* the niggers to escape, are you?"

"Well, now," she says: "Well, now, I didn't *say* that, did I?"

"No," I says, "You didn't. But I'll be danged if. . . ."

"Huckleberry Finn!" she says. "That was a naughty word. I'm going back and tell everybody what you said!" And she started off across the ice, and I chased her and caught her, and she was giggling like crazy and lost her balance and pulled me down and kissed me or I kissed her, I warn't never sure which. Anyway, it was the first time. And it was nice. I ain't never felt so proud and joyful.

She didn't say nothing more about the niggers escaping, or the North Star, and I didn't nuther. I figured she didn't know no better, and just let it slide. You see, Sarah warn't borned there in Missouri like the rest of us was, but had come from Ohio a year before with her ma and pa to live in St. Petersburg. There had been considerable many folks moving west, and everybody called them the "eastern

run," and said they had strange notions about
property and such, and wouldn't bring nothing but
trouble. So it warn't her fault, being brung up wrong.
Besides, it warn't but a little thing, and when it come
to skating and the rest, Sarah was just a cracker-jack,
so I warn't of a mind to chaw over a lot of gold-leaf
distinctions.

Well, Miss Watson hadn't nothing but bad to say
about girls like Sarah that went ice-skating and such.
She said the proper place for young ladies was at
home with their mothers and aunts, a-training for
the intolerable lot which Providence had give them as
a blessing out of His wisdom and mercy. She said
that they'd get more'n enough of men before they
was through, which was filthy, lecherous creturs,
worse than goats and only a hair better than hogs.
And girls that hung 'round boys warn't no better
than they was, like that Hellfire Hotchkiss. Miss
Watson said that if a girl would play games with
boys, she'd do worse things too, only she wouldn't
dirty her lips naming them, which was kept clean
for the name of the Lord.

Well, old Hotchkiss never done anything shameful
that I ever heard of. She was skinny as a pole anyway, and just another one of us, leastwise that's the
way we looked at it. Once we tried to get her to go
swimming with us, to find out if she warn't all the
way a boy, but she just got all red and angry and
threw stones at us. So I guess she was. A girl, I mean.

When Sarah and me was together we'd make plans
for the summer, when school was let out. She said
we could gather columbine on the cliffs and tie rose-
vine knots, and all that sweet-girlish stuff, and I said
I would if she'd go fishing with me, and she said of

course she would, and I knew she would too, and even bait her own hook, and I said we'd go swimming together when we was tired of fishing. She said all right, but we'd have to do it away off somewheres so that nobody would catch us, because she'd get a whipping sure. You can say what you want about them Ohio folks, but I liked Sarah fine.

We used to walk down to the landing, and sit there watching the river, and make all sorts of plans, and we was going to get married, too, and I'd be a pilot on a steamboat, which is what all the boys wanted to be, and come back to her at the end of every run, but she said no, she'd go with me, which was the kind of girl she was. But it didn't come to nothing, none of it. It warn't her fault, of course, and even now I get a sore throat when I think about her and the fine times we had and the better ones that never come.

You see, one morning I happened to turn over the son-a-bitchin' saltcellar at breakfast. I reached out for some of it as quick as I could to throw over my left shoulder and keep off the bad luck, but Miss Watson was in ahead of me, and crossed me off. She says, "Take your hands away, Huckleberry; what a mess you are always making!" I knowed that damn well enough.

I started out, after breakfast, feeling worried and shaky, and wondering where it was going to fall on me, and what it was going to be. There is ways to keep off some kinds of bad luck, but this warn't one of them kind; so I never tried to do anything, but just poked along low-spirited and on the watch-out.

I went down to the front garden and clumb over the stile where you go through the high board fence. There was an inch of new snow on the ground, and I seen somebody's tracks. They had come up from the quarry and stood around the stile awhile, and then went on around the garden fence. It was funny they hadn't come in, after standing around so. I couldn't make it out. It was very damn curious, somehow. I was going to follow them around, but stooped down to take a careful look at the tracks first. I didn't notice anything right away, but next I did. There was a cross in the left boot-heel made with big nails, to keep off the devil.

I was up in a second and shinning down the hill. I looked over my shoulder every now and then, but I didn't see nobody. I was at Judge Thatcher's as quick as I could get there. He said:

"Why, my boy, you are all out of breath. Did you come for your interest?"

"No, sir," I says; "is there some for me?"

"Oh, yes, a half-yearly is in last night—over a hundred and fifty dollars. Quite a fortune for you. You had better let me invest it along with your six thousand, because if you take it you'll spent it."

"No, sir," I says, "I don't want to spend it. I don't want it at all—nor the six thousand, nuther. I want you to take it; I want to give it to you—the six thousand, and all."

He looked surprised. He couldn't seem to make it out. He says:

"Why, what can you mean, my boy?" Now if'n I had asked to *borrow* some, he'd a understood that, but he couldn't get what I wanted through his head.

I says, "Don't ask me no questions about it, please. Jest take it, all of it. You will—won't you?"

He says:

"Well, I'm puzzled. Is something the matter?"

"Please take it," says I, "and don't ask me nothing—then I won't have to tell no lies."

He studied awhile, and then he says:

"Oho-o! I think I see. You want to *sell* all your property to me, not give it. That's the correct idea."

Then he wrote something on a paper and read it over, and says:

"There; you see it says 'for a consideration.' That means I have bought it of you and paid you for it. Here's a dollar for you. Now you sign it."

So I signed it, and left. I reckon he thought he had a bargain then, but he didn't think so for long.

Miss Watson's nigger, Jim, had a hair-ball as big as your fist, which had been took out of the fourth stomach of an ox, and he used to do magic with it. He said there was a spirit inside of it, and it knowed everything. So I went to him that night and told him pap was here again, for I found his tracks in the snow. What I wanted to know was, what was he going to do, and was he going to stay? Jim got out his hair-ball and said something over it, and then he held it up and dropped it on the floor. It fell pretty damn solid, and only rolled about an inch. Jim tried it again, and then another time, and it acted just the same. Jim got down on his knees, and put his ear against it and listened. But it warn't no use; he said it wouldn't talk. He said sometimes it wouldn't talk without money. I told him I had an old slick counterfeit quarter that warn't no good because the brass showed through the silver a little, and it wouldn't pass nohow, even if the brass didn't show, because it was so dern slick it felt greasy, and so that would tell on it every time. (I reckoned I wouldn't say nothing about the dollar I got from the judge.) I said it was pretty bad money, but maybe the hair-ball would take it, because maybe it wouldn't know the difference. Jim smelt it and bit it and rubbed it, and said he would manage so the hair-ball would think it was good. He said he would split open a raw Irish potato and stick the quarter in between and keep it there all night, and next morning you couldn't see no brass, and it wouldn't feel greasy no more, and anybody in town would take it in a minute, let along an old hair-ball. Well, I knowed a damn potato would do that before, but I had forgot it.

Jim put the quarter under the hair-ball, and got down and listened again. This time he said the hair-ball was all right. He said it would tell my whole fortune if I wanted it to. I says, go on. So the hair-ball talked to Jim, and Jim told it to me. He says:

"Yo' ole father doan' know yit what he's a-gwyne to do. Sometimes he spec he'll go 'way, en den ag'in he spec he'll stay. De bes' way is to res' easy en let de ole man take his own way. Dey's two angels hoverin' 'roun' 'bout him. One uv 'em is white en shiny, en t'other one is black. De white one gits him to go right a little while, den de black one sail in en bust it all up. A body can't tell yit which one gwyne to fetch him at de las'. But you is all right. You gwyne to have considable trouble in yo' life, en considable joy. Sometimes you gwyne to git hurt, and sometimes you gwyne to git sick; but every time you's gwyne to git well ag'in. Dey's two gals flyin' 'bout you in yo' life. One uv 'em's light en t'other one is dark. One is rich en t'other is po'. You gwyne to marry de po' one fust en de rich one by en by. You wants to keep 'way fum high places, but you don' run no resk fum de

water, 'kase it's down in de bills dat you's gwyne to
git hung."

Well, Jim said he had to keep the quarter because
the oracle told him to, but I didn't care none—it was
worth it. The only part that was pesky was the two
girls, the rich light girl and the poor dark one, because Sarah Winchell was light but she warn't rich.
She warn't exactly *poor*, nuther, so I guessed the
oracle had got her all scrambled up. Jim said that
happened sometimes, towards the end, and it was
because oracles get tired out, same as other folk.
That was all right too, because I warn't uncommon
fond of having to marry two wives. One was enough
for any man.

My own maw had died when I was small, but pap
never got himself another so far as I knowed. He
said he had had his share of marriage. It was like a
peck of dirt, pap said. Every man had to eat his'n
in a life-time, but it warn't necessary to take a liking
to it, and as for him, he hadn't ever craved another
man's. Wife, he meant, not dirt. Pap said a piece of
ass ever now and then was a good thing, but if he
wanted any he knew where he could get it just like
a rented room, by the day or week, and not get
snarled up in any long-term lease. He said he never
knew of a place getting any better the longer you
lived in it, and most times it got worse.

When I lit my candle and went up to my room
that night there he was—pap, his own self!

IV

Pap starts in on a new life

I had shut the door to. Then I turned around, and there he was. I used to be scared of him all the time, he tanned me so much. I reckoned I was scared now, too; but in a minute I see I was mistaken — that is, after the first jolt, as you may say, when my breath sort of hitched, he being so damn unexpected; but right away after I see I warn't scared of him worth bothering about.

He was most fifty, and he looked it. His hair was long and tangled and greasy, and hung down, and you could see his eyes shining through like he was behind vines. It was all black, no gray; so was his long, mixed-up whiskers. There warn't no color in his face, where his face showed; it was white; not like another man's white, but a white to make a body sick, a white to make a body's flesh crawl — a tree-toad white, a fish-belly white. As for his clothes — just rags, that was all. He had one ankle resting on t'other knee; the boot on that foot was busted, and two of his toes stuck through, and he worked them now and then. His hat was laying on the floor—an old black slouch with the top caved in, like a lid.

I stood a-looking at him; he set there a-looking at me, with his chair tilted back a little. I set the candle down. I noticed the window was up; so he had clumb in by the shed. He kept a-looking me all over. By and by he says:

"Starchy clothes—very. You think you're a god-damn big-bug, don't you?"

"Maybe I am, maybe I ain't," I says.

"Don't you give me none o' your lip," says he. "You've put on considerable many frills since I been away. I'll take you down a damn peg or two before I get done with you. You're educated, too, they say—can read and write. You think you're better'n your father, now, don't you, because he can't? I'll take it out of you. Who told you you might meddle with such damn hifalutin' foolishness, hey?—who told you you could?"

"The widow. She told me."

"The widow, hey?—and who in hell told the widow she could put in *her* frigging shovel about a thing that ain't none of her goddamn business?"

"Nobody ever told her."

"Well, by Christ, I'll learn her how to meddle. And looky here—you drop that damn school, you hear? I'll learn people to bring up a boy to put on airs over his own goddamn father and let on to be better'n what *he* is. You lemme catch you fooling around that frigging school again, you hear? Your mother couldn't read, and she couldn't write, nuther, before she died. None of the family couldn't before *they* died. *I* can't; and here you're a-swelling yourself up like this. I ain't the man to stand it—you hear? Say, lemme hear you read."

I took up a book and begun something about General Washington and the wars. When I'd read about half a minute, he fetched the book a whack with his hand and knocked it across the room. He says:

"It's so. You can do it. I had my doubts when you told me. Now looky here; you stop that putting on frills. I won't have it. I'll lay for you, my smart-ass, and if I catch you about that school I'll tan you good. First you know you'll get religion too. I never see such a son."

He took up a little blue and yaller picture of some cows and a boy, and says:

"What's this?"

"It's something they give me for learning my lessons good."

He tore it up, and says:

"I'll give you something better—I'll give you a goddamn cowhide."

He set there a-mumbling and a-growling a minute, and then he says:

"Well, by Jesus, *ain't* you a sweet-scented dandy, though? A goddamn bed; and bedclothes; and a look'n'-glass; and a piece of carpet on the frigging floor — an' your own father got to sleep with the stinking hogs in the damn tanyard. I never see such a son. I bet I'll take some o' these frills out o' you before I'm done with you. Why, there ain't no end to your airs—they say you're rich. Hey? —how's that?"

"They lie—that's how."

"Looky here—mind how you talk to me; I'm a-standing about all I can stand now—so don't give me no sass. I've been in town two days, and I hain't heard nothing but about you bein' rich. I heard about it away down the river, too. That's why I come. You git me that goddamn money tomorrow—I want it."

"I hain't got no money."

"It's a damn lie. Judge Thatcher's got it. You git it. I want it."

"I hain't got no damn money, I tell you. You ask Judge Thatcher; he'll tell you the same."

"All right. I'll ask him; and I'll make him pungle, too, or by God I'll know the reason why. Say, how much you got in your pocket? I want it."

"I hain't got only a dollar, and I want that to—"

"It don't make a damn what you want it for—you just shell it out."

He took it and bit it to see if it was good. And then he said he was going down-town to get some whiskey; said he hadn't had a drink all day. When he had got out on the shed he put his head in again, and cussed me for putting on frills and trying to be better than him; and when I reckoned he was gone he came back and put his head in again, and told me to mind about that school, because he was going to lay for me and lick me if I didn't drop that.

Next day he was drunk, and he went to Judge Thatcher's and bullyragged him, and tried to make him give up the money; but he couldn't, and then he swore he'd make the law force him.

The judge and the widow went to law to get the court to take me away from him and let one of them be my guardian; but it was a new judge that had just come, and he didn't know the old man; so he said courts mustn't interfere and separate families if they could help it; said he'd druther not take a child away from its father. So Judge Thatcher and the widow had to quit on the business.

That pleased the old man till he couldn't rest. He said he'd cowhide my ass till it was black and blue if I didn't raise some money for him. I borrowed three dollars from Judge Thatcher and pap took it and got drunk, and went a-blowing around and cussing and whooping and carrying on; and he kept it up all over town, with a tin pan, till most midnight; then they jailed him, and the next day they had him before court, and jailed him again for a week. But he said *he* was satisfied; said he was boss of his son, and he'd make it warm for *him*.

When he got out the new judge said he was a-going to make a man of him. So he took him to his own house, and dressed him up clean and nice, and had him to breakfast and dinner and supper with the family, and was just old pie to him, so to speak. And after supper he talked to him about temprance and such things till the old man cried, and said he'd been a fool, and fooled away his life; but now he was a-going to turn over a new leaf and be a man nobody wouldn't be ashamed of, and he hoped the judge would help him and not look down on him. The judge said he could hug him for them words; so *he* cried, and his wife she cried again; pap said he'd been a man that had always been misunderstood before, and the judge said he believed it. The old man said that what a man wanted that was down was sympathy, and the judge said it was so; so they cried again. And when it was bedtime, the old man rose up and held out his hand, and says:

"Look at it, gentlemen and ladies all; take a-hold of

it; shake it. There's a hand that was the hand of a hog; but it ain't so no more; it's the hand of a man that's started in on a new life, and'll die before he'll go back. You mark them words — don't forget I said them. It's a clean hand, now; shake it — don't be afeard."

So they shook it, one after the other, all around, and cried. The judge's wife she kissed it. Then the old man he signed a pledge — made his mark. The judge said it was the holiest time on record, or something like that. Then they tucked the old man into a beautiful room, which was the spare room, and in the night some time he got powerful thirsty and clumb out on to the porch roof and slid down a stanchion and traded his new coat for a jug of forty-rod, and clumb back again and had a good old time; and toward daylight he crawled out again, drunk as a fiddler, and rolled off the porch and broke his left arm in two places, and was damn near froze to death when somebody found him after sun-up. And when they come to look at that spare room they had to take soundings before they could navigate it.

The judge he felt kind of sore. He said he reckoned a body could reform the old man with a shotgun, maybe, but he didn't know no other way.

V

Pap struggles with the death angel

Well, pretty soon the old man was up and around again, and then he went for Judge Thatcher in the courts to make him give up that money, and he went for me, too, for not stopping school. He catched me a couple of times and thrashed me, but I went to school just the same, and dodged him or outrun him most of the time. I didn't want to go to school much before, but I reckoned I'd go now to spite pap.

The law trial was a damnation slow business — appeared like they warn't ever going to get started on it; so every now and then I'd borrow two or three dollars off of the judge for pap, to keep from getting a cowhiding. Every time he got money he got drunk; and every time he got drunk he raised hell around town; and every time he raised hell he got jailed. He was just suited — this kind of thing was right in his line.

He got to hanging around the widow's too much, and so she told him at last that if he didn't quit using around there she would make trouble for him. Well, *warn't* he mad? He said he would damn well show them who was Huck Finn's boss. So he watched out for me one day in the spring, and catched me, and took me up the river about three mile in a skiff, and crossed over to the Illinois shore where it was woody and there warn't no houses but an old log hut in a place where the timber was so dern thick you couldn't find it if you didn't know where it was.

He kept me with him all the time, and I never got a chance to run off. We lived in that old cabin, and he always locked the door and put the key under his head nights. He had a gun which he had stole, I reckon, and we fished and hunted, and that was what we lived on. Every little while he locked me in and went down to the store, three miles, to the ferry, and traded fish and game for whiskey, and fetched it home and got drunk and had a good time, and licked me. The widow she found out where I was by and by, and she sent a man over to try and get hold of me; but pap drove him off with the gun, and it warn't long after that till I was used to being where I was, and liked it — all but the danged cowhide part, that and not seeing Sarah Winchell.

I wouldn't a wished her there, by a damn sight, but there was times when I missed her and wondered where she was and what she was thinking and so on. After a long while, maybe three-four days, I didn't think about her so very much, and after a week had gone by I hardly thought about her at all. I guessed it was the same with her. I'd a writ her a letter but there warn't no paper or pencil there, and even if I had, pap wouldn't ever a took it in for me.

It was pretty good times up in the woods there,

take it all around; kind of lazy and jolly, laying off comfortable all day, smoking and fishing, and no books nor study. I had stopped cussing, because the widow didn't like it; but now I took to it again because pap hadn't no objections. Two months or more run along, and my clothes got to be all rags and dirt, and I didn't see how I'd ever got to like it so well at the widow's where you had to wash, and eat on a plate, and get combed all to hell, and go to bed and get up reglar, and be forever bothering over a dern book, and have old Miss Watson pecking at you all the time. I didn't want to go back no more. I had stayed because the widow's Providence seemed like a good thing, but it was just like I thought, He didn't hold no truck with the likes of me. I hadn't had nothing but bad luck since the widow took me in.

Well, by and by pap got too handy with his damn hick'ry, and I couldn't stand it no more. My ass was all over whelps, like corduroy. He got to going away so much, too, and locking me in. Once he locked me in and was gone three days. It was dreadful lonesome, lonely as hell out there. There warn't no way to empty the slop bucket, nuther, and the cabin got mighty ripe. I judged pap had got drownded, and I warn't ever going to get out any more. I was pretty derned scared, and I made up my mind I would fix up some way to leave there. I had tried to get out of that cabin many a time, but I couldn't find no way. There warn't a window to it big enough for a dog to get through. I couldn't get up the chimbly; it was too narrow. The door was thick as hell, solid oak slabs. Pap was pretty careful not to leave a knife or anything in the cabin when he was away; I reckon I had hunted the place over as much as a hundred times; well, I was 'most

all the time at it, because it was the only way to put
in the time. But this trip I found something at last; I
found an old rusty key-hole-saw without any handle;
it was laid in between a rafter and the clapboards of
the roof. I greased it up and went to work.

There was an old horse-blanket nailed against the
logs at the far end of the cabin behind the table, to
keep the wind from blowing through the chinks and
putting the candle out. I got under the table and
raised the blanket, and went to work to saw a section
of the big bottom log out — big enough to let me
through. Well, it was a dern long job, but I was getting
toward the end of it when I heard pap's gun in the
woods. I got rid of the mess, and dropped the blanket,
and hid my saw, and pretty soon pap came in.

Pap warn't in a good humor — so he was his natural self. He said he was down to town, and everything
was going wrong. His lawyer said he reckoned he
would win his lawsuit and get the money if they ever
got started on the trial; but then there was ways to
put it off a long time, and Judge Thatcher knowed
how to do it. And he said people allowed there'd be
another trial to get me away from him and give me
to the widow for my guardian, and they guessed it
would win this time. This shook me up considerable,
because I sure as hell didn't want to go back to the
widow's any more and be so cramped up and sivilized,
as they called it, or take any more chances with
Providence. Look where He had got me already.
Then the old man got to cussing, and cussed everything and everybody he could think of, and then
cussed them all over again to make sure he hadn't
skipped any, and after that he polished off with a kind
of a general cuss all round, including a considerable

parcel of people which he didn't know the names of, and so called them what's-his-name when he got to them, and went right along with his cussing.

He said he would like to *see* the goddamn widow get me. He said he would watch out, and if they tried to come any such goddamn game on him he knowed of a place six or seven mile off to stow me in, where they might hunt till they dropped and they couldn't find me. That made me pretty dern uneasy again, but only for a minute; I reckoned I wouldn't stay on hand till he got that chance.

The old man made me go to the skiff and fetch the things he had got. There was a fifty-pound sack of corn meal, and a side of bacon, ammunition, and a four-gallon jug of whisky, and an old book and two newspapers for wadding, besides some tow. I toted up a load, and went back and set down on the bow of the skiff to rest. I thought it all over, and I reckoned I would walk off with the gun and some lines, and take to the woods when I run away. I guessed I wouldn't stay in one place, but just tramp across the country, mostly night-times, and hunt and fish to keep alive, and so get so damn far away that the old man nor the widow couldn't ever find me any more. I judged I would saw out and leave that night if pap got drunk enough, and I reckoned he would. I got so full of it I didn't notice how long I was staying till the old man hollered and asked me whether I was asleep or drownded.

I got the things all up to the cabin, and then it was about dark. While I was cooking supper the old man took a swig or two and got sort of warmed up, and went to ripping again. He had been drunk over in town, and laid in the gutter all night, and he was a sight to look at. A body would a thought he was Adam—he was just all mud. Whenever his liquor began to work he most always went for the govment. This time he says:

"Call this a damn govment! why, just look at it and see what it's like. Here's the law a-standing ready to take a man's goddamn son away from him—a man's own goddamn son, which he has had all the damn trouble and all the damn anxiety and all the damn expense of raising. Yes, just as that man has got that goddamn son raised at last, and ready to go to work and begin to do suthin' for *him* and give him a rest, the frigging law up and goes for him. And they call *that* govment! That ain't all, nuther, by a damn sight. The law backs that old son-of-a-bitch Judge Thatcher up and helps him to keep me out o' my property. Here's what the goddamn law does: The goddamn law takes a man worth six thousand dollars and up'ards, and jams him into a damned old trap of a cabin like this, and lets him go round in clothes that ain't fitten for a damned hog. They call that govment! A man can't get his rights in a govment like this. By Christ, sometimes I've a mighty damn notion to just leave the frigging country for good and all. Yes, and I told 'em so; I told old son-a-bitch Thatcher to his face. Lots of 'em heard me, and can tell what I said. Says I, for two damn cents I'd leave the frigging country and never come a-near it ag'in. Them's the very words. I says, look at my hat—if you call it a hat—but the damn lid raises up and the rest of it goes down till it's below my frigging chin, and then it ain't rightly a hat at all, but more like my head was shoved up through a goddamn jint of stove-pipe. Look at it, says I—such a damned hat for me to wear—one of the wealthiest men in this goddamn town if I could git my frigging rights.

"Oh yes, this is a wonderful damn govment, wonderful. Why, looky here. There was a free nigger there from Ohio—a mulatter, most as white as a white man. He had the damnedest whitest shirt on you ever see, too, and the shiniest damn hat; and there ain't a man in that damned town that's got as fine clothes as what he had; and he had a gold watch and chain, and a silver-headed cane—the goddamnedest old gray-headed nabob in the frigging state. And what do you think? They said he was a p'fessor in a goddamn college, and could talk all kinds of goddamn languages, and knowed everything. And that ain't the wust. They said he could *vote* when he was at home. Well, by God, that let me out. Thinks I, sweet Jesus Christ, what in hell is the country a-coming to? It was 'lection day, and I was just about to go and vote myself if I warn't too drunk to get there. I had already voted twice and was jest getting warmed to it, but when they told me there was a state in this frigging country where they'd let that goddamn nigger nabob son-of-a-bitch vote, I drawed out. I says I'll never vote ag'in. Them's the very words I said; they all heard me; and the damn country may rot for all me—I'll never vote ag'in as long as I live. And to see the cool way of that damned nigger—why, he wouldn't a give me the road if I hadn't shoved him out o' the way. I says to people, why ain't this goddamned nigger put up at auction and sold? —that's what I want to know. And what in hell do you reckon they said? Why, they said he couldn't be sold till he'd been in the state six months, and he hadn't been there that long yet. There, now by God!—that's a specimen. They call that a damn govment that can't sell a free goddamn nigger till he's been in the state six frigging months. Here's a goddamned govment that calls itself a goddamned govment, and lets on to be a goddamned govment, and thinks it is a goddamned govment, and yet's got to set stock still on its frigging ass for six whole frigging months before it can take a-holt of a prowling, thieving, goddamn, white-shirted, son-of-a-bitching, free nigger barstid, and—"

Pap was a-going on so he never noticed where his old limber legs was taking him to, so he went head over heels over the tub of salt pork and barked both shins, and the rest of his speech was all the hottest kind of language—mostly hove at the nigger and the govment, though he give the tub some hell, too, all along, here and there. He hopped around the cabin considerable, first on one leg and then on the other, holding first one shin and then the other one, and at last he let out with his left foot all of a sudden and fetched the tub a rattling good kick. But it warn't very good judgment, because that was the boot that had a couple of his toes leaking out of the front end of it; so now he raised a howl that fairly made a body's hair raise, and down he went in the dirt, and rolled there, and held his toes; and the cussing he done then laid over anything he had ever done previous. He said so his own self, afterwards. He had heard old Sowberry Hagan in his best days, and he said it laid over him, too; but I reckon that was sort of piling it on, maybe.

After supper pap took the jug, and said he had enough whisky there for two drunks and one delirium tremens. That was always his word. I judged he

would be blind drunk in about an hour, and then I
would steal the key, or saw myself out, one or t'other.
He drank and drank, and tumbled down on his blankets by and by, but luck didn't run my way. He didn't
go sound asleep, but was uneasy. He groaned and
moaned and thrashed around this way and that for a
long time. At least I got so damn sleepy I couldn't
keep my eyes open, for all I could do, and so before I
knowed what I was about I was sound asleep, and the
candle burning.

I don't know how long I was asleep, but all of a
sudden there was an awful scream and I was up.
There was pap looking wilder'n hell, and skipping
around every which way and yelling about snakes.
He said they was crawling up his legs, and then he
would give a jump and scream, and say one had bit
him on the cheek—but I couldn't see no snakes. He
started and run round and round the cabin, hollering, "Oh Christ! Take him off! take him off! he's
biting me on the neck!" I never see a man look so
wild in the eyes. Pretty soon he was all fagged out,
and fell down panting; then he rolled over and over
wonderful fast, kicking things every which way, and
striking and grabbing at the air with his hands, and
screaming and saying there was devils a-hold of him.
He wore out by and by, and laid still awhile, moaning.
Then he laid stiller, and didn't make a sound. I could
hear the owls and the wolves away off in the woods,
and it seemed terrible damn still. He was laying over
by the corner. By and by he raised up part way and
listened, with his head to one side. He says, very low:

"Tramp—tramp—tramp; that's the dead; tramp—
tramp—tramp; they're coming after me; but I won't
go. Oh Lord, they're here! don't touch me—don't!

hands off—they're cold; let go. Oh, let a poor bugger alone!"

Then he went down on all fours and crawled off, begging them to let him alone, and he rolled himself, up in his blanket and wallowed in under the old pine table, still a-begging; and then he went to crying. I could hear him through the blanket.

By and by he rolled out and jumped up to his feet looking like a crazy man, and he sees me and went for me. He chased me round and round the place with a clasp-knife, calling me the Angel of Death, and saying he would kill me, and then I couldn't come for him no more. I begged, and told him I was only Huck; but he laughed *such* a screechy damn laugh, and roared and cussed, and kept on chasing me up. Once when I turned short and dodged under his arm he made a grab and got me by the jacket between my shoulders, and I thought I was gone; but I slid out of the jacket quick as greased lightning, and saved myself. Pretty soon he was all tired out, and dropped down with his back against the door, and said he would rest a minute and then kill me. He put his knife under him, and said he would sleep and get strong, and then he would see who in hell was who.

So he dozed off pretty soon. By and by I got the old split-bottom chair and clumb up as easy as I could, not to make any noise, and got down the gun. I slipped the ramrod down in to make sure it was loaded, and then I laid it across the turnip-barrel, pointing towards pap, and set down behind it to wait for him to stir. And how damnation slow and still the time did drag along.

VI

I fool pap and get away

G it up! What in hell you 'bout?"
I opened my eyes and looked around trying to make out where I was. It was after
sun-up, and I had been sound asleep. Pap was
standing over me looking sour—and sick, too. He
says:

"What you doin' with this damn gun?"

I judged he didn't know nothing about what he
had been doing, so I says:

"Somebody tried to get in, so I was laying for him."

"For Chrissakes! Why didn't you roust me out?"

"Well, I tried to, but I couldn't; I couldn't budge
you."

"Well, all right. Damn it, don't stand there palav-
ering all day, but out with you and see if there's a
fish on the lines for breakfast. I'll be along in a minute, soon's I shake a little dew off the lily."

He unlocked the door, and I cleared out up the
river bank. I noticed some pieces of limbs and such

things floating down, and a sprinkling of bark; so I knowed the river had begun to rise. I reckoned I would have great times now if I was over at the town. The June rise used to be always luck for me; because as soon as that rise begins here comes cordwood floating down, and pieces of log rafts — sometimes a dozen logs together; so all you have to do is catch them and sell them to the woodyards and the saw-mill.

I went along up the bank with one eye out for pap and t'other one out for what the rise might fetch along. Well, derned if all at once here comes a canoe; a dern beauty, too, about thirteen or fourteen foot long, riding high like a duck. I shot head-first off of the bank like a frog, clothes and all on, and struck out for the canoe. I just expected there'd be some-body laying down in it, because people often done that to fool folks, and when a chap had pulled a skiff out to it some bastard'd raise up and laugh at him. But it warn't so this time. It was a drift-canoe sure enough, and I clumb in and paddled her ashore. Thinks I, the old man will be damn glad when he sees this — she's worth ten dollars. But when I got to shore pap warn't in sight yet, and as I was running her into a little creek like a gully, all hung over with vines and willows, I struck another idea: I judged I'd hide her good, and then, 'stead of taking to the woods when I run off, I'd go down the river about fifty mile and camp in one place for good, and not have such a rough time tramping on foot.

It was pretty close to the shanty, and I thought I heard the old man coming all the time; but I got her hid; and then I out and looked around a bunch of wil-lows, and there was the old man down on the path a piece just drawing a bead on a bird with his gun. So he hadn't seen anything.

When he got along I was hard at it taking up a trot line. He give me a little hell for being so slow; but I told him I fell in the river, and that was what made me so long. I knowed he would see I was wet, and then he would be asking questions. We got five cat-fish off the lines and went home.

While we laid off after breakfast to sleep up, both of us being about wore out, I got to thinking that if I could fix up some way to keep pap and the widow from trying to follow me, it would be a certainer thing than trusting to luck to get far enough off before they missed me; you see, all kinds of things might happen. Well, I didn't see no way for a while, but by and by pap raised up a minute to drink another barrel of water, and he says:

"Another time some son-of-a-bitch comes a-prowl-ing round here you roust me out, you hear? That man warn't here for no damn good. I'd a shot the barstid. Next time you roust me out, you hear?"

Then he dropped down and went to sleep again; what he had been saying give me the very idea I wanted. I says to myself, I can fix it now so nobody won't think of following me.

About twelve o'clock we turned out and went along up the bank. The river was coming up pretty damn fast, and lots of driftwood going by on the rise. By and by along comes part of a log raft—nine logs fast to-gether. We went out with the skiff and towed it ashore. Then we had dinner. Anybody but pap would a waited and seen the day through, so as to catch more stuff; but that warn't pap's style. Nine logs was enough for one time; he must shove right over to town and sell. So he locked me in and took the skiff, and started off towing the raft about half past three. I judged he wouldn't come back that night. I waited till I reckoned he had got a good start; then I out with my saw, and went to work on that dern log again. Before he was t'other side of the river I was out of the hole; him and his raft was just a speck on the water away off yonder.

I took the sack of corn meal and took it to where the canoe was hid, and shoved the vines and branches apart and put it in; then I done the same with the side of bacon; then the whisky jug. I took all the coffee and sugar there was, and all the ammunition; I took the wadding; I took the bucket and gourd; took a dipper and a tin cup, and my old saw and two blankets, and the skillet and the coffee pot. I took fish lines and matches and other things — everything that was worth a dang cent. I cleaned out the place. I wanted an ax, but there warn't any, only the one out at the woodpile, and I knowed why I was going to leave that. I fetched out the gun, and now I was done. I had wore the ground a good deal crawling out of the hole and dragging out so many things. So I fixed that as good as I could from the outside by scattering dust on the place, which covered up the smoothness and the sawdust. Then I fixed the piece of log back into its place, and put two rocks under it and one against it to hold it there, for it was bent up at that place and didn't quite touch the ground. If you stood four or five foot away and didn't know it was sawed, you wouldn't never notice it; and besides, this was the back of the cabin, and it warn't very dern likely that anybody would go fooling around there.

It was all grass clear to the canoe, so I hadn't left

a track. I followed around to see. I stood on the bank and looked out over the river. All safe. So I took the gun and went up a piece into the woods, and was hunting around for some birds when I see a wild pig; hogs soon went wild in them bottoms after they had got away from the prairie farms. I shot this fellow and took him into camp.

I took the ax and smashed in the door. I beat it and hacked it all to hell a-doing it. I fetched the pig in, and took him back nearly to the table and hacked into his throat with the ax, and laid him down on the ground to bleed; I say ground because it *was* ground—hard packed, and no boards. Well, next I took an old sack and put a lot of big rocks in it—all I could drag—and I started it from the pig, and dragged it to the door and through the woods down to the river and dumped it in, and down it sunk, out of sight. You could easy see that something had been dragged over the ground. I did wish Tom Sawyer was there; I knowed he would take an interest in this kind of business, and try and throw in a few of his fancy touches. Nobody could spread himself like Tom Sawyer in such a thing as that.

Well, last I pulled out some of my hair, and blooded the ax good, and stuck it on the back side, and slung the ax in the corner. Then I took up the pig and dragged him along the trail I had made with my sack of rocks, so as to leave a little trace of blood here and there. When I was done I took him up and held him to my breast with my jacket (so he wouldn't drip) till I got a good piece below the house and then dumped him into the river. Now I thought of something else. So I went and got the bag of meal and my old saw out of the canoe, and fetched them to the house. I took

the bag to where it used to stand, and ripped a hole in
the bottom of it with the saw, for there warn't no
knives and forks on the place—pap done everything
with his clasp-knife about the cooking. Then I carried the sack about a hundred yards across the grass
and through the willows east of the house, to a shal-
low lake that was five mile wide and full of rushes—
and ducks, too, you might say, in the season. There
was a slough or a creek leading out of it on the other
side that went miles away, I don't know where, but
it didn't go to the river. The meal sifted out and made
a little track all the way to the lake. I dropped pap's
whetstone there too, so as to look like it had been
done by accident. Then I tied up the rip in the meal-
sack with a string, so it wouldn't leak no more, and
took it and my saw to the canoe again.

It was about dark now; so I dropped the canoe
down the river under some willows that hung over
the bank, and waited for the moon to rise. I made
fast to a willow; then I took a bite to eat, and by and
by laid down in the canoe to smoke a pipe and lay
out a plan. I says to myself, they'll follow the track of
that sackful of rocks to the shore and then drag the
river for me. And they'll follow that meal track to the
lake and go browsing down the creek that leads out of
it to find the robbers that killed me and took the
things. They won't ever hunt the river for anything
but my dead carcass. They'll damn soon get tired of
that, and won't bother no more about me. All right; I
can stop anywhere I want to. Jackson's Island is good
enough for me; I know that island pretty well, and
nobody ever comes there. And then I can paddle over
to town nights, and slink around and pick up things
I want. Jackson's Island's the place.

I was pretty damn tired, and the first thing I knowed I was asleep. When I woke up I didn't know where I was for a minute. I set up and looked around, a little scared. Then I remembered. The river looked miles and miles across. The moon was so bright I could a counted the drift-logs that went a-slipping along, black, and still, hundreds of yards out from shore. Everything was dead quiet, and it looked late, and *smelt* late. You know what I mean — I don't know the words to put it in.

I took a good gap and a stretch, and was just going to unhitch and start when I heard a sound away over the water. I listened. Pretty soon I made it out. It was that dull kind of a reglar sound that comes from oars working in rowlocks when it's a still night. I peeped out through the willow branches, and there it was — a skiff, away across the water. I couldn't tell how many was in it. It kept a-coming, and when it was abreast of me I see there warn't but one man in it. Thinks I, maybe it's pap, though I warn't expecting him. He dropped below me with the current, and by and by he came a-swinging up shore in the easy water, and he went by so dang close I could a reached out the gun and touched him. Well, it *was* pap, sure enough, and sober, too, by the way he laid to his oars.

I didn't lose no time. The next minute I was a-spinning downstream soft, but damn quick, in the shade of the bank. I made two mile and a half, and then struck out a quarter of a mile or more toward the middle of the river, because pretty soon I would be passing the ferry-landing, and people might see me and hail me. I got out amongst the driftwood, and then laid down in the bottom of the canoe and let her float. I laid there, and had a good rest and a smoke out of my pipe, looking away into the sky; not a cloud in it. The sky looks so damn deep when you lay down on your back in the moonshine; I never knowed it before. And how far a body can hear on the water such nights! I heard people talking at the ferry-landing. I heard what they said, too — every dern word of it. One man said it was getting towards the long days and the short nights now. T'other said *this* warn't one of the short ones, he reckoned — and then they laughed, and he said it over again, and they laughed again; then they waked up another fellow and told him, and laughed, but he didn't laugh; he told them to go to hell, and said let him alone. The first fellow he 'lowed to tell it to his old woman — she would think it was pretty good; but he said that warn't nothing to some things he had said in his time. I heard one man say it was damn near three o'clock, and he hoped daylight wouldn't wait more than about a week longer. After that the talk got further and further away, and I couldn't make out the words any more; but I could hear the mumble, and now and then a laugh, too, but it seemed a long ways off.

I was away below the ferry now. I rose up, and there was Jackson's Island, about two mile and a half down-stream, heavy-timbered and standing up out of the middle of the river, big and dark and solid, like a steamboat without any lights. There warn't any signs of the bar at the head — it was all under water now.

It didn't take me long to get there. I shot past the head faster'n hell, the current was so swift, and then I got into the dead water and landed on the side to-wards the Illinois shore. I run the canoe into a deep dent in the bank that I knowed about; I had to part the willow branches to get in; and when I made fast nobody could a seen the canoe from the outside.

I went up and took a pee off a log at the head of the island, and stood looking out on the big river and the black driftwood and away over to the town, three mile away, where there was three or four lights twinkling. A monstrous big lumber-raft was about a mile up-stream, coming along down, with a lantern in the middle of it. I watched it come creeping down, and when it most abreast of where I stood I heard a man say, "Stern oars, there! heave her head to stabboard!" I heard that just as plain as if the man was by my side.

There was a little gray in the sky now; so I stepped into the woods, and laid down for a nap before breakfast.

VII

I spare Miss Watson's Jim

The sun was up so high when I waked that I judged it was after eight o'clock. I laid there in the grass and the cool shade thinking about things, and feeling rested and ruther comfortable and satisfied. I could see the sun out at one or two holes, but mostly it was big trees all about, and gloomy as hell in there amongst them. There was freckled places on the ground where the light sifted down through the leaves, and the freckled places swapped about a little, showing there was a little breeze up there. A couple of squirrels set on a limb and jabbered at me very friendly.

I was mighty dern lazy and comfortable—didn't want to get up and cook breakfast. Well, I was dozing off again when I thinks I hears a deep sound of "boom!" away up the river. I rouses up, and rests on my elbow and listens; pretty soon I hears it again. I hopped up, and went and looked out at a hole in the leaves, and I see a bunch of smoke laying on the water a long ways up—about abreast of the ferry.

And there was the ferryboat full of people floating along down. I knowed what was the matter now. "Boom!" I see the white smoke squirt out of the ferryboat's side. You see, they was firing cannon over the water, trying to make my carcass come to the top.

I was pretty damn hungry by then, but it warn't going to do for me to start a fire, because they might see the smoke. So I set there and watched the cannon-smoke and listened to the boom. The river was a mile wide there, and it always looks pretty on a summer morning—so I was having a good enough time seeing them hunt for my remainders if only I had a damn bite to eat. Well, then I happened to think how they always put quicksilver in loaves of bread and float them off, because they always go right to the drownded carcass and stop there. So, says I, I'll keep a lookout, and if any of them's floating around after me I'll give them a show. I changed to the Illinois edge of the island to see what luck I could have, and I warn't disappointed. A big double loaf come along, and I most got it with a long stick, but my damn foot slipped and she floated out further. Of course I was where the current set in the closest to the shore—I knowed enough for that. But by and by along comes another one, and this time I won. I took out the plug and shook out the little dab of quicksilver, and set my teeth in. It was "baker's bread"—what the quality eat; none of your dern low-down cornpone.

I got a good place amongst the leaves, and set there on a log, munching the bread and watching the ferry-boat, and damn well satisfied. And then something struck me. I says, now I reckon the widow or the parson or somebody prayed that this bread would find me, and here it has gone and done it. So there ain't no doubt but there is something in it when a body like the widow or the parson prays, but it sure as hell don't work for me, and I reckon it don't work for only just the right kind.

I lit a pipe and had a good long smoke, and went on watching. The ferryboat was floating with the current, and I allowed I'd have a chance to see who was aboard when she come along, because she would come in close, where the bread did. When she'd got pretty well along down towards me, I put out my pipe and went to where I fished out the bread, and laid down behind a log on the bank in a little open place. Where the log forked I could peep through.

By and by she come along, and she drifted in so dang close that they could a run out a plank and walked ashore. Most everybody was on the boat. Pap, and Judge Thatcher, and Becky Thatcher, and Joe Harper, and Tom Sawyer, and his old Aunt Polly, and Sid and Mary, and plenty more. I looked hard for Sarah Ann, but she warn't aboard so far as I could tell, and I was sad first, thinking she didn't care enough, but then I was kind of glad, because I figured she cared so much she didn't want to come. Anyway, that was all over, so what the hell.

All the people was talking about the murder, but the captain broke in and says:

"Look sharp, now; the current sets in the closest here, and maybe he's washed ashore and got tangled amongst the brush at the water's edge. I hope so, anyway."

I damn well didn't hope so. They all crowded up and leaned over rails, nearly in my face, and kept still, watching with all their might. I could see them first-rate, but they couldn't see me — like a rabbit in the brush. The captain sung out: "Stand away!" and then the cannon let off such a reglar old ball-buster right before me that it made me deef with the noise and nearly blind with the smoke, and I judged I was a goner. If they'd a had some bullets in, I reckon they'd a got the corpse they was after. Well, I see I warn't hurt, thank God! and the boat floated on and went out of sight around the shoulder of the island. I could hear the booming now and then, further and further off, and by and by, after an hour, I didn't hear it no more. The island was three mile long. I judged they had got to the foot, and was giving it up. But they didn't yet awhile. They turned around the foot of the island and started up the channel on the Missouri side, under steam, and booming once in a while as they went. I crossed over to that side and watched them. When they got abreast the head of the island, they quit shooting and dropped over to the Missouri shore and went home to the town.

I knowed I was all right now. Nobody else would come a-hunting after me. I got my traps out of the canoe and made me a nice camp in the thick woods. I made a kind of tent out of my blankets to put my things under so the rain couldn't get at them. I catched a catfish and haggled him open with my saw, and towards sundown I started my camp-fire and had supper. Then I set out a line to catch some fish for breakfast.

When it was dark I set by my camp-fire smoking, and feeling damned well satisfied; but by and by it got sort of lonesome, and so I went and set on the bank and listened to the current swashing along, and counted the stars and drift-logs and rafts that come down, and then went to bed; there ain't no better way to put in time when you are lonesome; you can't stay so, you soon get over it.

And so for three days and nights. No difference — just the same thing. But the next day I went exploring around down through the island. I was boss of it; it all belonged to me, so to say, and I wanted to know all about it; but mainly I wanted to put in the time. I found plenty strawberries, ripe and prime; and green summer grapes, and green razberries; and the green blackberries was just beginning to show. Eat 'em now and I'd get the skitters for sure, but they would all come in handy by and by, I judged.

Well, I went fooling along in the deep woods till I judged I warn't far from the foot of the island. I had my gun along, but I hadn't shot nothing; it was for protection; though I would kill some game nigh home. About this time I damn near stepped on a good-sized snake, and it went sliding off through the grass and flowers, and I after it, trying to get a shot at it. I clipped along, and all of a sudden I bounded right on to the ashes of a camp-fire that was still smoking.

My dern heart jumped up amongst my lungs. I never waited for to look further, but uncocked my gun and went sneaking back on my tiptoes as fast as ever I could. Every now and then I stopped a second amongst the thick leaves and listened, but my breath come so hard I couldn't hear nothing else. I slunk along another piece further, then listened again; and so on, and so on. If I see a stump, I took it for a man; if I trod on a stick and broke it, it made me feel like a person had cut one of my breaths in two and I only got half, and the short half, too.

When I got to camp I warn't feeling very damned brash, there warn't much sand in my craw; but I says, this ain't no time to be fooling around. So I got all my traps into my canoe again so as to have them out of sight, and I put out the fire and scattered the ashes around to look like an old last-year's camp, and then clumb a tree.

I reckon I was up in the tree two hours; but I didn't see nothing, I didn't hear nothing—I only *thought* I heard and seen as much as a thousand things. Well, I couldn't stay up there forever; so at last I got down, but I kept in the thick woods and on the lookout all the time. All I could get to eat was strawberries and what was left over from break-fast. I dasn't eat many of the berries and there warn't much of the other, so by the time it was night I was pretty damn hungry.

When it was good and dark I slid out from shore before moonrise and paddled over to the Illinois bank—about a quarter of a mile. I went out in the woods and cooked a supper, and I had about made up my mind I would stay there all night when I hear a *plunkety-plunk*, *plunkety-plunk*, and says to myself, horses coming; and next I hear people's voices. I got everything into the canoe as quick as I could, and then went creeping through the woods to see what I could find out. I hadn't got far when I hear a man say:

"We better camp here if we can find a good place; the horses is about beat out. Let's look around."

I didn't wait, but shoved out and paddled away easy. I tied up in the old place, and reckoned I would sleep in the canoe.

I didn't sleep very darn much. I couldn't, some-how, for thinking. And every time I waked up I thought somebody had me by the neck. So the sleep didn't do me any good. I didn't want to leave the island till I had fetched some more truck from town, but I couldn't stand it having somebody else there without knowing who it was. By and by I says to myself, I can't live this way; I'm a-going to find out who the hell it is that's here on the island with me; I'll find it out or bust a gut trying. Well, I felt better right off.

So I took my paddle and slid out from shore just a step or two, and then let the canoe drop along down amongst the shadows. The moon was shining, and outside of the shadows it made it most as light as day. I poked along well on to an hour, everything still as rocks and sound asleep. Well, by this time I was most down to the foot of the island. A little ripply, cool breeze began to blow, and that was as good as saying the night was about done. I give her a turn with the paddle and brung her nose to shore; then I got my gun and slipped out and into the edge of the woods. I sat down there on a log, and looked out through the leaves. I see the moon go off watch, and the darkness begin to creep in deeper over the river. But in a little while I see a pale streak over the treetops, and knowed the day was coming. So I took my gun and slipped off towards where I had run across that camp-fire, stopping every minute or two to listen. But I hadn't no luck somehow; I couldn't seem to find the damned place. But by and by, sure enough, I catched a glimpse of fire away through the trees. I went for it, cautious and slow. By and by I was close enough to have a look, and there laid a man on the ground. It damn well most give me the fantods. He had a blanket around his head, and his head was

nearly in the fire. I set there behind a clump of
bushes in about six foot of him, and kept my eyes on
him steady. It was getting gray daylight now. Pretty
soon he gapped and stretched himself and hove off
the blanket, and it was Miss Watson's Jim, for
Christ's sake! I bet I was damn glad to see him.
I says:

"Hello, Jim!" and skipped out.

He bounced up and stared at me wild. Then he
drops down on his knees, and puts his hands together and says:

"Doan' hurt me — don't! I hain't ever done no harm
to a ghos'. I alwuz liked dead people, en done all I
could for 'em. You go en git in de river ag'in, whah
you belongs, en doan' do nuffn to ole Jim, 'at 'uz
awluz yo' fren'."

Well, I warn't long making him understand I
warn't dead. I was sure as hell glad to see Jim. I
warn't lonesome now. I told him I warn't afraid of
him telling the people where I was. I talked along,
but he only set there and looked at me; never said a
danged word. Then I says:

"It's good daylight. Let's get breakfast. Make up
your camp-fire good."

"What's de use er makin' up de camp-fire to cook
strawbries en sich truck? But you got a gun, hain't
you? Den we kin git sumfn better den strawbries."

"Strawberries and such truck," I says. "Is that
what you live on?"

"I couldn't git nuffn else," he says.

"Why, how long you been on the island, Jim?"

"I come heah de night arter you's killed."

"What, all that time?"

"Yes-indeedy."

"And ain't you had nothing but that kind of rubbage to eat?"

"No, sah—nuffn else," he says, squidging up his face, "En she goes t'rough mighty damn fas'."

"Well, you must be most starved, ain't you?"

"I reck'n I could eat a hoss. I think I could. How long you ben on de islan'?"

"Since the night I got killed."

"No! W'y, what has you lived on? But you got a gun. Oh, yes, you got a gun. Dat's good. Now you kill sumfn en I'll make up de fire."

So we went over to where the canoe was, and while he built a fire in a grassy open place amongst the trees, I fetched meal and bacon and coffee, and coffee-pot and frying-pan, and sugar and tin cups, and the nigger was set back considerable, because he reckoned it was all done with witchcraft. I catched a good big catfish, too, and Jim cleaned him with his knife, and fried him.

When breakfast was ready we lolled on the grass and eat it smoking hot. Jim laid it in with all his might, for he was damn near starved. Then when we had got pretty well stuffed, we laid off and lazied.

By and by Jim says:

"But looky here, Huck, who in hell wuz it dat 'uz killed in dat shanty ef it warn't you?"

Then I told him the whole thing, and he said it was danged smart. He said Tom Sawyer couldn't get up no better plan than what I had. Then I says:

"How do you come to be here, Jim, and how'd you get here?"

He looked damned uneasy, and didn't say nothing for a minute. Then he says:

"Maybe I better not tell."

"Why, Jim?"

"Well, dey's damn good reasons. But you wouldn't tell on me ef I 'uz to tell you, would you, Huck?"

"Danged if I would, Jim."

"Well, I b'lieve you, Huck. I—I *run off*."

"Jim!"

"But mind, you said you wouldn' tell—you know you said you wouldn' tell, Huck."

"Well, I did. I said I wouldn't, and I'll stick to it. Honest to Christ, I will! People would call me a god-damn low-down Ab'litionist and despise me for keeping mum—but that don't make no difference. I ain't a-going to tell, and I ain't a-going back there anyways. So, now, let's know all about it."

"Well, you see, it 'uz dis way. Ole missus—dat's Miss Watson—she pecks on me all de time, en treats me pooty damn rough, but she awluz said she wouldn' sell me down to Orleans. But when she ups and dies—"

"Miss Watson died, Jim?"

" 'Bout a month arter yo' pappy come en tuck you away. She uz jes' setting' dar in de privy arter Sunday dinner, en *bim*, she keel over daid. Jes' like dat. Hain't you heerd?"

"How in hell could I hear, Jim? I been locked up in a dern cabin for more'n two months."

"Well, anyways, all her propity went to de widder, you know, en de widder tells me dat she ain't a-goin' to sell me souf', neider, but she don' know egzactly what to do wid me, seein' how she got all de niggers she can feed. And so when I see a damn nigger trader hangin' roun' de place, I begins to get oneasy. Dem traders'll talk de bark off'n a tree, en once't dey has dey han's on you, it's Orleans sho' as hell. Well, one night I see de widder an' him a-sittin' in de parlor, en he wuz a-jawin' away, all smiles en sweet-talk, so I seen de signs. I didn't need no ole ha'r-ball to tell *me* what to do.

"Dar 'uz dis Ab'litionis' name Winchell I hears 'bout. Him en some other men come f'um Ohier to he'p de po' slave-niggers get free. . . ."

"Why," says I. "That's Sarah Ann Winchell's pa!"

"You knows de genlman? Den I got bad news fo' you, Huck."

He told me all about it, how they had caught the three together and took him to the jail, and that it was some niggers they was going to help that told on them. There was a bunch of men with ropes outside the courthouse, and Jim said if the new judge hadn't give them twelve years at hard labor each, they'd a been hung.

"What fo' dem niggers 'peach on 'um?" he says. "Heah's white men a-gwyne he'p 'um git free, en dey turns 'round en does sum'pin' like dat. It don' make no damn sense, do it?"

"Hang it all, Jim," I says. "It was the only honest thing they *could* do. It's the law."

"Blame de damn law," he says. "What kin' er law take a man 'way fum his fambly? What kin' er law put a black man in chains en put a white man over him wid a whip? You tell me dat."

Well, I could see that them damn Ab'litionists had been a-talking to him, and giving him rascally notions. I didn't care if Mr Winchell *was* Sarah's pa, he hadn't no right messing around and getting the niggers of some people all stirred up which hadn't ever done nothing to *him*. It warn't no concern of *his*. But I let it drop. I asked Jim what happened to Sarah and her ma, and he told me that they was all right, that everybody felt sorry for them and understood it warn't none of *their* fault, and when the trial was over the courtroom passed the hat and got enough to buy them passage back to Ohio.

He said that Mr Winchell made a speech afterwards, and said that twelve years hard labor warn't nothing to what a slave sold South had to face, and that he hadn't no regrets. He said in such a state as Missouri was, the only place for an honest man was in prison anyways. He said if they was satisfied, he was, and that they should call it a draw. Well, that entertained them considerable, and they paid their respects with whatever was handy. Miz Winchell was there and seen it all. She didn't say nothing, but Jim said she was white as any sheet, and had bit her lip so danged hard the blood come. Only Sarah was crying, though she was trying not to. Say what you want, that girl *had* sand.

Jim heard that when they went down to get aboard the boat there warn't nobody at the landing but the clerks and niggers which did the loading and unloading, and they was all as still as death. He said that Miz Winchell and Sarah had to take their own baggage on board. They'd had a nigger servant of their own, a free nigger it turned out, but he'd been sent on ahead when the trouble broke.

Well, I knew then why it was Sarah warn't on the *other* steamboat, and it made me sad to think about it, her being the daughter of Ab'litionists and all. Jim said he was sorry it had to be him to bring me the bad news, but I said he warn't to blame. It all come from skating on the river, because if Miss Watson's Providence didn't have a hand in it, they could hang *me*.

Jim says:

"When dey took de genlmen which was Ab'lition-ists up to de State Prisom, it look bad fo' ole Jim. Who gwyne he'p him now? Who gwyne tell him wheah to go, en who to see? No use headin' No'th, but no damn good in jes' a-settin' 'roun waitin' to be traded Souf', nuther.

"De on'y thing lef' wuz jes' to git movin', some-wheres, so next night I tuck out en shin down de hill, en 'spec to steal a skift 'long de sho' som'ers 'bove de town, but dey wuz people a-stirring yit, so I hid in de ole tumbledown cooper shop on de bank to wait for everybody to go 'way. Well, I wuz dah all night. Dey wuz somebody roun' all de time. 'Long 'bout six in de mawnin' skifts begin to go by, en 'bout eight er nine every skift dat went 'long wuz talkin' 'bout how yo' pap come over to de town en say you's killed. Dese las' skifts wuz full o' ladies en genlmen a-goin' over fo' to see de place. Sometimes dey'd pull up at de sho' en take a res' b'fo' dey started acrost, so by de talk I got to know all 'bout de killin'. I 'uz powerful sorry you's killed, Huck, but I ain't no mo' now.

"I laid dah under de shavin's all day. I 'uz hungry as hell, but I warn't afeard; bekase I knowed de widder wuz goin' to start to de camp-meet'n' right arter breakfas' en be gone all day, en she knows I goes off wid de cattle 'bout daylight, so she wouldn' 'spec to see me roun' de place, en so dey wouldn' miss me tell arter dark in de evenin'. De yuther serv-ants wouldn' miss me, kase dey'd shin out en take holiday soon as de ole lady 'uz out'n de way.

"Well, when it come dark I tuck out up de river

road, en went 'bout two mile er more to whah dey
warn't no houses. I'd made up my mine 'bout what I's
a-gwyne to do. You see, ef I kep' on tryin' to git away
afoot, de damn dogs 'ud track me; ef I stole a skift
to cross over, dey'd miss dat skift, you see, en dey'd
know 'bout whah I'd lan' on de yuther side, en whah
to pick up my track. So I says, a raff is what I's arter;
it doan' *make* no damn track.

"I see a light a-comin' roun' de p'int by en by, so I
wade' in en shove' a log ahead o' me en swum more'n
half-way acrost de river, en got in 'mongst de driftwood, en kep' my head down low, en kinder swum
agin de current tell de raff come along. Den I swum
to de stern uv it en tuck a-holt. It clouded up en 'uz
pooty dark for a little while. So I clumb up en laid
down on de planks. De men 'uz all 'way yonder in de
middle, whah de lantern wuz. De river wuz a-risin',
en dey wuz a damn good current; so I reck'n'd 'at by
fo' in de mawnin' I'd be twenty-five mile down de
river, en den I'd slip in jis b'fo' daylight en swim
asho', en take to de woods on de Illinois side.

"But I didn' have no luck. When we 'uz mos' down
to de head er de islan' a man begin to come aft wid de
lantern. I see it warn't no damn use fer to wait, so I
slid overboard en struck out fer de islan'. Well, I had
a notion I could lan' mos' anywhers, but I couldn't—
bank too bluff. I 'uz mos' to de foot er de islan' b'fo' I
foun' a good place. I went into de woods en jedged I
wouldn' fool wid raffs no mo', long as dey move de
lantern roun' so. I had my pipe en a plug er dogleg en
some matches in my cap, en dey warn't wet, so I 'uz
all right."

"And so you ain't had no meat nor bread to eat all
this time? Why didn't you get mud-turkles?"

"How'n hell you gwyne to git 'm? You can't slip up on um en grab um; en how's a body gwyne to hit um wid a damn rock? How could a body do it in de night? En I warn't gwyne to show mysef on de bank in de daytime?"

"Well, that's so. You've had to keep in the woods all the time, I guess. Did you hear 'em shooting the cannon?"

"Oh, yes. I knowed dey was arter you. I see um go by heah—watched um thoo de bushes."

Some young birds come along, flying a yard or two at a time and lighting. Jim said it was a sign it was going to rain. He said it was a sign when young chickens flew that way, and so he reckoned it was the same when young birds done it. I was going to catch some of them, but Jim wouldn't let me. He said it was death, sure as hell. He said his father laid mighty sick once, and some of them catched a bird, and his old granny said his father would die, and he did.

And Jim said you mustn't count the things you are going to cook for dinner, because that would bring bad luck. The same if you shook the tablecloth after sundown. And he said if a man owned a beehive and that man died, the bees must be told about it before sun-up next morning, or else the bees would all weaken down and quit work and die. I had heard about some of these things before, but not all of them. Jim knowed all kinds of signs. He said he knowed most everything. I said it looked to me like all the signs was about bad luck, and so I asked him if there warn't any good-luck signs. He says:

"Mighty few—an' *dey* ain't no damn use to a body. What you want to know when good luck's a-comin' for? Want to keep it off?" And he said: "Ef you's got hairy arms en a hairy breas', it's a sign dat you's a-gwyne to be rich. Well, dey's some use in a sign like dat, 'kase it's so fur ahead. You see, maybe you's got to be po' a long time fust, en so you might git discourage' en kill yo' sef 'f you didn' know by de sign dat you gwyne to be rich by en by."

I told Jim that he had a hairy breast and hairy arms and I didn't see how he was very damn rich, and he says:

"No, and you doan' see me killin' mysef', neider." Then he thought for a minute and says: "I *is* rich, come to look at it. I owns mysef, doan' I? En I's wuth eight hund'd dollars. I wisht I had de money, I wouldn' want no mo'."

I told him he was damn well off without it. I said I was rich once, and ought to know.

VIII

The house of death floats by

I wanted to go and look at a place right about the middle of the island that I'd found when I was exploring; so we started and soon got to it, because the island was only three miles long and a quarter of a mile wide.

This place was a tolerable long, steep hill or ridge about forty foot high. We had a rough time getting to the top, the sides was so dern steep and the bushes so thick. We tramped and clumb around all over it, and by and by found a good big cavern in the rock, most up to the top on the side towards Illinois. The cavern was as big as two or three rooms bunched together, and Jim could stand up straight in it. It was cool in there. Jim was for putting our traps in there right away, but I said we didn't want to be climbing up and down there all the time.

Jim said if we had the canoe hid in a good place, and had all the traps in the cavern, we could rush there if anybody was to come to the island, and they would never find us without dogs. And, besides, he said them little birds had said it was going to rain, and did I want the things to get wet?

So we went back and got the canoe, and paddled up abreast the cavern, and lugged all the damn traps up there. Then we hunted up a place close by to hide the canoe in, amongst the thick willows. We took some fish off the lines and set them again, and begun to get ready for dinner.

The door of the cavern was big enough to roll a hogshead in, and on one side of the door the floor stuck out a little bit, and was flat and a good place to build a fire on. So we built it there and cooked dinner.

We spread the blankets inside for a carpet, and eat our dinner in there. We put all the other things handy at the back of the cavern. Pretty soon it darkened up, and begun to thunder and lighten; so the birds was right about it. Directly it begun to rain, and it rained like all hell let loose, too, and I never see the wind blow so. It was one of these reglar summer storms. It would get so dark that it looked all blue-black outside, and lovely; and the rain would thrash along by so damn thick that the trees off a little ways looked dim and spider-webby; and here would come a blast of wind that would bend the trees down and turn up the pale underside of the leaves; and then a perfect damn ripper of a gust would follow along and set the branches to tossing their arms as if they was wild; and next, when it was just about the bluest and blackest—*fst!* it was as bright as glory, and you'd have a little glimpse of treetops a-plunging about away off yonder in the storm, hundreds of yards further than you could see before; dark as sin again in a second, and now you'd hear the thunder let go with an awful darn crash, and then go rumbling, grumbling, tumbling, down the sky towards the underside of the world, like rolling empty barrels down-stairs — where it's long stairs and they bounce a good deal, you know.

"Goddamn, Jim, this is nice," I says. "I wouldn't want to be nowhere else but here. Pass me along another danged hunk of fish and some hot corn-bread."

"Well, you wouldn't a ben here 'f it hadn't a ben for Jim. You'd a ben down dah in de woods widout any dinner, en gittin' damn neah drownded, too; dat you would honey. Chickens knows when it's gwyne to rain, en so do de birds, chile."

The river went on raising and raising for ten or twelve days, till at last it was over the banks. The water was three or four foot deep on the island in the low places and on the Illinois bottom. On that side it was a good many miles wide, but on the Missouri side it was the same old distance across — a half a mile — because the Missouri shore was just a wall of high bluffs.

Daytimes we paddled all over the island in the canoe. It was mighty cool and shady in the deep woods, even if the sun was blazing outside. We went winding in and out amongst the trees, and sometimes the vines hung so damn thick we had to back away and go some other way. Well, on every old broken-down tree you could see rabbits and snakes and such things; and when the island had been overflowed a day or two they got so dern tame, on account of being hungry, that you could paddle right up and put your hand on them if you wanted to; but not the snakes and turkles — they would slide off in the water. The ridge our cavern was in was full of them. We could a had pets enough if we'd wanted them.

One night we catched a little section of a lumber-raft—nice pine planks. It was twelve foot wide and about fifteen or sixteen foot long, and the top stood above water six or seven inches—a solid, level floor. We could see saw-logs go by in the daylight sometimes, but we let them go; we didn't show ourselves in daylight.

Another night when we was up at the head of the island, just before daylight, here comes a frame-house down, on the west side. She was a two-story, and tilted over considerable. We paddled out and got aboard—clumb in at an upstairs window. But it was too dark to see yet, so we made the canoe fast and set in her to wait for daylight.

The light begun to come before we got to the foot of the island. Then we looked in at the window. We could make out a bed, and a table, and two old chairs, and lots of things around about on the floor, and there was clothes hanging against the wall. There was something laying in the far corner that looked like a man. So Jim says:

"Hullo, you!"

I could tell by his voice he was skairt. But when the man didn't budge, I give an even louder shout, and then Jim says:

"Dat man ain't asleep—he's daid. You hold still—I'll go en see."

He went, and bent down and looked, and says:

"It's a daid man. Yes, indeedy; naked, too. He's ben shot in de back. I reck'n he's ben daid two er three days. Come in, Huck, but doan' look at his face—it's too damn gashly."

I didn't look at him at all. Jim threw some old rags over him, but he needn't a done it; I sure as hell didn't want to see him. There was heaps of old greasy playing cards scattered around over the floor, the kind with pictures of naked men and women doing all sorts of wild things to one another so's to get your pecker stiff, and old whisky bottles, and a couple of masks made out of black cloth; and all over the walls was the dirtiest kind of words and drawings made with charcoal. Somebody had writ "FUK YOU" across one wall so's it was the first thing you see when you come in, that and the dead man. I took a bit of burnt wood out of the stove and blacked it over because it didn't seem right, somehow. No matter who he was he deserved kinder words than them. They was probably writ there before he died, but that didn't make no difference. Hell, he might a writ them hisself.

There was two dirty calico dresses, and a sunbonnet, and some women's underclothes hanging against the wall, and some men's clothes, too. We put the whole dang lot into the canoe—it might come good. There was a boy's old speckled straw hat on the floor; I took that, too. And there was a bottle that had had milk in it, and it had a rag stopper for a baby to suck. We would a took the bottle, but it was broke. There was a seedy old chest, and an old hair trunk with the hinges broke. They stood open, but there warn't nothing left in them that was worth a damn. The way things was scattered about we reckoned the people left in a hell of a hurry and warn't fixed so as to carry off most of their stuff.

We got an old tin lantern, and a butcher knife without any handle, and a bran-new Barlow knife worth two bits in any store, and a lot of tallow candles, and a tin candlestick, and a gourd, and a tin cup, and a ratty old bedquilt off the bed, and a little box with needles and pins and beeswax and buttons and thread and all such truck in it, and a hatchet and some nails, and a fish-line as thick as my little finger with some monstrous hooks on it, and a roll of buckskin, and a leather dog-collar, and a horseshoe, and some little jars of medicine that didn't have no label on them; and just as we was leaving I found a tolerable good currycomb, and Jim he found a ratty old fiddle-bow, and a wooden leg. The straps was broke off of it, but, barring that, it was a good enough leg, though it was too long for me and not long enough for Jim, and we couldn't find the other one, though we hunted everywhere.

And so, take it all around, we made a pretty damn good haul. When we was ready to shove off we was a quarter of a mile below the island, and it was broad day; so I made Jim lay down in the canoe and cover up with a quilt, because if he set up people could tell he was a nigger a good ways off. I paddled over to the Illinois shore, and drifted down most a half a mile doing it. I crept up the dead water under the bank, and hadn't no accidents and didn't see nobody. We got home all safe.

IX

What comes of handlin' snake-skin

After breakfast I wanted to talk about the dead man and guess out how he come to be killed, but Jim didn't want to. He said it would fetch bad luck; and besides, he said, he might come and ha'nt us; he said a man that warn't buried was more likely to go a-ha'nting around than one that was planted and comfortable. That sounded pretty damn reasonable, so I didn't say no more.

We rummaged the clothes we'd got, and found eight dollars in silver sewed up in the lining of an old blanket overcoat. Jim said he reckoned the people in that house stole the coat, because if they'd a knowed the money was there they wouldn't a left it. I said I reckoned they killed him, too; but Jim didn't want to talk about that. I says:

"Now you think, it's bad luck; but what did you say when I fetched in the snake-skin that I found on the top of the ridge day before yesterday? You said it was the worst bad luck in the world to touch a snake-skin with my hands. Well, here's your damned bad luck!

We've raked in all this truck and eight dollars besides. I wish we could have some bad luck like this
every damn day."

"Never you mind, honey, never you mind. Don't
you git too damn peart. It's a-comin'. Mind I tell you,
it's a-comin'."

It did come, too. It was a Tuesday that we had that
talk. Well, after dinner Friday we was laying around
in the grass at the upper end of the ridge, and got out
of tobacco. I went to the cavern to get some, and
found a rattlesnake in there. I killed him, and curled
him up on the foot of Jim's blanket, ever so natural,
thinking there'd be one hell of a lot of fun when Jim
found him there. Well, by night I forgot all about the
dern snake, and when Jim flung himself down on the
blanket while I struck a light the snake's mate was
there, and bit him.

He jumped up yelling, and the first thing the light
showed was the damned varmit curled up and ready
for another spring. I laid him out in a second with a
stick, and Jim grabbed pap's whisky-jug and begun
to pour it down.

He was barefooted, and the damn snake bit him
right on the heel. That all comes of my being such a
goldang fool as to not remember that wherever you
leave a dead snake its mate always comes there and
curls around it. Jim tole me to chop off the snake's
head and roast a piece of it. I done it, and he eat it
and said it would help cure him. He made me take off
the rattles and tie them around his wrist, too. He
said that that would help. Then I slid out quiet and
throwed the snakes clear away amongst the bushes;
for I sure as hell warn't going to let Jim find out it
was my fault, not if I could help it.

Jim sucked and sucked at the jug, and now and then he got out of his head and yelled; but every time he come to himself he went to sucking at the jug again. His foot swelled up pretty damn big, and so did his leg; but by and by the drunk begun to come, and so I judged he was all right; but I'd druther been bit with a snake than pap's whisky.

Jim was laid up for four days and nights. Then the swelling was all gone and he was around again. I made up my mind I wouldn't ever take a-holt of a danged snake-skin again with my hands, now that I see what had come of it. Jim said he reckoned I would believe him next time. And he said that handling a snake-skin was such awful damn bad luck that maybe we hadn't got to the end of it yet. He said he druther see the new moon over his left shoulder as much as a thousand times than take up a snake-skin in his hand. Well, I was getting to feel that way myself, though I've always reckoned that looking at the new moon over your left shoulder is one of the carelessest and foolishest things a body can do. Old Hank Bunker done it once, and bragged about it; and in less than two years he got drunk and fell off of the shot-tower, and spread himself out so dang thin that he was just a kind of layer, as you might say; and they slid him edgeways between two barn doors for a coffin, and buried him so, so they say, but I didn't see it. Pap told me. But anyway it all come of looking at the moon that way, like a darn fool.

Well, the days went along, and the river went down between its banks again; and about the first thing we done was to bait one of the big hooks with a skinned rabbit and set it and catch a catfish that was damn well big as a man, being six foot two inches long, and weighed over two hundred pounds. We couldn't handle him, of course; he would a flung us into Illinois. We just set there and watched him rip and tear around till he drownded. We found a brass button in his stomach and a round ball, and lots of rubbage. We split the ball open with a hatchet, and there was a spool in it. Jim said he'd had it there one hell of a long time, to coat it over so and make a ball of it. It was as big a dern fish as was ever catched in the Mississippi, I reckon. Jim said he hadn't ever seen a bigger one. He would a been worth a good deal over at the village. They peddle out such a fish as that by the pound in the market-house there; everybody buys some of him; his meat's white as snow and makes a damn good fry.

Next morning I said it was getting slow times and duller'n hell, and I wanted to get a stirring-up some way. I said I reckoned I would slip over the river and find out what was going on. Jim liked that notion; but he said I must go in the dark and look sharp. Then he studied it over and said, couldn't I put on some of them old things and dress up like a girl? That was a good notion, too. So we shortened up one of the calico gowns, and I turned up my trouser-legs to my knees and got into it. Jim hitched it behind with the hooks, and it was a fair fit. I put on the sun-bonnet and tied it under my chin, and then for a body to look in and see my face was like looking down a joint of stove-pipe. Jim said nobody would know me, even in the daytime, hardly. I practised around all day to get the hang of the things, and by and by I could do pretty well in them, only Jim said I didn't walk like a girl, I should throw my ass around a little more. I told him I was going into town after news, not trouble.

I started up the Illinois shore in the canoe just after dark.

I started across to the town from a little below the ferry-landing, and the drift of the current fetched me in at the bottom of the town. I tied up and started along the bank. There was a light burning in a little shanty that hadn't been lived in for a long time, and I wondered who had took up quarters there. I slipped up and peeped in at the window. There was a woman about forty year old in there knitting by a candle that was on a pine table. I didn't know her face; she was a stranger, for you couldn't start a face in that town that I didn't know. Now this was damn lucky, because I was weakening; I was getting afraid I had come; people might know my voice and find me out. But if this woman had been in such a little town two days she could tell me all I wanted to know; so I knocked at the door, and made up my mind I wouldn't forget I was a girl.

X

They're after us!

"C ome in," says the woman, and I did. She says: "Take a cheer."

I done it. She looked me all over with her little shiny eyes, and says:

"What might your name be?"

"Sarah Williams."

"Where 'bouts do you live? In this neighborhood?"

"No'm. In Hookerville, seven mile below. I've walked all the way and I'm all tired out."

"Hungry, too, I reckon. I'll find you something."

"No'm, I ain't hungry. I was so hungry I had to stop two miles below here at a farm; so I ain't hungry no more. It's what makes me so late. My mother's down sick, and out of money and everything, and I come to tell my uncle Abner Moore. He lives at the upper end of the town, she says. I hain't ever been here before. Do you know him?"

"No; but I don't know everybody yet. I haven't lived here quite two weeks. It's a considerable ways to the upper end of the town. You better stay here all night. Take off your bonnet."

"No," I says; "I'll rest awhile, I reckon, and go on. I ain't afeard of the dark."

She said it warn't the dark I should be afeard of, but it was all right, because her husband would be in by and by, maybe in an hour and a half, and she'd send him along with me. Then she got talking about her husband, and about her relations up the river, and her relations down the river, and about how much better off they used to be, and how they didn't know but they'd made a mistake coming to our town, instead of letting well alone—and so on and so on, till I was afeard *I* had made a mistake coming to her to find out what was going on in the town; but by and by she dropped on to pap and the murder, and then I was pretty willing to let her clatter right along. She told about me and Tom Sawyer finding the twelve thousand dollars (only she got it twenty) and all about pap and what a hard lot he was, and what a hard lot I was, and at last she got down to where I was murdered. I says:

"Who done it? We've heard considerable about these goings-on down in Hookerville, but we don't know who 'twas that killed Huck Finn."

"Well, I reckon there's a right smart chance of people *here* that'd like to know who killed him. Some think old Finn done it himself."

"No—is that so?"

"Most everybody thought it at first. He'll never know how nigh he come to getting lynched. But before night they changed around and judged it was done by a runaway nigger named Jim."

"Why *he*—" I stopped. I reckoned I damn well better keep still. She run on, and never noticed I had put in at all:

"The nigger run off the very night Huck Finn was killed. So there's a reward out for him—three hundred dollars. And there's a reward out for old Finn, too—two hundred dollars. You see, he come to town the morning after the murder, and told about it, and was out with 'em on the ferryboat hunt, and right away after he up and left. Before night they wanted to lynch him, but he was gone, you see. Well, next day they found out the nigger was gone; they found out he hadn't ben seen sence ten o'clock the night the murder was done. So then they put it on him, you see; and while they was full of it, next day, back comes old Finn, and went boo-hooing to Judge Thatcher to get money to hunt for the nigger all over Illinois with. The judge gave him some, and that evening he got drunk, and was around till after midnight with a couple of mighty hard-looking strangers, and then went off with them. Well, he hain't come back sence, and they ain't looking for him back till this thing blows over a little, for people thinks now that he killed his boy and fixed things so folks would think robbers done it, and then he'd get Huck's money without having to bother a long time with a lawsuit. People do say he warn't any too good to do it. Oh, he's sly, I reckon. If he don't come back for a year he'll be all right. You can't prove anything on him, you know; everything will be quieted down then, and he'll walk into Huck's money as easy as nothing."

"Yes, I reckon so, 'm. I don't see nothing in the way of it. Has everybody quit thinking the nigger done it?"

"Oh, no, not everybody. A good many thinks he done it. But they'll get the nigger pretty soon now, and maybe they can scare it out of him."

"Why, are they after him yet?"

"Well, you're innerscent, ain't you! Does three hundred dollars lay around every day for people to pick up? Some folks think the nigger ain't far from here. I'm one of them—but I hain't talked it around. A few days ago I was talking with an old couple that lives next door in the log shanty, and they happened to say hardly anybody ever goes to that island over yonder that they call Jackson's Island. Don't anybody live there? says I. No, nobody, says they. I didn't say any more, but I done some thinking. I was pretty near certain I'd seen smoke over there, about the head of the island, a day or two before that, so I says to myself, like as not that nigger's hiding over there, waiting for things to quiet down so he can move on over to the Illinois side. Lord knows, the bushes over there is full just now with men looking for that three hundred dollars."

"But ain't Illinois a free state?"

She winked one of them bright eyes at me, and says: "Oh, yes, it's a free state all right. But if a couple of men should come across a three hundred dollar nigger, why I don't reckon Illinois would know she was that much poorer, do you?"

"No 'm."

"Well, I don't think so, neither. Anyway, it's my notion that the nigger is hiding on the island. I ain't seen any smoke sence that first time, but it's worth the trouble to give the place a hunt. Husband's going over to see—him and another man. He was gone up the river; but he got back today, and I told him about the smoke as soon as he got here two hours ago."

I had got so damned uneasy I couldn't set still. I had to do something with my hands; so I took up a needle off of the table and went to threading it. My hands shook, and I was making a bad job of it. When the woman stopped talking I looked up, and she was looking at me pretty curious and smiling a little. I put down the needle and thread, and let on to be interested — and I was, too — and says:

"Three hundred dollars is a power of money. I wish my mother could get it. Is your husband going over there tonight?"

"Oh, yes. He went up-town with the man I was telling you of, to get a boat and see if they could borrow another gun. They'll go over after midnight."

"Couldn't they see better if they was to wait till daytime?"

"Yes. And couldn't the nigger see better, too? After midnight he'll likely be asleep, and they can slip around through the woods and hunt up his camp-fire all the better for the dark, if he's got one."

"I didn't think of that."

The woman kept looking at me pretty curious, and I didn't feel a bit comfortable. Pretty soon she says:

"What did you say your name was, honey?"

"M — Mary Williams."

Somehow it didn't seem to me that I said it was Mary before, so I didn't look up — seemed to me I said it was Sarah; so I felt sort of cornered, and was afeard maybe I was looking it too. I wished the woman would say something more; the longer she set still the uneasier I was. But now she says:

"Honey, I thought you said it was Sarah when you first come in?"

"Oh, yes'm, I did. Sarah Mary Williams. Sarah's my first name. Some calls me Sarah, some calls me Mary."

"Oh, that's the way of it?"

"Yes'm."

I was feeling better then, but I sure as hell wished I was out of there. I couldn't look up yet.

Well, the woman fell to talking about how hard times was, and how poor they had to live, and how the rats was as free as if they owned the place, and so forth and so on, and then I got easy again. She was right about the damn rats. You'd see one stick his nose out of a hole in the corner every little while. She said she had to have things handy to throw at them when she was alone, or they wouldn't give her no peace. She showed me a bar of lead twisted up into a knot, and said she was a good shot with it generly, but she'd wrenched her arm a day or two ago, and didn't know whether she could throw true now. But she watched for a chance, and directly banged away at a rat; but she missed him wide, and said "Ouch!" it hurt her arm so. Then she told me to try for the next one. I wanted to be getting away before the old man got back, but of course I didn't let on. I got the thing, and the first rat that showed his nose I let drive, and if he'd a stayed where he was he'd a been one damn sick rat. She said that was first-rate, and she reckoned I would hive the next one. She went and got the lump of lead and fetched it back, and brought along a hank of yarn which she wanted me to help her with. I held up my two hands and she put the hank over them, and went on talking about her and her husband's matters. But she broke off to say:

"Keep your eye on the rats. You better have the lead in your lap, handy."

So she dropped the lump into my lap just at that

moment, and I clapped my legs together on it and she went on talking. But only about a minute. Then she took off the hank and looked me straight in the face, and very pleasant, and says:

"Come, now, what's your real name?"

"Wh-at, mum?" I damn near went through the floor.

"What's your real name? Is it Bill, or Tom, or Bob?—or what is it?"

I reckon I shook like a leaf, and I didn't know hardly what to do. But I says:

"Please to don't poke fun at a poor girl like me, mum. If I'm in the way here, I'll—"

"No, you won't. Set down and stay where you are. I ain't going to hurt you, and I ain't going to tell on you, nuther. You just tell me your secret, and trust me. I'll keep it; and, what's more, I'll help you. So'll my old man if you want him to. You see, you're a runaway 'prentice, that's all. It ain't anything. There ain't no harm in it. You've been treated bad, and you made up your mind to cut. Bless you, child, I wouldn't tell on you. Tell me all about it now, that's a good boy."

So I said it wouldn't be no use to try to play it any longer, and I would just make a clean breast and tell her everything, but she mustn't go back on her promise. Then I told her my father and mother was dead, and the law had bound me out to a mean old farmer in the country thirty mile back from the river, and he treated me so bad I couldn't stand it no longer; he went away to be gone a couple of days, and so I took my chance and stole some of his daughter's old clothes and cleared out, and I had been three nights coming the thirty miles. I traveled nights, and hid daytimes and slept, and the bag of bread and meat I carried from home lasted me all the way, and I had a-plenty. I said I believed my uncle Abner Moore would take care of me, and so that was why I struck out for this town of Goshen.

"Goshen, child? This ain't Goshen. This is St. Petersburg. Goshen's ten mile further up the river. Who told you this was Goshen?"

"Why, a man I met at daybreak this morning, just as I was going to turn into the woods for my reglar sleep. He told me when the roads forked I must take the right hand, and five mile would fetch me to Goshen."

"He was drunk, I reckon. He told you just exactly wrong."

"Well, he did act like he was drunk, but it ain't no matter now. I got to be moving along. I'll fetch Goshen before daylight."

"Hold on a minute. I'll put you up a snack to eat. You might want it."

So she put me up a snack, and says:

"Say, when a cow's laying down, which end of her gets up first? Answer up prompt now — don't stop to study over it. Which end gets up first?"

"The hind end, mum."

"Well, then, a horse?"

"The forrard end, mum."

"Which side of a tree does the moss grow on?"

"North side."

"If fifteen cows is browsing on a hillside, how many of them eats with their heads pointed the same direction?"

"The whole fifteen, mum."

"Well, I reckon you *have* lived in the country. I thought maybe you was trying to hocus me again. What's your real name, now?"

"George Peters, mum."

"Well, try to remember it, George. Don't forget and tell me it's Elexander before you go, and then get out by saying it's George Elexander when I catch you. And don't go about women in that old calico. You do a girl tolerable poor, but you might fool men, maybe. Bless you, child, when you set out to thread a needle don't hold the thread still and fetch the needle up to it; hold the needle still and poke the thread at it; that's the way a woman most always does, but a man always does t'other way. And when you throw at a rat or anything, hitch yourself up a-tiptoe and fetch your hand up over your head as awkward as you can, and miss your rat about six or seven foot. Throw stiff-armed from the shoulder, like there was a pivot there for it to turn on, like a girl; not from the wrist and elbow, with your arm out to one side, like a boy. And, mind you, when a girl tries to catch anything in her lap she throws her knees apart; she don't clap them together, the way you did when you catched the lump of lead. Why, I spotted you for a boy when you was threading the needle; and I rigged the other things just to make certain. Now trot along to your uncle, Sarah Mary Williams George Elexander Peters, and if you get into trouble you send word to Mrs. Judith Loftus, which is me, and I'll do what I can to get you out of it. Keep the river road all the way, and next time you tramp take shoes and socks with you. The river road's a rocky one, and your feet'll be in a condition when you get to Goshen, I reckon."

I went up the bank about fifty yards, and then I doubled on my tracks and slipped back to where my canoe was, a good piece below the house. I jumped in, and was off in a hurry. I went up-stream far enough to make the head of the island, and then started across. I took off the sun-bonnet, for I didn't want no damn blinders on. When I was about the middle I heard the clock begin to strike, so I stops and listens; the sound come faint over the water but clear—eleven. When I struck the head of the island I never waited to blow, though I was most winded, but I shoved right into the timber where my old camp used to be, and started a good fire there on a high and dry spot.

Then I jumped in the canoe and dug out for our place, a mile and a half below, as hard as I could go. I landed, and slopped through the timber and up the ridge, and into the cavern. There Jim laid, sound asleep on the ground. I roused him out and says:

"Git up and hump yourself, Jim! There ain't a damn minute to lose. They're after us!"

Jim never asked no questions, he never said a word; but the way he worked for the next half an hour showed about how he was scared. By that time everything we had in the world was on our raft, and she was ready to be shoved out from the willow cove where she was hid. We put out the camp-fire at the cavern the first thing, and didn't show a candle outside after that.

I took the canoe out from the shore a little piece, and took a look; but if there was a boat around I couldn't see it, for stars and shadows ain't good to see by. Then we got out the raft and slipped along down in the shade, toward the foot of the island dead still—never saying a word. It was powerful quiet there, no sound but the water hissing along the bank, and dark, too. You couldn't hardly see the island, but you could *feel* it, looming up over you like it was about to fall.

Jim and I didn't say a word, just stood there whilst the island slipped along past us. He had a-holt of the sweep, hard over so's to keep us from being drawed in to shore, and then when the island dropped off astern, he brung it back amidships and give a little sigh. I knowed he was glad that we warn't still back there, and that he was on his way to freedom, but somehow I couldn't feel very gay. The further astern the island got the nervouser I got a-thinking over what I had done. For here I was on a raft with a goddamned runaway nigger slave, and of my own free will, too. There warn't no excuse for it, and if'n you had held a gun on me, I couldn't a thought one up.

Well, fuck it, says I, there hain't nothing to be done now. A pisoned rat feels chipper to how I felt then, but there warn't nothing I could do about it, short of jumping overboard, and I ain't never been partial to swimming at night. There's something about that deep darkness under you that makes you keep close to shore, and it was half a mile from where we was to the nearest land.

Jim had begun to push and haul on the sweep, and pretty soon he started in humming a hymn tune, the way niggers will when they're a-working. I says:

"Damn it, Jim, will you stow that! We ain't to the Promised Land yet, not by a damn sight."

Jim bit it right off and swallered it, and didn't say a word more. "There'll be plenty of time later for camp-meetings," I says, but he didn't say nothing, so I didn't nuther. Pretty soon I crept forward where our traps was and rolled up in my blanket and went to sleep, but it warn't a good sleep, and I reckoned Miss Watson's Providence had a hand it it somewheres, even though she was dead.

XI

"Better let damn well alone"

It must a been close on to one o'clock when we got below the island at last, and the raft did seem to go mighty damn slow. If a boat was to come along we was going to take to the canoe and break for the Illinois shore and take our chances over there. It was well a boat didn't come, for we hadn't ever thought to put the gun in the canoe, or a fishing-line, or anything to eat. We was in ruther too much of a sweat to think of so many things. It warn't good judgment to put *everything* on the raft.

If the men went to the island I just expect they found the camp-fire I built, and watched it all night for Jim to come. Anyways, they stayed away from us, and if my building the fire never fooled them, it warn't no damned fault of mine. I played it as low down on them as I could.

When the first streak of day began to show we tied up to a towhead in a big bend on the Illinois side, and hacked off cottonwood branches with the hatchet and covered up the raft with them so she looked like there had been a cave-in in the bank there. A tow-head is a sand-bar that has cottonwoods on it as thick as harrow-teeth.

We had mountains on the Missouri shore and heavy timber on the Illinois side, and the channel was down the Missouri shore at that place, so we warn't afraid of anybody running across us. We laid there all day, and watched the rafts and steamboats spin down the Missouri shore, and up-bound steam-boats fight the big river in the middle. I told Jim all about the time I had jabbering with that dern old woman; and Jim said she was a smart one, and if she was to start after us herself *she* wouldn't set down and watch a camp-fire — no, sir, she'd fetch a dog. Well, then, I said, why couldn't she tell her husband to fetch a dog? Jim said he bet she did think of it by the time the men was ready to start, and he believed they must a gone up-town to get a dog and so they lost all that time, or else we wouldn't be here on a towhead sixteen or seventeen mile below the vil-lage — no, indeedy, we would be in that same old town again. So I said I didn't give a damn what the reason was they didn't get us as long as they didn't. Being catched with a runaway nigger ain't no picnic, but I didn't say that.

When it was beginning to come on dark we poked our heads out of the cottonwood thicket, and looked up and down and across; nothing in sight; so Jim took up some of the top planks of the raft and built a snug wigwam to get under in blazing weather and rainy, and to keep the things dry. Jim made a floor for the wigwam, and raised it a foot or more above the level of the raft, so now the blankets and all the traps was out of reach of steamboat waves. Right in the middle of the wigwam we made a layer of dirt about five or six inches deep with a frame around it for to hold it to its place; this was to build a fire on in sloppy weather or chilly; the wigwam would keep it from being seen. We made an extra steering-oar, too, because one of the others might get broke on a damn snag or something. We fixed up a short forked stick to hang the old lantern on, because we must always light the lantern whenever we see a steamboat coming down-stream, to keep from getting run over; but we wouldn't have to light it for up-stream boats unless we see we was in what they call a "crossing"; for the river was pretty high yet, very low banks being still a little under water; so up-bound boats didn't always run the channel, but hunted easy water.

This second night we run between seven and eight hours, with a current that was making over four mile an hour. We catched fish and talked, and we took a swim now and then to keep off sleepiness. It was kind of solemn, drifting down the big, still river, laying on our backs looking up at the stars, and we didn't ever feel like talking loud, and it warn't often that we laughed—only a little kind of a low chuckle. We had mighty damn good weather as a general thing, and nothing ever happened to us at all—that night, nor the next, nor the next.

Every night we passed towns, some of them away up on black hillsides, nothing but just a shiny bed of lights; not a house could you see. The fifth night we passed St. Louis, and it was like the whole damned world lit up. In St. Petersburg they used to say there was twenty or thirty thousand people in St. Louis, but I never believed it till I see that wonderful dang spread of lights at two o'clock that still night. There warn't a sound there; everybody was asleep.

Every night now I used to slip ashore toward ten o'clock at some village, and buy ten or fifteen cents worth of meal or bacon or other stuff to eat; and some-times I lifted a chicken that warn't roosting comfort-able, and took him along. Pap always said, take a chicken when you get a chance, because if you don't want him yourself you can easy find somebody that does, and a good deed ain't ever forgot. I never see pap when he didn't want the damn chicken himself, but that is what he used to say, anyway.

Mornings before daylight I slipped into corn-fields and borrowed a watermelon, or a mushmelon, or a punkin, or some new corn, or things of that kind. Pap always said it warn't no harm to borrow things if you was meaning to pay them back some time; but the widow said it warn't anything but a soft name for stealing, and no decent body would do it. Jim said he reckoned the widow was partly right and pap was partly right; so the best way would be for us to pick out two or three things from the list and say we wouldn't borrow them any more—then he reckoned it wouldn't be no harm to borrow the others. So we talked it over all one night, drifting along down the river, trying to make up our minds whether to drop the watermelons, or the mushmelons, or what. But toward daylight we got all settled satisfactory, and concluded to drop crabapples and p'simmons. We warn't feeling just right before that, but it was all comfortable now. I was glad the way it come out, too, because crabapples ain't ever good, and the p'sim-mons wouldn't be ripe for two or three months yet.

We shot a water-fowl now and then that got up too early in the morning or didn't go to bed early enough in the evening. Take it all round, we lived pretty darn high.

The fifth night below St. Louis we had a big storm after midnight, with a power of thunder and lightning, and the rain poured down in a solid damn sheet. We stayed in the wigwam and let the raft take care of itself. When the lightning glared out we could see a big straight river ahead, and high, rocky bluffs on both sides. By and by says I, "Hel-*lo*, Jim, looky yonder!" It was a steamboat that had killed herself on a rock. We was drifting straight down for her. The lightning showed her very clear. She was leaning over, with part of her upper deck above water, and you could see every little chimbly-guy clean and clear, and a chair by the big bell, with an old slouch hat hanging on the back of it, when the flashes come.

Well, even if it was away in the night and stormy, and all so mysterious-like, with the wreck laying there so damned mournful and lonesome in the middle of the river, I see that here was a chance to have some real adventures, the kind Tom Sawyer was always talking about. Besides, there warn't no telling what people might a left on board. So I says:

"Let's land on her Jim, and slink around a little and see what's there."

But Jim was dead against it at first. He says:

"I doan' want to go fool'n' 'long er no wrack. We's doin' damn well, en we better let damn well alone. Like as not dey's a watchman on dat wrack."

"Watchman your grandmother," I says; "there hain't nothing to watch but the texas and the pilot-house; and do you reckon anybody's going to resk his

life for a dern texas and a pilot-house such a night as
this, when it's likely to break up and wash off down
the river any minute?" Jim couldn't say nothing to
that, so he didn't try. "And besides," I says, "we
might borrow something worth having out of the captain's stateroom. Seegars, *I* bet you—and cost five
cents apiece, solid cash. Steamboat captains is always rich, and get sixty dollars a month, and *they*
don't care a cent what a thing costs, you know, long
as they want it. Stick a candle in your pocket; I can't
rest, Jim, till we give her a rummaging."

Jim he grumbled a little, but give in. He said we
mustn't talk any more than we could help, and then
mighty damn low. The lightning showed us the wreck
again just in time, and we fetched the stabboard
derrick, and made fast there.

The deck was high out here. We went sneaking
down the slope of it to labboard, in the dark, towards
the texas, feeling our way slow with our feet, and
spreading our hands out to fend off the guys, for it
was so damned dark we couldn't see no sign of them.
Pretty soon we struck the forrard end of the skylight, and clumb on it; and the next step fetched us
in front of the captain's door, which was open, and
then by Jesus, away down through the texas-hall we
see a light! and all in the same second we seem to
hear low voices in yonder!

Jim whispered and said he was feeling mighty
damn sick, and told me to come along. I says, all
right, and was going to start for the raft; but just then
I heard a voice wail out and say:

"Oh, please don't, boys; I swear I won't ever tell!"

Another voice said, pretty loud:

"It's a goddamn lie, Jim Turner. You've acted this

way before. You always want to hog more'n your
share of the truck, and you've always got it, too, because you've swore't if you didn't you'd tell. But this
time you've said it jest one time too many. You're the
meanest, treacherousest son-of-a-bitch in this country."

By this time Jim was gone for the raft. I was just
a-biling with curiosity; and I says to myself, I'm a
going to see what's going on here. So I dropped on my
hands and knees in the little passage, and crept aft
in the dark till there warn't but one stateroom betwixt me and the cross-hall of the texas. Then in
there I see a man stretched on the floor and tied hand
and foot, and two men standing over him, and one of
them had a dim lantern in his hand, and the other
one had a pistol. This one kept pointing the pistol
at the man's head on the floor, and saying:

"I'd *like* to! And I orter, too—a mean, goddamn
skunk!"

The man on the floor would shrivel up and say,
"Oh, please don't, Bill; I hain't ever goin' to tell."

And every time he said that the man with the
lantern would laugh and say:

" 'Deed you ain't, you barstid! You never said no
truer thing 'n that, you bet you." And once he said:
"Hear the son-of-a-bitch beg! and yit if we hadn't got
the best of him and tied him he'd a killed us both.
And what *for*? Jist for noth'n'. Jist because we stood
on our friggin' *rights*—that's what for. But I lay you
ain't a-goin' to threaten nobody any more, Jim Turner.
Put *up* that damn pistol, Bill."

Bill says:

"I don't want to, Jake Packard. I'm for killin' him—

and didn't he kill old Hatfield just the same way—and
don't he goddamn well deserve it?"

"But I don't *want* him killed, and I've got my
reasons for it."

"Bless yo' heart for them words, Jake Packard! I'll
never forgit you long's I live!" says the man on the
floor, sort of blubbering.

Packard didn't take no notice of that, but hung up
his lantern on a nail and started toward where I was,
there in the dark, and motioned Bill to come. I craw-
fished as fast as I could about two yards, but the boat
slanted so that I couldn't make very good time; so to
keep from getting run over and catched I crawled
into a stateroom on the upper side. The man came
a-pawing along in the dark, and when Packard got
to my stateroom, he says:

"Here—come in here."

And in he come, and Bill after him. But before they
got in I was up in the upper berth, cornered, and
goddamn sorry I come. Then they stood there, with
their hands on the ledge of the berth, and talked. I
couldn't see them, but I could tell where they was by
the whisky they'd been having. I was glad I didn't
drink whisky; but it wouldn't made much difference
anyway, because most of the time I didn't breathe. I
was too damn scared. And, besides, a body *couldn't*
breathe and hear such talk. They talked low and
earnest. Bill wanted to kill Turner. He says:

"He's said he'll tell, and he shore'n hell will. If we
was to give both our shares to him *now* it wouldn't
make no difference after the row and the way we've
served him. Shore'n shit, he'll turn state's evidence;
now you hear *me*, I'm for putting him out of his
troubles."

"So'm I," says Packard, very quiet.

"Damnation! I'd sorter begun to think you wasn't. Well, then, that's all right. Le's go and do it."

"Hold on a goddamn minute; I hain't had my say yit. You listen to me. Shooting's good, but there's quieter ways if the thing's *got* to be done. But what *I* say is this: it ain't good sense to go court'n' around after a friggin' halter if you can git at what you're up to in some way that's jist as good and at the same time don't bring you into no damn resks. Ain't that so?"

"You bet it is. But how in Christ's name you goin' to manage it this time?"

"Well, my idea is this: we'll rustle around and gather up whatever pickin's we've overlooked in the staterooms, and shove for shore and hide the truck. Then we'll wait. Now I say it ain't a-goin' to be more'n two hours befo' this damn wrack breaks up and washes off down the river. See? He'll be drownded, and won't have nobody to blame for it but his own goddamn self. I reckon that's a considerable sight better 'n killin' of him. I'm unfavorable to killin' a man as long as you can git aroun' it; it ain't good sense, it ain't good morals. Ain't I right?"

"Yes, I reck'n you are. But s'pose she *don't* break up and wash off?"

"Well, we can wait the two hours anyway and see, can't we?"

"All right, then; come along."

So they started, and I lit out, all in a cold sweat, and scrambled forward. It was dark as pitch there; but I said, in a kind of a coarse whisper, "Jim!" and he answered up, right at my elbow, with a sort of a moan, and I says:

"Quick, Jim, it ain't no time for farting around and moaning; there's a gang of murderers in yonder, and if we don't hunt up their boat and set her drifting down the river so these sons-a-bitches can't get away from the wreck, there's one of 'em going to be in a goddamn fix. But if we find their boat we can put *all* of 'em in a fix—for the sheriff 'll get 'em. Quick—hurry! I'll hunt the labboard side, you hunt the stabboard. You start at the raft, and—"

"Oh, my lordy, lordy! *Raf'*? Dey ain' no raf' no mo'; she done broke loose en gone! —en here we is!"

XII

Honest loot from the "Walter Scott"

Well, I catched my breath and goddamn near fainted. Shut up on a wreck with such a gang as that! But it warn't no time to be sentimentering. We'd *got* to find that boat now—had to have it for ourselves. So we went a-quaking and shaking down the stabboard side, and slow work it was, too—seemed a week before we got to the stern. No sign of a boat. Jim said he didn't believe he could go any farther—so scared he hadn't hardly any strength left, he said. But I said, come on, if we get left on this wreck we are in a fix, sure'n hell. So on we prowled again. We struck for the stern of the texas, and found it, and then scrabbled along forwards on the skylight, hanging on from shutter to shutter, for the edge of the skylight was in the water. When we got pretty close to the cross-hall door there was the skiff, sure enough! I could just barely see her. I felt mighty dern thankful. In another second I would a been aboard of her, but just then the door opened. One of the men stuck his head out only about a couple of foot from me, and I thought I was gone; but he jerked it in again, and says:

"Heave that friggin' lantern out o' sight, Bill!"

He flung a bag of something into the boat, and then got in himself and set down. It was Packard. Then Bill *he* come out and got in. Packard says, in a low voice:

"All ready — shove off!"

I couldn't hardly hang on to the shutters, I was so godamighty weak. But Bill says:

"Hold on — 'd you go through him?"

"Hell, no. Didn't you?"

"No, goddamn it. So he's got his share o' the cash yet."

"Well, then, shin back up there and get it; no use to take truck and leave money."

Bill got up but then he stood still in the skiff a minute. Finally he says:

"Hold on, Jake Packard. How do I know you won't hive out of here soon's I'm back on board?"

Packard, he cursed, and says:

"Damn it all, Bill, what kind of man do you take me for? You think I'd leave you on board with your share of the swag *and* his'n?"

"Maybe you already *took* his'n."

"You *are* a suspicious son of a bitch, hain't you? I suppose noth'n' will do but for me to git back on board with you. Come along."

So they got out and went in.

The door slammed to because it was on the careened side; and in a half second I was in the boat, and Jim come tumbling after me. I out with my knife and cut the rope, and away we went!

We didn't touch an oar, and we didn't speak nor

whisper, nor hardly even breathe. We went gliding swift along, dead silent, past the tip of the paddlebox, and past the stern; then in a second or two more we was a hundred yards below the wreck, and the darkness soaked her up, every last sign of her, and we was safe, and knowed it.

When we was three or four hundred yards downstream we see the lantern show like a little spark at the texas door for a second, and we knowed by that that the rascals had missed their boat, and was beginning to understand that they was in just as much trouble now as Jim Turner was.

Then Jim manned the oars, and we took out after our raft. Now was the first time that I begun to worry about the men—I reckon I hadn't had time to before. I begun to think how dreadful it was, even for murderers, to be in such a damn fix. I says to myself, there ain't no telling but I might come to be a murderer myself yet, and then how would I like it? So says I to Jim:

"The first light we see we'll land a hundred yards below it or above it, in a place where it's a good hiding-place for you and the skiff, and then I'll go and fix up some kind of a yarn, and get somebody to go for that gang and get them out of their scrape, so they can be hung when their time comes."

But that idea was a failure; for pretty soon it begun to storm again, and this time worse than ever. The dern rain poured down, and never a light showed; everybody in bed, I reckon. We boomed along down the river, watching for lights and watching for our raft. After a long time the rain let up, but the clouds stayed, and the lightning kept whimpering, and by

and by a flash showed us a black thing ahead, floating, and we made for it.

It was the raft, and mighty damn glad was we to
get aboard of it again. We seen a light now away
down to the right, on shore. So I said I would go for
it. The skiff was half full of loot which that gang had
stole there on the wreck. We hustled it on to the raft
in a pile, and I told Jim to float along down, and show
a light when he judged he had gone about two mile,
and keep it burning till I come; then I manned my
oars and shoved for the light. As I got down towards
it three or four more showed—up on a hillside. It was
a village. I closed in above the shore light, and laid
on my oars and floated. As I went by I see it was a
lantern hanging on the jackstaff of a double-hull
ferryboat. I skimmed around for the watchman,
a-wondering whereabouts he slept; and by and by I
found him roosting on the bitts forward under a bit
of canvas he had tied to the rail for shelter. His head
was down between his knees, so I gave his shoulder
two or three little shoves, and begun to cry.

He stirred up in a kind of startlish way, and
tossed aside the canvas; but when he see it was
only me he took a good gap and stretch, and then
he says:

"Hello, what's up? Don't cry, bub. What's the
trouble?"

I says:

"Pap, and mam, and sis, and—"

Then I broke down. He says:

"Oh, damn it now, *don't* take on so; we all has to
have our troubles, and this 'n 'll come out all right.
What's the matter with 'em?"

"They're—they're—are you the watchman of the boat?"

"Yes," he says, kind of pretty-well-satisfied like. "I'm the captain and the owner and the mate and the pilot and watchman and head deck-hand; and sometimes I'm the freight and passengers. I ain't as rich as old Jim Hornback, and I can't be so damn generous and good to Tom, Dick, and Harry as what he is, and slam around money the way he does; but I've told him a many a time 't I wouldn't trade places with him; for, says I, a sailor's life's the life for me, and I'm damned if *I'd* live two mile out o' town, where there ain't nothing ever goin' on, not for all his spondulicks and as much more on top of it. Says I—"

I broke in and says:

"They're in an awful peck of trouble, and—"

"*Who* is?"

"Why, pap and mam and sis and Miss Hooker; and if you'd take your ferryboat and go up there—"

"Up where? Where are they?"

"On the wreck."

"What wreck?"

"Why, there ain't but one."

"What, you don't mean the *Walter Scott*?"

"Yes."

"Good Christ! What are they doin' there, for God-sakes?"

"Well, they didn't go there a-purpose."

"I bet they didn't! Why, Christamighty, there ain't no chance for 'em if they don't git off mighty quick! Why, how in hell did they ever git into such a scrape?"

"Easy enough. Miss Hooker was a-visiting up there to the town"

"Yes. Booth's Landing—go on."

"She was a-visiting there at Booth's Landing, and just in the edge of the evening she started over with her nigger woman in the horse-ferry to stay all night at her friend's house, Miss What-you-may-call-her—I disremember her name—and they lost their steering-oar, and swung around and went a-floating down, stern first, about two mile, and saddle-baggsed on the wreck, and the ferry man and the nigger woman and the horses was all lost, but Miss Hooker she made a grab and got aboard the wreck. Well, about an hour after dark we come along down in our trading-scow, and it was so dark we didn't notice the wreck till we was right on it; and so *we* saddle-baggsed; but all of us was saved but Bill Whipple—and oh, he *was* the best cretur!— I most wish't had been me, I do,"

"I'll be damned if that ain't the goddamnedest thing I ever struck! And *then* what did you all do?"

"Well, we hollered and took on, but it's so wide there we couldn't make nobody hear. So pap said somebody got to get ashore and get help somehow. I was the only one that could swim, so I made a dash for it, and Miss Hooker she said if I didn't strike help sooner, come here and hunt up her uncle, and he'd fix the thing. I made the land about a mile below, and been fooling along ever since, trying to get people to do something, but they said, 'What, in such a night and such a current? There ain't no sense in it; go for the steam-ferry.' Now if you'll go and—"

"By Jesus, I'd *like* to, and, goldarn, I don't know

but I will; but who in the damnation's a-going to *pay* for it? Do you reckon your pap—"

"Why, *that's* all right. Miss Hooker she tole me, *particular*, that her Uncle Hornback—"

"Jesus H. Christ! is *he* her uncle? Looky here, you break for that light over yonder-way, and turn out west when you git there, and about a quarter of a mile out you'll come to the tavern; tell 'em to dart you out to Jim Hornback's, and he'll foot the bill. And don't you fool around any, because he'll want to know the news. Tell him I'll have his niece all safe before he can get to town. Hump yourself, now; I'm a-going up around the corner here to roust out my engineer."

I struck for the light, but as soon as he turned the corner I went back and got into my skiff and bailed her out, and then pulled up shore in the easy water about six hundred yards, and tucked myself in among some woodboats; for I couldn't rest easy till I could see the ferryboat start. But take it all around, I was feeling ruther comfortable on accounts of taking all this damn trouble for that gang, for not many would a done it. I wished the widow knowed about it. I judged she would be proud of me for helping these danged rapscallions, because rapscallions and dead-beats is the kind the widow and good people takes the most interest in.

Well, before long here comes the wreck, dim and dusky, sliding along down! A kind of cold shiver went through me, and then I struck out for her. She was very deep, and I see in a minute there warn't much chance for anybody being alive in her. I pulled all around her and hollered a little, but there warn't any answer; all dead still. I felt a little bit heavy-hearted about the gang, but not much, for I reckoned if they could stand it I sure as hell could.

Then here comes the ferryboat; so I shoved for the middle of the river on a long down-stream slant; and when I judged I was out of eye-reach I laid on my oars, and looked back and see her go and smell around the wreck for Miss Hooker's remainders, because the captain would know her Uncle Hornback would want them; and then pretty soon the ferryboat give it up and went for the shore, and I laid into my work and went a-booming down the river.

It did seem a damned powerful long time before Jim's light showed up; and when it did show it looked like it was a thousand mile off. By the time I got there the sky was beginning to get a little gray in the east; so we struck for an island, and hid the raft, and sunk the skiff, and turned in and slept like dead people.

XIII

Fooling poor old Jim

By and by, when we got up, we turned over the truck the gang had stole off of the wreck, and found boots, blankets, and clothes, and all sorts of other things, and a spy-glass, and three boxes of seegars. We hadn't ever been this danged rich before in neither of our lives. The seegars was prime, and so we laid off all the afternoon in the woods, smoking and talking, and having a general good time. I told Jim all about what happened inside the wreck and at the ferryboat, and I said these kinds of things was adventures, like those Tom Sawyer read about in his books, only for real. Jim said he didn't want no more damned adventures. He said that when I went in the texas and he crawled back to get on the raft and found her gone he damn near died, because he judged it was all up with *him* anyway it could be fixed; for if he didn't get saved he would get drownded; and if he did get saved, whoever saved him would send him back home so's to get the reward, and then if he didn't get hung, the widow would most likely sell him South, anyhow, which was just as bad.

Well, he was right; he was most always right. He had an uncommon level head, for a nigger, and I told him we wouldn't have no more adventures unless we couldn't help it. There was some books in the boodle the thieves had took from the *Walter Scott*, and from what I could make out from the words and the pictures, *they* was all about adventures, too, the doings of kings and such, and useless. I was all for chucking them, but Jim said no, the paper might always come in handy for starting fires and what-not. After that, whenever he went aft to take a crap, he always toted one of them books along, to look at the pictures and when he was done tear out a page or two to finish his business with.

There was one picture all in colors he was tolerable fond of, which showed a lovely yaller-haired gal standing on top of a castle with a little bird perched on one finger. Her lips was stuck out like she was trying to whistle to it or kiss it or maybe blow dust off it, but the book didn't say which. Her name was "Fair Rowena," which was printed underneath. Jim took such a liking to Fair Rowena that he eased her out and stuck her up in the wigwam next to his tick. Well, I didn't much cotton to that. Pap used to say that a nigger who's hankering for trouble will most likely try to find it under a white gal's dress. It was bad enough Jim was a runaway, but now he was laying on his tick with the Fair Rowena next to him, a-thinking things that got my danged blood in a boil just wondering what they was.

It was just one more case of books bringing nothing but mischief, and I was damned sorry we didn't throw them away. But we didn't, we snugged them down with the rest of the truck, and when night come on, we cut loose from the island, and went a-drifting on down-stream. We judged that three nights more would fetch us to Cairo, at the bottom of Illinois, where the Ohio River comes in. Jim said that was his best chance. Instead of heading right across Illinois, which was full of sheriffs on the lookout for runaways, he reckoned we should sell the raft and get on a steamboat and go way up the Ohio amongst the free states, and then be out of trouble. He spent the next day laying out his plan, and it was a good one so far as it went. He said that with us dressed up in the fine clothes we took off the *Walter Scott*, I could pass as quality and him as my nigger. Being on a steamboat ain't like tramping cross country. Everybody is a stranger on a boat and nobody das't ask questions. Pap used to say there hain't no place like a river-boat crowd to hide in, and he ought to know.

So it was a fine plan, only I didn't care much about being in it. It did seem to me that I done my share and more already, and now here Jim was a-talking about my helping him get the rest of the way clear, right into the free states. I didn't like it worth shucks, and I'd a told him so, only it wouldn't a done no good. Once a nigger gets a damn notion in his head, no matter how foolish, there ain't no way of getting it out again, because you just can't learn a nigger to argue. If he ain't wrong, he's right, and there ain't no shaking him. So I decided to keep mum till a chance come for me to slide.

Well, the second night a fog begun to come on, and we made for a towhead to tie to, for it wouldn't do to try to run in a fog; but when I paddled ahead in the

canoe, with the line to make fast, there warn't anything but some damn little saplings to tie to. I passed
the line around one of them right on the edge of the
cut bank, but there was a stiff current, and the raft
come booming down so lively she tore it out by the
roots and away she went. I see the fog closing down,
and it made me so goddamn sick and scared I couldn't
budge for most a half a minute it seemed to me — and
then there warn't no raft in sight; you couldn't see
twenty yards.

Then the thought come to me, here's your chance!
All I had to do was sit tight, and when the fog
lifted, I could cross over to the Missouri side and
light out cross-country. Jim would be most to
Cairo by then, and I'd give him my blessing. But then
I remembered that all my traps was on the raft, and
the money, too. That damn nigger had it all, even the
musket. There warn't nothing for me to do but hive
after him, and quick! I jumped into the canoe and
scuttled back to the stern, and grabbed the paddle
and set her back a stroke. But she didn't come. I was
in such a goddamn hurry I hadn't untied her. I got
up and scrabbled at the knot, but my danged hands
was shaking so I couldn't hardly do anything with
them.

As soon as I got started I took out after the raft,
hot and heavy, right down the towhead. That was all
right as far as it went, but the damn towhead warn't
sixty yards long, and the minute I flew by the foot of
it I shot out into the solid white fog, and hadn't no
more idea which way I was going than a dead man.

Thinks I, it won't do to paddle; first I know I'll
run into the frigging bank or a towhead or something;
I got to set still and float, and yet it's a damn fidgety

business to have to hold your hands still at such a time. I whooped and listened. Away down there some-wheres I hears a small whoop, and up comes my spirits. I went tearing after it, listening sharp to hear it again. The next time it come I see I warn't heading for it, but heading away to the left of it — and not gaining on it much either, for I was flying around, this way and that and t'other, but it was going straight ahead all the time.

I did wish the goddamn fool would think to beat a tin pan, and beat it all the time, but he never did, and it was the still places between the whoops that was making the trouble for me. Well, I fought along, and directly I hears the whoop *behind* me. I was tangled all to hell, now. That was somebody else's whoop, or else I was turned around.

I throwed the damn paddle down. I heard the whoop again; it was behind me yet, but in a differ-ent place; it kept coming, and kept changing its place, and I kept answering, till by and by it was in front of me again, and I knowed the current had swung the canoe's head down-stream, and I was all right if that was Jim and not some other raftsman hollering. I couldn't tell nothing about voices in a fog, for nothing don't look natural nor sound natural in a fog.

The whooping went on, and in about a minute I come a-booming down on a cut bank with smoky ghosts of big trees on it, and the current throwed me off to the left and shot by, amongst a lot of snags that fairly roared, the current was tearing by them so danged swift.

In another second or two it was solid white and still again. I set perfectly still then, listening to my heart thump, and I reckon I didn't draw a breath while it thumped a hundred.

I just give up then. I knowed what the matter was. That cut bank was on a goddamn island, and Jim had gone down t'other side of it. It warn't no towhead that you could float by in ten minutes. It had the big timber of a regular island; it might be five or six miles long and more than half a mile wide.

I kept quiet, with my ears cocked, about fifteen minutes, I reckon. I was floating along, of course, four or five miles an hour, but you don't ever think of that. No, you *feel* like you are laying dead still on the water; and if a little glimpse of a snag slips by you don't think to yourself how fast *you're* going, but you catch your breath and think, Jesus! how that snag's tearing along. If you think it ain't dismal and lonesome as hell out in a fog that way by yourself at night, you try it once—you'll see.

Next, for about a half an hour, I whoops now and then; at last I hears the answer a long ways off, and tries to follow it, but I couldn't do it, and directly I judged I'd got into a regular dang nest of towheads, for I had little dim glimpses of them on both sides of me—sometimes just a narrow channel between, and some that I couldn't see I knowed was there because I'd hear the wash of the current against the old dead brush and trash that hung over the banks. Well, I warn't long losing the whoops down amongst the towheads; and I only tried to chase them a little while, anyway, because it was worse than chasing a damn Jack-o'-lantern. You never knowed a sound dodge around so, and swap places so quick and so much.

I had to claw away from the bank pretty dern lively four or five times, to keep from knocking the islands out of the river; and so I judged the raft must be butting into the bank every now and then, or else it would get further ahead and clear out of hearing— it was floating a little faster than what I was.

Well, I seemed to be in the open river again by and by, but I couldn't hear no sign of a whoop nowheres. I reckoned Jim had fetched up on a snag, maybe, and it was all up with him. I was good and tired, so I laid down in the canoe and said I wouldn't bother no more. I didn't want to go to sleep, of course; but I was so damn sleepy I couldn't help it; so I thought I would take just one little cat-nap.

But I reckon it was more than a cat-nap, for when I waked up the stars was shining bright, the fog was all gone, and I was spinning down a big bend stern first. First I didn't know where I was; I thought I was dreaming; and when things began to come back to me they seemed to come up dim out of last week.

It was a monstrous big river there, with the tallest and thickest kind of timber on both banks; just a solid wall, as well as I could see by the stars. I propped myself in the stern to take a piss, and as I was at it, I noticed a black speck on the water away down-stream. I took after it; but when I got to it it warn't nothing but a couple of damn saw-logs made fast together. Then I see another speck, and chased that; then another, and this time I was right. It was the raft.

When I got to it Jim was setting there with his head down between his knees, and his right arm hanging over the steering-oar. The other oar was smashed off, and the raft was littered up with leaves and branches and dirt. So she'd had a rough time.

I see that Jim was asleep, and figured Providence was on my side for once. So I slipped alongside and tied up, thinking I would just sneak on, get the money and the musket, and be gone before Jim woke up. But it warn't no good. That nigger slept like a dang cat, and I hadn't no more'n stepped aboard when he begun to stir. Quick as a flash I lay down next to him and begun to gap and stretch my fists out. I says: "Hello, Jim, have I been asleep? Why didn't you stir me up?"

"Godamighty, is dat you, Huck?" he says. "En you ain' dead—you ain' drownded—you's back ag'in? It's too good for true, honey, it's too good for true. Lemme look at you, chile, lemme feel o' you. No, you ain' dead! You's back ag'in, 'live en soun', jis de same ole Huck—de same ole Huck, thanks to de Lawd!"

"What in hell's the matter with you, Jim," I says. "You been a-drinkin'?"

"Drinkin'? Has I ben a-drinkin'? Has I had a chance to be a-drinkin'?"

"Well, then, what makes you talk so damn wild?"

"How does I talk wild?"

"*How*? Why, hain't you been talking about my coming back, and all that stuff, as if I'd been gone away?"

"Huck—Huck Finn, you look me in de eye; look me in de damn eye. *Hain't* you ben gone away?"

"Gone away? Why, what in hell do you mean? *I* hain't been gone anywheres. Where would I go to?"

"Well, looky here, boss, dey's sumfn wrong, dey is. Is I *me*, or who *is* I? Is I heah, or whah in hell *is* I? Now dat's what I wants to know."

"Well, I think you're here, plain enough, but I think you're a goddamn tangle-headed old fool, Jim."

"I is, is I? Well, you answer me dis: Didn' you tote out de line in de canoe fer to make fas' to dat damn towhead?"

"No I didn't. What towhead? I hain't seen no damn towhead."

"You hain't seen no damn towhead? Looky here, didn' de line pull loose en de raf' go a-hummin' down de river, en leave you en de canoe behine in de fog?"

"What fog?"

"Why, *de* fog! — de damn fog dat's been aroun' all night. En didn' you whoop, en didn' I whoop, tell we got mix' up in de damn islands en one un us got los' en t'other one was jis' as good as los', 'kase he didn' know whah he wuz? En didn' I bust up agin a lot er dem islands en have a turrible time en mos' git drownded? Now ain't dat so, boss — ain't it so? You answer me dat."

"Well, this is too dang many for me, Jim. I hain't seen no fog, nor no islands, nor no troubles, nor nothing. I been setting here talking with you all night till you went to sleep about ten minutes ago, and I reckon I done the same. You couldn't a got drunk in that time, so of course you've been dreaming."

"Aw hell, Huck, how is I gwyne to dream all dat in ten minutes?"

"Well, dern it all, you did dream it, because there didn't any of it happen."

"But, Huck, it's all jis' as plain to me as —"

"It don't make no damn difference how plain it is; there ain't nothing in it. I know, because I've been here all the time."

Jim didn't say nothing for about five minutes, but set there studying over it. Then he says:

"Well, den, I reck'n I did dream it, Huck; but dog my cats ef it ain't de powerfulest damn dream I ever see. En I hain't ever had no dream b'fo' dat's tired me like dis one."

"Oh, well, that's all right, because a dream does tire a body like everything sometimes. But this one was a staving dream; tell me all about it, Jim."

So Jim went to work and told me the whole thing right through, just as it happened, only he painted it up considerable. Then he said he must start in and "'terpret" it, because it was sent for a warning. He said the first towhead stood for a man that would try to do us some good, but the current was another man that would get us away from him. The whoops was warnings that would come to us every now and then, and if we didn't try hard to make out to understand them they'd just take us into bad luck, 'stead of keeping us out of it. The lot of towheads was troubles we was going to get into with quarrelsome people and all kinds of mean folks, but if we minded our business and didn't talk back and aggravate them, we would pull through and get out of the fog and into the big clear river, which was the free states, and wouldn't have no more trouble.

It had clouded up pretty dark just after I got on to the raft, but it was clearing up again now.

"Oh, well, that's all interpreted well enough as far as it goes, Jim," I says; "but what does *these* things stand for?"

It was the leaves and rubbish on the raft and the smashed oar. You could see them first-rate now.

Jim looked at the trash, and then looked at me, and back at the trash again. He had got the dream fixed so strong in his head that he couldn't seem to shake it loose and get the facts back into its place again right away. But when he did get the thing straightened around he looked at me steady without ever smiling, and says:

"What do dey stan' for? I's gwyne to tell you. When I got all wore out wid work, en wid de callin' for you, en went to sleep, my heart wuz mos' broke bekase you wuz los', en I didn' k'yer no' mo' what become er me en de raf'. En when I wake up en find you back ag'in, all safe en soun', de tears come, en I could a got down on my knees and kiss yo' foot, I's so thankful. En all you wuz thinkin' 'bout wuz how you could make a fool uv ole Jim wid a damn lie. Dat truck dah is *trash*; en trash is what people is dat puts shit on de head er dey fren's en makes 'em ashamed."

Then he got up slow and walked to the wigwam, and went in there without saying anything but that. But that was enough. It made me feel so goddamn mean I could almost kissed *his* foot to get him to take it back.

It was fifteen minutes before I could work myself up to go and humble myself to a nigger; but I done it, and I warn't ever sorry for it afterward, nuther. I didn't do him no more mean tricks, and I wouldn't a done that one if I'd a knowed it would make him feel that way, and I told him so.

"Dat's awright, honey," he says. "You's jes' a chile en doan' know no better. But you is a *good* chile,

Huck, en you got a good heart — not like dat mean Tom Sawyer, al'us playin' tricks on a poor nigger out'n meanness. He gonna be a mean man someday."

Well, I didn't much care for that kind of talk, but I didn't say nothing, and Jim didn't nuther, we just lay there in the wigwam a-listening to the birds singing around the place where we had run in. After a while I seen that Jim had rolled over and was looking at Fair Rowena again, and that scratched me some, but then he says:

"Hucky, I once't had a li'l bird like dat 'un, a yaller bird it 'uz. She fell out'n de nes', en I raise her by han'. By en by she grow up, en I want to keep dat bird, but my mammy say I cain't, 'kase she say it ain't right to keep nuffin' shet up in no cage. She make me take dat yaller bird out inter de woods and let her go, en I wuz powerful sad den, but I ain't sad no mo'."

"But Jim," I says. "That ain't no yaller bird."

"What diff'rence dat make?" he says. "De gal got yaller ha'r, hain't she?"

Well, it warn't no use to argue. I just let it slide.

XIV

The child of calamity

We slept most all day, and started out at night, a little ways behind a monstrous long raft that was as long going by as a dern parade. She had four long sweeps at each end, so we judged she carried as many as thirty men, likely. She had five big wigwams aboard, wide apart, and an open camp-fire in the middle, and a flag-pole at each end. There was a power of style about her. It damn well *amounted* to something being a raftsman on such a craft as that.

We went drifting down into a big bend, and the night clouded up and got hot. The river was very wide, and was walled with solid timber on both sides; you couldn't see a break in it hardly ever, or a light. We talked about Cairo, and wondered whether we would know it when we got to it. I said likely we wouldn't, because I had heard say there warn't but about a dozen houses there, and if they didn't happen to have them lit up, how was we going to know we was passing a town? Jim said if the two big rivers

joined together there, that would show. But I said
maybe we might think we was passing the foot of an
island and coming into the same old river again.
That disturbed Jim—and me too. So the question
was, what in hell to do?

We talked it over, and by and by Jim said it was
such a black night, now, that it wouldn't be no risk
to swim down to the big raft and crawl aboard and
listen—they would talk about Cairo, because they
would be calculating to go ashore there for a spree,
maybe; or anyway they would send boats ashore to
buy whisky or fresh meat or something. Jim had a
danged wonderful level head for a nigger: he could
most always start a good plan when you wanted one.
They didn't have the style of a Tom Sawyer plan, but
then they most always worked.

I stood up and shook my rags off and jumped into
the river, and struck out for the raft's light. By and
by, when I got down nearly to her, I eased up and
went slow and cautious. But everything was all
right—nobody at the sweeps. So I swum down along
the raft till I was most abreast the camp-fire in the
middle, then I crawled aboard and inched along and
got in among some bundles of shingles on the
weather side of the fire, so I wouldn't get sparks on
my bare hide. There was thirteen men there—they
was the watch on deck of course. And a damned
rough-looking lot, too. They had a jug, and tin cups,
and they kept the jug moving. One man was singing—
roaring, you may say; and it was a tiresome old dirty
song pap used to sing about a riverman that had a
whore in every town on the river, and there was a
verse for every town, and how he done it different
every time. He roared through his nose, and strung

out the last word of every line very long. When he was done they all fetched a kind of Injun war-whoop, and then another was sung. It begun:

"There was a woman in our towdn,
      In our towdn did dwed'l [dwell],
She loved her husband dear-i-lee,
      But another man twyste as wed'l.

"Singing too, riloo, riloo, riloo,
      Ri-too, riloo, rilay — e,
She loved her husband dear-i-lee,
      But another man twyste as wed'l."

And so on — fourteen verses. There was some interesting parts, but it was generally kind of poor, and when he was going to start on the next verse one of them said it was the tune the old cow died on; and another one said: "Oh Christ, give us a rest!" And another one told him to take a walk. They made fun of him till he got mad and jumped up and began to cuss the crowd, and said he could lam any goddamn thief in the lot.

They was all about to make a break for him, but the biggest man there jumped up and says:

"Set whar you are, gentlemen. Leave him to me; he's my meat."

Then he jumped up in the air three times, and cracked his heels together every time. He flung off a buckskin coat that was all hung down with fringes, and says, "You lay thar tell the chawin-up's done"; he flung his hat down, which was all over ribbons, and says, "You lay thar tell his sufferins is over."

Then he jumped in the air and cracked his heels together again, and shouted out:

"Whoo-oop! I'm the old original iron-jawed, brass-mounted, copper-assed corpse-maker from the wilds of Arkansaw! Look at me! I'm the man they call Sudden Death and General Desolation. Sired by a hurricane, damned by an earthquake, half-brother to the cholera, nearly related to the smallpox on the mother's side! Look at me! I take nineteen fucking alligators and a bar'l of whisky for breakfast when I'm in robust health, and a bushel of rattlesnakes and a dead body when I'm ailing. I split the ever-lasting rocks with my glance, and I squench the thunder when I speak! Whoo-oop! Stand back and give me room according to my strength! Blood's my natural drink, and the wails of the dying is music to my ear. Cast your eye on me, gentlemen! and lay low and hold your goddamn breath, for I'm 'bout to turn myself loose!"

All the time he was getting this off, he was shaking his head and looking fierce, and kind of swelling around in a little circle, tucking up his wristbands, and now and then straightening up and beating his breast with his fist, saying, "Look at me, gentlemen!" When he got through, he jumped up and cracked his heels together three times, and let off a roaring "Whoo-oop! I'm the bloodiest son of a wildcat that lives."

Then the man that had started the row tilted his old slouch hat down over his right eye; then he bent stooping forward, with his back sagged and his ass end sticking out far, and his fists a-shoving out and drawing in front of him, and so went around in a little circle about three times, swelling himself up and breathing hard. Then he straightened, and jumped up and cracked his heels together three times before he lit again (that made them cheer), and he began to shout like this:

"Whoo-oop! bow your goddamned neck and spread, for the kingdom of sorrow's a-coming! Hold me down to the earth, for I feel my powers a-working! Whoo-oop! I'm a child of hell-fire, *don't* let me get a start! Smoked glass, here for all! Don't attempt to look at me with the naked eye, gentlemen! When I'm playful I use the meridians of longitude and parallels of latitude for a seine and drag the Atlantic Ocean for whales! I scratch my head with the lightning and purr myself to sleep with the thunder! When I'm cold, I bile the Gulf of Mexico and bathe in it; when I'm hot I fan myself with an equinoctial storm; when I'm thirsty I reach up and suck a cloud dry like a sponge; when I range the earth hungry, famine follows in my tracks! Whoo-oop! Bow your goddamned neck and spread! I put my hand on the sun's face and make it night in the earth; I bite a piece out of the moon and hurry the seasons; I shake myself and crumble the mountains! Contemplate me through leather—*don't* use the naked eye! I'm the man with a petrified heart and biler-iron guts! The massacre of isolated communities is the pastime of my idle moments, the destruction of whole damn nationalities the serious business of my life! The boundless vastness of the great American desert is my inclosed property, and I bury my dead on my own premises!" He jumped up and cracked his heels together again three times before he lit (they cheered him again), and as he come down he shouted out: "Whoo-oop! bow your goddamned neck and spread, for the Pet Child of Calamity's a-coming to bust your boil-covered ass!"

Then the other one went to swelling around and blowing again—the first one—the one they called

Bob; next, the Child of Calamity chipped in again, bigger than ever; then they both got at it at the same time, swelling round and round each other and punching their fists most into each other's faces, and whooping and jawing like Injuns; then Bob called the Child names, and the Child called him names back again.

"You hain't nothin'," says Bob, "You hain't but a fart in a windstorm. Why, if I was to cut five inches off your pecker, you'd have a six-inch hole in your belly. And you're ugly. Intolerably ugly. If I had a dog with a face like yours, why I'd shave its ass and teach it to walk backwards."

"Whoo-oop!" cries the Child, grinding his teeth and making awful faces. "Yes, I'm ugly. Indeed I am. I was the original Ugly Man, and proud of it, but I give up the title now. I see I met my match. You're so goddamned, all-fired ugly, it hain't decent for you to leave your face exposed to this here company. I reckon your mother was a purple-assed baboon and your father the two-headed barstid son of a half-breed oh-rang-u-tang. Mirrors and clocks hain't safe in your vicinity. Women faint and strong men puke."

All this time Bob was doing an imitation of a biler with the safety-valve stuck, and finally he blew. "Whoo-oop! Hold me back, gentlemen, or I'll mess up this here raft with the remainders of an aborted giraffe. Why, you little greasy-nosed cocksucker, I'm a-going to have your balls for an ornament. I'm a-going to reach into your mouth till I got my finger through your ass-hole, and then I'm a-going to turn you inside out. You pre-sump-tous little mongrel son-of-a-bitch, it won't make no difference if you don't have friends here to cover up what's left with a little decent dirt, because I'm a-going to pound the living shit out of you, and that won't leave much to mourn over."

Well, the Child come back at him with the very worst kind of language; and next, Bob knocked the Child's hat off, and the Child picked it up and kicked Bob's ribbony hat about six foot; Bob went and got it and said never mine, this warn't going to be the last of this thing, because he was a man that never forgot and never forgive, and so the Child better damn well look out, for there was a time a-coming just as sure as he was a living man, that he would have to answer to him with the best blood in his body. The Child said no man was willinger than he for that time to come, and he would give Bob fair warning, *now*, never to cross his path again, for he could never rest till he had waded in his blood, for such was his nature, though he was sparing him now on account of his family, if he had one.

Both of them was edging away in different directions, growling and going on about what they was going to do; but a little black-whiskered chap skipped up and says:

"Come back here, you couple of goddamned chicken-livered cowards, and I'll thrash the two of ye!"

And he done it, too. He snatched them, he jerked them this way and that, he booted them around, he knocked them sprawling faster than they could get up. Why, it warn't two minutes till they begged like dogs — and how the other lot did yell and laugh and clap their hands all the way through, and shout, "Sail in, Corpse-Maker!" "Hi! at him again, Child of Calamity!" "Bully for you, little Davy!" Well, it was a perfect pow-wow for a while. Bob and the Child had bloody noses and black eyes when they got through. Little Davy made them own up that they was yellow-belly sneaks and cowards and not fit to eat with a dog or drink with a nigger; then Bob and the Child shook hands with each other, very solemn, and said they had always respected each other and was willing to let bygones be bygones. So then they washed their faces in the river; and just then there was a loud order to stand by for a crossing, and some of them went forrard to man the sweeps there, and the rest went aft to handle the after sweeps.

I lay still and waited for fifteen minutes, and had a smoke out of a pipe that one of them left in reach; then the crossing was finished, and they stumped back and had a drink around and went to talking and singing again. Next they got out an old fiddle, and one played, and another patted juba, and the rest turned themselves loose on a reglar old-fashioned keelboat breakdown. They couldn't keep that up very long without getting winded, so by and by they settled around the jug again.

They sung "Jolly, Jolly Raftsman's the Life for Me," with a rousing chorus, and then they got to talking about differences between hogs, and their different kind of habits; and next about women and their different ways, and from what they said the women they knowed didn't have much of an edge on the hogs; and next about the best ways to put out houses that was afire; and next about what ought to be done with the Injuns; and next about what a king had to do, and how much he got; and next about how to make cats fight; and next about what to do when a man has fits; and next about differences betwixt clear-water rivers and muddy-water ones. The man they called Ed said the muddy Mississippi water was wholesomer to drink than the clear water of the Ohio; he said if you let a pint of this yaller Mississippi water settle, you have about a half to three-quarters of an inch of mud in the bottom, according to the stage of the river, and then it warn't no better than Ohio water—what you wanted to do was keep it stirred up—and when the river was low, keep mud on hand to put in and thicken the water up the way it ought to be.

The Child of Calamity said that was so; he said there was nutrishusness in the mud, and a man that drunk Mississippi water could grow corn in his belly if he wanted to. He says:

"You look at the graveyards; that tells the tale. Trees won't grow worth shit in a Cincinnati grave-yard, but in a Sent Louis graveyard they grow upwards of eight hundred foot high. It's all on account of the water the people drunk before they laid up. A Cincinnati corpse don't richen a soil any."

And they talked about how Ohio water didn't like to mix with Mississippi water, no more than a white man with a nigger. Ed said if you take the Mississippi on a rise when the Ohio is low, you'll find a wide band of clear water all the way down the east side of the Mississippi for a hundred mile or more, and the minute you get out a quarter of a mile from shore and pass the line, it is all thick and yaller the rest of the way across. Then they talked about how to keep to-bacco from getting moldy, and from that they went into ghosts and told about a lot that other folks had seen; but Ed says:

"Why don't you tell something that you've seen

yourselves? Now let me have a damn say. Five years ago I was on a raft as big as this, and right along here it was a bright moonshiny night, and I was on watch and boss of the stabboard oar forrard, and one of my pards was a man named Dick Allbright, and he come along to where I was sitting, forrard — gaping and stretching, he was — and stopped down on the edge of the raft and washed his face in the river, and come and set down by me and got out his pipe, and had just got it filled, when he looks up and says:

" 'Why, looky-here,' he says, 'ain't that Buck Miller's place, over yander in the bend?'

" 'Yes,' says I, 'it is — why?' He laid his pipe down and leaned his head on his hand, and says:

" 'I thought we'd be furder down.' I says:

" 'I thought it too, when I went off watch' — we was standing six hours on and six off — 'but the boys told me,' I says, 'that the raft didn't seem to hardly move, for the last hour,' says I, 'though she's a slipping along all right now,' says I. He give a kind of groan, and says:

" 'I've seed a raft act so before, along here,' he says, " 'pears to me the current has most quit above the head of this bend durin' the last two years,' he says.

"Well, he raised up two or three times, and looked away off and around on the water. That started me at it, too. A body is always doing what he sees somebody else doing, though there mayn't be no sense in it. Pretty soon I see a black something floating on the water away off to stabboard and quartering behind us. I see he was looking at it, too.

"I says: 'What's that?'

"He says, sort of pettish:

" 'Tain't nothing but an old empty bar'l.'

" 'An empty bar'l!' says I, 'why,' says I, 'a damn spy-glass is a fool to *your* eyes. How can you tell it's an empty bar'l?' He says:

" 'I don't know; I reckon it ain't a bar'l, but I thought it might be,' says he.

" 'Yes,' I says, 'so it might be, and it might be any-thing else, too; a body can't tell nothing about it, such a distance as that,' I says.

"We hadn't nothing else to do so we kept watching it. By and by I says: 'Why looky-here, Dick Allbright, that damned thing's a-gaining on us, I believe.'

"He never said nothing. The thing gained and gained, and I judged it must be a dog that was about tired out. Well, we swung down into the crossing, and the thing floated across the bright streak of the moonshine, and by Christ, it *was* a bar'l!

" 'Dick Allbright, what made you think that thing was a bar'l, when it was half a mile off?' says I.

"Says he: 'I don't know.'

"Says I: 'You tell me, Dick Allbright.'

"Says he: 'Well, I knowed it was a bar'l; I've seen it before; lots has seen it; they says it's a ha'nted bar'l.'

"I called the rest of the watch, and they come and stood there, and I told them what Dick had said. It floated right along abreast, now, and didn't gain any more. It was about twenty foot off. Some was for having it aboard, but the rest didn't want to. Dick Allbright said rafts that had fooled with it had got bad luck by it. The captain of the watch said he didn't believe in it. He said he reckoned the bar'l gained on us because it was in a little better current than what we was. He said it would leave by and by.

"So then we went to talking about other things, and we had a song, and then a breakdown; and after that the captain of the watch called for another song; but it was clouding up now, and the damned bar'l stuck right thar in the same place, and the song didn't seem to have much warm-up to it, somehow, and so they didn't finish it, and there warn't any cheers, but it sort of dropped flat, and nobody said anything for a minute. Then everybody tried to talk at once, and one chap got off a joke, but it warn't no use, they didn't laugh, and even the chap that made the joke didn't laugh at it, which ain't usual. We all just settled down glum, and watched the bar'l, and was damned oneasy and oncomfortable. Well, sir, it shut down black and still, and the wind began to moan around, and next the lightning began to play and the thunder to grumble. And pretty soon there was a reglar storm, and in the middle of it a man that was running aft stumbled and fell and sprained his ankle so that he had to lay up. This made the boys shake their heads. And every time the lightning come, there was that dammed bar'l with the blue lights winking around it. We was always on the lookout for it. But by and by, toward dawn, she was gone. When the day come we couldn't see her anywhere, and we warn't sorry, either.

"But the next night about half past nine, when there was songs and high jinks going on, here she comes again, and took her old roost on the stabboard side. There warn't no more high jinks. Everybody got solemn; nobody talked; you couldn't get anybody to do anything but set around moody and look at the bar'l. It begun to cloud up again. When the watch changed, the off watch stayed up, 'stead of turning in. The storm ripped and roared around all night, and in the middle of it another man tripped and sprained his ankle, and had to knock off. The bar'l left toward day, and nobody see it go.

"Everybody was sober and down in the mouth all day. I don't mean the kind of sober that comes of leaving liquor alone—not that. They was quiet, but they all drunk more than usual—not together, but each man sidled off and took it in private, by himself.

"After dark the off watch didn't turn in; nobody sung, nobody talked; the boys didn't scatter around, neither; they sort of huddled together, forrard; and for two hours they set there, perfectly still, looking steady in the one direction, and heaving a sigh once in a while. And then, here comes the bar'l again. She took up her old place. She stayed there all night; nobody turned in. The storm come on again, after midnight. It got darker'n hell; the rain poured down; hail, too; the thunder boomed and roared and bellowed; the wind blowed like a frigging hurricane; and the lightning spread over everything in big sheets of glare, and showed the whole goddamned raft as plain as day; and the river lashed up white as milk as far as you could see for miles, and there was that damned bar'l jiggering along, same as ever. The captain ordered the watch to man the after sweeps for a crossing, and nobody would go—no more sprained ankles for them, they said. They wouldn't even *walk* aft. Well, then, just then the sky split wide open, with a hell of a crash, and the lightning killed two men of the after watch and crippled two more.

Crippled them how, say you? Why, *sprained their damned ankles*!

"The bar'l left in the dark betwixt lightnings, toward dawn. Well, not a body eat a damn bite at breakfast that morning. After that the men loafed around, in twos and threes, and talked low together. But none of them herded with Dick Allbright. They all give him the cold shake. If he come around where any of the men was, they split up and sidled away. They wouldn't man the sweeps with him. The captain had all the skiffs hauled up on the raft, alongside of his wigwam, and wouldn't let the dead men be took ashore to be planted. He didn't believe a man that got ashore would come back; and he was right.

"After night come, you see pretty plain that there was going to be trouble if that damned bar'l come again; there was such a muttering going on. A good many wanted to kill Dick Allbright, because he'd seen the bar'l on other trips, and that had an ugly look. Some wanted to put him ashore. Some said: 'Let's all go ashore in a pile, if the bar'l comes again.'

"This kind of whispers was still going on, the men being bunched together forrard watching for the bar'l, when Jesus Christ! here she comes again. Down she comes, slow and steady, and settles into her old tracks. You could a heard a damn pin drop. Then up comes the captain, and says:

" 'Boys, don't be a pack of goddamned children and fools; I don't want this bar'l to be dogging us all the way to Orleans, and *you* don't: Well, then, how's the best way to stop it? Burn it up—that's the way. I'm going to fetch it aboard,' he says. And before anybody could say a damned word, in he went.

"He swum to it, and as he came pushing it to the

raft, the men spread to one side. But the old man got it aboard and busted in the head, and there was a goddamn baby in it! Yes, sir; a stark-naked baby. It was Dick Allbright's baby; he owned up and said so.

" 'Yes,' he says, a-leaning over it, 'yes, it is my own lamented darling, my poor lost Charles William Allbright deceased,' says he — for he could curl his tongue around the bulliest damned words in the language when he was a mind to, and lay them before you without a jint started anywheres. Yes, he said, he used to live up at the head of this bend, and one night he choked his child, which was crying, not intending to kill it — which was prob'ly a goddamn lie — and then he was scared, and buried it in a bar'l, before his wife got home, and off he went, and struck the northern trail and went to rafting; and this was the third year that the bar'l had chased him. He said the bad luck always begun light, and lasted till four men was killed, and then the bar'l didn't come any more after that. He said if the men would stand it one more night — and was a-going on like that — but the men had got enough. They started to get out a boat to take him ashore and lynch him, but he grabbed the little child all of a sudden and jumped overboard with it, hugged up to his breast and shedding tears, and we never seed him again in this life, poor suffering bastard, nor Charles William neither."

"*Who* was shedding tears?" says Bob; "was it Allbright or the damn baby?"

"Allbright, for Chrissakes! Didn't I tell you the baby was dead? Been dead three frigging years — how in hell could it cry?"

"Well, never mind how it could cry — how could it

keep all that damn time?" says Davy. "You answer me that."

"I don't know how it done it," says Ed. "It done it, though—that's all I know about it."

"Say—what did they do with the dern bar'l?" says the Child of Calamity.

"Why, they hove it overboard, and it sunk like a damned chunk of lead."

"Edward, did the child look like it was choked?" says one.

"Did it have its hair parted?" says another.

"What was the brand on that bar'l, Eddy?" says a fellow they called Bill.

"Have you got the papers for them statistics, Edmund?" says Jimmy.

"Say, Edwin, was you one of the men that was killed by the lightning?" says Davy.

"Him? Hell, no! He was both of 'em," says Bob. Then they all haw-hawed.

"Say, Edward, don't you reckon you'd better take a pill? You look bad—don't you feel pale?" says the Child of Calamity.

"Oh, come, now, Eddy," says Jimmy, "show up; you must a kept part of that bar'l to prove the thing by. Show us the bunghole—*do*—and we'll all believe you."

"Say, boys," says Bill, "less divide it up. Thar's thirteen of us. I can swaller a thirteenth of the yarn, if you can worry down the rest."

Ed got up mad and said *they* was thirteen bung-holes, or maybe something worse. He walked off aft, cussing to himself, and they yelling and jeering at him, and roaring and laughing so you could hear them a mile.

"Boys, we'll split a watermelon on that," says the Child of Calamity; and he came rummaging around in the dark amongst the shingle bundles where I was, and put his hand on me. I was warm and soft and naked; so he says "Ouch!" and jumped back.

"Fetch a lantern or a chunk of fire here, boys — there's a snake here as big as a goddamn cow!"

So they run there with a lantern, and crowded up and looked in on me.

"Come out of that, you little barstid!" says one.

"Who in hell are you?" says another.

"What are you after here? Speak up prompt, or overboard you go."

"Snake the little son-of-a-bitch out, boys. Snatch him out by the heels."

I began to beg, and crept out amongst them trembling. They looked me over, wondering, and the Child of Calamity says:

"A god-dammed thief! Lend me a hand and less heave him overboard!"

"No," says Big Bob, "less get out the paint-pot and paint his ass and balls a sky-blue, and *then* heave him over."

"Shit! that's great! Go for the paint, Jimmy."

When the paint come, and Bob took the brush and was just going to begin, the others laughing and rubbing their hands. I begun to cry, and that sort of worked on Davy, and he says:

" 'Vast there. He's nothing but a cub. I'll paint the first son-of-a-bitch that tetches him!"

So I looked around on them, and some of them grumbled and growled, but Bob put down the paint, and the others didn't take it up.

"Come here to the fire, and less see what you're

up to here," says Davy. "Now set down there and give an account of yourself. How long have you been aboard here?"

"Not over a quarter of a minute, sir," says I.

"How did you get dry so damn quick?"

"I don't know, sir. I'm always that way, mostly."

"Oh, you are, are you? What's your name?"

I sure as hell warn't going to tell my name. I didn't know what to say, so I just says:

"Charles William Allbright, sir."

Then they roared — the whole crowd; and I was mighty damn glad I said that, because, maybe, laughing would get them in a better humor.

When they got done laughing, Davy says:

"It won't hardly do, Charles William. You couldn't have growed this much in five year, and you was a baby when you come out of the bar'l, you know, and dead at that. Come, now, tell a straight story, and nobody'll hurt you, if you ain't up to anything wrong. What is your name?"

"Aleck Hopkins, sir. Aleck James Hopkins."

"Well, Aleck, where did you come from, here?

"From a trading-scow. She lays up the bend yonder. I was born on her. Pap has traded up and down here all his life; and he told me to swim off here, because when you went by he said he would like to get some of you to speak to a Mr. Jonas Turner, in Cairo, and tell him — "

"Oh, bullshit!"

"Yes, sir, it's as true as the world. Pap he says — "

"Oh, *balls!*"

They all laughed, and I tried again to talk, but they broke in on me and stopped me.

"Now, looky-here," says Davy; "you're scared,

and so you talk wild. Honest, now, do you live in a scow, or is it a bunch of crap?"

"Yes, sir, in a trading scow. She lays up at the head of the bend. But I warn't born in her. It's our first trip."

"Now you're talking! What did you come aboard here for? To steal?"

"No, sir, I didn't. It was only to get a ride on the raft. All boys does that."

"Well, I know that. But what in hell did you hide for?"

"Sometimes they drive the boys off."

"So they do. The little bastards might steal. Looky-here, if we let you off this time, will you keep out of these damn silly scrapes hereafter?"

" 'Deed I will, boss. You try me."

"All right, then. You ain't but little ways from shore. Overboard with you, and don't you make a jackass of yourself another time this way. Damn it, boy, some raftsmen would rawhide your tail till it was black and blue!"

I didn't wait to kiss good-by, but went overboard and broke for shore. When Jim come along by and by, the big raft was away out of sight around the point. I swum out and got aboard, and was mighty darn glad to see home again.

XV

The rattlesnake-skin
does its work

W ell, I could see now there warn't much profit
in pestering other people about Cairo, and
told Jim we'd better just stick to our own
raft and keep low. There warn't nothing to do but
look out sharp for the town, and not pass it without
seeing it. Jim said that was all right, and that he'd
be mighty sure to see it, because he'd be a free man
the minute he seen it, but if he missed it he'd be in
the slave country again and no more show for freedom. Every little while he jumps up and says:
"Dah she is!"

But it warn't. It was Jack-o'-lanterns, or lightning
bugs; so he set down again, and went to watching,
same as before. Jim said it made him all over trembly
and feverish to be so close to freedom. Well, I can
tell you it made me all over trembly and feverish, too,
to hear him, because I begun to get it through my
head that he *was* most free — and who was to blame
for it? Why, goddamn it, *me*. I couldn't get that out of
my conscience, no how nor no way. It got to troubling

me so I couldn't rest; I couldn't stay still in one place. It hadn't ever come home to me before, what this thing was that I was doing. But now it did; and it stayed with me, and scorched me more and more. I tried to make out to myself that *I* warn't to blame, because *I* didn't run Jim off from his rightful owner; but it warn't no damn use, conscience up and says, every time, "But you knowed he was running for his freedom, and you could a paddled ashore and told somebody." That was so—I couldn't get around that no way. That was where it pinched. Conscience says to me, "What had that widow done to you that you could see her rightfully inherited nigger go off right under your eyes and never say one single word? What did that poor old woman do to you that you could treat her so mean? Warn't she always good to you, and didn't she take you in even after you run off that first time? Why, she tried to learn you your book, she tried to learn you your manners, she tried to reg'larize you in every way she knowed how. *That's* what she done."

I got to feeling so mean and so damn miserable I most wished I was dead. I fidgeted up and down the raft, cussing myself to myself, and Jim was fidgeting up and down past me. We neither of us could keep still. Every time he danced around and says, "Dah's Cairo!" it went through me like a shot, and I thought if it *was* Cairo I reckoned I would die of miserableness.

Jim talked out loud all the time while I was talking to myself. He was saying how the first thing he would do when he got to a free state he would go to saving up money and never spend a single darn cent, and when he got enough he would buy his wife, which was

owned on a farm close to where Miss Watson had
lived; and then they would both work to buy the two
children, and if their master wouldn't sell them,
they'd get an Ab'litionist to go and steal them.

It most froze me to hear such goddamn talk. He
wouldn't ever dared to talk such talk in his life before. Just see what a difference it made in him the
minute he judged he was about free. Like they say,
"Give a nigger an inch and he'll take an ell." Thinks
I, this is what comes of my not thinking. Here was
this damn nigger, which I had as good as helped to
run away, coming right out flat-footed and saying he
would steal his children — children that belonged to
a man I didn't even know; a man that hadn't ever
done me no harm.

I was sorry to hear Jim say that, it was such a
lowering of him. My damned conscience got to stirring me up hotter than ever, until at last I says to
it, "Let up on me — it ain't too late yet — I'll paddle
ashore at the first light and tell." I felt easy and
happy and light as a dern feather right off. All my
troubles was gone. I went to looking out sharp for a
light, and sort of singing to myself. By and by one
showed. Jim sings out:

"We's safe, Huck, we's safe! Jump up and crack
yo' heels! Dat's de good ole Cairo at las', I jis' knows
it!"

I says:

"I'll take the canoe and go and see, Jim. It mightn't
be, you know."

He jumped and got the canoe ready, and put his
old coat in the bottom for me to set on, and give me
the paddle; and as I shoved off, he says:

"Pooty soon I'll be a-shout'n for joy, en I'll say,

it's all on accounts o' Huck; I's a free man, en I couldn't ever ben free ef it hadn't ben for Huck; Huck done it. Jim won't ever forgit you, Huck; you's de bes' damn fren' Jim ever had; en you's de only fren' ole Jim's got now."

I was paddling off, all in a sweat to tell on him; but when he says this, it seemed to kind of take the tuck all out of me. I went along slow then, and I warn't right down certain whether I was glad I started or whether I warn't. When I was fifty yards off, Jim says:

"Dah you goes, de ole true Huck; de on'y white genlman dat ever kep' his promise to ole Jim."

Well, I just felt sick. But I says, hell, I *got* to do it—I can't get *out* of it. So away I went paddling on towards the light, feeling all snarled up inside and miserable. Pretty soon I saw another light, drifting down towards the first one, close in to the bank. I edged off, but they must of heard me or seen me, because the light come a-booming down onto me, and I saw it was two men in a skiff with a bulls-eye lantern. The one with the light flashed it in my eyes and says:

"What's that yonder?" He gave the lamp a wobble out towards our raft, and I cussed Jim for not putting the lantern out when we was so close in to shore.

"A piece of raft," I says.

"Do you belong on it?"

"Yes, sir."

"Any men on it?"

"Only one, sir."

"Well, there's five niggers run off tonight up yonder, above the head of the bend. Is your man white or black?"

I didn't answer up promptly. I tried for a second or two to brace up and out with it, but I warn't man enough—hadn't the spunk of a dang rabbit. I see I was weakening; so I just give up trying, and up and says:

"He's white."

"I reckon we'll go and see for ourselves." He lay the bull's-eye down, and I seen they both had guns.

"I wish you would," says I, "because it's pap that's there, and maybe you'd help me tow the raft ashore where the light is. He's sick—and so is mam and Mary Ann."

"Oh, hell! we're in a hurry, boy. But I s'pose we've got to. Come, buckle to your paddle, and let's get along."

I buckled to my paddle and they laid to their oars. When we had made three hundred yards or so, and was getting near the raft, I says:

"Pap'll be mighty much obleeged to you, I can tell you. Everybody goes away when I want them to help me tow the raft ashore, and I can't do it by myself."

"Well, that's damned mean," says one. After a couple more strokes, he stopped rowing and says:

"Say, boy, what's the *matter* with your father?"

"It's the—a—the—well, it ain't anything much."

They both stopped pulling then. It warn't but a mighty little ways to the raft now. The man flashed the lantern on me again, and says:

"Boy, that's a damned lie. What *is* the matter with your pap? Answer up square now, and it'll be the better for you."

"I will, sir, I will, honest—but don't leave us, please. It's the—the— Gentlemen, if you'll only pull ahead, and let me heave you the headline, you won't have to come a-near the raft—please do."

"Set her back, John, set her back!" says the man with the bull's-eye, and the other backed water. "Keep away, boy, keep to looard. Goddamn it, I just expect the wind has blowed it to us. Your pap's got the smallpox, and you know it damnation well. Why didn't you come out and say so? Do you want to spread it all over?"

"Well," says I, a-blubbering, "I've told everybody before, and they just went away and left us."

"Poor devil, there's something in that. We are right down sorry for you, but we—well, hang it, we don't want the smallpox, you see. Look here, I'll tell you what to do. Don't you try to land by yourself, or you'll smash everything to pieces. You float along down about twenty miles, and you'll come to a town on the left-hand side of the river. It will be long after sun-up then, and when you ask for help you tell them your folks are all down with chills and fever. Don't be a dammed fool again, and let people guess what is the matter. Now we're trying to do you a kindness; so you just put twenty miles between us, that's a good boy. It wouldn't do any good to land yonder where the light is—it's only a wood-yard. Say, I reckon your father's poor, and I'm bound to say he's in pretty hard luck. Here, I'll put a twenty-dollar gold piece on this board, and you get it when it floats by. I feel damn mean to leave you; but my Christ! it won't do to fool with smallpox, don't you see?"

"Hold on, Parker," says the other man, "here's a twenty to put on the board for me. Good-by, boy; you do as Mr. Parker told you, and you'll be all right."

"That's so, my boy—good-by, good-by. If you see any runaway niggers you get help and nab them, and you can make some money by it."

"Good-by, sir," says I; "I won't let no runaway niggers get by me if I can help it."

They went off back to the shore mighty fast, and I got aboard the raft, feeling bad and low, because they was such kind and good men and I was so wicked. I knowed damn well I had done wrong, and I see it warn't no use for me to try to learn to do right; a body that don't get *started* right when he's little ain't got no show—when the pinch comes there ain't nothing to back him up and keep him to his work, and so he gets beat. Then I thought a minute, and says to myself, hold on; s'pose you'd a done right and give Jim up, would you've felt better than what you do now? No, says I, I'd feel bad—I'd feel just the same way I do now. Well, then, says I, what's the use you learning to do right when it's so damned troublesome to do right and ain't no trouble to do wrong, and the wages is the same? I was stuck. I couldn't answer that. So I reckoned I wouldn't bother no more about it, but after this always do whichever come handiest at the time.

I went into the wigwam; Jim warn't there. I looked all around; he warn't anywhere. I says:

"Jim!"

"Here I is, Huck. Is dey out o' sight yit? Don't talk loud."

He was in the river under the stern oar, with just his nose out. I told him they were out of sight, so he come aboard. He says:

"I was a-listenin' to all de talk, en I slips into de

river en was gwyne to shove for sho' if dey come aboard. Den I was gwyne to swim to de raf' agin when dey was gone. But lawsy, how you did fool 'em, Huck! Dat *wuz* de smartes' dodge! I tell you, chile, I 'spec it save' ole Jim—ole Jim ain't going to forgit you for dat, honey."

Well, I begun to feel uncomfortable again, but then we talked about the money, and my spirits picked up considerable. It was a damn good raise—twenty dollars apiece. Jim said we could take deck passage on a steamboat now, and the money would last us as far as we wanted to go in the free states. He said twenty mile more warn't far for the raft to go, but he wished we was already there.

Towards daybreak we tied up, and Jim was mighty particular about hiding the raft good. Then he worked all day fixing things in bundles, and getting all ready to quit rafting.

That night about ten we hove in sight of the lights of a town away down in a left-hand bend. I went off in a canoe to ask about it, and pretty soon I found a man out in the river with a skiff, setting a trot-line. I ranged up and says:

"Mister, is that town Cairo?"

"Cairo? No. You must be a derned fool."

"What town is it, mister?"

"For Christ's sake, if you want to know, go and find out. If you stay here botherin' around me for about a half a minute longer you'll get something you damn well won't want."

I paddled to the raft. Jim was awfully disappointed, but I said never mind, Cairo would be the next place, I reckoned.

We passed another town before daylight, and I was going out again; but it was high ground, so I didn't go. No high ground about Cairo, Jim said. I had forgot it. We laid up for the day on a towhead tolerable close to the left-hand bank, and snugged down in the wigwam for night to come, as always.

But Jim was having a hard time of it, tossing and a-turning, so neither of us could get much sleep. Then, about an hour after sunrise, he set up and says:

"Godamighty! Whyn't I never think o' dat befo'?"

"Think of *what*, Jim?"

"Why, de river, Huck, de river!" He hopped out of the wigwam and took one look at the water, and then hopped back. He didn't say anything, just squatted down and began to rock back and forth, a-moaning so it set a body's teeth on edge.

"What's the matter, Jim?" I says.

"Matter? Oh, Lawd-God, matter a-plenty! Jes' look at dat river out dar, en den ask me what de matter is."

Well, I began to suspicion what it was, but I went out anyhow, and sure enough, here was the clear Ohio water inshore, and outside was the old regular Muddy. Both of us had clean forgot about that, and sleeping days and traveling nights, we hadn't either of us been able to see the change, and there warn't no way of telling how far back it had happened. So it was all up with Cairo.

I went back into the wigwam and tried to comfort poor Jim. I says:

"It hain't your fault. If anybody's to blame, it's me. I knowed about the Ohio water jest as much as you, and I never had no dang excuse to forget about it." Which warn't strickly true, but it didn't help

Jim, anyways. He just kept a-rocking back and forth, moaning all the while.

I says:

"Maybe we went by Cairo in the fog that night."

He says:

"Doan' le's talk about it, Huck. Po' niggers cain't have no luck. I alwuz 'spected dat damn rattle-snake skin warn't done wid its work."

"I wish I'd never seen that consarn snake-skin, Jim—I do wish I'd never laid eyes on it."

"It ain't yo' fault, Huck; you didn't know. Don't you blame yo'self 'bout it."

We didn't say another word for a good while. There warn't anything to say. We both knowed well enough it was some more work of the damn rattle-snake skin; so what was the use to talk about it? It would only look like we was finding fault, and that would be bound to fetch more bad luck—and keep on fetching it, too, till we knowed enough to keep still.

By and by we talked about what we better do. Jim was for taking to the canoe, and for starting back up to Cairo as soon as we could get moving. But I thought it would be better to go on down-stream till we passed a sizeable town. Then we could dress up in the fine clothes we took off the *Walter Scott* and paddle back to the town and get on a steamboat for Cairo, which was a lot less work than paddling a damn canoe for maybe a hundred miles or so up-stream.

When night come on, we pushed off again, but pretty soon wished we hadn't. It got gray and ruther thick, which is the next meanest thing to fog. You can't tell the shape of the river, and you can't see no distance. It got to be very late and still, and then along comes a steamboat up the river. We lit the lantern, and judged she would see it. Up-stream boats didn't generly come close to us; they go out and follow the bars and hunt for easy water under the reefs; but nights like this they bull right up the channel against the whole river.

We could hear her pounding along, but we didn't see her good till she was close. She seemed to be aimed right for us. Often those bastards do that and try to see how close they can come without touching; sometimes the wheel bites off a sweep, and then the pilot sticks his head out and laughs, and thinks he's mighty dang smart. Well, here she comes, and we said she was going to try and shave us; but she didn't seem to be sheering off a bit. She was a big son-of-a-bitch, and she was coming in a damn big hurry, too, looking like a black cloud with rows of glow-worms around it; but all of a sudden she bulged out, big and scary, with a long row of wide-open furnace doors shining like red-hot teeth, and her monstrous bows and guards hanging right over us. There was a yell at us, and a jingling of bells to stop the engines, a powwow of cussing and whistling of steam, and she come smashing right down on the raft.

I dived—and I aimed to find the damn bottom, too, for a thirty-foot wheel had got to go over me, and I wanted it to have plenty of room. I could always stay under water a minute; this time I reckoned I stayed under a minute and a half. Then I bounced for the top in a hurry, for I was nearly busting. I popped out to my armpits and blowed the water out of my nose, and puffed a bit. Of course there was a booming current; and of course that goddamn boat started her engines again ten seconds after she stopped them, for they never cared much for raftsmen; so now she was churning along up the river, out of sight in the thick weather, though I could hear her.

I looked around for Jim, but the night was so heavy you couldn't see in any direction for more than a few feet. I sung out for him about a dozen times, but there warn't no answer. It seemed to me that he had been right under the damn guards when she hit us, so I reckoned it was all up with poor old Jim. I couldn't help blubbering a little, because he was a mighty fine man for a nigger, and had always been good to me. But then, I thought, all that talk about Ab'litionists *was* wicked, and I figured as how Providence had had a hand in the business. It looked like that damned snake skin had been sent as a warning, and what had happened come from not paying it proper heed. When that steamboat come a-booming down on us, all blackness and fire, it was Providence having His say about slave-stealing, and if I had ever known He was a-going to take things *that* hard, I never would a helped Jim in the first place. I was mighty damn grateful that He had decided to let me off this once, and swore out loud that it would be a cold day in hell before I'd ever help *another* nigger escape.

I never much cottoned to swimming at night, and as I lay there treading water, thinking about Jim drownded somewheres nearby, and Providence, and the snake skin, I begun to feel lonely and scared. I felt like I was floating in a blackness. There warn't a danged light anywhere, nor a sound except for the deep growl the river makes out there in the channel. I couldn't get rid of the idea that there was something deep down in that black water a-laying for me, and it warn't long before my balls had shrunk into little wrinkled peas. I wanted to tuck my legs up tight and lift myself right out of that river, and when something come along just then and bumped me from behind, I damn near did it. I give a whoop and a twist and climbed out nearly to my waist, thinking it was Jim's corpse, or Providence, or maybe Charles William Allbright, but it was just a piece of the raft that had floated up, nothing more.

Well, it *was* good to see that old chunk of raft, even though it was just a few foot of splintered board. It was an old friend, or part of one anyways, and I begun to feel better. I took a-holt of the plank and struck out for shore, shoving it ahead of me. But I made out to see that the drift of the current was towards the left-hand shore, which meant that I was in a crossing; so I changed off and went that way.

It was one of these long, slanting, two-mile crossings; so I was a good long time in getting over. I made a safe landing, and clumb up the bank. I couldn't see but a little ways, but I went poking along over rough ground for a quarter of a mile or more, and then I run across a big old-fashioned double log house before I noticed it. I was going to rush by and get away, but a lot of danged dogs jumped out and went to howling and barking at me, and I knowed better than to move another peg.

XVI

The Grangerfords
take me in

In about a minute somebody spoke out of a window without putting his head out, and says:

"Be done, boys! Who's there?"

I says:

"It's me."

"Whose me?"

"George Jackson, sir."

"What do you want?"

"I don't want nothing, sir. I only want to go along by, but the dogs won't let me."

"What are you prowling around here this time of night for — hey?"

"I warn't prowling around, sir; I fell overboard off of the steamboat."

"Oh, you did, did you? Strike a light there, somebody. What did you say your name was?"

"George Jackson, sir. I'm only a boy."

"Look here, if you're telling the truth you needn't be afraid — nobody'll hurt you. But don't try to budge; stand right where you are. Rouse out Bob and Tom,

some of you, and fetch the guns. George Jackson, is
there anybody with you?"

"No, sir, nobody."

I heard the people stirring around in the house now,
and see a light. The man sung out:

"Snatch that light away, Betsy, you old fool—
ain't you got any sense? Put it on the floor behind
the front door. Bob, if you and Tom are ready, take
your places."

"All ready."

"Now, George Jackson, do you know the Shepherdsons?"

"No, sir; I never heard of them."

"Well, that may be so, and it mayn't. Now, all
ready. Step forward, George Jackson. And mind,
don't you hurry—come mighty slow. If there's anybody with you, let him keep back—if he shows himself he'll be shot. Come along now. Come slow; push
the door open yourself—just enough to squeeze in,
d'you hear?"

I didn't hurry; I couldn't if I'd a wanted to. I took
one slow step at a time and there warn't a sound, only
I thought I could hear my heart. The dogs were as
still as the humans, but they followed a little behind me. When I got to the three log doorsteps I
heard them unlocking and unbarring and unbolting.
I put my hand on the door and pushed it a little and
a little more till somebody said, "There, that's
enough—put your head in." I done it, but I judged
they would take it off.

The candle was on the floor, and there they all was,
looking at me, and me at them, for about a quarter
of a minute: Three big men with guns pointed at me,
which made me wince, I tell you; the oldest, gray and

about sixty, the other two thirty or more — all of them fine and handsome — and the sweetest old gray-headed lady, and back of her two young women which I couldn't see right well. The old gentleman says:

"There; I reckon it's all right. Come in."

As soon as I was in the old gentlemen he locked the door and barred it and bolted it, and told the young men to come in with their guns, and they all went in a big parlor that had a new rag carpet on the floor, and got together in a corner that was out of the range of the front windows — there warn't none on the side. They held the candle, and took a good look at me, and all said, "Why *he* ain't a damn Shepherdson — no, there ain't any Shepherdson about him." Then the old man said he hoped I wouldn't mind being searched for arms, because he didn't mean no harm by it — it was only to make sure. So he didn't pry into my pockets, but only felt outside with his hands, and said it was all right. He told me to make myself easy and at home, and tell all about myself; but the old lady says:

"Why, bless you, Saul, the poor thing's as wet as he can be; and don't you reckon it may be he's hungry?"

"True for you, Rachel — I forgot."

So the old lady says:

"Betsy" (this was a nigger woman), "you fly around and get him something to eat as quick as you can, poor thing; and one of you girls go and wake up Buck and tell him — oh, here is himself. Buck, take this little stranger and get the wet clothes off from him and dress him up in some of yours that's dry."

Buck looked about as old as me — thirteen or fourteen or along there, though he was a little bigger than me. He hadn't on anything but a shirt, and he was very frowzy-headed. He came in gaping and digging one fist in his eyes, and he was dragging a gun along with the other one. He says:

"Ain't they no dern Shepherdsons around?"
They said no, 'twas a false alarm.

"Well," he says, "if they'd a ben some, I reckon I'd a got one."

They all laughed, and Bob says:

"Why, Buck, they might have scalped us all, you've been so slow in coming."

"Well, nobody come after me, and it ain't right. I'm always kept down; I don't get no dang show."

"Never mind, Buck, my boy," says the old man, "you'll have show enough, all in good time, don't you fret about that. Go 'long with you now, and do as your mother told you."

When we got up-stairs to his room he got me a coarse shirt and a roundabout and pants of his, and I put them on. While I was at it he asked me what my name was, but before I could tell him he started to tell me about a bluejay and a young rabbit he had catched in the woods day before yesterday, and he asked me where Moses was when the candle went out. I said I didn't know; I hadn't heard about it before, no way. He says:

"Why, he was in the *dark*! That's where he was!"

He laughed, so I laughed too, but it beat me what was funny about a man being in the dark when the candle went out. He says:

"Say, how long are you going to stay here? You got to stay always. We can just have booming times — they don't have no school now. Do you own a dog?

I've got a dog—and he'll go in the river and bring out
chips that you throw in. Do you like to comb up
Sundays, and all that kind of crap? You bet I don't,
but ma she makes me. Damn these ole britches! I
reckon I'd better put 'em on, but I'd ruther not, it's
so warm. Are you all ready? All right. Come along,
old hoss."

Cold corn-pone, cold corn-beef, butter and buttermilk—that is what they had for me down there, and
there ain't nothing better than ever I've come across
yet. Buck and his ma and all of them smoked cob
pipes, except the nigger woman, which was gone, and
the two young women. They all smoked and talked,
and I eat and talked. The young women had quilts
around them, and their hair down their backs. They
was mighty damn good-looking females, and it was
all I could do to keep from staring at them. The whole
family asked me questions, and I told them how pap
and me and all the family was living on a little farm
down at the bottom of Arkansaw, and my sister Mary
Ann run off and got married and never was heard of
no more, and Bill went to hunt them and he warn't
heard of no more, and Tom and Mort died, and then
there warn't nobody but just me and pap left, and he
was just trimmed down to nothing, on account of his
troubles; so when he died I took what there was left,
because the farm didn't belong to us, and started
up the river, deck passage, and fell overboard; and
that was how I come to be here. So they said I could
have a home there as long as I wanted it. Then it was
most daylight and everybody went to bed, and I went
to bed with Buck, and when I waked up in the morning, damn it all, I had forgot what my name was. So

I laid there about an hour trying to think, and when Buck waked up I says:

"Can you spell, Buck?"

"Yes," he says.

"I bet you can't spell my name," says I.

"I bet you what you dare I can," says he.

"All right," says I, "go ahead."

"G-e-o-r-g-e J-a-x-o-n — there now," he says.

"Well," says I, "you done it, but I didn't think you could. It ain't no slouch of a name to spell — right off without studying."

I set it down, private, because somebody might want *me* to spell it next, and so I wanted to be handy with it and rattle it off like I was used to it.

It was a mighty nice family, and a mighty nice house, too. I hadn't seen no log house out in the country before that was so damn nice and had so much damn style. It didn't have an iron latch on the front door, nor a wooden one with a buckskin string, but a brass knob to turn, the same as houses in town. There warn't no bed in the parlor, nor a sign of a bed; but heaps of parlors in towns has beds in them. There was a big fireplace that was bricked on the bottom, and the bricks was kept clean and red by pouring water on them and scrubbing them with another brick; sometimes they wash them over with red water-paint that they call Spanish-brown, same as they do in town. They had big brass dog-irons that could hold up a saw-log. There was a clock on the middle of the mantelpiece, with a picture of a town painted on the bottom half of the glass front, and a round place in the middle of it for the sun, and you could see the pendulum swinging behind it. It was beautiful to hear the clock tick; and sometimes when one of these peddlers had been along and scoured her up and got her in good shape, she would start in and strike a hundred and fifty before she got tuckered out. They wouldn't a took any money for her.

Well, there was a big outlandish damn parrot on each side of the clock, made out of something like chalk, and painted up gaudy. By one of the parrots was a cat made of crockery, and a crockery dog by the other; and when you pressed down on them they squeaked, but didn't open their mouths nor look different nor interested. They squeaked through underneath where there was a little whistle stuck in their bellies, sort of like a misplaced ass-hole. There was a couple of big wild-turkey-wing fans spread out behind those things. On the table in the middle of the room was a kind of lovely crockery basket that had apples and oranges and peaches and grapes piled up in it, which was much redder and yellower and prettier than real ones is, but they warn't real because you could see where pieces had got chipped off and showed the white chalk, or whatever it was, underneath.

This table had a cover made out of beautiful oilcloth, with a red and blue spread-eagle painted on it, and a painted border all around. It come all the way from Philadelphia, they said. There was some books, too, piled up perfectly exact, on each corner of the table. One was a big family Bible full of pictures. One was *Pilgrim's Progress*, about a man that left his family, it didn't say why. I read considerable in it, about five pages. The statements was interesting, but tough. Another was *Friendship's Offering*, full of beautiful stuff and poetry; but I didn't read the poetry. Another was Henry Clay's *Speeches*, and another was Dr. Gunn's *Family Medicine*, which told you all about what to do if a body was sick or dead. There was a hymn-book, and a lot of other books. And there was several nice split-bottom chairs, and perfectly sound, too—not bagged down in the middle and busted, like an old basket.

They had pictures hung on the walls—mainly Washingtons and Lafayettes, and battles, and Highland Marys, and one called "Signing the Declaration." There was some that they called crayons, which one of the daughters which was dead made her own self when she was only fifteen years old. They was different from any picture I ever see before— blacker, mostly, than is common. One was a woman in a slim black dress, belted small under the armpits, with bulges like a cabbage in the middle of the sleeves, and a large black scoop-shovel bonnet with a black veil and white slim ankles crossed about with black tape, and very wee black slippers, like a chisel, and she was leaning pensive on a tombstone on her right elbow, under a weeping willow, and her other hand hanging down her side holding a white handkerchief and a reticule, and underneath the picture it said "Shall I Never See Thee More Alas." Another one was a young lady with her hair all combed up straight to the top of her head, and knotted there in front of a comb like a chair-back, and she was crying into a handkerchief and had a dead bird laying on its back in her other hand with its heels up, and underneath the picture it said "I Shall Never Hear Thy Sweet Chirrup More Alas." There was one where a young lady was at a window looking up at the moon, and tears running down her cheeks; and she had an open letter in one hand with black sealing-wax showing on one edge of it, and she was mashing a locket with a chain to it against her mouth, and underneath the picture it said "And Art Thou Gone Yes Thou Art Gone Alas." These was all damn fine pictures, I reckon, but I didn't somehow seem to take to them, because if ever I was down a little, maybe thinking about poor old Jim, they always give me the fantods. Everybody was sorry she died, because she had laid out a lot more of these pictures to do, and a body could see by what she had done what they had lost. But I reckoned that with her disposition, she was having a better time in the dang graveyard. She was at work on what they said was her greatest picture when she took sick, and every day and every night it was her prayer to be allowed to live till she got it done, but she never got the chance. It was a picture of a young woman in a long white gown, standing on the rail of a bridge all ready to jump off, with her hair all down her back, and looking up to the moon, with the tears running down her face, and she had two arms folded across her breast, and two arms stretched out in front, and two more reaching up toward the moon— and the idea was to see which pair would look best, and then scratch out all the other arms; but, as I was saying, she died before she got her mind made up, and now they kept this picture over the head of the bed in her room, and every time her birthday come they hung flowers on it. Other times it was hid with a little curtain. The young woman in the picture had a kind of nice sweet face, but there was so many damn arms it made her look too spidery, seemed to me.

This young girl kept a scrap-book when she was alive, and used to paste obituaries and accidents and cases of patient suffering in it out of the *Presbyterian Observer*, and write poetry after them out of her own head. It was very good poetry, especially one she wrote about a boy by the name of Stephen Dowling Bots that fell down a well and was drownded. If Emmeline Grangerford could make poetry like that before she was fourteen, there ain't no telling what she could a done by and by.

Buck said she could rattle off poetry like nothing. She didn't even have to stop to think. He said she would slap down a line, and if she couldn't find anything to rhyme with it, would just scratch it out and slap down another one, and go ahead. She warn't particular; she could write about any damn thing you choose to give her to write about just so it was sadful. Every time a man died, or a woman died, or a child died, she would be on hand with her poem—"tributes" she called 'em—before he was cold. The neighbors said it was the doctor first, then Emmeline, then the undertaker—the undertaker never got in ahead of Emmeline but once, so to speak, and that was at her own funeral.

They kept Emmeline's room trim and nice, and all the things fixed in it just the way she liked to have them when she was alive, and nobody ever slept there. The old lady took care of the room herself, though there was plenty of niggers, and she sewed there a good deal and read her Bible there mostly. Sometimes when there warn't anybody about, I'd go up there myself and get out her poor old scrap-book and read in it. It was so quiet up there, like a reglar church it was, only without all the coughing and snuffling and screaking of chairs. Reading about all them miserable suffering dead people got me to thinking about poor old Jim, and since there was considerable blank space left in Emmeline's book, I thought I'd stick in one for him, being careful not to say nothing about his being a nigger and all.

It was easy enough, at first. Emmeline give me a sort of shove so to speak, and away I went.

> Poor Jim, thou are gone for good, alas!
> Buried where there is no dirt nor grass.
> Drownded in the Mississippi,

Well, "Mississippi" done me in. I must a sweated over that damn word for two hours, trying to think up another that matched. It was like a steamboat stuck on a sand bar, I couldn't go forrards or back. So I quit poetry for good. It just warn't in me.

Anyway, as I was saying about the parlor, there was beautiful curtains on the windows; white, with pictures painted on them of castles with vines all down the walls, and cattle coming down to drink. There was a little old piano, too, that had tin pans in it, I reckon, and nothing was ever so lovely as to hear the young ladies singing "The Last Link is Broken" and play "The Battle of Prague" on it. The walls of all the rooms was plastered, and most had carpets on the floors, and there warn't a loose board about the place that hadn't been whitewashed.

It was a double house, like I said, and the big open place betwixt the log houses was roofed and floored with reglar puncheon planks—none of your dirt floors for them! Sometimes the table was set there in the middle of the day, and it was a cool comfortable place. Nothing couldn't be better. And warn't the cooking good, and just bushels of it too!

XVII

Why Harney rode away
for his hat

For the first time since I left Jackson's Island
my conscience left off getting me all in a sweat,
and times was fine, mostly. But every now and
then I'd remember the raft, and poor Jim, and what a
good cretur he was, and then I'd get to feeling so blue
and lowdown miserable that I'd have to go off into the
woods and cry. Once Col. Grangerford found me out
there and asked me what the matter was, and I told
him it was my pap and all my family which was dead
or disappeared. I felt mean telling such a lie to a man
who had took me in for his own son, but it wouldn't
a done to tell him I was crying over a dead nigger.

Col. Grangerford was a gentleman, you see. He
was a gentleman all over; and so was his family. He
was well born, as the saying is, and that's worth as
much in a man as it is in a horse, so the Widow
Douglas said, and nobody ever denied that she was
of the first aristocracy in our town; and pap he always
said it, too, though he warn't no more quality than a
damn mudcat himself. Col. Grangerford was very tall

and very slim, and had a darkish-paly complexion, not a sign of red in it anywheres; he was clean-shaved every morning all over his thin face, and he had the thinnest kind of lips, and the thinnest kind of nostrils, and a high nose, and heavy eyebrows, and the blackest kind of eyes, sunk so deep back that they seemed like they was looking out of caverns at you, as you may say. His forehead was high, and his hair was gray and straight and hung to his shoulders. His hands was long and thin, and every day of his life he put on a clean shirt and a full suit from head to foot made out of linen so dern white it hurt your eyes to look at it; and on Sundays he wore a blue tail-coat with brass buttons on it. He carried a mahogany cane with a silver head to it. There warn't no friv-olishness about him, not a damn bit, and he warn't ever loud. He was as kind as he could be — you could feel that, you know, and so you had confidence. Sometimes he smiled, and it was good to see; but when he straightened himself up like a liberty-pole, and the lightning begun to flicker out from under his eyebrows, you wanted to climb a tree first, and find out what the matter was afterwards. He didn't ever have to tell anybody to mind their manners — every-body was always good-mannered where he was. Everybody loved to have him around, too; he was sunshine most always — I mean he made it seem like good weather. When he turned into a cloud-bank it was awful damn dark for half a minute, and that was enough; there wouldn't nothing go wrong again for a week.

When him and the old lady come down in the morning all the family got up out of their chairs and give them good day, and didn't set down again till

they had set down. Then Tom and Bob went to the
sideboard where the decanter was, and mixed a
glass of bitters and handed it to him, and he held
it in his hand and waited till Tom's and Bob's was
mixed, and then they bowed and said, "Our duty to
you, sir, and madam"; and *they* bowed the least bit
in the world and said thank you, and so they drank,
all three, and Bob and Tom poured a spoonful of
water on the sugar and the mite of whisky or apple-
brandy in the bottom of their tumblers, and give it to
me and Buck, and we drank to the old people too.

Bob was the oldest and Tom next — tall, beautiful
men with very broad shoulders and brown faces, and
long black hair and black eyes. They dressed in white
linen from head to foot, like the old gentleman, and
wore broad Panama hats.

Then there was Miss Charlotte; she was twenty-
five, and tall and proud and grand, but as good as she
could be when she warn't stirred up; but when she
was she had a look that would make you wilt in your
danged tracks, like her father. She was beautiful.

So was her sister, Miss Sophia, but it was a different kind. She was gentle and sweet like a dove,
and she was only twenty.

Each person had their own nigger to wait on them —
Buck too. My nigger had a monstrous easy time,
because I warn't used to having anybody do anything for me, but Buck's was on the jump most of
the time.

This was all there was of the family now, but there
used to be more — three sons; they got killed; and
Emmeline that died.

The old gentleman owned a lot of farms and over
a hundred niggers. Sometimes a stack of people

would come there, horseback, from ten or fifteen miles around, and stay five or six days, and have such junketings round about and on the river, and dances and picnics in the woods daytimes, and balls at the house nights. These people was mostly kinfolks of the family. The men brought their guns with them. It was a damn handsome lot of quality, I tell you.

There was another clan of aristocracy around there—five or six families—mostly of the name of Shepherdson. They was as high-toned and well born and rich and grand as the tribe of Grangerfords. The Shepherdsons and Grangerfords used the same steamboat-landing, which was about two mile above our house; and one time when I went up there with a lot of our folks I see a lot of the Shepherdsons there on their fine horses.

One day Buck and me was away out in the woods hunting, and heard a horse coming. We was crossing the road. Buck says:

"Quick! Jump for the woods!"

We done it, and then peeped down the woods throught the leaves. Pretty soon a splendid young man came galloping down the road, setting his horse easy and looking like a soldier. He had his gun across his pommel. I had seen him before. It was young Harney Shepherdson. I heard Buck's gun go off at my ear, and Harney's hat tumbled off from his head. He grabbed his gun and rode straight to the place where we was hid. But we didn't wait. We started through the woods on a run. The woods warn't thick, so I looked over my shoulder to dodge the bullet, and twice I seen Harney cover Buck with his gun; and then he rode away the way he come—to get his hat, I reckon, but I couldn't see. We never stopped running till we got home. The old gentleman's eyes blazed a minute—'twas pleasure, mainly, I judged—then his face sort of smoothed down, and he says, kind of gentle:

"I don't like that shooting from behind a bush. Why don't you step into the road, my boy?"

"The Shepherdson's don't, father. They always take advantage."

Miss Charlotte she held her head up like a queen while Buck was telling his tale, and her nostrils spread and her eyes snapped. The two young men looked dark, but never said nothing. Miss Sophia she turned pale, but the color come back when she found the man warn't hurt.

Soon as I could get Buck down by the corncribs under the trees by ourselves, I says:

"Did you want to kill him, Buck?"

"Well, you're damn right I did."

"What did he do to you?"

"Him? He never done nothing to me."

"Well, then, what in hell did you want to kill him for?"

"Why, nothing—only it's on account of the feud 'twixt us and them. I'm bound to shoot any Shepherdson whenever I get a decent chance."

"Has this feud been going on very long, Buck?"

"Well, I should *reckon*! It started thirty year ago, or som'ers along there. There was trouble 'bout something, and then a lawsuit to settle it; and the suit went agin one of the men, and so he up and shot the man that won the suit—which he would naturally do, of course. Anybody would."

"What was the trouble about?"

"About? I don't know. Land, maybe."

"Well, who done the shooting? Was it a Granger-ford or Shepherdson?"

"Hell, how do *I* know? I warn't even *borned* yet!"

"Don't anybody know?"

"Oh, pa knows, I reckon, and some of the other old folks; but they don't much like to talk about it. They say we're in it, and it don't matter how we got there, because we're in it to stick. They say it's *got* to be so, there ain't no other way. No Grangerford *ever* backed out."

"Has there been many killed, Buck?"

"Yes; right smart chance of funerals. But they don't always get killed. Pa's got a few buckshot in him; but he don't mind it 'cuz he don't weigh much, anyway. Bob's been carved up some with a bowie, and Tom's been hurt once or twice."

"Has anybody been killed this year, Buck?"

"Yes; we got one and they got one. 'Bout three months ago my cousin Bud, fourteen year old, was riding through the woods on t'other side of the river, and didn't have no weapon with him, which was damn foolishness, and in a lonesome place he hears a horse a-coming behind him, and sees old Baldy Shep-herdson a-linkin' after him with his gun in his hand and his white hair a-flying in the wind; and 'stead of jumping off and taking to the brush, Bud 'lowed he could outrun him; so they had it, nip and tuck, for five mile or more, the old man a-gaining all the time; so at last Bud seen it warn't any use, so he stopped and faced around so as to have the bullet-holes in front, you know, and the old man he rode up and shot him down. But he didn't get much chance to enjoy his luck, for inside of a week our folks laid *him* out."

"I reckon that old man was a damn coward, Buck."

"I reckon he *warn't* a coward. Not by a damn sight. There ain't a coward amongst them Shepherdsons—not a one. And there ain't no cowards amongst the Grangerfords either. Why, that old man kep' up his end in a fight one day for half an hour against three Grangerfords, and come out winner. They was all a-horseback; he lit off of his horse and got behind a little woodpile, and kep' his horse before him to stop the bullets; but the Grangerfords stayed on their horses and capered around the old man, and peppered away at him, and he peppered away at them. Him and his horse both went home pretty leaky and crippled, but the Grangerfords had to be *fetched* home—and one of 'em was dead, and another died the next day. No, sir; if a body's out hunting for cowards he don't want to fool away any time among them Shepherdsons, becuz they don't breed any of that *kind*."

Next Sunday we all went to church, about three mile, everybody a-horseback. The men took their guns along, so did Buck, and kept them between their knees or stood them handy against the wall. The Shepherdsons done the same. It was pretty ornery preaching—all about brotherly love, and such-like rotton tiresomeness; but everybody said it was a good sermon, and they all talked it over going home, and had such a powerful lot to say about faith and good works and free grace and preforeordestination, and I don't know what-all, that it did seem to me to be one of the roughest dern Sundays I had run across yet.

About an hour after dinner everybody was dozing around, some in their chairs and some in their rooms, and it got to be pretty dull. Buck and his dog was stretched out on the grass in the sun sound asleep. I went up to our room, and judged I would take a nap myself. I found that sweet Miss Sophia standing in her door, which was next to ours, and she took me in her room and shut the door very soft, and asked me if I liked her, and I said I did, and she asked me if I would do something for her and not tell anybody, and I said I would. Then she said she'd forgot her Testament, and left it in the seat at church between two other books, and would I slip out quiet and go there and fetch it to her, and not say nothing to nobody. I said I would. So I slid out and slipped off up the road, and there warn't anybody at the church, except maybe a dern hog or two, for there warn't any lock on the door, and hogs likes a puncheon floor in summer-time because it's cool. If you notice, most folks don't go to church only when they've got to; but a hog is different.

Says I to myself, something's up; it ain't natural for a girl to be in such a damn sweat about a Testament. So I give it a shake, and out drops a little piece of paper with "*Half past two*" wrote on it with a pencil. I ransacked it, but couldn't find anything else. I couldn't make anything out of that, so I put the paper in the book again, and when I got home and upstairs there was Miss Sophia in her door waiting for me. She pulled me in and shut the door; then she looked in the Testament till she found the paper, and as soon as she had read it she looked glad; and before a body could think she grabbed me and give me a squeeze, and said I was the best boy in the world, and not to tell anybody. She was mighty red in the face for a minute, and her eyes lighted up, and it made her powerful damn pretty. I was a good deal astonished, but when I got my breath I asked her what the paper was about, and she asked me if I had read it, and I said no, and she asked me if I could read writing, and I told her "no, only coarse-hand," and then she said the paper warn't anything but a bookmark to keep her place, and I was to run along, unless I wanted to read a little bit with her from the Testament.

Well, I'd had enough of that for one Sunday, so I went off down to the river, studying over this thing, and pretty soon I noticed that my nigger was following along behind. When we was out of sight of the house he looked back and around a second, and then comes a-running, and says: "Mars Jawge, if you'll come down into de swamp I'll show you a whole stack o' water-moccasins."

Thinks I, that's mighty damn curious; he said that yesterday. He oughter know a body don't love water-moccasins enough to go around hunting for them. What is he up to, anyway? So I says:

"All right; trot ahead."

I followed a half a mile; then he struck out over the swamp, and waded ankle-deep as much as another half-mile. We come to a little flat piece of land which was dry and very thick with trees and bushes and vines, and he says:

"You shove right in dah jist a few steps, Mars Jawge; dah's whah dey is. I's seed 'm befo'; I don't k'yer to see 'em no mo'."

Then he slopped right along and went away, and

pretty soon the trees hid him. I poked into the place a ways and come to a little open patch as big as a bedroom all hung around with vines, and found a man laying there asleep—and, by Jesus, it was my old Jim! He warn't dead after all.

I waked him up, and I reckoned it was going to be a grand surprise to him to see me again, but it warn't. He nearly cried he was so glad, but he warn't surprised. Said that the niggers had told him there was a strange boy up at the house, and he reckoned on how it was me.

Well, didn't I have a lot of questions to ask him! I says:

"Why didn't you yell out that night, Jim, after we dove off the raft?"

"Dove off de raf'? Why, Huck, I never *dove* off. I jump for de g'yards when she hit, en' hung on. Oh, Lordy, I wuz skairt! Wid dem damn paddles blim-blammin' along de raf' like dey done, I tho't you wuz a goner, sho'."

Then he got all choked up and I began to feel a little damp myself, so I says:

"Well, dang it all Jim, *then* what happened. If you'd kept holdin' onto them guards, you'd be in St. Louis by now."

"I kep' a-holt on'y tell de peoples run astern to see what happen to de raf', en den I shin abo'd en mix in wid de black gang, en when I gits a chanst, I snuck away and swim for de sho'. Den I struck out for de woods to wait for day, en when de niggers come along, gwyne to de fields early in de mawnin', dey tuck me en showed me dis place, whah de dogs can't track me on accounts o' de water, en dey brings me truck to eat every night, en tells me 'bout dis boy who gittin'

'long famous up at de big house. Oh, Huck honey, I
know'd it 'uz you, an' here you is, big as life!"

"Why didn't you get my Jack to fetch me here
sooner, Jim?"

"De niggers 'ud hide me heah fo' ever, but dey
don't want ter get mixed up wid white folks. I tried
to 'splain how you is *different*, but dey jes' shake dey
haids. They cain't understand why a white genlman
would go ter all dat trouble jes' to help a nigger run
away, les'n he wuz an Ab'litionist, en I set 'm straight
on dat score right off. Dey's mighty good to me, dese
niggers is, en whatever I wants 'm to do fur me I
doan' have to ast 'm twice. But dey stops sho't uv
fotchin' you. Howsomever, I see dat Jack's a pooty
smart nigger, wid ambition, en I talks wid him now
and den, en finally gives him a nice new silver dollar,
en he say he'll fotch you all right when de time
comes."

"When the time comes?"

"Sho'. 'Twarn't no use to 'sturb you, Huck, tell we
could do sumfn—but we're all right now. I ben a-
buyin' pots en pans en vittles, as I got a chanst, en
a-patchin' up de raf' nights when—"

"*What* raft, Jim?"

"Our ole raf'."

Well, that one stopped me. I had to sit down.
I says:

"You mean to say our old raft warn't smashed all to
flinders?"

"No, she warn't. She was tore up a good deal—one
en' uv her wuz; but dey warn't no great harm done,
on'y some uv our traps 'uz los'. But now she's all fixed
up ag'n mos' as good as new, en we's got a new lot o'
stuff in de place o' what 'uz los'."

"Why, how did you get hold of the raft again, Jim — did you catch her?"

"How in hell I gwyne to ketch her en I out in de woods? No; some er de niggers foun' her ketched on a snag along heah in de ben', en dey hid her in a crick 'mongst de willows, en dey wuz so much jawin' 'bout which un 'um she b'long to de mos' dat I come to heah 'bout it pooty soon, so I ups en settles de trouble by tellin' 'um she don't b'long to none uv 'um, but to you en me; en I ast 'm if dey gwyne to grab a young white genlman's propety, en git a hid'n for it? Den I gin 'm ten cents apiece, en dey 'uz mighty well satisfied, en wisht some mo' raf's 'ud come along en make 'm rich ag'in."

Well, so Jim warn't dead after all. That took some getting used to and all the time he was talking, I was thinking, because I could feel my conscience a-chewing on me so as to get his strength back. Whilst I was mighty glad to see good old Jim and to find out he hadn't drownded, I didn't much relish bucking Providence once again. But Jim was so happy and full of plans and talk that I didn't have the heart to tell him. Instead, I begun to feel ornery and mean and a little sad, wondering what in damnation I was a-going to do next.

"Well," I says when Jim stopped long enough to draw a breath, "I got to get back before they miss me."

"Ain't we gwyne tuck out'n heah, honey?" I never see a nigger so for pestering a body once he had hold of an idea.

"Oh, *yes*," I says. "Right now, and with all my things up at the house, and people asking questions and all."

Jim was proper sorry then, and hung his head and
looked foolish. So I got to feeling even ornerier, and
wished I was most anyplace but there. There was this
little thought trying to push through all the rest,
a mean, creeping, low-down thought it was, too, and it
kept telling me that things would a been a whole lot
easier if Jim had really drownded when that steamboat hit our raft.

I says:

"Oh, hell, Jim, something will come along. Something always does, you know."

"Sho, I knows dat," he says. "But dis damn
waitin' do git a man down. An' de loneliness, settin'
here in dis ol' swamp."

"It ain't for ever," I says. "I'll set to a-studying,
Jim, and figure out some kind of plan so's we can get
out of here without any ruckus."

Well, that perked him up a little, and I see he was
about to start in again, so I told him I just *had* to get
back to the house before somebody began asking
around.

I got up then, and started to crawl out of the
thicket, but Jim caught a-holt of my sleeve. He says:

"Huck, you hain't a-goin' ter leave old Jim, is you?"

"Damn it, I already told you. I *got* to get home."

"I mean, you is comin' back, hain't you?"

"Haven't I said I would? Haven't I *said* I'd study
up a plan?"

"I believes you, den," he says. "I believes you."
So he let go of me and I crawled through the vines
that hung down around his hide-out. But I hadn't
gone more'n a few feet before he calls out to me:

"Don't fergit, now! Ol' Jim is a-countin' on you,
Huck. He knows dat you's a-gwyne ter come back to

de raf' ag'in, en he'p him. He knows dat. He knows you's a-gwyne ter come back to de raf' ag'in, Huck honey, kase you *said* you 'uz."

Well, I had got up onto my feet by then, and some of my brashness had come back, but now it all went out of me like piss down a hole. It would a been just as well if I had stayed down on all fours and crawled out of that swamp like some varmit, I felt so rotten mean, and humble, and to blame, somehow—though I hadn't *done* nothing. But that's always the way; it don't make no difference whether you do something or not, a person's conscience ain't got no sense, and just goes for him *anyway*. If I had a yaller dog that didn't know no more than a person's conscience does I would pison him. It takes up more room than all the rest of a person's insides, and yet ain't no damned good, nohow.

XVIII

What comes of fetching a Bible

I don't want to talk much about the next day. I reckon I'll cut it pretty short. I waked up about dawn, and was a-going to turn over and go to sleep again when I noticed how still it was—didn't seem to be anybody stirring. That warn't usual. Next I noticed that Buck was up and gone. Well, I gets up, a-wondering, and goes downstairs—nobody around; everything as still as a mouse. Just the same outside. Thinks I, what does it mean? Down by the woodpile I comes across my Jack and says:

"What's it all about?"

"Don't you know, Mars Jawge? Why, Miss Sophia's run off! 'deed she has. She run off in de night some time—nobody don't know jis' when; run off to get married to dat young Harney Shepherdson, you know—leastwise, so dey 'spec. De fam'ly foun' it out 'bout half an hour ago—maybe a little mo'—en I tell you dey warn't no time los'. Sich another hurryin' up guns en hosses you never see! De women folks has gone for to stir up de relations, en ole Mars Saul en de boys tuck dey guns en rode up de river road for to try to ketch dat young man en kill him 'fo' he kin git acrost de river wid Miss Sophia. I reck'n dey's gwyne to be mighty rough times."

"Buck went off 'thout waking me up?"

"Well, I reck'n he *did*! Dey warn't gwyne to mix you up in it. Mars Buck he loaded up his gun en 'lowed he's gwyne to fetch home a blame Shepherdson or bust. Well, dey'll be plenty un 'm dah, I reck'n, en you bet you he'll fetch one ef he gits a chanst."

I took up the river road as hard as I could put. By and by I begin to hear guns a good ways off. When I came in sight of the log store and the woodpile where the steamboats lands, I worked along under the trees and brush till I got to a good place, and then I clumb up into the forks of a cottonwood that was out of reach, and watched. There was a wood-rank four foot high a little ways in front of the tree, and first I was going to hide behind that; but maybe it was luckier I didn't.

There was four or five men cavorting around on their horses in the open place before the log store, cussing and yelling, and trying to get at a couple of young chaps that was behind the wood-rank alongside of the steamboat-landing; but they couldn't come it. Every time one of them showed himself on the river side of the woodpile he got shot at. The two boys was squatting back to back behind the pile, so they could watch both ways.

By and by the men stopped cavorting around and yelling. They started riding towards the store; then up gets one of the boys, draws a steady bead over the wood-rank, and drops one of them out of his saddle. All the men jumped off their horses and grabbed the hurt one and started to carry him to the store; and that minute the two boys started on the run. They got half-way to the tree I was in before the men noticed. Then the men see them, and jumped on their horses and took out after them. They gained on the boys, but it didn't do no good, the boys had too good a headstart; they got to the woodpile that was in front of my tree, and slipped in behind it, and so they had the bulge on the men again. One of the boys was Buck, and the other was a slim young chap about nineteen years old.

The men ripped around awhile, and then rode away. As soon as they was out of sight I sung out to Buck and told him. He didn't know what to make of my voice coming out of the tree at first. He was awful surprised. He told me to watch out sharp and let him know when the men come in sight again; said they was up to some devilment or other — wouldn't be gone long. I wished I was out of that damn tree, but I dasn't come down. Buck begun to cry and rip, and 'lowed that him and his cousin Joe (that was the other young chap) would make up for this day yet. He said his father and his two brothers was killed, and two or three of the enemy. Said the Shepherdsons laid for them in ambush. Buck said his father and brothers ought to waited for their relations — the Shepherdsons was too strong for them. I asked what was become of young Harney and Miss Sophia. He damned them north, south, east, and west, and then around the points of the compass, and said she warn't no better than a slut and that Harney wouldn't marry her and that it was all probably some kind of trick. Then he began to rip on about that son-of-a-bitch Harney, and I hain't ever heard anything like the way Buck took on because he didn't manage to kill Harney that day he shot at him.

All of a sudden, *bang*! *bang*! *bang*! goes three or four guns—the men had slipped around through the woods and come in from behind without their horses! The boys jumped for the river—both of them hurt— and as they swum down the current the men run along the bank shooting at them and singing out, "Kill them, kill them!" It made me so sick I almost fell out of the tree. I ain't a-going to tell *all* that happened—it would make me sick again if I was to do that. I wished I hadn't ever come ashore that night to see such terrible damned things. I ain't ever going to get shut of them—lots of times I dream about them.

I stayed in the tree till it begun to get dark, afraid to come down. Sometimes I heard guns away off in the woods; and twice I seen little gangs of men gallop past the log store with guns; so I reckoned the trouble was still a-going on. I was mighty down-hearted; so I made up my mind I wouldn't ever go near that house again, because I reckoned I was to blame somehow. I judged that that piece of paper meant that Miss Sophia was to meet Harney some-wheres at half past two and run off; and I judged I ought to told her father about that paper and the curious way she acted, and then maybe he would a locked her up, and this goddamned awful mess wouldn't ever a happened.

When I got down out of the tree I crept along the river-bank a piece, and found the two bodies laying in the edge of the water, and tugged at them till I got them ashore; then I covered up their faces, and got away as quick as I could. I cried a little when I was covering up Buck's face, for he was mighty damn good to me.

It was just dark now. I never went near the house, but struck through the woods and made for the swamp. Jim warn't on his island, so I tramped off in a hurry for the crick, and crowded through the willows, red-hot to jump aboard and get out of that awful country. The raft was gone! My Christ, but I was scared! I couldn't get my breath for most a minute. Then I raised a yell. A voice not twenty-five foot from me says:

"Good lan'! Is dat you, honey? Doan' make no noise."

It was Jim's voice—nothing ever sounded so good before. I run along the bank a piece and got aboard, and Jim he grabbed me and hugged me, he was so glad to see me. He says:

"God bless you, chile, I 'uz right down sho' you's dead ag'in. Jack's been heah; he say he reck'n you's ben shot, kase you didn' come home no mo'; so I's jes' dis minute a startin' de canoe down towards de mouf er de crick, so's to be all ready for to shove out en leave soon as Jack comes ag'in en tells me for certain you *is* dead. Lawsy, I's mighty damn glad to get you back ag'in, honey."

I says:

"All right—that's mighty good; they won't find me, and they'll think I've been killed, and floated down the river—there's something up there that'll help them think so—so don't you lose no time, Jim, but haul that canoe aboard and shove off for the big water as fast as ever you can."

I never felt easy till the raft was two mile below there and out in the middle of the Mississippi. Then

184 : The true adventures of Huckleberry Finn

we hung up our signal lantern, and judged we was free and safe once more. I hadn't had a bite to eat since yesterday, so Jim he got out some corn-dodgers and buttermilk, and pork and cabbage and greens — there ain't nothing in the world so good when it's cooked right — and whilst I eat my supper we talked about what we was a-going to do next. I explained to Jim about Providence, and he got very solemn and agreed that there was something to it, but he put the snake skin first and Providence second. He said he'd known good men a-plenty who got bad luck after handling snake skin and plenty of bad men that Providence never even touched. He said he was willing to take his chances with Providence, and that maybe He had done His worst by now anyways. He said that from what he'd heard there warn't nothing Providence could do which was up to the style of them down-river overseers.

Well, I see there warn't no use arguing with him. Once that nigger had made up his mind, there was no changing it. There warn't nothing to do but go along with him, and see what happened, though that close call with the steamboat had cooled me off considerable about helping him get to the free states, where there was nothing but Ab'litionists and trouble. But I was powerful damn glad to get away from the feuds, and I guess Jim was happy to get shut of the swamp.

After dinner I got out my pipe and tobacco for a smoke, and Jim got out his pipe too. He filled up and struck a light and began to puff away, and I noticed right off he warn't doing it the reglar way. He would sort of drag on the stem and then keep a-holt of his

breath till there warn't nothing left to puff out. Well, I
didn't say nothing. I figured maybe he needed a
smoke worse than I did. But then some of it drifted
over my way, and it was the strangest smelling
stuff—kind of sweet but musty. Not like no tobacco
I ever smelt before. I says:

"Where in hell did you get that tobacco, Jim?"

He rolled over slow and smiled. He said:

"Why, Huck, dishere ain't terbacker, dis is *hemp*."

"Hemp?"

"Yes indeedy. Dat Jack brung me a sack er mighty
fine weed day befo' yesterday. Dey got an ole man dat
knows jes' whar de good stuff grow."

"Why, dang it all Jim, I thought hemp was what
they made rope out of."

Jim began to laugh. I had always knowed he was
the laughingest nigger, but the performance he put
on that night beat all for laughing I ever see. He
would just quiet down when he would say "rope,"
and away he'd go again. I never see anything like it.

Finally he says:

"Huck, didn't yo' pap never give you no hemp to
smoke?"

"Hell, the only hemp he ever give me was across
my ass."

Jim shook his head and took my pipe away. He
knocked out the tobacco and filled it with shreds of
stuff he took out of the puckermouth sack he had.
Then he give it back.

"Jes' light up and do like I do, Huck. Den you see
what *hemp* is fo'."

Well, I done it. The smoke burned my throat something fierce, and holding it in like that made me

sweat like a danged Turk, but I kept it up. Jim was puffing away too, and every now and then he'd look over at me.

"You *feel* anything yet, Huck? Dat hemp tuck a-holt yet?"

"I dunno," I said. "What am I s'posed to feel?" I had a little trouble getting the words out.

Jim laughed.

"You's feelin' it all right. You's comin' along fine. Dis ole hemp's mighty good stuff."

"Well, what's it s'posed to *do*, Jim? I mean, it's different than tobacco."

"Oh, yes, indeedy! Terbacker now, is all right if'n yo' wants to chaw er smoke a bit jes' to pass time, but *hemp*, she's sumfn special. She makes you *think*. She's fo' serious smokin'."

I didn't know what he meant then, but I kept quiet. I didn't feel much like talking or asking questions any more. I just felt happy and chuckly deep inside, and I guessed that the hemp was taking holt or whatever it was supposed to do. No tobacco ever made me feel like that. I never felt so good and so full of friendship, laying there smoking hemp and listening to Jim talk. I was happy all over.

Jim says:

"Dey's sumfn 'bout hemp dat nothin' else has got. You take likker. Likker gits yo' all fired up, on a rampage, laffin' en singin' en carryin' on wid de gals, but den she'll let you down, bim! Or else she gits yo' mad, en you ends up poundin' on somebody. Allus gits you *doin'* sumfn, and gittin' into trouble. But not de ole hemp, de good ole hemp, what alus makes you feel *good*, and think *clear*. No, sir, Huck, dey's nufn like it."

Well, I begun to see what he meant. Take the raft,
for instance. For the first time I begun to *feel* that
raft, and it was like Jim and me was floating in a bub-
ble, just a-drifting along, broke loose from the world.
I give up worrying about what was going to happen,
or worrying over what had already happened. I just
let myself float. I says:

"Jim, there just ain't no home like a raft, is there?"
He says:

"Huck, honey, it do seem dat *raf's* uz one er de
things de Lawd had in mind when he made de good
ole *hemp*."

Well, I guess he was right. Other places do seem
so cramped up and smothery, but a raft don't. You
feel mighty free and easy and comfortable on a raft.
And hemp, well it somehow fits, like Jim said.

XIX

The duke and the
dauphin come aboard

Two or three days and nights went by; I reckon
I might say they swum by, they slid along so
quiet and smooth and lovely. Here is the way
we put in the time. It was a monstrous big river down
there—sometimes a mile and a half wide; we run
nights, and laid up and hid daytimes; soon as night
was most gone we stopped navigating and tied up—
nearly always in the dead water under a towhead;
and then cut young cottonwoods and willows, and
hid the raft with them. Then we set out the lines.
Next we slid into the river bare-ass and had a swim,
so as to freshen up and cool off; then we set down on
the sandy bottom where the water was about knee-
deep, and watched the daylight come. Not a sound
anywheres—perfectly still—just like the whole darn
world was asleep, only sometimes the bull-frogs
a-cluttering, maybe. The first thing to see, looking
away over the water, was a kind of dull line—that
was the woods on t'other side; you couldn't make
nothing else out; then a pale place in the sky; then

more paleness spreading around; then the river softened up away off, and warn't black any more, but gray; you could see little dark spots drifting along ever so far away—trading scows, and such things; and long black streaks—rafts; sometimes you could hear a sweep screaking; or jumbled-up voices, it was so still, and sounds come so far; and by and by you could see a streak on the water which you know by the look of the streak that there's a snag there in a swift current which breaks on it and makes that streak look that way; and you see the mist curl up off of the water, and the east reddens up, and the river, and you make out a log cabin in the edge of the woods, away on the bank on t'other side of the river, being a wood-yard, likely, and piled by them damn cheats so you can throw a dog through it anywheres; then the nice breeze springs up, and comes fanning you from over there, so cool and fresh and sweet to smell on account of the woods and the flowers; but sometimes not that way, because they've left dead fish laying around, gars and such, and they do get awful dern rank; and next you've got the full day, and everything smiling in the sun, and the song-birds just going it!

A little smoke couldn't be noticed now, so we would take some fish off of the lines and cook up a hot breakfast. And afterwards we would watch the lonesome-ness of the river, and kind of lazy along, and by and by lazy off to sleep. Wake up by and by, and look to see what done it, and maybe see a steamboat cough-ing along up-stream, so far off towards the other side you couldn't tell nothing about her only whether she was a stern-wheel or side-wheel; then for about an hour there wouldn't be nothing to hear nor nothing to

see—just solid lonesomeness. Next you'd see a raft
sliding by, away off yonder, and maybe a galoot on it
chopping, because they're most always doing it on a
raft; you'd see the ax flash and come down—you
don't hear nothing; you see that ax go up again, and
by the time it's above the man's head then you hear
the *k'chunk!*—it had took all that time to come over
the water. So we would put in the day, lazying
around, listening to the stillness. Once there was a
thick fog, and the rafts and things that went by was
beating tin pans so the steamboats wouldn't run over
them. A scow or a raft went so danged close we could
hear them talking and cussing and laughing—heard
them plain; but we couldn't see no sign of them; it
made you feel crawly; it was like spirits carrying on
that way in the air. Jim said he believed it was spirits;
but I says:

"No: spirits wouldn't say 'Damn the damned fog.'"

Soon as it was night out we shoved; when we got
her out to about the middle we let her alone, and let
her float wherever the current wanted her to; then
we got out the bag of hemp and lit up our pipes, and
dangled our legs in the water, and talked about all
kinds of things. We was always naked, day and night,
whenever the skeeters would let us. The new
clothes Buck's folks made for me was too good to be
comfortable, and besides I didn't go much on clothes,
nohow.

It was considerable big and empty down there.
Sometimes we'd have that whole damned river all to
ourselves for the longest time. Yonder was the banks
and the islands, across the water; and maybe a
spark—which was a candle in a cabin window; and

sometimes on the water you could see a spark or two—on a raft or a scow you know; and maybe you could hear a fiddle or a song coming over from one of them crafts. It's lovely to live on a raft. We had the sky up there, all speckled with stars, and we used to lay there smoking and look up at them, and discuss about whether they was made or only just happened. Jim he allowed they was made, but I allowed they happened; I judged it would have took too long to *make* so dern many. Jim said the moon could a laid them; well, that looked kind of reasonable, so I didn't say nothing against it, because I've seen a frog lay most as many, so of course it could be done. We used to watch the stars that fell, too, and see them streak down. Jim allowed they'd got spoiled and was hove out of the nest.

Once or twice of a night we would see a steamboat slipping along in the dark, and now and then she would belch a whole world of sparks up out of her chimbleys, and they would rain down in the river and look awful danged pretty, for all the world like when a sky-rocket lets go and everybody goes Aahhhh! because it's so dern lovely you just can't keep still; then she would turn a corner and her lights would wink out and her powwow shut off and leave the river still again; and by and by her waves would get to us, a long time after she was gone, and would joggle the raft a bit, and after that you wouldn't hear nothing for you couldn't tell how long, except maybe frogs or something.

After midnight the people on shore went to bed, and then for two or three hours the shores was black—no more sparks in the cabin windows. These sparks was our clock—the first one that showed again meant morning was coming, so we hunted a place to hide and tie up right away.

It seemed like things would go on like that forever, just drifting and smoking and talking, but then one afternoon, after we had ate and slept and was feeling a mite restless, we tried to get a game going with them cards we had found in the floating house off Jackson's Island. We got nearly a full deck by filling in with the ones that had naked people on their backs, but I couldn't keep my mind on the game and neither could Jim. It warn't long before we both had a couple of hard 'uns, and Jim he started giggling and then I begun to snigger a little, too, and pretty soon we both dove into the water to cool down a bit. We hung onto the edge of the raft, so as to stay in under the cottonwoods, not looking at each other and not talking for a while.

Then Jim says:

"It sho' has been a long time, Huck."

He give a sort of sigh and I knowed he was thinking about his wife, so like a damn fool I puts my shovel in. I says:

"We ought to be coming to a sizeable town any day now, Jim. Don't you fret."

"What good dat gwyne ter do? All de fine clo's wuz spiled when dat steamboat run us down. Don't talk no foolishness, Huck."

I says:

"Well, we got money hain't we? What's to stop me going ashore and *buying* us some new duds?"

That done it. He got going again, a-clattering on about the free states and getting a job and what-all. He didn't say nothing more about Ab'litionists, but

I knew where he stood. I was dern sorry I had brung the subject up. For a day or more he kept it going, and I was in a sweat for fear that Providence was going to give us another swipe. First chance I got I took all them cards with the pictures on their backs and tossed them overboard, so's to keep Jim's mind off that sort of thing, and when no towns biggern a half dozen cabins come along, he slacked off and seemed to forget all about it. Leastwise he didn't talk no more about it, and I begun to relax a little.

One morning about daybreak I took the canoe and crossed over a chute to the main shore — it was only two hundred yards — and paddled about a mile up a crick amongst the cypress woods, to see if I couldn't get some berries. Just as I was passing a place where a kind of cowpath crossed the crick, here comes a couple of men tearing up the path as tight as they could foot it. I thought I was a goner, for whenever anybody was after anybody I judged it was *me* — or maybe Jim. I was about to dig out from there in a hurry, but they was pretty close to me then, and sung out and begged me to save their lives — said they hadn't been doing nothing, and was being chased for it — said there was men and dogs a-coming. They wanted to jump right in, but I says:

"Don't you do it. I don't hear the dogs and horses yet; you've got time to crowd through the brush and get up the crick a little ways; then you take to the water and wade down to me and get in — that'll throw the dogs off the scent."

They cussed considerable but they done it, and as soon as they was aboard I lit out for our towhead, and in about five or ten minutes we heard the dogs and the men away off, shouting. We heard them come along towards the crick but couldn't see them; they seemed to stop and fool around awhile; then, as we got further and further away all the time, we couldn't hardly hear them at all; by the time we had left a mile of woods behind us and struck the river, everything was quiet, and we paddled over the tow-head and hid in the cottonwoods and was safe.

One of these fellows was about seventy or up-wards, and had a bald head and very gray whiskers. He had an old battered-up slouch hat on, and a greasy blue woolen shirt, and ragged old blue jeans britches stuffed into his boot-tops, and home-knit galluses — no, he only had one. He had an old long-tailed blue jeans coat with slick brass buttons flung over his arm, and both of them had big, fat, ratty-looking carpet-bags.

The other fellow was about thirty, and dressed about as ornery. After breakfast we all laid off and talked, and the first thing that come out was that these chaps didn't know one another.

"What got you into trouble?" says the bald-head to t'other chap.

"Well, I'd been selling an article to take the tartar off the teeth — and it does take it off, too, and generly the enamel along with it — but I stayed about one night longer than I ought to, and was just in the act of sliding out when I ran across you on the trail this side of town, and you told me they were coming, and begged me to help you to get off. So I told you I was expecting trouble myself, and would scatter out *with* you. That's the whole yarn — what's yourn?"

"Well, I'd ben a-running' a little temprance revival thar 'bout a week, and was the pet of the women folks, big and little, for I was makin' it mighty damn warm for the rummies, I *tell* you, and takin' as much as five or six dollars a night—ten cents a head, children and niggers free—and business a-growin' all the time, when somehow or another a little report got around last night that I had a way of puttin' in my time with a private jug on the sly. A nigger rousted me out this mornin', and told me the people was getherin' on the quiet with their dogs and horses, and they'd be along pretty soon and give me 'bout half an hour's start, and then run me down if they could; and if they got me they'd tar and feather me and ride me on a rail, sure. I didn't wait for no breakfast—I warn't hungry."

"Old man," said the young one, "I reckon we might double-team it together; what do you think?"

"I ain't undisposed. What's your line—mainly?"

"Jour printer by trade; do a little in patent medicines; theater-actor—tragedy, you know; take a turn to mesmerism and phrenology when there's a chance; teach singing-geography school for a change; sling a lecture sometimes—oh, I do lots of things—most any damn thing that comes handy, so it ain't work. What's your lay?"

"I've done considerable in the doctoring way in my time. Layin' on o' hands is my best holt—for cancer and paralysis, and sich things; and I k'n tell a fortune pretty good when I've got somebody along to find out the facts for me. Preachin's my line, too, and workin' camp-meetin's, and missionaryin' around."

Nobody never said anything for a while; then the young man hove a sigh and says:

"Alas!"

"What 'n hell you alassin' about?" says the bald-head.

"To think I should have lived to be leading such a life, and be degraded down into such company." And he begun to wipe the corner of his eye with a rag.

"Damn your hide, ain't the company good enough for you?" says the baldhead, pretty pert and uppish.

"Yes, it *is* good enough for me; it's as good as I deserve; for who fetched me so low when I was so high? *I* did it myself. I don't blame *you*, gentlemen — far from it; I don't blame anybody. I deserve it all. Let the cold world do its worst; one thing I know — there's a grave somewhere for me. The world may go on just as it's always done, and take everything from me — loved ones, property, everything; but it can't take that. Some day I'll lie down in it and forget it all, and my poor broken heart will be at rest." He went on a-wiping.

"Cuss your pore broken heart," says the bald-head; "what are you heaving your damn pore broken heart at *us* f'r? *We* hain't done nothing."

"No, I know you haven't. I ain't blaming you, gentlemen. I brought myself down — yes, I did it myself. It's right I should suffer — perfectly right — I don't make any moan."

"Brought you down from whar, fer Chrissakes? Whar was you brought down from?"

"Ah, you would not believe me; the world never believes — let it pass — 'tis no matter. The secret of my birth —"

"The secret of your birth! Do you mean to say —"

"Gentlemen," says the young man, very solemn,

"I will reveal it to you, for I feel I may have confidence in you. By rights I am a duke!"

Jim's eyes bugged out when he heard that; and I reckon mine did, too. Then the baldhead says: "No! you can't mean it?"

"Yes. My great-grandfather, eldest son of the Duke of Bridgewater, fled to this country about the end of the last century, to breathe the pure air of freedom; married here, and died, leaving a son, his own father dying about the same time. The second son of the late duke seized the titles and estates — the infant real duke was ignored. I am the lineal descendant of that infant — I am the rightful Duke of Bridgewater; and here am I, forlorn, torn from my high estate, hunted of men, despised by the cold world, ragged, worn, heart-broken, and degraded to the companionship of felons on a raft!"

Jim pitied him ever so much, and so did I. We tried to comfort him, but he said it warn't much use, he couldn't be much comforted; said if we was a mind to acknowledge him, that would do him more good than most anything else; so we said we would, if he would tell us how. He said we ought to bow when we spoke to him, and say "Your Grace," or "My Lord," or "Your Lordship" — and he wouldn't mind it if we called him plain "Bridgewater," which, he said, was a title anyway, and not a name; and one of us ought to wait on him at dinner, and do any little thing for him he wanted done.

Well, that was all easy, so we done it. All through dinner Jim stood around and waited on him, and says, "Will yo' Grace have some o' dis or some o' dat?" and so on, and a body could see it was mighty damn pleasing to him.

But the old man got pretty silent by and by—didn't have much to say, and didn't look pretty comfortable over all that petting that was going on around that duke. He seemed to have something on his mind. So, along in the afternoon, he says:

"Looky here, Bilgewater," he says, "I'm damnation sorry for you, but you ain't the only pore bastard that's had troubles like that."

"No?"

"No, you ain't. You ain't the only pore bastard that's ben snaked down wrongfully out'n a high place."

"Alas!"

"No, you ain't the only pore bastard that's had a secret of his birth." And, by Jesus, *he* begins to cry.

"Hold! What do you mean?"

"Bilgewater, kin I trust you?" says the old man, still sort of sobbing.

"To the bitter death!" He took the old man by the hand and squeezed it, and says, "That secret of your being: speak!"

"Bilgewater, I am the late Dauphin!"

You bet you, Jim and me stared this time. A duke was something, but a *dauphin*! why, we hadn't even *heard* of that one.

"You are what?"

"Yes, my friend, it is too true—your eyes is lookin' at this very moment on the pore disappeared Dauphin, Looy the Seventeen, son of Looy the Sixteen and Mary Antonette."

"You! At your age! No! You mean you're the late Charlemagne; you must be six or seven hundred years old, at the very least."

"Trouble has done it, Bilgewater, trouble has done

it; trouble has brung these gray hairs and this pre-
mature balditude. Yes, gentlemen, you see before
you, in blue jeans and misery, the wanderin', exiled,
trampled-on, and suffern' rightful King of France."

Well, he cried and took on so that me and Jim
didn't know hardly what to do, we was so sorry—
and so glad and proud we'd got him with us, too. So
we set in, like we done before with the duke, and
tried to comfort *him*. But he said it warn't no use,
nothing but to be dead and done with it all could do
him any good; though he said it often made him feel
easier and better for a while if people treated him
according to his rights, and got down on one knee to
speak to him, and always called him "Your Majesty,"
and waited on him first at meals, and didn't set
down in his presence till he asked them. So Jim and
me set to majestying him, and doing this and that
and t'other for him, and standing up till he told us
we might set down. This done him heaps of good, and
so he got cheerful and comfortable. But the duke
kind of soured on him, and didn't look a bit satisfied
with the way things was going; still, the king acted
real friendly towards him, and said the duke's great-
grandfather and all the other Dukes of Bilgewater
was a good deal thought of by *his* father, and was
allowed to come to the palace considerable; but the
duke stayed huffy a good while, till by and by the
king says:

"Like as not we got to be together a tol'able long
time on this h-yer raft, Bilgewater, and so what's
the use o' your bein' sour? It'll only make things
oncomfortable. It ain't my fault I warn't born a duke,
it ain't your fault you warn't born a king—so what's
the use to worry? Make the best o' things the way

you find 'em, says I — that's my motto. This ain't no bad thing that we've struck here — plenty grub and an easy life — come, give us your hand, duke, and le's all be friends."

The duke done it, and Jim and me was pretty glad to see it. It took away all the uncomfortableness and we felt mighty good over it, because it would a been a miserable damn business to have any unfriendliness on the raft, for what you want, above all things, on a raft, is for everybody to be satisfied, and feel right and kind towards the others.

It didn't take me long to make up my mind that these liars warn't no kings nor dukes at all, but just damn low-down humbugs and frauds. But I never said nothing, never let on; kept it to myself; it's the best way; then you don't have no quarrels, and don't get into no trouble. If they wanted us to call them kings and dukes, I hadn't no objections, long as it would keep peace in the family; and it warn't no use to tell Jim, so I didn't tell him. If I never learnt nothing out of pap, I learnt that the best way to get along with his kind of people is to let them have their own way. I warn't keen on having rapscallions of that sort aboard our raft, but now they were with us, I couldn't see how we was to get free of them without causing a row, so the best thing to do was sit tight and see what come along.

XX

What royalty did to Pokeville

They asked us considerable many questions; wanted to know what we covered the raft that way for, and laid by in the daytime instead of running—was Jim a runaway nigger? Says I:

"Goodness sakes! Would a runaway nigger run *south*?"

No, they allowed he wouldn't. I had to account for things some way, so I says:

"My folks was living in Pike County, in Missouri, where I was born, and they all died off but me and pa and my brother Ike. Pa, he 'lowed he'd break up and go down and live with Uncle Ben, who's got a little one-horse place on the river forty-four mile below Orleans. Pa was pretty poor, and had some debts; so when he squared up there warn't nothing left but sixteen dollars and our nigger, Jim. That warn't enough to take us fourteen hundred mile, deck passage nor no other way. Well, when the river rose pa had a streak of luck one day; he ketched this piece of a raft; so we reckoned we'd go down to Orleans on it. Pa's luck didn't hold out; a steamboat run over the forrard corner of the raft one night, and we all went overboard and dove under the wheel; Jim and me come up all right, but pa was drunk, and Ike was only four years old, so they never come up no more. Well, for the next day or two we had considerable trouble, because people was always coming out in skiffs and trying to take Jim away from me, saying they believed he was a runaway nigger. We don't run daytimes no more now; nights they don't bother us."

The duke says:

"Leave me alone to cipher out a way so we can run in the daytime if we want to. I'll think the thing over—I'll invent a plan that'll fix it. We'll let it alone for today, because of course we don't want to go by that town yonder in daylight—it mightn't be healthy."

I seen how Jim pricked up his ears and took a long look across the water, and then give a sigh, knowing that with them two others on board we couldn't never sneak aboard a riverboat, and I felt sorry for him. But deep down inside I was sort of glad that there warn't nothing I could do, and that we would pass that town by as soon as it got dark. As it turned out, it warn't much show as a town anyways.

Towards night it begun to darken up and look like rain; the heat-lightning was squirting around low down in the sky, and the leaves was beginning to shiver—it was going to be damned ugly, it was easy to see that. So the duke and the king went to overhauling our wigwam, to see what the beds was like. My bed was a straw tick—better than Jim's, which was a corn-shuck tick; there's always cobs around about in a shuck tick, and they poke into you and hurt; and when you roll over the dry shucks sound like you was rolling over in a dern pile of dead leaves; it makes such a damn rustling that you wake up. Well, the duke allowed he would take my bed; but the king allowed he wouldn't. He says:

"I should a reckoned the difference in rank would a sejested to you that a corn-shuck bed warn't just fitten for me to sleep on. Your Grace'll take the shuck bed yourself."

Jim and me was in a sweat again for a minute, being afraid there was going to be some more trouble amongst them; so we was pretty glad when the duke says:

" 'Tis my fate to be always ground into the mire under the iron heel of oppression. Misfortune has broken my once haughty spirit; I yield, I submit; 'tis my accursed fate. I am alone in the world—let me suffer; I can bear it."

We got away as soon as it was good and dark. The king told us to stand well out towards the middle of the river, and not show a light till we got a long ways below the town. We come in sight of the little bunch of lights by and by—that was the town, you know— and slid by, about a half a mile out, all right. When we was three-quarters of a mile below we hoisted up our signal lantern; and about ten o'clock it come on to rain and blow and thunder and lighten like all hell was busting loose, so the king told us to both stay on watch till the weather got better; then him and the duke crawled into the wigwam and turned in for the night. It was my watch below till twelve, but I wouldn't a turned in anyway if I'd had a bed, because a body don't see such a storm as that every day in the week, not by a damn sight. Godamighty, how the wind did scream along! And every second or two there'd come a glare that lit up the white-caps for a half a mile around, and you'd see the islands looking dusty through the rain, and the trees thrashing around in the wind; then comes a *h-whack!* — bum! bum! bumble-umble-um-bum-bum-bum-bum — and the thunder would go rumbling and grumbling away, and quit — and then *rip* comes another flash and another sockdolager. The waves most washed me off the raft sometimes, but I hadn't any clothes on, and didn't mind. We didn't have no trouble about snags; the lightning was glaring and flittering around so constant that we could see them plenty soon enough to throw her head this way or that and miss them.

I had the middle watch, you know, but I was pretty sleepy by that time, so Jim he said he would stand the first half of it for me; he was always mighty damn good that way, Jim was. I crawled into the wigwam and sort of got myself a place half on the shuck tick and half on the straw. The king was a-sawing away considerable, but I was plumb tuckered out and fell right to sleep.

Then I had this dream, and it was wild. I dreamt I was all alone on an island, like Jackson's Island, only smaller, and the river was rising. The island was all covered with creturs, like before, only this time there was a squiggly, squirming mess of black *things*, sort of like snakes and bugs all mixed up, and with faces like people. I was perched way up on the topmost rock, so's to keep away from them, but they kept on creeping up towards me all the while, a-whispering and a-bubbling something awful. I could see faces I knew amongst all the rest. There was Tom

Sawyer and Miss Watson, and pap and Judge
Thatcher, and lots of others. There was a kind of
thing like a hair-ball, only I seen it warn't a hair-ball,
it was Jim, and he had legs like a spider and was
weeping and carrying on because he couldn't get
up where I was on the rock away from the rising
water. Then all of a sudden he was on my leg and was
crawling up toward me, smiling and bubbling, and
I couldn't move. I wanted to shake my leg but I
couldn't, and I wanted to brush him away but
I couldn't do that either. And as soon as the rest of
the things seen Jim up there, they set up a dreadful
damned howl, and began to squirm and jump around
and screech and holler, and then I found I *could*
shake my leg, and I give it a powerful kick and woke
up, all a-tremble.

I lay there shaking like a leaf, and for a minute
I was sure the spider was still on my leg. Then I
thought it was like it sometimes is after a dream,
when things seem to go on for a bit after you wake up,
and you still aren't sure whether you're in the dream
or out of it, but then, sure enough, the crawling
started in again, only it warn't no spider, it was the
king's hand. The duke he was snoring away as if to
put the thunder to shame, but the old man was
breathing hard and making a little slobbering sound,
that hand of his feeling along my leg like a live thing.
It made a body's flesh crawl so, it was *worse* than any
spider. There warn't nothing to do but creep back
outside and make the best of it there, so I slid away
from under the king's hand, and the minute I done
it he started in snoring like his pard, only you could
tell it warn't real. I like to a puked.

Well, it was still raining aplenty, but I didn't mind

because it was warm, and the waves warn't running so high now. After what happened in the wigwam, it felt pretty good. I lay there and let the water slosh over me and went to sleep that way, until all of a sudden along comes a regular ripper and washed me overboard. It most killed Jim a-laughing. He was the easiest damn nigger to laugh that ever was, anyway. I took the watch then, and let Jim lay down for a spell; and by and by the storm let up for good and all; and the first cabin-light that showed I rousted him out, and we slid the raft into hiding quarters for the day.

The king got out an old ratty deck of cards after breakfast, and him and the duke played seven-up awhile, five cents a game. Then they got tired of it, and allowed they would "lay out a campaign," as they called it. The duke went down into his carpet-bag, and fetched up a lot of little printed bills and read them out loud. One bill said, "The celebrated Dr. Armand de Montalban, of Paris," would "lecture on the Science of Phrenology" at such and such a place, on the blank day of blank, at ten cents admission, and "furnish charts of character at twenty-five cents apiece." The duke said that was *him*. In another bill he was the "world-renowned Shakespearian tragedian, Garrick the Younger, of Drury Lane, London." In other bills he had a lot of other names and done other wonderful things, like finding water and gold with a "divining-rod," "dissipating witch spells," and so on. By and by he says:

"But the histryonic muse is the darling. Have you ever trod the boards, Royalty?"

"No," says the king.

"You shall, then, before you're three days older, Fallen Grandeur," says the duke. "The first good

town we come to we'll hire a hall and do the sword-
fight in 'Richard III.' and the balcony scene in
'Romeo and Juliet.' How does that strike you?"

"I'm in, up to the hub, for anything that will pay,
Bilgewater; but, you see, I don't know a damn thing
about play-actin', and hain't ever seen much of it. I
was too small when pap used to have 'em at the
palace. Do you reckon you can learn me?"

"Easy!"

"All right. I'm jist a-freezin' for something fresh,
anyway. Le's commence right away."

So the duke told him all about who Romeo was and
who Juliet was, and he said he was used to being
Romeo, so the king could be Juliet.

"But if Juliet's such a young gal, duke, my peeled
head and my white whiskers is goin' to look on-
common odd on her, maybe."

"No, don't you worry; these damned country
jakes won't ever think of that. Besides, you know,
you'll be in costume, and that makes all the difference in the world; Juliet's in a balcony, enjoying
the moonlight before she goes to bed, and she's got
on her nightgown and her ruffled nightcap. Here are
the costumes for the parts."

He got out two or three curtain-calico suits, which
he said was meedyevil armor for Richard III. and
t'other chap, and a long white cotton nightshirt and
a ruffled nightcap to match. The king was satisfied;
so the duke got out his book and read the parts over
in the most splendid dern spread-eagle way, pranc-
ing around and acting at the same time, to show how
it had to be done; then he give the book to the king
and told him to get his part by heart.

There was a little one-horse town about three mile

down the bend, and after dinner the duke said he
had ciphered out his idea about how to run in daylight without it being dangersome for Jim; so he
allowed he would go down to the town and fix that
thing. The king allowed he would go, too, and see
if he couldn't strike something. I seen how this was
our chance, so I said I would stay with Jim and tidy
things up a bit, but the king gives me a long look and
says:

"I guess the nigger can take keer o' that. You
hop along with us."

I says:

"What about Jim? S'pose somebody comes along
while we're in town and finds him here?"

The king give a little snort. He says:

"There ain't likely anybody come along in a god-
forsaken spot like this. You get yourself ready to go
with us."

I begun to cry a little, and the duke took another
dive into his carpet bag and come up with some more
costumes. "Ahah!" he says. "Just the ticket."

He was uncommon bright, the duke was. He
dressed Jim up in King Lear's outfit—it was a long
curtain-calico gown, and white horse-hair wig and
whiskers; and then he took his theater paint and
painted Jim's face and hands and ears and neck all
over the dead, dull solid blue, like a man that's been
drownded nine days. Damned if he warn't the hor-
riblest-looking outrage I ever see. Then the duke took
and wrote out a sign on a shingle so:

SICK ARAB—
BUT HARMLESS WHEN NOT OUT OF HIS HEAD.

And he nailed that shingle to a lath, and stood the

lath up four or five foot in front of the wigwam. Jim was satisfied. He said it was a damn sight better than running back into the woods every time a boat or raft come in view. This way maybe he could get a little sleep. The duke told him to make himself free and easy, and if anybody ever come meddling around, he must hop out of the wigwam, and carry on a little, and fetch a howl or two like a wild beast, and he reckoned they would light out and leave him alone. Which was sound enough judgment; but you take the average man, and he wouldn't wait for him to howl. Why, he didn't only look like he was dead, he looked like he was mortified.

When we got into town there warn't nobody stirring; streets empty, and perfectly dead and still, like Sunday. We found a sick nigger sunning himself in a back yard, and he said everybody that warn't too young or too sick or too old was gone to camp-meeting, about two mile back in the woods. The king got the directions, and allowed he'd go and work that camp-meeting for all it was worth, and I might go, too. Well, I warn't particularly warm for that idea, but I figured I'd be all right as long as kept a little space between him and me.

The duke said what he was after was a printing-office. We found it; a little bit of a concern, up over a carpenter-shop—carpenters and printers all gone to the meeting, and no doors locked. It was a dirty, littered-up place, and had ink-marks, and handbills with pictures of horses and runaway niggers on them, all over the walls. The duke shed his coat and said he was all right now. So me and the king lit out for the camp-meeting.

We got there in about a half an hour fairly dripping,

for it was a danged awful hot day. There was as much as a thousand people there from twenty mile around. The woods was full of teams and wagons, hitched everywheres, feeding out of the wagon-troughs and stomping to keep off the flies. There was sheds made out of poles and roofed over with branches, where they had lemonade and ginger-bread to sell, and piles of watermelons and green corn and such-like truck.

The preaching was going on under the same kinds of sheds, only they was bigger and held crowds of people. The benches was made out of outside slabs of logs, with holes bored in the round side to drive sticks into for legs. They didn't have no backs. The preachers had high platforms to stand on at one end of the sheds. The women had on sun-bonnets; and some had linsey-woolsey frocks, some gingham ones, and a few of the young ones had on calico. Some of the young men was barefooted, and some of the children didn't have on any clothes but just a tow-linen shirt. Some of the old women was knitting, and some of the young folks was courting on the sly. Out in the woods you could hear a lot of giggling and carryings on where some other young folks was courting, but not so sly.

That's always how it is at a camp-meeting. It does seem that there's something about salvation that gets young folks all excited in more ways than one, and the preacher that holds them meetings can generally count on coming back for considerable many weddings some months hence. And if he's smart, he'll come around again for all the baptizings, too.

The first shed we come to the preacher was lining

out a hymn. He lined out two lines, everybody sung
it, and it was kind of grand to hear it, there was so
many of them and they done it in such a rousing way;
then he lined out two more for them to sing—and so
on. The people woke up more and more, and sung
louder and louder; and towards the end some begun
to groan, and some begun to shout. Then the preacher
begun to preach, and begun in earnest, too; and went
weaving first to one side of the platform and then the
other, and then a-leaning down over the front of it,
and his arms and his body going all the time, and
shouting his words out with all his might, and every
now and then he would hold up his Bible and spread
it open, and kind of pass it around this way and that,
shouting, "I'ts the brazen serpent in the wilderness!
Look upon it and live!" And people would shout out,
"Glory!—A-a-*men*!" And so he went on, and the
people groaning and crying and saying amen:
  "Oh, come to the mourners' bench! come, black
with sin (*amen*!) come, sick and sore! (*amen*!) come,
lame and halt and blind! (*amen*!) come, pore and
needy, sunk in shame! (*a-a-men*!) come, all that's
worn and soiled and suffering!—come with a broken
spirit! come with a contrite heart! come in your rags
and sin and dirt! the waters that cleanse is free, the
door of heaven stands open—oh, enter in and be at
rest!" (*a-a-men! glory, glory hallelujah!*)
  And so on. You couldn't hardly make out what the
preacher was saying any more, on account of all the
dang shouting and crying. Folks got up everywheres
in the crowd, and worked their way just by pushing
and shoving to the mourners' bench, with the tears
running down their faces; and when all the mourners
had got up there to the front benches in a crowd, they

sung and shouted and flung themselves down on the straw, just crazy and wild.

Well, the first thing I knowed the king got a-going, and you could hear him over everybody; and next he went a-charging up onto the platform, dragging me along, and the preacher he begged him to speak to the people, and he done it. He told them he was just traveling through with his son, here, and that he had been robbed last night and put ashore off of a steamboat with no more than the price of a drink in his pocket and the clothes on his back. He told how he had come into town looking for a doggery so's he could get up a crooked game of cards and win enough for passage down to Orleans where he was a gambler ever since his dearest darling wife had died, which was a year ago, and that he had been a hardened sinner from that day forth because of the terrible loss. And when he found that all the gin-mills was closed on account of the camp-meeting, he got mad and come up here with deviltry and ill-will in his heart, intending to do what he could to break up the proceedings. But now he thanked his stars that he had been put off the steamboat at *that* town, and that the doggeries *was* all closed up, and that there was *this* camp-meeting going on, and that *this* preacher — and he reached out and took a-holt of the preacher's arm that had asked him up on the platform — was exhorting, because he had no sooner heard about the brazen serpent in the wilderness before he knew where he stood and what he was. For the first time in six months he remembered his dear departed wife and thought what he must like in her pure eyes, and what a life such as his was doing to her darling boy, and he was

going down on his knees right *now* and beg my pardon, which he done, and I give it to him, because
there warn't much choice. And then he gets up once
more and says that from that day forth he was a
changed man, and happy for the first time in a year;
and, poor as he was, he was going to start right off
and work his way back into respectability with his
own two hands—which he held up—and it was all
because of the dear people in the Pokeville camp-
meeting.

And then he busted into tears, and so did everybody. Then somebody sings out, "Take up a collection for him, take up a collection." Well, a half a
dozen made a jump to do it, but somebody sings out,
"Let *him* pass the hat around!" Then everybody
said it, the preacher too.

So the king went all through the crowd with his
hat, swabbing his eyes, and blessing the people and
praising them and thanking them for being so good to
him; and every little while the prettiest kind of girls,
with the tears running down their cheeks, would up
and ask him would he let them kiss him for to remember him by; and he always done it, taking care
to catch them full on the mouth and get a squeeze
in, and maybe if the crowd was pushing and shoving
enough, accidentally grab himself a handful of something on the side. Some of them girls he hugged and
kissed as many as five or six times, enjoying himself
considerable the whole while, and they didn't seem
to mind it neither, but sort of wriggled around and
stood right there taking it. Afterwards they was always red in the face, but it warn't from shame. The
king was invited to stay a week, and everybody

wanted him to live in their houses, and said they'd
think it was an honor; but he said as this was the last
day of the camp-meeting he couldn't do no good,
and besides he was in a sweat to get down to Orleans
and go to work convincing his fellow gamblers of the
folly of their ways.

When we got back to the raft and he come to count
up he found he had collected eighty-seven dollars
and seventy-five cents. And then he had fetched
away a three-gallon jug of whiskey, too, that he found
under a wagon when he was starting home through
the woods. The king said, take it all around, it laid
over any day he'd ever put in in the missionarying
line. He said it warn't no use talking, heathens don't
amount to shucks alongside of reformed gamblers
to work a camp-meeting with.

The duke was thinking *he'd* been doing pretty well
till the king come to show up, but after that he didn't
think so so much. He had set up and printed off two
little jobs for farmers in that printing office — horse
bills — and took the money, four dollars. And he had
got in ten dollars' worth of advertisements for the
paper, which he said he would put in for four dollars
if they would pay in advance — so they done it. The
price of the paper was two dollars a year, but he took
in three subscriptions for half a dollar apiece on
condition of them paying him in advance; they were
going to pay in cordwood and onions as usual, but
he said he had just bought the concern and knocked
down the price as low as he could afford it, and was
going to run it for cash. He set up a little piece of
poetry, which he made, himself, out of his own
head — three verses — kind of sweet and sadish — the
name of it was, "Yes, crush, cold world, this break-

ing heart"—and he left that all set up and ready to print in the paper, and didn't charge nothing for it. Well, he took in nine dollars and a half, and said he'd done a damn square day's work for it.

Then he showed us another little job he'd printed and hadn't charged for, because it was for us. It had a picture of a runaway nigger with a bundle on a stick over his shoulder, and "$200 reward" under it. The reading was all about Jim and just described him to a dot. It said he run away from St. Jacques's plantation, forty mile below New Orleans, last winter, and likely went north, and whoever would catch him and send him back he could have the reward and expenses.

"Now," says the duke, "after tonight we can run in the daytime if we want to. Whenever we see anybody coming we can tie Jim hand and foot with a rope, and lay him in the wigwam and show this handbill and say we captured him up the river, and were too poor to travel on a steamboat, so we got this little raft on credit from our friends and are going down to get the reward. Handcuffs and chains would look still better on Jim, but it wouldn't go well with the story of us being so poor. Too much like julery. Ropes are the correct thing—we must preserve the unities, as we say on the boards."

We all said the duke was pretty darn smart, and there couldn't be no trouble about running daytimes. We judged we could make miles enough that night to get out of the reach of the powwow we reckoned the duke's work in the printing-office was going to make in that little town; then we could boom right along if we wanted to.

We laid low and kept still, and never shoved out

till nearly ten o'clock; then we slid by, pretty wide away from the town, and didn't hoist our lantern till we was clear out of sight of it.

When Jim called me to take the watch at four in the morning, he says:

"Huck, I bin thinkin' 'bout dis here plan of de Duke's, en I doan' mind bein' tied up en all, but I 'uz wonderin' how it's gwyne ter git me back up de river. Why, we's furder souf' every day, honey, en purty soon we's gwyne ter be in Orleans. Den what's gwyne happen ter ol' Jim?"

Well, I never heard such ungratefulness in all my days, and I told him so. I says:

"Jim, you ought to be damn thankful the Duke took such good care of you. Why, with that poster we can go anywheres we got a mind to, as long as it's South, and once we get to Orleans, something else is bound to turn up."

But Jim was the stubbornest nigger born. He says:

"Yes, you *says* sumfn gwyne turn up. Dat's fine. But fo' de life o' me, I cain't figure out *what*."

"Well, something has come along every time so far, hain't it? And something's sure to come along later on, too."

But Jim just give a sigh and shrugged his shoulders, so I knew he still warn't convinced. Let a nigger get a-holt of a worry, and he'll chew it right to the bone. After a while he lay down and went to sleep, but every now and then he'd give a little moan and a twitch and I reckoned his dreams warn't sweet. Long toward the middle of my watch he started mumbling and then he said right out clear, "Come back to de raf', Huck honey! Come back, li'l Huck!"

Well, I begun to feel bad then, remembering how

glad Jim had been to see me when I got away from the feud, and how much he trusted me and depended on me. So I set to work to figure out a plan that would get us to the free states, but nothing came. It did look like the king and the duke was our best hope, even though they was scalawags and frauds. Pap used to say that dirty socks will do if 'n you hain't got a clean pair, and even though he never owned any socks, dirty or clean, that I knowed of, I guess he was right.

XXI

An Arkansaw difficulty

It was after sun-up now, but we went right on and didn't tie up. The king and the duke turned out by and by looking pretty damn rusty; but after they'd jumped overboard and took a swim it chippered them up a good deal. After breakfast the king he took a seat on the corner of the raft, and pulled off his boots and rolled up his britches, and let his legs dangle in the water, so as to be comfortable, and lit his pipe, and went to getting his "Romeo and Juliet" by heart. When he had got it pretty good him and the duke begun to practise it together. The duke had to learn him over and over again how to say every speech; and he made him sigh, and put his hand on his heart, and after a while he said he done it pretty well; "only," he says, "you mustn't bellow out *Romeo!* that way, like a bull in heat — you must say it soft and sick and languishy, so — R-o-o-meo! that is the idea; for Juliet's a dear sweet mere child of a girl, you know, and she doesn't bray like a jackass."

Well, next they got out a couple of long swords that

the duke make out of oak laths, and begun to practise the sword-fight—the duke called himself
Richard III.; and the way they laid on and pranced
around the raft was grand to see. But by and by the
king tripped and fell overboard, and after that they
took a rest, and had a talk about all kinds of adventures they'd had in other times along the river.

After dinner the duke says:

"Well, Capet, we'll want to make this a first-class
show, you know, so I guess we'll add a little more to it.
We want something to answer onkors with, anyway."

"What's onkors, Bilgewater?"

The duke told him how actors always come out
after the applause and give the audience something
a little extra for their money. He says:

"I'll answer by doing the Highland fling or the
sailor's hornpipe; and you—well, what *can* you do
in the entertainment line?"

The king thought a minute and then says he used
to be quite a man at a shuffle-and-break-down, but
the duke says no, what these country clowns wanted
was something gaudy, like musical glasses or the
burning of Moscow. The king scratched his bald head
and thought some more, and the duke he thought,
and finally the duke snapped his fingers and went to
fishing around in his carpet bag until he come up
with a greasy pack of cards.

"Divination is the thing," he says. "It'll lay them
out every time. Take a card," he says to the king, who
took one. Then the duke shut his eyes and put the
pack against his forehead and rocked back and
forth for a bit. Finally he opened his eyes and says:
"It's the six of clubs."

"Keerect!" shouts the king, and shows it around.

Well, Jim and I were bugging our eyes out considerable at that one, but the duke just laughs and opens the deck for us. They was *all* six of clubs, by Jesus! Then the duke pulls out three more decks of cards, one that was all four of diamonds, another that was king of spades, and the third was the deuce of diamonds. He said the only trick was in keeping the jakes occupied so they didn't notice you changing packs between draws, but he didn't imagine it would be any trouble for an old stager like the king, and I reckon he was right.

"One more thing, Capet," he says to the king. "You want to misfire on the third draw, so they think they got you, and then take a second shot and nail it firm."

Well, the king was mighty tickled by that divination trick, and he spent the rest of the day slipping packs of cards in and out of his pockets, and asking Jim and me to draw out a card. It warn't no fun, once you knowed the secret, but we drew 'em out anyway.

The first chance we got the duke he had some show-bills printed; and after that, for two or three days as we floated along, the raft was a most uncommon lively place, for there warn't nothing but sword-fighting and rehearsing—as the duke called it—going on all the time. I told Jim it was a shame Tom Sawyer warn't along, because this sort of thing was nuts to him. One morning, when we was pretty well down the state of Arkansas, we come in sight of a little one-horse town in a big bend; so we tied up about three-quarters of a mile above it, in the mouth of a crick which was shut in like a tunnel by the cypress trees, and the two of them got dressed up for town. I said I would stay behind to keep Jim company, but the king said no, I was to come with them, so I did. Jim we left all painted up in his sick Arab costume.

We hadn't gone but a few steps from the raft, when the king took a-holt of my arm and stuck his face down close to mine so as to give me a treat of his breath — which warn't no violets. He told me I should stick by them the whole while, and if I got the notion to run off, why he would track me down and slit my gizzard out no matter where we went. Then he took one of them nigger posters the duke had printed up and sort of tucked it into my shirt front and give me the evilest damn eye I ever saw.

"Jist think on it," he says. I didn't have to.

I told him there warn't no place I wanted to be but where I was, and him and the duke seemed satisfied. But I felt pretty damn sick, because it looked like it would be a considerable long while before Jim and me got rid of them rapscallions. There warn't nothing to do in the meanwhile but go along with them, because I knew that those two wouldn't think twice about selling their own grandmother if it might help them over a rough spot. If we was to run off and they was to track us down, why it was our word against theirs about whether Jim was a runaway or not, and I had a feeling that our word wouldn't amount to shucks in a showdown with them two slicks.

They struck it mighty lucky in town; there was going to be a circus there that afternoon, and the country-people was already beginning to come in, all kinds of shackly wagons, and on horses. The circus wasn't to perform at night, so our show would have a pretty good chance. The duke he hired the court-house, and we went around and stuck up our

222 : The true adventures of Huckleberry Finn

bills. It was hot and dusty work, and I got dern tired
of it soon enough, and when the king and the duke
got into a hassle with some fellow that didn't want
their bills on his store window which they had already
pasted there, I snuck off and went loafing around
town by myself.

The stores and houses was most all old, shackly,
dried-up frame concerns that hadn't ever been
painted; they was set up three or four foot above
ground on stilts, so as to be out of reach of the water
when the river was overflowed. The houses had little
gardens around them, but they didn't seem to raise
hardly anything in them but jimpson-weeds, and sun-
flowers, and ash-piles, and old curled-up boots and
shoes, and pieces of bottles, and rags, and played-out
tinware. The fences was made of different kinds of
boards, nailed on at different times; and they
leaned every which way, and had gates that didn't
generly have but one hinge—a leather one. Some of
the fences had been whitewashed, some time or
another, but the duke said it was in Columbus's time,
like enough. There was generly hogs in the garden,
and people driving them out.

All the stores was along one street. They had
white awnings in front and the country people
hitched their horses to the awning-posts. There was
empty dry-goods boxes under the awnings, and
loafers roosting on them all day long, whittling them
with their Barlow knives; and chawing tobacco, and
gaping and yawning and stretching—a danged ornery
lot. They generly had on yellow straw hats most as
wide as an umbrella, but didn't wear no coats nor
waistcoats; they called one another Bill, and Buck,
and Hank, and Joe, and Andy, and talked lazy and

drawly, and used considerable many cuss-words. There was as many as one loafer leaning up against every awning-post, and he most always had his hands in his britches pockets, except when he fetched them out to lend a chaw of tobacco or stretch or scratch.

All the streets and lanes was just mud; they warn't nothing else *but* mud—mud as black as tar and nigh about a foot deep in some places, and two or three inches deep in *all* the places. The hogs loafed and grunted around everywheres. You'd see a muddy sow and a litter of pigs come lazying along the street and whollop herself right down in the way, where folks had to walk around her, and she'd stretch out and shut her eyes and wave her ears whilst the pigs was sucking her tits, and look as happy as if she was on salary. And pretty soon you'd hear a loafer sing out, "Hi! *so* boy! sick him, Tige!" and away the sow would go, squealing most horrible, with a dog or two swinging to each ear, and three or four dozen more a-coming, and then you would see all the loafers get up and watch the thing out of sight, and laugh at the fun and look grateful for the noise. Then they'd settle back again till there was a dog-fight. There couldn't anything wake them up all over, and make them happy all over, like a dog-fight—unless it might be putting turpentine on a stray dog and setting fire to him, or tying a tin pan to his tail and see him run himself to death.

I noticed how the niggers went out of their way just to keep from walking past them loafers, and if they had to go near because of being sent to the store for something, they was always quiet all the time. A nigger might come up the street a-singing his lungs out, but when he got near them awnings, he quieted right down till his business was over. The loafers never paid them no heed, but you sort of felt they was just waiting for a chance to pay them more heed than a nigger wanted.

On the river-front some of the houses was sticking out over the bank, and they was bowed and bent, and about ready to tumble in. The people had moved out of them. The bank was caved away under one corner of some others, and that corner was hanging over. People lived in them yet, but it was damned dangersome, because sometimes a strip of land as wide as a house caves in at a time. Sometimes a belt of land a quarter of a mile deep will start in and cave along and cave along till it all caves into the river in one summer. Such a town as that has to be always moving back, and back, and back, because the river's always gnawing at it.

The nearer it got to noon that day the thicker and thicker was the wagons and horses in the streets, and more coming all the time. Families fetched their dinners with them from the country, and eat them in the wagons. There was considerable whisky-drinking going on, and I seen three fights. By and by somebody sings out:

"Here comes old Boggs!—in from the country for his little old monthly drunk; here he comes, boys!"

All the loafers looked glad; I reckoned they was used to having fun out of Boggs. One of them says:

"Wonder who the old barstid's a-gwyne to chaw up this time. If he'd a-chawed up all the men he's been a-gwyne to chaw up in the last twenty year, he'd have considerable reputation now."

Another one says, "I wisht old Boggs'd threaten

me, b'Gawd, 'cuz then I'd know I warn't gwyne to die for a thousan' year."

Boggs comes a-tearing along on his horse, hell-bent for election, whooping and yelling like an Injun. He pulled up in a big cloud of dust and sung out:

"Cler the track, thar. I'm on the waw-path, and the price uv coffins is a-gwyne to raise."

He was drunk, and weaving about in his saddle; he was over fifty year old, and had a very red face. Everybody yelled at him and laughed at him and sassed him, and he sassed back, and said he'd attend to them and lay them out in their regular turns, but he couldn't wait now because he'd come to town to kill old Colonel Sherburn, and his motto was, "Meat first, and spoon vittles to top off on."

He see me, and rode up and says:

"Whar'd you come f'm, boy? You prepared to die?"

Then he rode on. I was scared, but a man says:

"He don't mean nothing; he's always a-carrying on like that when he's drunk. He's the best-naturdest dern fool in Arkansaw—never hurt nobody, drunk nor sober."

Boggs rode up before the biggest store in town, and bent his head down so he could see under the awning and yells:

"Come out here, Sherburn! Come out and meet the man you've swindled once too many damn times. You're the son-of-a-bitch I'm after, and I'm a-gwyne to have you, too!"

And so he went on, calling Sherburn everything he could lay his tongue to, and the whole street packed with people listening and laughing and going on. By and by a proud-looking man about fifty-five—and he was a heap the best-dressed man in that town, too—steps out of the store, and the crowd drops back on each side to let him come. He says to Boggs, mighty calm and slow—he says:

"I'm tired of this, but I'll endure it till one o'clock. Till one o'clock, mind—no longer. If you open your mouth against me only once after that time you can't travel so far but I will find you."

Then he turns and goes in. The crowd looked mighty dern sober; nobody stirred, and there warn't no more laughing. Boggs rode off blackguarding Sherburn as loud as he could yell, all down the street; and pretty soon back he comes and stops before the store, still keeping it up. Some men crowded around him and tried to get him to shut up, but he wouldn't; they told him it would be one o'clock in about fifteen minutes, and so he *must* go home—he must go right away. But it didn't do no good. He cussed away with all his might, and throwed his hat down in the mud and rode over it, and pretty soon away he went a-raging down the street again, with his gray hair a-flying. Everybody that could get a chance at him tried their best to coax him off his horse so they could lock him up and get him sober; but it warn't no use—up the street he would tear again, and give Sherburn another cussing. By and by somebody says:

"Go for his daughter!—quick, go for his daughter; sometimes he'll listen to her. If anybody can persuade him, she can."

So somebody started on a run. I walked down street a ways and stopped. In about five or ten minutes here comes Boggs again, but not on his horse.

He was a-reeling across the street towards me, bare-headed, with a friend on both sides of him a-holt of his arms and hurrying him along. He was quiet, and looked uneasy; and he warn't hanging back any, but was doing some of the hurrying himself. Somebody sings out:

"Boggs!"

I looked over there to see who said it, and it was that Colonel Sherburn. He was standing perfectly still in the street, and had a pistol raised in his right hand — not aiming it, but holding it out with the barrel tilted up towards the sky. The same second I see a young girl coming on the run, and two men with her. Boggs and the men turned round to see who called him, and when they see the pistol the men jumped to one side, and the pistol-barrel come down slow and steady to a level — both barrels cocked. Boggs throws up both of his hands and says, "O Lord, don't shoot!" Bang! goes the first shot, and he staggers back, clawing at the air — bang! goes the second one, and he tumbles backward onto the ground, heavy and solid, with his arms spread out. That young girl screamed out and comes rushing, and down she throws herself on her father, crying, and saying, "Oh, he's killed him, he's killed him!" The crowd closed up around them, and shouldered and jammed one another, with their necks stretched, trying to see, and people on the inside trying to shove them back and shouting:

"Back, back! give him air, give him air!"

Colonel Sherburn he tossed his pistol onto the ground, and turned around on his heels and walked off.

They took Boggs to a little drug store, the crowd

pressing around just the same, and the whole town
following, and I rushed and got a good place at the
window, where I was close to him and could see in.
They laid him on the floor and put one large Bible
under his head, and opened another one and spread
it on his breast; but they tore open his shirt first,
and I seen where one of the bullets went in. He made
about a dozen long gasps, his breast lifting the Bible
up when he drawed in his breath, and letting it down
again when he breathed it out — and after that he laid
still; he was dead. Then they pulled his daughter
away from him, screaming and crying, and took her
off. She was about sixteen, and very sweet and gentle-
looking, but awful pale and scared.

Well, pretty soon the whole dang town was there,
squirming and scrouging and pushing and shoving to
get at the window and have a look, but people that
had the places wouldn't give them up, and folks
behind them was saying all the time, "Say, now,
you've looked enough, you fellows; 'tain't right and
'tain't fair for you to stay thar all the time, and never
give nobody a damn chance; other folks has their
rights as well as you."

There was considerable jawing back, so I slid out,
thinking maybe there was going to be trouble. The
streets was full, and everybody was excited. Everybody that seen the shooting was telling how it happened, and there was a big crowd packed around
each one of these fellows, stretching their necks and
listening. One long, lanky man, with long hair and a
big white fur stovepipe hat on the back of his head,
and a crooked-handled cane, marked out the places
on the ground where Boggs stood and where Sherburn stood, and the people following him around from

one place to t'other and watching everything he done, and bobbing their heads to show they understood, and stooping a little and resting their hands on their thighs to watch him mark the places on the ground with his cane; and then he stood up straight and stiff where Sherburn had stood, frowning and having his hat-brim down over his eyes, and sung out, "Boggs!" and then fetched his cane down slow to a level, and says "Bang!" staggered backward, says "Bang!" again, and fell down flat on his back. The people that had seen the thing said he done it perfect; said it was just exactly the way it all happened. Then as much as a dozen people got out their bottles and treated him.

Well, by and by somebody said Sherburn ought to be lynched. In about a minute everybody was saying it; so away they went, mad and yelling to beat hell, and snatching down every damn clothesline they come to to do the hanging with. They swarmed up towards Sherburn's house, a-whooping and raging like Injuns, and everything had to clear the way or get run over and tromped to mush, and it was awful to see. Children was heeling it ahead of the mob, screaming and trying to get out of the way; and every window along the road was full of women's heads, and there was nigger boys in every tree, and bucks and wenches looking over every fence; and as soon as the mob would get nearly to them they would break and skaddle back out of reach. Lots of the women and girls was crying and taking on, scared most to death.

They swarmed up in front of Sherburn's palings as thick as they could jam together and you couldn't hear yourself think for the racket. It was a little

twenty-foot yard. Some sung out "Tear down the
fence! tear down the fence!" Then there was a
ripping and tearing and smashing, and down she
goes, and the front wall of the crowd begins to roll in
like a damn wave.

Just then Sherburn steps out onto the roof of his
little front porch, with a double-barrel gun in his
hand, and takes his stand, perfectly calm and deliberate, not saying a word. The racket stopped, and the
wave sucked back.

Sherburn never said a word—just stood there,
looking down. The stillness was awful damn creepy
and uncomfortable. Sherburn run his eyes slow along
the crowd; and wherever it struck the people tried
a little to outgaze him, but they couldn't; they
dropped their eyes and looked sneaky. Then pretty
soon Sherburn sort of laughed; not the pleasant kind,
but the kind that makes you feel like when you are
eating greens that's got sand in them.

Then he started in to talk, slow and scornful. He
told them that the idea of *them* lynching anybody
was amusing, and that they had the idea that they
could lynch a *man* was even funnier. He said just
because they was up to tar and feathering poor
friendless cast-out whores that come along, trying to
earn a bite to eat by lowering themselves to *their*
level, that didn't mean they had grit enough to lay
their hands on a *man*. He allowed that a *man* was
safe in the hands of ten thousand of their kind, so
long as it was daytime and they warn't behind him.

He told 'em they'd brought *part* of a man with
them, and he called out "Buck Harkness," and
pointed to a big man with a jaw like a side of beef
and button-blue eyes half hid under pale eyebrows,

that had been doing considerable shouting recently
but now looked like he wished he was anywhere else
but there. He had on a red flannel shirt and his
face began to creep up on it. Sherburn told 'em that
if they hadn't had Buck Harkness to start them,
they'd a taken it out in blowing, nothing more. He
told 'em they didn't really want to come. He said he'd
been born and raised in the South, and lived in the
North, so he knew the average all round, and that the
average man was a coward. He said that the average
man don't like trouble and danger, and that *they*
didn't like trouble and danger. But if only *half* a
man — like Buck Harkness, there — shouts "Lynch
him! lynch him!" they was afraid to back down —
afraid they'd be found out to be what they was —
cowards — and so they'd raise hell, and hang onto
another man's coat-tail, and come raging up to his
house, swearing what big things they was a-going to
do.

Then he stopped for a minute, and smiled sort of
sad and scornful. He set the gun stock down and
leaned on the barrel like it was a cane. Then he
started in again, and his voice was very low, as if he
was talking to himself. He said that the pitifulest
thing out was a mob, and that an army warn't nothing but a mob, because they didn't fight with courage
that was born in them nuther, but with courage
that's borrowed from the others, and from their
officers. But a mob without any *man* at the head
of it is *beneath* pitifulness.

He straightened up then, and begun to raise his
voice. He told them the thing for *them* to do was to
droop their tails and go home and crawl in a hole. He
said that if any real lynching's going to be done it will

be done in the dark, Southern style; and when they come they'll bring their masks, and fetch a *man* along to lead 'em. Then Sherburn tossed his gun up across his left arm and cocked it. He says:

"Now *leave*—and take your half-a-man with you."

The crowd washed back sudden, and then broke all apart, and went tearing off every which way, and Buck Harkness he heeled it after them, looking tolerable damn cheap. I could a stayed if I wanted to, but I didn't want to.

I went to the circus and loafed around the back side till the watchman went by, and then dived in under the tent. I had my twenty-dollar gold piece and some other money, but I reckoned I better save it, because there ain't no telling how soon you are going to need it, away from home and amongst strangers that way. You can't be too careful. I ain't opposed to spending money on circuses when there ain't no other way, but there ain't no use in *wasting* it on them.

It was a damn bully circus. It was the splendidest sight that ever was when they all come riding in, two and two, and gentleman and lady, side by side, the men just in their drawers and undershirts, and no shoes nor stirrups, and resting their hands on their thighs easy and comfortable—there must a been twenty of them—and every lady with a white skin and beautiful, and looking just like a gang of real sure-enough queens, and dressed in clothes that cost millions of dollars, and just littered with diamonds. It was a powerful fine sight; I never see anything so darned lovely. And then one by one they got up and stood, and went a-weaving around the ring so gentle and wavy and graceful, the men looking ever so tall and airy and straight, with their heads bobbing and skimming along, away up there under the tent-roof, and every lady's rose-leafy dress flapping soft and silky around her hips, and she looking like the most loveliest parasol.

And then faster and faster they went, all of them dancing, first one foot out in the air and then the other, the horses leaning more and more, and the ringmaster going round and round the center pole, cracking his whip and shouting "Hi—hi!" and the clown cracking jokes behind him; and by and by all hands dropped the reins, and every lady put her knuckles on her hips and every gentleman folded his arms, and then how the horses did lean over and hump themselves. And so one after the other they all skipped off into the ring, and made the sweetest bow I ever see, and then scampered out, and everybody clapped their hands and went just about wild.

Well, all through the circus they done the most astonishing things; and all the time that clown carried on so it most killed the people. The ringmaster couldn't ever say a word to him but he was back at him quick as a wink with the funniest things a body ever said; and how he ever *could* think of so many of them, and so sudden and so pat, was what I couldn't no way understand. Why, I couldn't a thought of them in a year. And by and by a drunken man tried to get into the ring—said he wanted to ride; said he could ride as well as anybody that ever was. They argued and tried to keep him out, but he wouldn't listen, and the whole show come to a standstill. Then the people begun to holler at him and make fun of him, and that made him mad, and he begun to rip and tear; so that stirred up the people, and a lot of men begun to pile down off of the benches and swarm toward the ring, saying, "Knock him down! throw him out!" and one or two women begun to scream. So, then, the ringmaster he made a little speech, and said he hoped there wouldn't be no disturbance, and if the man would promise he wouldn't make no more trouble he would let him ride if he thought he could stay on the horse. So everybody laughed and said all right, and the man got on. The minute he was on, the horse begun to rip and tear and jump and cavort around, with two circus men hanging on to his bridle trying to hold him, and the drunken man hanging on to his neck, and his heels flying in the air every jump, and the whole crowd of people standing up shouting and laughing till tears rolled down. And at last, sure enough, all the circus men could do, the horse broke loose, and away he went like the very damnation, round and round the ring, with that sot laying down on him and hanging to his neck, with first one leg hanging most to the ground on one side, and then t'other one on t'other side, and the people just crazy. It warn't very damn funny to me, though; I was all of a tremble to see his danger. But pretty soon he struggled up astraddle and grabbed the bridle, a-reeling this way and that; and the next minute he sprung up and dropped the bridle and stood! and the horse a-going like a house afire, too. He just stood up there, a-sailing around as easy and comfortable as if he warn't ever drunk in his life — and then he began to pull off his clothes and sling them. He shed them so thick they kind of clogged up the air, and altogether he shed seventeen suits. And, then, there he was, slim and handsome, and dressed the gaudiest and prettiest you ever saw, and he lit into that horse with his whip and made him fairly hum — and finally skipped off, and made his bow and danced off to the dressing-room, and everybody just a-howling with pleasure and astonishment.

Then the ringmaster he see how he had been fooled, and he *was* the sickest damn ringmaster you ever see, I reckon. Why, it was one of his own men! He had got up that joke all out of his own head, and never let on to nobody. Well, I felt sheepish enough to be took in so, but I wouldn't a been in that ring-master's shoes, not for a thousand dollars. I don't know; there may be bullier circuses than what that one was, but I never struck them yet. Anyways, it was plenty good enough for *me*; and wherever I run across it, it can have all of *my* custom every time.

Well, when I got back warn't the king furious! He lammed me around a bit and told me if I ever run off like that again he'd have my hide. I blubbered some and told him it warn't *my* fault. I said I had seen a man who looked like my lost brother, Sam, the one that had gone off with the circus, and I had run after him but he warn't, and then some boy stole my hat and I chased him all over town before I got it back. The king just laughed. He said there warn't no trusting boys these days, and it was all because of the way they was brought up. And the duke got his shovel in too, saying how he and the king had worked hard all day getting that show up and the whole time I was galavanting around town instead of helping. He said he would keep a sharp eye on me after that and he done it, too.

That night we had *our* show; but there warn't only about twelve people there—just enough to pay expenses. And they laughed all the time, and that made the duke mad; and everybody left, anyway, before the show was over, but one boy which was asleep. The king had to wake him up to ask him to take a card, and he got scared and begun to cry and then run out of the place without taking one. The duke said these damn Arkansaw lunkheads couldn't come up to Shakespeare; what they wanted was low comedy—and maybe something ruther gamier than low comedy, he reckoned. He said he could size their style—he judged he could caper to their base instincts, if that was what was wanted. So next morning he got some big sheets of wrapping paper and some black paint, and drawed off some handbills, and stuck them up all over the village.

These was something like the other bills, all about the world-renowned David Garrick the Younger, which was the duke, and the illustrious Edmund Kean the Elder, which was the king, but instead of telling about Romeo and Juliet and the sword fight in Richard III., it had in big letters "THE KING'S CAMELEOPARD, or THE BURNING SHAME!!" —which was a thrilling tragedy or some such. Then at the bottom was the biggest line of all, which said: "LADIES AND CHILDREN NOT ADMITTED."

"There," says the duke, "if that line don't fetch the bastards, I don't know Arkansaw!"

XXII

The Burning Shame

Well, we had got the posters up by early afternoon, and then the duke said it was time
for rehearsal. He wouldn't let me hang
around to watch. He said it was pretty strong milk
for babes, and that I was to stay close to the stage
entrance and keep anybody from getting in, and if I
took a notion to wander off, he'd hide me good. Well,
it was damnation dull work, but when night come he
put me to helping him sell tickets at the door and
that was considerable better. Then, when the house
begun to fill, up he sent me around to the stage door
again, and told me to stick there until the performance was over. After he finished out front and went
in himself, I shinned up a tree where there was a
bunch of other boys looking in the windows, which
was open because of the heat. It was better'n a gal-
lery, and a damn sight cooler.

The house was jam full of men by then, and the
ones that hadn't got seats was standing around the
walls. The duke he come onto the stage and stood

up before the curtain that was there and made a little speech, and praised up this tragedy, and said it was the most thrillingest one that ever was; and so he went on a-bragging about the tragedy, and about Edmund Kean the Elder, which was to play the main principal part in it; and at last when he'd got everybody's expectations up high enough, he rolled up the curtain, and the next minute the king comes a-prancing out on all fours, naked; and he was painted all over, ring-streaked-and-striped, all sorts of colors, as splendid as a rainbow, but the wildest part of his outfit was a lit candle that was stuck upright in his ass. Well, it was outrageous, but it was awful derned funny. The people most killed themselves laughing; and when the king got done capering and capered off behind the scenes, they roared and clapped and stormed and haw-hawed till he come back and done it over again, and after that they made him do it another time. Well, it would make a cow laugh to see the shines that old idiot cut.

Then the duke he lets the curtain down, and bows to the people, and says the great tragedy will be performed only two nights more, on accounts of pressing London engagements, where the seats is all sold already for it in Drury Lane; and then he makes them another bow, and says if he has succeeded in pleasing them and enlightening them, he will be deeply obleeged if they will mention it to their friends and get them to come and see it.

Twenty people sings out:

"What, is it over? Is that *all*?"

The duke says yes, they'd seen what they paid to see, and if they wanted to see more of it, they'd have to come back the next night. Well, then there was a fine time. Everybody sings out, "Sold!" and rose up mad, and was a-going for that stage and them tragedians. But a big, fine-looking man jumps on a bench and shouts:

"Hold on! Just a word, gentlemen." They stopped to listen. "We are sold—mighty badly sold. But we don't want to be the laughing-stock of this whole town, I reckon, and never hear the last of this thing as long as we live. *No*. What we want is to go out of here quiet, and talk this show up, and sell the *rest* of the town! Then we'll all be in the same boat. Ain't that sensible?" ("You bet it is!—the jedge is right!" everybody sings out.) "All right, then—not a word about any sell. Go along home, and advise everybody to come and see the tragedy."

The next day the duke and the king lazied around the raft, and in the early afternoon they sent me up to town to see how the talk went. Well, I went up and walked around, and you couldn't hear nothing but how splendid that show was. While I was there I went out to the cemetary where they was burying old Boggs but there warn't nobody at his funeral except his daughter and a couple of old ladies like them that always turns out for such affairs. It was tolerable dull and I didn't stick around for the finish. When I went by Sherburn's store, he was standing there under the awning smoking a seegar, and all the people when they walked by or went in they tipped their hats and said their good afternoons, and he stood there, every now and then raising a couple of fingers in return. I'm damned if he warn't the coolest man *ever*.

Come nightfall the duke and the king come up and got ready for the next show. They put me outside again, but I didn't care any more since I'd already seen all there was to see. The house was jammed again that night, and they sold this crowd the same way. When me and the king and the duke got home to the raft we all had a supper, and listened to the two of them a-crowing about their success. By and by, about midnight, they made Jim and me back the raft out and float her down the middle of the river, and fetch her in and hide her about two mile below town. The next day I thought we would lay around again, but the duke and the king took me along with them up to town early. The duke said we was all to get fitted out for some new clothes. I told him I liked the ones I had fine, but he told me to shut up and come along sharp, and I did. We all got new suits and shirts and shoes, but we didn't get to wear them none. The duke had them put in a box and give it to me to tote along. I couldn't see the sense in it, but it warn't no business of mine.

That night the house was crammed again—and they warn't newcomers this time, but people that was at the show before. I stood by the duke at the door, and I see that every man that went in had his pockets bulging, or something muffled up under his coat—and I see it warn't no perfumery, neither, not by a damn sight. I smelt rotten eggs by the barrel, and rotten cabbages and such things; and if I know the smell of a dead cat, and I bet I do, there was sixty-four of them went in. I shoved in there for a minute, but it was too rancid for me; I couldn't stand it. Well, when the place couldn't hold no more people, the duke shut the doors and stuck up a big "SOLD OUT" sign there. He told me to stand by the door and count up to a hundred, and then put the bolt through the hasp and start walking slowly out of town. If anybody came along, I was to tell them to come back the next night for the big free show. Then he cut around the corner towards the stage door.

Well, I done what he told me, but I hadn't got very far before he caught up to me in the dark and says:

"Walk fast now till you get away from the houses, and then shin for the raft like all hell was after you!"

I done it, and he done the same. We struck the raft at the same time, and in less than two seconds was gliding down-stream, all dark and still, and edging towards the middle of the river, nobody saying a word. I reckoned the poor king was in for a damned gaudy time of it with the audience, but nothing of the sort; pretty soon he crawls out from under the wigwam, and says:

"Well, how'd the old thing pan out this time, duke?" He hadn't been up-town at all.

We never showed a light till we was about ten mile below the village. Then we lit up and had a supper, and the king and the duke fairly laughed their bones loose over them people being locked in the hall with all them putrid cabbages and eggs and cats. The duke says:

"Greenhorns, flatheads! *I* knew the first house would keep mum and let the rest of the town get roped in; and I knew they'd lay for us the third night, and consider it was *their* turn now. Well, it *is* their turn, and I'd give something to know how much they'd take for it. I *would* just like to know how they're putting in their opportunity. They can turn it into a picnic if they want to — they brought plenty provisions."

Them derned rapscallions took in four hundred

and sixty-five dollars in that three nights. I never see money hauled in by the wagon-load like that before.

Well, the king and duke had themselves a celebration that lasted almost all night, and it was all that Jim and I could do to keep them from rolling off the raft. The king *did* fall off once, as he was taking a pee to windward and trying to dodge his own spray, but we got him back on board all right, even though the duke felt that he ought to help and kept getting in the damn way. The wetting sort of sobered up the king and he went to sleep and the duke passed out pretty soon after, so there warn't nothing left to do but mind the sweeps.

I went to sleep myself after a bit, and Jim didn't call me when it was my turn. He often done that. When I waked up just at daybreak he was sitting there with his head down betwixt his knees, moaning and mourning to himself. I didn't take no notice nor let on. I knowed what it was about, this time. He was thinking about his wife and children again, away up yonder, and he was low and homesick. He was a mighty good nigger, Jim was, but I warn't about to let on that I knew about his troubles. The last time I done it, I was sorry I had.

But he caught me looking at him and turned sheepish and embarrassed, like I had caught him at something shameful, which I hadn't. After all, he hadn't ever been away from home before in his life; and I do believe he cared just as much for his people as white folks does for their'n. It don't seem natural, but I reckon it's so. He says:

"What makes me feel so bad 'uz bekase I hear sumpn over yonder on de bank like a whack, er a

slam, while ago, en it mine me er de time I treat my
little 'Lizabeth so ornery. She warn't on'y 'bout fo'
year ole en she tuck de sk'yarlet fever, en had a
powerful rough spell; but she got well, en one day
she was a-stannin' aroun', en I says to her, I says:

" 'Shet de do'.' "

"She never done it; jis' stood dah, kiner smilin' up
at me. It make me mad; en I says ag'in, mighty loud,
I says:

" 'Doan you hear me? Shet dat damn do'!'

"She jis' stood de same way, kiner smilin' up. I
was a-bilin'! I says:

" 'I lay I *make* you mine!'

"En wid dat I fetch' her a slap side de head dat
sont her a-sprawlin'. Den I went into de yuther room,
en 'uz gone 'bout ten minutes; en when I come back
dah was dat do' a-stannin' open *yit*, en dat chile
stannin' mos' right in it, a-lookin' down and mournin',
en de tears runnin' down. My, but I *wuz* mad! I wuz
a-gwne for de chile, but jis' den — it wuz a do' dat
open innerds — jis' den, 'long come de wind en slam
it to, behine de chile, ker-*blam*! — en my lan', de
chile never move'! My breff mos' hop outer me; en I
feel so — so — I doan' know *how* I feel. I crope out,
all a-tremblin', en poke my head in behine de chile,
sof' en still, en all uv a sudden I says *pow*! jis' as loud
as I could yell. *She never budge!* Oh, Huck, I bust out
a-cryin' en grab her up in my arms, en say, 'Oh, de
po' little thing! De Lawd God Almighty fo'give po'
ole Jim, kaze he never gwyne to fogive hisself as long
as he live!' Oh, she was plum deef en dumb, Huck,
plumb deef en dumb — en I'd ben a-treat'n her so!"

And then he started in a-moaning and mourning to
himself, rocking back and forth and saying, "Po'

little 'Lizabeth! po' little Johnny! it's mighty hard; I spec' I ain't ever gwyne to see you no mo', no mo'!" After a while he fell asleep and didn't wake up till the duke and king began stirring around asking for breakfast.

XXIII

The king turns parson

All that next day them two rapscallions didn't feel very chipper, but mostly lay around the raft with their heads wrapped up in wet rags. But come nightfall, they had picked up considerable, and when we come to a little willow towhead out in the middle, where there was a village on each side of the river, they had us put up there, and begun to lay out a plan for working them towns. They wanted to try the Burning Shame again, because there was so much money in it, but they judged it wouldn't be safe, because maybe the news might a already worked along down. They couldn't hit no project that suited exactly; so at last the duke said he reckoned he'd lay off and work his brains an hour or two and see if he couldn't put up something on the Arkansaw village; and the king he allowed he would drop over to t'other village without any plan, but just trust in Providence to lead him the profitable way—meaning the devil, I reckon, because the widow's Providence wouldn't a had nothing to do with a damn rascal like that.

They had me break out the box of store clothes we had bought, and the king put his'n on, and he told me to put mine on. I done it, of course. The king's duds was all black, and he did look real swell and starchy. Before, he looked like the dangdest old rip that ever was; but now, when he'd take off his new white beaver and make a bow and do a smile, he looked that grand and good and pious that you'd swear he walked right out of the Bible. Pap used to say if you scratched a preacher you would bleed a thief, and he was most usually right in such matters.

Jim cleaned up the canoe, and I got my paddle ready. there was a big steamboat laying at the shore away up under the point, about three mile above the town—been there a couple of hours, taking on freight. Says the king:

"Seein' how I'm dressed, I reckon maybe I better arrive down from St. Louis or Cincinnati, or some other big place. Go for the steamboat, Huckleberry; we'll come down to the village on her."

I didn't have to be ordered twice to go and take a steamboat ride. I fetched the shore a half a mile above the village, and then went scooting along the bluff bank in the easy water. Pretty soon we come to a nice innocent-looking young country jake setting on a log swabbing the sweat off of his face, for it was damnation hot weather; and he had a couple of big carpet-bags by him.

"Run her nose inshore," says the king. I done it. "Wher' you bound for, young man?"

"For the steamboat; going to Orleans."

"Git aboard," says the king. "Hold on a minute, my servant'll he'p you with them bags. Jump out and he'p the gentleman, Adolphus."—meaning me, I see.

I done so, and then we all three started on again.
The young chap was mighty dern thankful; said it
was tough work toting his baggage such weather. He
asked the king where he was going, and the king told
him he'd come down the river and landed at the other
village this morning, and now he was going up a few
mile to see an old friend on a farm up there. The
young fellow says:

"When I first see you I says to myself, 'It's Mr.
Wilks, sure, and he come mighty near getting here
in time.' But then I says again, 'No, I reckon it ain't
him, or else he wouldn't be paddling up the river.'
You *ain't* him, are you?"

"No, my name's Blodgett—Elexander Blodgett—
Reverend Elexender Blodgett, I s'pose I must say, as
I'm one o' the Lord's poor servants. But still I'm just
as able to be sorry for Mr. Wilks for not arriving
in time, all the same, if he's missed anything by it—
which I hope he hasn't."

"Well, he don't miss any property by it, because
he'll get that all right; but he's missed seeing his
brother Peter die—which he mayn't mind, nobody
can tell as to that—but his brother would a give anything in this world to see *him* before he died; never
talked about nothing else all these three weeks;
hadn't seen him since they was boys together—and
hadn't ever seen his brother William at all—that's
the deef and dumb one—William ain't more than
thirty or thirty-five. Peter and George were the only
ones that come out here; George was the married
brother; him and his wife both died last year. Harvey
and William's the only ones that's left now; and, as
I was saying, they haven't got here in time."

"Did anybody send 'em word?"

"Oh, yes; a month or two ago, when Peter was first took; because Peter said then that he sorter felt like he warn't going to get well this time. You see, he was pretty old, and George's g'yirls was too young to be much company for him, except Mary Jane, the red-headed one; and so he was kinder lonesome after George and his wife died, and didn't seem to care much to live. He most desperately wanted to see Harvey—and William, too, for that matter—because he was one of them kind that can't bear to make a will. He left a letter behind for Harvey, and said he'd told in it where his money was hid, and how he wanted the rest of the property divided up so George's g'yirls would be all right—for George didn't leave nothing. And that letter was all they could get him to put a pen to."

"Why do you reckon Harvey don't come? Wher' does he live?"

"Oh, he lives in England—Sheffield—preaches there—hasn't ever been in this country. He hasn't had any too much time—and besides he mightn't a got the letter at all, you know."

"Too bad, too bad he couldn't a lived to see his brothers, poor soul. You going to Orleans, you say?"

"Yes, but that ain't only a part of it. I'm going in a ship, next Wednesday, for Ryo Janeero, where my uncle lives."

"It's a pretty long journey. But it'll be lovely; I wisht I was a-going. Is Mary Jane the oldest? How old is the others?"

"Mary Jane's nineteen, Susan's fifteen, and Jo-anna's about fourteen—that's the one that gives herself to good works and has a hare-lip."

"Poor things! to be left alone in the cold world so."

"Well, they could be worse off. Old Peter had friends, and they ain't going to let them come to no harm. There's Hobson, the Baptis' preacher; and Deacon Lot Hovey, and Ben Rucker, and Abner Shackleford, and Levi Bell, the lawyer; and Dr. Robinson, and their wives, and the widow Bartley, and—well, there's a lot of them; but these are the ones that Peter was thickest with, and used to write about sometimes, when he wrote home; so Harvey'll know where to look for friends when he gets here."

Well, the old man went on asking questions till he just fairly emptied that young fellow. Danged if he didn't inquire about everybody and everything in that derned town, and all about the Wilkses; and about Peter's business—which was a tanner; and about George's—which was a carpenter; and about Harvey's—which was a dissentering minister; and so on, and so on. Then he says:

"Was this Peter Wilks well off?"

"Oh, yes, pretty well off. He had houses and land, and it's reckoned he left three or four thousand in cash hid up som'ers."

"When did you say he died?"

"I didn't say, but it was last night."

"Funeral tomorrow, likely?"

"Yes, 'bout the middle of the day."

"Well, it's all terrible sad; but we've all got to go, one time or another. So what we want to do is to be prepared; then we're all right."

"Yes, sir, it's the best way. Ma used to always say that."

When we struck the boat she was about done loading, and pretty soon she got off. The king never said nothing about going aboard, so I lost my ride, after all. When the boat was gone the king made me paddle up another mile to a lonesome place, and then he got ashore and says:

"Now hustle back, right off, and fetch the duke up here, and the new carpet-bags. And if he's gone over to t'other side, go over there and git him. And tell him to git himself up regardless. Shove along, now."

I see what *he* was up to; but I never said nothing, of course. I went a-booming down to the raft, and there the duke was, still thinking of some way to work the village on the other side. When I told him what the king wanted, he jumped into his new clothes in jiffy time, and whilst he was doing that, I got Jim into his sick Arab costume. Then the duke and me got into the canoe, and hot as it was, we lay into those paddles and went humming along back upstream. I never seen anybody work so hard as that duke when there was deviltry afoot.

When we got back to the king we hid the canoe, and then they set down on a log and the king told him everything, just like the young fellow had said it — every last word of it. And all the time he was a-doing it he tried to talk like an Englishman; and he done it pretty damn well, too, for a slouch. I can't imitate him, and so I ain't a-going to try to; but he really done it pretty good. Then he says:

"How are you on the deef and dumb, Bilgewater?"

The duke said, leave him alone for that; said he had played a deef and dumb person on the his-tryonic boards. So then they waited for a steamboat.

About the middle of the afternoon a couple of little boats come along, but they didn't come from high enough up the river; but at last there was a big one, and they hailed her. She sent out her yawl, and we went aboard, and she was from Cincinnati; and when they found we only wanted to go four or five mile they were booming mad, and gave us a cussing, and said they wouldn't land us. But the king was calm. He says:

"If gentlemen kin afford to pay a dollar a mile apiece to be took on and put off in a yawl, a steamboat kin afford to carry 'em, can't it?"

So they softened down and said it was all right; and when we got to the village they yawled us ashore. About two dozen men flocked down when they see the yawl a-coming, and when the king says:

"Kin any of you gentlemen tell me wher' Mr. Peter Wilks lives?" they give a glance at one another, and nodded their heads, as much as to say, "What'd I tell you?" Then one of them says, kind of soft and gentle:

"I'm sorry, sir, but the best we can do is to tell you where he *did* live yesterday evening."

Sudden as winking the ornery old cretur went all to smash, and fell up against the man, and put his chin on his shoulder, and cried down his back, and says:

"Alas, alas, our poor brother—gone, and we never got to see him; oh, it's too, *too* hard."

Then he turns around, blubbering, and makes a lot of idiotic signs to the duke on his hands, and damned if *he* didn't drop a carpet-bag and bust out a-crying. If they warn't the goddamnedest lot, them two frauds, that ever I struck, I'll be dipped.

Well, the men gathered around and sympathized with them, and said all sorts of kind things to them, and carried their carpet-bags up the hill for them, and let them lean on them and cry, and told the king all about his brother's last moments, and the king he told it all over again on his hands to the duke, and both of them took on about that dead tanner like they'd lost the twelve disciples. Well, if ever I struck anything like it, I'm a danged nigger. It was enough to make a body ashamed of the human race.

XXIV

All full of tears and flapdoodle

The news was all over town in two minutes, and you could see the people tearing down on the run from every which way, some of them putting on their coats as they come. Pretty soon we was in the middle of a crowd, and the noise of the tramping was like a soldier march. The windows and dooryards was full; and every minute somebody would say, over a fence:

"Is it *them*?"

And somebody trotting along with the gang would answer back and say:

"You bet it is."

"When we got to the house the street in front of it was packed, and the three girls was standing in the door. Mary Jane *was* red-headed, but that don't make no difference, she was awful darn beautiful, and her face and her eyes was all lit up, she was so glad her uncles had come. The king he spread his arms, and Mary Jane she jumped for them, and Susan she jumped for the duke, and there they *had* it!

Them two rips give it to the girls smack on the
mouth, and they hung on so long I thought sure somebody would get suspicions, but everybody, leastwise
the women, was crying for joy to see them meet at
last and have such good times. Joanna—that was the
hare-lip—was there too, and I noticed she was fidgeting around, having sort of been left out of the general smooch, so to speak. Right in the middle of it
all she give a little yip and let me have it good, right
on the mouth and considerable inside it, too. It's
always that way with them girls that gives themselves
to good works. They get so used to the idea of being
generous, that all it takes is for them to see you as a
deserving case, and you'll get all the bread they got
and a heap of molasses, beside. Well, I didn't fight
back none, but laid into my work as if I was borned
to it. She warn't bad looking, take it all around, save
for being a trifle rabbity. And her kissing—well, it
was different, but it was rattling good.

We broke clean, all three of us, and I see the
king hunch the duke private-like, and then he looked
around and spied the coffin, over in the corner on
two chairs; so then him and the duke, with a hand
to their eyes, walked slow and solemn over there,
everybody dropping back to give them room, and all
the talk and noise stopping, people saying, " 'Sh!"
and all the men taking their hats off and drooping
their heads, so you could a heard a pin fall. And when
they got there they bent over and looked in the coffin,
and took one sight, and then they bust out a-crying so
you could a heard them to Orleans, most; and then
they put their arms around each other's necks, and
hung their chins over each other's shoulders; and
then for three minutes, or maybe four, I never seen

two men leak the way they done. And, mind you, everybody was doing the same; and the place was that damp I never see anything like it. Even a dog that had wandered in with the rest give out a howl or two until somebody kicked him back outside.

Then the king he got on one side of the coffin, and the duke on t'other side, and they kneeled down and rested their foreheads on the coffin, and let on to pray all to themselves. Well, when it come to that it worked the crowd like you never see anything like it, and everybody broke down and went to sobbing right out loud—the poor girls, too; and every woman, nearly, went up to the girls, without saying a word, and kissed them, solemn, on the forehead, and then put their hand on their head, and looked up towards the sky—which was the ceiling, of course—with the tears running down, and then busted out and went off sobbing and swabbing, and give the next woman a show. I never see anything so damn disgusting.

Well, by and by the king he gets up and comes forward a little, and works himself up and slobbers out a speech, all full of tears and flapdoodle, about its being a sore trial for him and his poor brother to lose the diseased, and to miss seeing diseased alive after the long journey of four thousand mile, but it's a trial that's sweetened and sanctified to us by this dear sympathy and these holy tears, and so he thanks them out of his heart and out of his brother's heart, because out of their mouths they can't, words being too weak and cold, and all that kind of dern rot and slush, till it was enough to make you puke; and then he blubbers out a pious goody-goody Amen, and turns himself into a reglar damn water-works, crying fit to bust.

And the minute the words were out of his mouth somebody over in the crowd struck up the doxolojer and everybody joined in with all their might, and it just warmed you up and made you feel as good as church letting out. Music *is* a good thing; and after all that soul-butter and hogwash I never see it freshen up things so, and sound so honest and bully.

Then the king begins to work his jaw again, and says how him and his nieces would be glad if a few of the main principle friends of the family would take supper here with them this evening; and help set up with the ashes of the diseased; and says if his poor brother laying yonder could speak he knows who he would name, for they was names that was very dear to him, and mentioned often in his letters, and so he will name the same, to wit, as follows, viz.:—Rev. Mr Hobson, and Deacon Lot Hovey, and Mr Ben Rucker, and Abner Shackleford, and Levi Bell, and Dr Robinson, and their wives, and the widow Bartley.

Rev. Hobson and Dr Robinson was down to the end of the town a-hunting together—that is, I mean the doctor was shipping a sick man to t'other world, and the preacher was pinting him right. Lawyer Bell was away up to Louisville on business. But the rest was on hand, and so they all come and shook hands with the king and thanked him and talked to him; and then they shook hands with the duke, and didn't say nothing, but just kept a-smiling and bobbing their heads like a passel of damn sapheads whilst he made all sorts of signs with his hands and said "Goo-goo—goo-goo-goo" all the time, like a baby that can't talk.

So the king he blatted along, and managed to inquire about pretty much everybody and dog in town, by his name, and mentioned all sorts of little things that happened one time or another in the town, or to George's family, or to Peter. And he always let on that Peter wrote him the things; but that was a lie: he got every dinged one of them out of that young flat-head that we canoed up to the steamboat.

Then Mary Jane she fetched the letter her father left behind, and the king he read it out loud and cried over it. It give the dwelling-house and three thousand dollars, gold, to the girls; and it give the tanyard (which was doing a good business), along with some other houses and land (worth about seven thousand), and three thousand dollars in gold to Harvey and William, and told where the six thousand cash was hid down cellar. So these two damn frauds said they'd go and fetch it up, and have everything square and above-board; and told me to come with a candle We shut the cellar door behind us, and when they found the bag they spilt it out on the floor, and it was a lovely sight, all them yaller-boys. My, the way the king's eyes did shine! He slaps the duke on the shoulder and says:

"Oh, *this* ain't bully nor noth'n'! Oh, no, I reckon not! Why, Biljy, it beats the Shame all to hell *don't* it?"

The duke he allowed it did. They pawed the yaller-boys, and sifted them through their fingers and let them jingle down on the floor; and the king says:

"It ain't no use talkin'; bein' brothers to a rich dead man and representatives of furrin heirs that's got left is the line for you and me, Bilge. Thish yer comes of trust'n to Providence. It's the best way, in the long run. I've tried 'em all, and ther' ain't no better way."

Most everybody would a been satisfied with the pile, and took it on trust; but no, they must count it. So they counts it, and it comes out four hundred and fifteen dollars short. Says the king:

"Damn him, I wonder what he done with that four hundred and fifteen dollars?"

They worried over that awhile, and ransacked all around for it. Then the duke says:

"Well, he was a pretty sick man, and likely he made a mistake—I reckon that's the way of it. The best way's to let it go, and keep still about it. We can spare it."

"Oh, hell, yes, we can *spare* it. I don't k'yer noth'n 'bout that—it's the *count* I'm thinkin' about. We want to be awful square and open and above-board here, you know. We want to lug this h'yer money upstairs and count it before everybody—then ther' ain't noth'n suspicious. But when the dead man says ther's six thous'n dollars, you know, we don't want to—"

"Hold on," says the duke. "Le's make up the deffisit," and he begun to haul out yaller-boys out of his pocket.

"It's a most amaz'n' good idea, duke—you *have* got a rattlin' clever head on you," says the king. "Damned if the old Shame ain't a-heppin' us out ag'in," and *he* begun to haul out yaller-jackets and stack them up.

It most busted them, but they made up the six thousand clean and clear.

"Say," says the duke, "I got another idea. Le's go up-stairs and count this money, and then take and *give it to the girls.*"

"Good land, duke, lemme hug you! It's the most dazzling damn idea 'at ever a man struck. You have cert'nly got the most astonishin' head I ever see. Oh, this is the boss dodge, ther' ain't no mistake 'bout it. Let 'em fetch along their suspicions now if they want to—this'll lay 'em out."

When we got up-stairs everybody gethered around the table, and the king he counted it and stacked it up, three hundred dollars in a pile—twenty elegant little piles. Everybody looked hungry at it, and licked their chops. Then they raked it into the bag again, and I see the king begin to swell himself up for another speech. He says:

"Friends all, my poor brother that lays yonder has done generous by them that's left behind in the vale of sorrers. He has done generous by these yer poor little lambs that he loved and sheltered, and that's left fatherless and motherless. Yes, and we that knowed him knows that he would a done *more* generous by 'em if he hadn't ben afeard o' woundin' his dear William and me. Now, *wouldn't* he? Ther' ain't no question 'bout it in *my* mind. Well, then, what kind o' brothers would it be that'd stand in his way at sech a time? And what kind o' uncles would it be that'd rob—yes, *rob*—sech poor sweet lambs as these 'at he loved so at sech a time? If I know William—and I *think* I do—he—well, I'll jest ask him." He turned around and began to make a lot of signs to the duke with his hands, and the duke he looks at him stupid and leather-headed awhile; then all of a sudden he seems to catch his meaning, and jumps for the king, goo-gooing with all his might for joy, and hugs him about fifteen times before he lets up. Then the king says, "I knowed it; I reckon *that*'ll convince anybody the way *he* feels about it. Here, Mary Jane, Susan, Joanner, take the money—take it *all*. It's the gift of him that lays yonder, cold but joyful."

Mary Jane she went for him, Susan went for the duke, and the hare-lip was on me in three shakes of a sheep's tail. There was another spell of hugging and kissing, and I took my share and then some, because when Joanna found out I was just hired help, she might not be so free and easy with it. Everybody crowded up with the tears in their eyes, and most shook the hands off of them dang frauds, saying all the time:

"You *dear* good souls!—how *lovely*!—how *could* you!"

Well, then, pretty soon all hands got to talking about the diseased again, and how good he was, and what a loss he was, and all that; and before long a big iron-jawed man worked himself in there from outside, and stood a-listening and looking, and not saying anything; and nobody saying anything to him either, because the king was talking and they was all busy listening. The king was saying—in the middle of something he'd started in on—

"—they bein' partickler friends o' the diseased. That's why they're invited here this evenin'; but tomorrow we want *all* to come—everybody; for he respected everybody, he liked everybody, and so it's fitten that his funeral orgies sh'd be public."

And so he went a-mooning on and on, liking to hear himself talk, and every little while he fetched in his funeral orgies again, till the duke he couldn't stand it no more; so he writes the right word on a little scrap of paper, and folds it up, and goes to goo-gooing and reaching it over people's heads to him. The king he reads it and puts it in his pocket, and says:

"Poor William, afflicted as he is, his *heart's* aluz right. Asks me to invite everybody to come to the funeral—wants me to make 'em all welcome. But he needn't a worried—it was just what I was at."

Then he weaves along again, perfectly calm, and goes to dropping in his funeral orgies again every now and then, just like he done before. And when he done it the third time he says:

"I say orgies, not because it's the common term, because it ain't—obsekwees bein' the common term—but because orgies is the right term. Obsekwees ain't used in England no more now—it's gone out. We say orgies now in England. Orgies is better, because it means the thing you're after more exact. It's a word that's made up out'n the Greek *orgo*, outside, open, abroad; and the Hebrew *jeesum*, to plant, cover up; hence in*ter*. So, you see, funeral orgies is an open er public funeral."

He was the *worst* I ever struck. Well, the iron-jawed man he laughed right in his face. Everybody was shocked. Everybody says, "Why, *doctor!*" and Abner Shackleford says:

"Why, Robinson, hain't you heard the news? This is Harvey Wilks."

The king he smiled eager, and shoved out his flapper, and says:

"*Is* it my poor brother's dear good friend and physician? I—"

"Keep your hands off me!" says the doctor. "*You* talk like an Englishman, *don't* you? It's the worst imitation I ever heard. *You* Peter Wilks's brother! You're a blasted fraud, that's what you are!"

Well, how they all took on! They crowded around the doctor and tried to explain to him and tell him how Harvey's showed in forty ways that he *was* Harvey, and knowed everybody by name, and the names of the very dogs, and begged and *begged* him not to hurt Harvey's feelings and the poor girls' feelings, and all that. But it warn't no use; he stormed right along, and said any man that pretended to be an Englishman and couldn't imitate the lingo no better than what he did was a fraud and a liar. The poor girls was hanging to the king and crying; and all of a sudden the doctor ups and turns on *them*. He says:

"I was your father's friend, and I'm your friend; and I warn you *as* a friend, and an honest one that wants to protect you and keep you out of harm and trouble, to turn your backs on that scoundrel and have nothing to do with him, the ignorant tramp, with his idiotic Greek and Hebrew, as he calls it. He is the thinnest kind of an impostor—has come here with a lot of empty names and facts which he picked up somewheres; and you take them for *proofs*, and are helped to fool yourselves by these foolish friends here, who ought to know better. Mary Jane Wilks, you know me for your friend, and for your unselfish friend, too. Now listen to me; turn this pitiful rascal out—I *beg* you to do it. Will you?"

Mary Jane straightened herself up, and damnation! if she warn't a stunner! She says:

"*Here* is my answer." She hove up the bag of money and put it in the king's hands, and says, "Take this six thousand dollars, and invest for me and my sisters any way you want to, and don't give us no receipt for it."

Then she put her arm around the king on one side, and Susan done the same on the other. Everybody clapped their hands and stomped on the floor like a perfect storm, whilst the king held up his head and smiled proud. The doctor says:

"All right; I wash *my* hands of the matter. But I warn you all that a time's coming when you're going to feel sick whenever you think of this day." And away he went.

"All right, doctor," says the king, kinder mocking him; "we'll try and get 'em to send for you"; which made them all laugh, and they said it was a prime good hit.

XXV

I steal the king's plunder

Well, when they was all gone the king he asks Mary Jane how they was off for spare rooms, and she said she had one spare room, which would do for Uncle William, and she'd give her own room to Uncle Harvey, which was a little bigger. Then she looked at me, and stopped, not knowing who I was, of course. The king see what the trouble was and said she warn't to bother herself about me, since I was only Adolphus, his valley. Well, Mary Jane said there *was* a little cubby with a pallet in it up garret, and the king said that would do fine for me. I see that Joanna turned a little red, having been a-giving of her good works to a valley, but she carried it off with style, and I admired her grit.

Mary Jane took us up, and she showed them their rooms, which was plain but nice. She said she'd have her frocks and a lot of other traps took out of her room if they was in Uncle Harvey's way, but he said they warn't. The frocks was hung along the wall, and before them was a curtain made out of calico that hung down to the floor. There was an old hair trunk in one corner, and a guitar-box in another, and all sorts of little knicknacks and jimcracks around, like girls brisken up a room with. The king said it was all the more homely and more pleasanter for these fixings, and so don't disturb them. The duke's room was pretty small, but plenty good enough, and so was my cubby. Toward midday it got middling hot up there, of course, but that didn't trouble me none.

That night they had a big supper, and all them men and women was there, and I stood behind the king and the duke's chairs and waited on them, and the niggers waited on the rest. Mary Jane she set at the head of the table, with Susan alongside of her, and said how bad the biscuits was, and how mean the preserves was, and how ornery and tough the fried chickens was — and all that kind of rot, the way women always do for to force out compliments; and the people all knowed everything was tiptop, and said so — said "How *do* you get biscuits to brown so nice?" and "Where, for the land's sake, *did* you get these amaz'n pickles?" and all that kind of humbug talky-talk, just the way people always does at a supper, you know.

And when it was all done me and the hare-lip had supper in the kitchen off of the leavings, whilst the others was helping the niggers clean up the things. I found out later that Joanna always done that. She never ate at the table with her sisters, but always kept at her good works till the others was done, and then she would eat back there by herself. She had read about some lady that had done the same a couple hundred years back, and had gone to heaven because of it.

Well, Joanna was coolish towards me at first,

because of what had happened, but I let on that valleys was something special in England—several notches above niggers, and well on the way to royalty. Taking the king and the duke for a gauge, I figures I warn't stretching it much; maybe they warn't royalty for real, but then I warn't no valley, nuther. Her interest perked up considerable, and she got to pumping me about England, and damned if I didn't think the ice was getting mighty thin. She says:

"Did you ever see the queen?"

"Well, I bet I have. More than I keer to admit. Whenever they're in town, she and the king send for me, and he—"

"The king? Oh, you must mean Prince Albert."

Hell! there she had me and let me go in the same breath. I says:

"Well, we calls him 'king' around the palace. He wants it that way. He—"

"The palace? I thought the palace was in London."

"Well, it is. Where would it be?"

"But I thought *you* lived in Sheffield?"

I see I was up a stump. I had to let on to get choked with a chicken-bone, so as to get time to think how to get down again. Then I says:

"If you'd ever let me finish, I could explain all that. You see, when the queen is in town, she and the king they send for me down in Sheffield, and I go up to London and visit them in the palace."

That seemed to satisfy her. She says:

"Does Uncle Harvey let you go whenever she asks?"

"Does he? I *guess* he does. I reckon if'n he didn't, she'd have his head off quicker'n you c'd say Jack Robinson."

"Goodness! I didn't know they *did* that any more."

"Well, I guess they don't, usually. But the queen said she'd make an exception in my case. You see, she couldn't stand for the idea of me not showing up when they wanted me around."

"Think of that!" Her eyes was fairly popping out.

"Well, it's a blame nuisance, if you must know. The queen, she's all right, but that ole king, he's the worst sort. Why the sun don't set but he ain't done some mischief or other.

Well, her face was a study when she heard that one. You'd a thought I had told her the king was a nigger. She says:

"Why, I hain't never read nothing but what a good and pious man he is. I'm jest amazed to hear all this." She buckled to the table and leaned forward. "What kind of mischief do you mean?"

I see what she wanted, so I give it to her. I says:

"Well, he ain't particular how often he washes, for one thing. Most of the people around the palace kind of keeps to windward, and on a hot day, they tend to hang around the open windows a lot."

"My gracious! I never imagined!"

"That ain't all, nuther. He's mighty fond of the bottle, too, and when his steam is up, he goes after them ladies-in-waiting like a bull . . . a bull in a china-shop."

"My land!" She blushed, but she kept listening.

"And he don't stop with girls, no indeed. He's got an eye for boys, too. If I don't look sharp when I'm at the palace, why he —"

That done it. Joanna turned red as a beet and covered up her ears. "Oh! oh!" she hollered. "I don't believe it!"

"Well," I said. "It's the plain truth." And it *was* all true about the king. Our king, leastwise. And from what I hear tell there ain't much difference between him and the reglar ones. Take them all around, kings is a mighty ornery lot. It's the way the sons-a-bitches is raised.

"Honest injun, now," she says. "Hain't you been telling me a lot of lies?"

"Honest injun," says I, crossing my fingers in my pocket.

"None of it at all?"

"None of it at all." I snuck my other hand behind my back and double-crossed. "Not a lie in it."

"Lay your hand on this book and say it."

Well, that meant I had to uncross, but I see it warn't nothing but a dictionary, so I laid my hand on it and said it. So then she looked a little better satisfied, and says:

"Well, then, I'll believe some of it; but I hope to gracious if I'll believe the rest."

"What is it you won't believe, Jo?" says Mary Jane, stepping in with Susan behind her. "It ain't right nor kind for you to talk so to him, and him a stranger and so far from his people. How would you like to be treated so?"

"Why, Maim, he said—"

"I don't care what he said; he's here in our house and a stranger, and it wasn't good of you to say it. If you was in his place it would make you feel ashamed; and so you oughtn't to say a thing to another person that will make *them* feel ashamed. My goodness, you read the Bible enough to know the thing for you to do is treat him *kind*, and not be saying things to make him remember he ain't in his own country and amongst his own folks. You are always one for charity and good works, Jo, but sometimes you forget to start right here, at home."

I says to myself, *this* is a girl that I'm letting that goddamned old reptile rob of her money!

Then Susan *she* waltzed in; and if you'll believe me, she did give Hare-lip hark from the tomb!

Says I to myself, and this is *another* one that I'm letting him rob of her money!

Then Mary Jane she took another inning, and went in sweet and lovely again—which was her way; but when she got done there warn't hardly anything left o' poor Hare-lip. So she hollered.

"All right, then," says the other girls; "you just ask his pardon."

She done it, too; and she done it beautiful. She done it so beautiful it was good to hear; and I wished I could tell her a thousand lies, so she could do it again.

I says to myself, this is *another* one that I'm letting that old bastard rob of her money. And when she got through they all just laid theirselves out to make me feel at home and know I was amongst friends. I felt so ornery and low down and mean that I says to myself, my mind's made up; I'll hive that money for them or bust.

So then I lit out—for bed, I said, meaning some time or another. When I got by myself I went to thinking the thing over. I says to myself, shall I go to that doctor, private, and blow on these dang frauds? No—that won't do. He might tell who told him; then the king and the duke would make it warm for me and Jim. Shall I go, private, and tell Mary Jane? No—I dasn't do it. Her face would give them a hint, sure; They've got the money, and they'd slide right out and get away with it. If she was to fetch in help I'd get mixed up in the business before it was done with, I judge. No; there ain't no good way but one. I got to steal that damn money, somehow; and I got to steal it some way that they won't suspicion that I done it. They've got a good thing here, and they ain't a-going to leave till they've played this family and this town for all they're worth, so I'll find a chance time enough. I'll steal it and hide it; and by and by, when I'm away down the river, I'll write a letter and tell Mary Jane where it's hid. But I better hive it tonight if I can, because the doctor maybe hasn't let up as much as he lets on he has; he might scare them out of here yet.

So thinks I, I'll go and search them rooms. Upstairs the hall was dark, but I found the duke's room, and started to paw around it with my hands; but I recollected it wouldn't be much like the king to let anybody else take care of that money but his own self; so then I went to his room and begun to paw around there. But I see I couldn't do nothing without a candle, and I dasn't light one, of course. So I judged I'd got to do the other thing—lay for them and eavesdrop. About that time I heard their footsteps coming, and was going to skip under the bed; I reached for it, but it warn't where I thought it would be; but I touched the curtain that hid Mary Jane's frocks, so I jumped in behind that and snuggled in amongst the gowns, and stood there perfectly still. It was scary, but pleasant, being hid in there amidst all that girl scent.

They come in and shut the door; and the first thing the duke done was to get down and look under the bed. Then I was glad I hadn't found the bed when I wanted it. And yet, you know, it's kind of natural to hide under the bed when you are up to anything private. They sets down then, and the king says:

"Well, what is it? And cut it middlin' short, because it's better for us to be down there a-whooping up the mournin' than up here givin' 'em a chance to talk us over."

"Well, this is it, Capet. I ain't easy; I ain't comfortable. That damned doctor lays on my mind. I wanted to know your plans. I've got a notion, and I think it's a sound one."

"What is it, Bilgey?"

"That we better glide out of this before three in the morning, and clip it down the river with what we've got. Specially, seeing we got it so damned easy—*given* back to us, flung at our head, as you may say, when of course we allowed to have to steal it back. I'm for knocking off and lighting out."

That made me feel pretty bad. About an hour or two ago it would a been a little different, but now it made me feel bad and disappointed. The king rips out and says:

"What! And not sell out the rest o' the propety? March off like a passel o' damn fools and leave eight or nine thous'n' dollars wuth o' propety layin' around just sufferin' to be scooped in?—and all good, salable stuff, too."

The duke he grumbled; said the bag of gold was enough, and he didn't want to go no deeper—didn't want to rob a lot of orphans of *everything* they had.

"Why, how you talk!" says the king. "We sha'n't

rob 'em of nothing at all but jest this money. The people that *buys* the propety is the suff'rers; because as soon's it's found out 'at we didn't own it—which won't be long after we've slid—the sale won't be valid; and it'll all go back to the estate. These yer orphans'll git their house back ag'in, and that's enough for *them*; they're young and spry, and k'n easy earn a livin!. *They* ain't a-goin to suffer. Why, jest think—there's thous'n's and thous'n's that ain't nigh so well off. Bless you, *they* ain't got noth'n to complain of."

Well, the king he talked him blind; so at last he give in, and said he believed it was damned foolishness to stay, and that doctor hanging over them. But the king says:

"T'hell with the doctor! What do we k'yer for *him*? Hain't we got all the fools in town on our side? And ain't that a big enough majority in any damn town?"

So they got ready to go downstairs again. The duke says:

"I don't think we put that money in a good place."

That cheered me up. I'd begun to think I warn't going to get a hint of no kind to help me. The king says:

"Why?"

"Because Mary Jane'll be in mourning from this out; and first you know the nigger that does up the rooms will get an order to box these duds up and put 'em away; and do you reckon a nigger can run across money and not borrow some of it?"

"Your head's level ag'in, duke," says the king; and he comes a-fumbling under the curtain two or three foot from where I was. I stuck tight to the wall and kept mighty damn still, though quivery; and

I wondered what them fellows would say to me if they catched me; and I tried to think what I'd better do if they did catch me. But the king he got the bag before I could think more than about a half a thought, and he never suspicioned I was around. They took and shoved the bag through a rip in the straw tick that was under the feather-bed, and crammed it in a foot or two amongst the straw and said it was all right now, because a nigger only makes up the featherbed, and don't turn over the straw tick only about twice a year, and so it warn't in no danger of getting stole now.

But I knowed better. I had it out of there before they was half-way downstairs. I groped along up to my cubby, and hid it there till I could get a chance to do better. I judged I better hide it outside of the house somewheres, because if they missed it they would give the house a damn good ransacking: I knowed that very well. Then I turned in, with my clothes all on; but I couldn't a gone to sleep if I'd a wanted to, I was in such a dern sweat to get through with the business. By and by I heard the king and the duke come up; so I rolled off my pallet and laid with my chin at the top of the ladder, and waited to see if anything was going to happen. But nothing did.

So I held on till all the late sounds had quit and the early ones hadn't begun yet; and then I slipped down the ladder.

XXVI

Dead Peter has his gold

I crept to their doors and listened; they was snoring. So I tiptoed along, and got downstairs all right. There warn't a sound anywheres. I peeped through a crack of the dining-room door, and see the men that was watching the corpse all sound asleep on their chairs. The door was open into the parlor, where the corpse was laying, and there was a candle in both rooms. I passed along, and the parlor door was open; but I see there warn't nobody in there but the remainders of Peter; so I shoved on by; but the front door was locked, and the key warn't there. Just then I heard somebody coming down the stairs, back behind me. I run in the parlor and took a swift look around, and the only place I see to hide the bag was in the coffin. The lid was shoved along about a foot, showing the dead man's face down in there, with a wet cloth over it, and his shroud on. I tucked the money-bag in under the lid, just down beyond where his hands was crossed, which made me creep, they was so cold. The smell was a little ripe, also, it being well along into summer, and I figured they warn't getting him under ground any too soon. All in all I was glad when the damn job was done, and I run back across the room and in behind the door.

The person coming was Mary Jane. She went to the coffin, very soft, and kneeled down and looked in; then she put up her handkerchief, and I thought it was because of the smell until I see she begun to cry, though I couldn't hear her, and her back was to me. I slid out, and as I passed the dining-room I thought I'd make sure them watchers hadn't seen me; so I looked through the crack, and everything was all right. They hadn't stirred.

I slipped up to bed, feeling ruther blue, on accounts of the thing playing out that way after I had took so much dern trouble and run so much resk about it. Says I, if it could stay where it is, all right; because when we get down the river a hundred mile or two I could write back to Mary Jane, and she could dig him up again and get it; but that ain't the thing that's going to happen; the thing that's going to happen is, the money'll be found when they come to screw on the lid. Then the king'll get it again, and it'll be a cold day in hell before he gives anybody another chance to snitch it from him. Of course I *wanted* to slide down and get it out of there, but I dasn't try it. Every minute it was getting earlier now, and pretty soon some of them watchers would begin to stir, and I might get catched — catched with six thousand dollars in my hands that nobody hadn't hired me to take care of. I don't wish to be mixed up in no such damn business as that, I says to myself.

When I got down-stairs in the morning the parlor was shut up, and the watchers was gone. There warn't nobody around but the family and the widow Bartley and our tribe. I watched their faces to see if anything had been happening, but I couldn't tell.

Towards the middle of the day the undertaker come with his man, and they set the coffin in the middle of the room on a couple of chairs, and then set all our chairs in rows, and borrowed more from the neighbors till the hall and the parlor and the dining-room was full. I see the coffin lid was the way it was before, but I dasn't go to look in under it, with folks around.

Then the people begun to flock in, and the beats and the girls took seats in the front row at the head of the coffin, and for a half an hour the people filed around slow, in single rank, and looked down at the dead man's face a minute, and some dropped in a tear, and it was all very still and solemn, only the girls and the beats holding handkerchiefs to their eyes and keeping their heads bent, and sobbing a little. There warn't no other sound but the scraping of the feet on the floor and blowing noses — because people always blows them more at a funeral than they do at other places except church.

When the place was packed full the undertaker he slid around in his black gloves with his softy soothering ways, putting on the last touches, and getting people and things all ship-shape and comfortable, and making no more sound than a dang cat. He never spoke; he moved people around, he squeezed in late ones, he opened up passageways, and done it with nods, and signs with his hands. Then he took his place over against the wall. He was the softest, glidingest, stealthiest man I ever see; and there warn't no more smile to him than there is to a dern ham.

They had borrowed a melodeum — a sick one; and when everything was ready a young woman set down and worked it, and it was pretty skreeky and colicky, and everybody joined in and sung, and Peter was the only one that had a good thing, according to my notion. Then the Reverend Hobson opened up, slow and solemn, and begun to talk; and straight off the most outrageous row busted out in the cellar a body ever heard; it was only one dog, but he made a most powerful damn racket, and he kept it up right along; the parson he had to stand there, over the coffin, and wait — you couldn't hear yourself think. It was right down awkward, and nobody didn't seem to know what to do. But pretty soon they see that long-legged undertaker make a sign to the preacher as much as to say, "Don't you worry — just depend on me." Then he stooped down and begun to glide along the wall, just his shoulders showing over the peoples heads. So he glided along, and the powwow and racket getting more and more outrageous all the time; and at last, when he had gone around two sides of the room, he disappears down cellar. Then in about two seconds we heard a whack, and the dog he finished up with a most amazing howl or two, and then everything was dead still, and the parson begun his solemn talk where he left off. In a minute or two here comes this undertaker's back and shoulders gliding along the wall again; and so he glided and glided around three sides of the room, and then rose up, and stretched his neck out towards the preacher, over the people's heads, and says, in a kind of coarse whisper, "*He had a rat!*" Then he dropped down and glided along the wall again to his place. You could see it was a great satisfaction to the people, because naturally they wanted to know. A little thing like that don't cost nothing, and it's just the little things that makes a man to be looked up to and liked. There warn't no more popular man in town than what that undertaker was.

Well, the funeral sermon was very good, but pison long and tiresome; and then the king he shoved in and got off some of his usual damn rubbage, and at last the job was through, and the undertaker begun to sneak up on the coffin with his screwdriver. I was in a sweat then, and watched him pretty keen. But he never meddled at all; just slid the lid along as soft as mush, and screwed it down tight and fast. So there I was! I didn't know whether the money was in there or not. So, says I, s'pose somebody has hogged that bag on the sly? —now how do *I* know whether to write to Mary Jane or not? S'pose she dug him up and didn't find nothing, what would she think of me? Damn it, I says, I might get hunted up and jailed; I'd better lay low and keep dark, and not write at all; the thing's awful mixed now; trying to better it, I've worsened it a hundred times, and I wish to Christ I'd just let it alone, goddamn the whole business!

They buried him, and we come back home, and I went to watching faces again—I couldn't help it, and I couldn't rest easy. But nothing come of it; the faces didn't tell me nothing.

The king he visited around in the evening, and

sweetened everybody up, and made himself ever so friendly; and he give out the idea that his congregation over in England would be in a sweat about him, so he must hurry and settle up the estate right away and leave for home. He was very sorry he was so pushed, and so was everybody; they wished he could stay longer, but they said they could see it couldn't be done. And he said of course him and William would take the girls home with them; and that pleased everybody too, because then the girls would be well fixed and amongst their own relations; and it pleased the girls, too—tickled them so they clean forgot they ever had a trouble in the world; and told them to sell out as quick as he wanted to, they would be ready. Them poor things was that glad and happy it made my heart ache to see them getting fooled and lied to so, but I didn't see no safe way for me to chip in and change the general tune.

Well, damned if the king didn't bill the house and the niggers and all the property for auction straight off—sale two days after the funeral; but anybody could buy private beforehand if they wanted to.

So the next day after the funeral, along about noontime, the girl's joy got the first jolt. A couple of nigger-traders come along, and the king sold them the niggers reasonable, for three-day drafts as they called it, and away they went, the two sons up the river to Memphis, and their mother down the river to Orleans. I thought them poor girls and them niggers would break their hearts for grief; they cried around each other, and took on so it most made me down sick to see it. The girls said they hadn't ever dreamed of seeing the family separated or sold away from the town. I can't ever get it out of my memory, the sight of them poor miserable girls and the niggers hanging around each other's necks and crying; and I reckoned I couldn't a stood it all, but would a had to bust out and tell on our gang if I hadn't knowed the sale warn't no account and the niggers would be back home in a week or two.

The thing made a big stir in the town, too, and a good many come out flatfooted and said it was scandalous to separate the mother and the children that way. It injured the frauds some; but the old peckerhead he bulled right along, spite of all the duke could say or do, and I tell you the duke was powerful uneasy.

Next day was auction day. About broad day in the morning the king and the duke come up in the garret and woke me up, and I see by their look that there was trouble. The king says:

"Was you in my room night before last?"

"No, your majesty" — which was what I always called him when nobody but our gang warn't around.

"Was you in there yisterday er last night?"

"No, your majesty."

He lay his finger on my chest and made as if to cock his thumb. "No damned lies, now."

"Honest, your majesty. I'm telling you the truth. I hain't been a-near your room since Miss Mary Jane took you and the duke and showed it to you."

The duke says:

"Have you seen anybody else go in there?"

"No, your grace, not as I remember, I believe."

"Stop and think."

I studied awhile and see my chance; then I says:

"Well, I see the niggers go in there several times."

Both of them gave a little jump, and looked like

they hadn't ever expected it, and then like they *had*. Then the duke says:

"What, *all* of them?"

"No—leastways, not all at once—that is, I don't think I ever see them all come *out* at once but just one time."

"Hello! When was that?"

"It was the day we had the funeral. In the morning. It warn't early, because I overslept. I was just starting down the ladder, and I see them."

"Well, go on, *go* on! What did they do? How'd they act?"

"They didn't do nothing. And they didn't act anyway much, as fur as I see. They tiptoed away; so I seen, easy enough, that they'd shoved in there to do up your majesty's room, or something, s'posing you was up; and found you *warn't* up, and so they was hoping to slide out of the way of trouble without waking you up, if they hadn't already waked you up."

"Jeesus! this *is* a go!" says the king; and both of them looked pretty sick and tolerable damn silly. They stood there a-thinking and scratching their heads a minute, and the duke he bust into a kind of a little raspy chuckle, and says:

"It does beat all hell how neat those damned niggers played their hand. They let on to be *sorry* they was going out of this region! And I believed they *was* sorry, and so did you, and so did everybody. Don't ever tell *me* any more that a nigger ain't got any histryonic talent. Why, the way they played that thing it would fool *anybody*. In my opinion, there's a fortune in 'em. If I had capital and a theater, I wouldn't want a better layout than that—and here we've gone and sold 'em for a song. Yes, and ain't privileged to sing the song yet. Say, where *is* that song—that draft?"

"In the bank for to be collected. Where *would* it be?"

"Well, *that's* all right then, thank God."

Says I, kind of timid-like:

"Is something gone wrong?"

The king whirls on me and rips out:

"None o' your goddamn business! You keep your friggin' head shet, and mind y'r own affairs—if you got any. Long as you're in this town don't you for-git *that*—you hear?" Then he says to the duke, "We got to just swaller it and say noth'n': mum's the word for *us*."

As they was starting down the ladder the duke he chuckles again, and says:

"Quick sales *and* small profits! It's a good busi-ness—yes."

The king snarls around on him and says:

"I was trying to do for the best in sellin' 'em out so quick. If the profits has turned out to be none, lackin' considable, and none to carry, is it my damn fault any more'n it's yourn?"

"Well, *they'd* be in this house yet and we *wouldn't* if I could a got my advice listened to, you old son-of-a-bitch!"

The king sassed back as much as was safe for him, and then swapped around and lit into me again. He give me down the banks for not coming and telling him I see the niggers come out of his room acting that way—said any fool would a *knowed* something was up. And then he waltzed in and cussed himself awhile, and said it all come of him not laying late and taking his natural rest that morning, and he'd be damned if he'd ever do it again. Pretty soon he hit on the girls, and said it was *their* fault he'd got up so early, because of their goddamned funeral, and it was *their* damn niggers that had come sneaking into his room whilst he was downstairs a-comforting everybody, and if it hadn't been for them everything would still be all right. He cussed some more and then he said he hadn't planned to take the girls with him when he had said it, but now he warn't so sure. He grinned an awful grin and said they was all going to need jobs and he reckoned he could find 'em jobs down in Orleans, all right. He knew just the place, and he'd be the first customer.

Well, the duke didn't like that one bit, and he called the king a damned old toad, and a lot worse. He said he should a sized him up for what he was long ago, and as soon as this business was over, he was through with the old lecher for good. Then the king said if *he* was a lecher, then he knowed what the duke was, and he guessed the girls was safe enough around *him*, meaning the duke. So they went off down the ladder a-jawing; and I felt dreadful, seeing them two in such a temper. I had worked it off onto the niggers, knowing I wouldn't do them no harm by it, but now look what was happening! The king was down on the girls, and what he had in mind for them made me most puke. And if he wanted to do it, I didn't see how the duke could stop him, without giving the whole show away, and himself with it. Mary Jane and Susan and Joanna in a damn whorehouse, and it was all my fault. I wished I was dead.

XXVII

Overreaching don't pay

By and by it was getting-up time. I didn't want to budge, but anything was better than lying there thinking about what would happen to them girls if the king ever got 'em to Orleans, so I clumb down the ladder and started for downstairs. But as I come to the girls' room the door was part open, and I see Mary Jane standing in the window looking at the outside. It was to the east, and the sun come in full through her dress — it warn't nothing but her sleeping shift — and my damn pecker nearly jumped out of its socket. Well, I drew back a little, and just in time, because she turned away from the window then, and I could see she was crying. Her old hair trunk was open on the floor, and she'd been packing things in it — getting ready to go to England. She hiked up her shift to dry her eyes and I seen everything there was and damn near come in my britches. She was a beauty, red hair and all.

Well, next thing she done was to sit down in a little rocker there and bust out crying even more. I felt awful bad to see it; of course anybody would. The show was over anyhow, so I went in there and says:

"Miss Mary Jane, you can't a-bear to see people in trouble, and *I* can't—most always. Tell me about it."

So she done it. And it was the niggers—I just expected it. She said the beautiful trip to England was most about spoiled for her; she didn't know *how* she was ever going to be happy there, knowing the mother and the children warn't ever going to see each other no more—and then busted out bitterer than ever, and flung up her hands, and says:

"Oh, dear, dear, to think they ain't *ever* going to see each other any more!"

"But they *will*—and inside of two weeks—and I *know* it!" says I.

Hell, it was out before I could think! And before I could budge she throws her arms around my neck and told me to say it *again*, say it *again*, say it *again*! It was just like when I was back in her closet and the king and duke was outside in her room; I was too nervous to really enjoy all that lovely girl smell, and here there was the girl herself, to boot.

I see I had spoke too sudden and said too much, and was in a close place. I asked her to let me think a minute; and she set there in that flowery night-gown of hers, very impatient and excited and handsome, but looking kind of happy and eased-up, like a person that's had a tooth pulled out. I says to myself, I reckon a body that ups and tells the truth when he is in a tight place is taking considerable many resks, though I ain't had much experience, and can't say for certain; but it looks so to me, anyway; and yet here's a case where I'm damned if it don't look to me like the truth is better and downright *safer* than a lie. I laid it by in

my mind, to think over some time or other, it seemed
so kind of strange and unreglar. I never seen nothing like it. Well, I says to myself at last, I'm a-going
to chance it; I'll up and tell the truth this time, though
it does seem most like setting down on a damn kag of
powder and touching it off just to see where you'll
go to. Then I says:

"Miss Mary Jane, is there any place out of town
a little ways where you could go and stay three or
four days?"

"Yes; Mr. Lothrop's. Why?"

"Never mind why yet. If I'll tell you how I know the
niggers will see each other again — inside of two
weeks — here in this house — and *prove* how I know
it — will you go to Mr. Lothrop's and stay four days?"

"Four days!" she says; "I'll stay a year!"

"All right," I says, "I don't want nothing more out
of *you* than just your word — I druther have it than
another man's kiss-the-Bible." She smiled and red-
dened up very sweet, and I says, "If you don't mind
it, I'll shut the door — and bolt it."

Then I come back and set down again, and says:

"Don't you holler. Just set still and take it like a
man. I got to tell the truth and you want to brace up,
Miss Mary, because it's a bad kind, and going to be
hard to take, but there ain't no help for it. These
uncles of yourn ain't no uncles at all; they're a couple
of frauds — reglar dead-beats. There, now we're over
the worst of it, you can stand the rest middling easy."

It jolted her up like everything, of course; but I was
over the shoal water now, so I went right along, her
eyes a-blazing higher and higher all the time, and told
her every goddamn thing, from where we first struck
that young fool going up to the steamboat, clear

through to where she flung herself into the king's
arms at the front door and he kissed her sixteen or
seventeen times — and then up she jumps, with her
face afire like sunset. For a minute she didn't say
anything just twisted a little this way and that, as if
she could hardly keep from running out the door to
get at them scalawags. Christ-all-mighty, but she
looked handsome, with her green eyes and red hair.
Her night gown was one of them full-length cottons,
that starts at the neck and goes to the feet, and where
she was standing now you couldn't see a thing; it
might a been a robe and her a queen — that's the kind
of girl Mary Jane Wilks was. Finally she says:

"The brute! Come, don't waste a minute — not a
second — we'll have them tarred and feathered, and
flung in the river."

Says I:

"Cert'nly. But do you mean before you go to Mr.
Lothrop's, or — "

"Oh," she says, "what am I *thinking* about!"
she says, and set right down again. "Don't mind what
I said — please don't — you *won't* now, *will* you?"
Laying her silky hand on mine in that kind of way
that I said I would die first. It warn't just her touching
me, nuther, she just had a *way* about her, that Mary
Jane. "I never thought, I was so stirred up," she says;
"now go on, and I won't do so any more. You tell me
what to do, and whatever you say I'll do it."

"Well," I says, "it's a rough gang, them two frauds,
and I'm fixed so I got to travel with them a while
longer, whether I want to or not — I druther not tell
you why; and if you was to blow on them this town
would get me out of their claws, and *I'd* be all right;
but there'd be another person that you don't know

about who'd be in big trouble. Well, we got to save *him*, hain't we? Of course. Well, then, we won't blow on them."

Saying them words put a good idea in my head. I see how maybe I could get me and Jim rid of those damn frauds; get them jailed here, and then leave. But I didn't want to run the raft in the daytime without anybody aboard to answer questions but me; so I didn't want the plan to begin working till pretty late tonight. I says:

"Miss Mary Jane, I'll tell you what we'll do, and you won't have to stay at Mr. Lothrop's so long, nuther. How fur is it?"

"A little short of four miles—right out in the country, back here."

"Well, that'll answer. Now you go along out there, and lay low till nine or half past tonight, and then get them to fetch you home again—tell them you've thought of something. If you get here before eleven put a candle in this window, and if I don't turn up wait *till* eleven, and *then* if I don't turn up it means I'm gone, and out of the way, and safe. Then you come out and spread the news around, and get these beats jailed."

"Good," she says, "I'll do it."

"And if it just happens so that I don't get away, but get took up along with them, you must up and say I told you the whole thing beforehand, and you must stand by me all you can."

"Stand by you! indeed I will. They sha'n't touch a hair of your head!" she says, jumping up and making a pass or two by that window. *Jesus!*

"If I get away I sha'n't be here," I says, "to prove these rapscallions ain't your uncles, and I couldn't

do it if I *was* here. I could swear they was beats and
worse, that's all, though that's worth something.
Well, there's others can do that better than what I
can, and they're people that ain't going to be doubted
as quick as I'd be. I'll tell you how to find them.
Gimme a pencil and a piece of paper." She done it,
and I wrote down "*Burning Shame, Bricksville,*" and
told her to put it away until the people here wanted
something on those two. All they had to do was send
up to Bricksville and say they'd got the men that
played the "Burning Shame," and ask for some
witnesses, and they'd have the whole town down on
them in three shakes of a sheep's tail. And they'd
come a-biling, too.

I judged we had got everything fixed about right
now, so I says:

"Just let the auction go right along, and don't
worry. Nobody don't have to pay for the things they
buy till a whole day after the auction on accounts of
the short notice, and they ain't going out of this till
they get that money; and the way we've fixed it the
sale ain't going to count, and they ain't going to *get*
no money. It's just like the way it was with the
niggers—it warn't no sale, and the niggers will be
back before long. Why, they can't collect the money
for the *niggers* yet—they're in the worst kind of a fix,
Miss Mary."

"Well," she says, "I'll run down to breakfast now,
and then I'll start straight for Mr. Lothrop's."

" 'Deed, *that* ain't the ticket, Miss Mary Jane," I
says, "by no manner of means; go *before* breakfast."

"Why?"

"What did you reckon I wanted you to go at all
for, Miss Mary?"

"Well, I never thought—and come to think, I don't know. What was it?"

"Why, it's because you ain't one of these leather-faced people. I don't want no better book than what your face is. A body can set down and read it off like print in a book. Do you reckon you can go and face you uncles when they come to kiss you good-morning, and never—"

"There, there, don't! Yes, I'll go before breakfast—I'll be glad to. And leave my sisters with them?"

"Yes; never mind about them. They've got to stand it yet awhile. They might suspicion something if all of you was to go. I don't want you to see them, nor your sisters, nor nobody in this town; if a neighbor was to ask how is your uncles this morning your face would tell something. No, you go right along, Miss Mary Jane, and I'll fix it with all of them. I'll tell Miss Susan to give your love to your uncles and say you've went away for a few hours for to get a little rest and change, or to see a friend, and you'll be back tonight or early in the morning."

"Gone to see a friend is all right, but I won't have my love given to them."

"Well, then, it sha'n't be." It was well enough to tell *her* so—no harm in it. It was only a little thing to do, and no trouble; and it's the little things that smooths people's roads the most; it would make Mary Jane comfortable, and it wouldn't cost nothing. Then I says: "There's one more thing—that bag of money."

"Well, they've got that; and it makes me feel pretty silly to think *how* they got it."

"No, you're out, there. They hain't got it."

"Why, who's got it?"

"I wish I knowed, but I don't. I *had* it, because I stole it from them; and I stole it to give to you; and I know where I hid it, but I'm afraid it ain't there no more. I'm awful sorry, Miss Mary Jane, I'm just as sorry as I can be; but I done the best I could; I did, honest. I come nigh getting caught, and I had to shove it into the first place I come to, and run — and it warn't a good place."

"Oh, stop blaming yourself — it's too bad to do it, and I won't allow it — you couldn't help it; it wasn't your fault. Where *did* you hide it?"

I didn't want to set her to thinking about her troubles again; and I couldn't seem to get my mouth to tell her what would make her see that corpse laying in the coffin with that bag of money on his stomick. So for a minute I didn't say nothing; then I says:

"I'd ruther not *tell* you where I put it, Miss Mary Jane, if you don't mind letting me off; but I'll write it for you on a piece of paper, and you can read it along the road to Mr. Lothrop's, if you want to. Do you reckon that'll do?"

"Oh, yes."

So I wrote: "I put it in the coffin. It was in there when you was crying there, away in the night. I was behind the door, and I was mighty sorry for you, Miss Mary Jane."

It made my eyes water a little to remember her crying there all by herself in the night, and them bastards laying there right under her own roof, shaming her and robbing her; and when I folded it up and give it to her I see the water come into her eyes, too; and she shook me by the hand, hard, and says:

"*Good*-by. I'm going to get dressed now, and then

I shall do everything just as you've told me; and if I don't ever see you again, I sha'n't ever forget you, Adolphus, and I'll think of you a many and a many a time, and I'll *pray* for you, too!"

Pray for me! I reckoned if she knowed me she'd take a job that was more nearer her size. But I bet she done it, just the same — she was just that kind. She had the grit to pray for Judas if she took the notion — there warn't no back-down to her, I judge. You may say what you want to, but in my opinion she had more damned sand in her than any girl I ever see; in my opinion she was just full of sand. It sounds like flattery, but it ain't no flattery. And when it comes to beauty, both inside and out, she lays over them all. I hain't ever seen her since she let me out of her room that morning and shut the door behind me; no, I hain't ever seen her since, but I reckon I've thought of her a many and a many a million times. All I have to do is close my eyes and I can see her there, standing in front of that window in a glory of light and nothing else, or rising up in her cotton nightgown like a queen and telling me she would pray for me; and if ever I'd a thought it would do any good for me to pray for *her*, damned if I wouldn't a done it or bust.

Well, I felt squoggy as a sponge when I left her, and I crept down the back stairs and out into the yard. There was her window, and there was a big oak tree growing hard by it, and I knew all I had to do was scramble up it to get a look at Mary Jane jay-bird naked. Time was I'd a been powerful curious what she looked like in nothing but her red hair, but now I just couldn't do it. Lots of fellers would have jumped at the chance, I know. Hellfire, many's the time I've

clumb a tree to do the same back in St. Petersburg.
Tom Sawyer and me used to shin up a clothes pole
regular to take a look at Miss Hattie Pettigrew getting
ready for bed, and she warn't a patch on Mary Jane.
And if I had just been passing through, and some
feller had come up and told me for a nickel he'd
show me where I could get a look at a naked red-
haired lady, you can bet I'd a paid and come a-running. But this was different. This was Mary Jane
Wilks, and I'd a punched the eyes out of any son-of-a-
bitch that I see creeping around *her* window, you
can bet!

Still, I was powerful randy, just the same, so I lit
out into the woods behind the tanyard and pulled
pudding. It didn't take long, but I warn't doing it
for fun, just to ease my burden a bit. Hell, I could
feel it in my *teeth*, that's how bad it was, and I knew
I would spend the whole day mooning about thinking
of Mary Jane in her nightgown unless I done it.

Well, I felt much better afterwards, all kind of
happy and relaxed. When I got back, Mary Jane had
already gone, and Susan and the hare-lip was looking for her and asked me if I had seen her. I says:

"Yes, and I brung a message from her to you.
She says, 'Tell them to give Uncle Harvey and William my love and a kiss, and say I've run over the
river to see Mr. — Mr. — what *is* the name of that rich
family your uncle Peter used to think so much of? — I
mean the one that —

"Why, you must mean the Apthorps, ain't it?"

"Of course; bother them kind of names, a body
can't ever seem to remember them, half the time,
somehow. Yes, she said, say she has run over for to
ask the Apthorps to be sure and come to the auction

and buy this house, because she allowed her uncle Peter would ruther they had it than anybody else; and she's going to stick to them till they say they'll come, and then, if she ain't too tired, she's coming home; and if she is, she'll be home in the morning anyway. She said, don't say nothing about it to anybody else, because she didn't want the neighbors to find out, because it warn't none of their business who she wanted to buy the house."

"All right," they said, and cleared out to lay for their uncles, and give them the love and the kisses, and tell them the message. It went against me to give them bastards such sweet dessert and coffee, but I knew it would hold them, thinking Mary Jane was off working for the auction. There hadn't been too much interest in the town for the sale ever since they busted up that nigger family.

I felt pretty damn good; I judged I had done it very neat — I reckoned Tom Sawyer couldn't a done it no neater himself. Of course he would a throwed more style into it, but I can't do that very handy, not being brung up to it.

Well, they held the auction in the public square, along towards the end of the afternoon, and it strung along, and strung along, and the old man he was on hand and looking his level pisonest, up there alongside of the auctioneer, and chipping in a little Scripture now and then, or a little goody-goody saying of some kind, and whenever things warn't going too well, he would say Jest wait till my brother's good friend Apthorp shows up, and then you'll see some fancy bidding, which was what he warn't supposed to mention, but what can you expect of such a damned rapscallion as him! I was in a sweat the whole time, for fear that the Apthorps *would* show up, but they didn't. The duke, of course, he was around too, goo-gooing for sympathy all he knowed how, and just spreading himself generly. It was an uncomfortable time, all around.

But by and by the thing dragged through, and everything was sold—everything but a little old trifling lot in the graveyard. So they'd got to work *that* off—I never see such a goddamned billy-goat as the king was for wanting to swallow *everything*. Well, whilst they was at it a steamboat landed, and in about two minutes up comes a crowd a-whooping and yelling and laughing and carrying on, and singing out:

"*Here's* your opposition line! here's your two sets o' heirs to old Peter Wilks—and you pays your money and you takes your choice!"

XXVIII

I light out in the storm

They was fetching a very nice-looking old gentleman along, and a nice-looking younger one, with his right arm in a sling. And, my Christ, how the people yelled and laughed, and kept it up. But I didn't see no damn joke about it, and I judged it would strain the duke and the king some to see any. I reckoned they'd turn pale. But no, nary a pale did *they* turn. The duke he never let on he suspicioned what was up, but just went a goo-gooing around, happy and satisfied, like a jug that's googling out buttermilk; and as for the king, he just gazed and gazed down sorrowful on them newcomers like it give him the stomick-ache in his very heart to think there could be such frauds and rascals in the world. Oh, he done it admirable. Lots of the principal people gethered around the king, to let him see they was on his side. That old gentleman that had just come looked all puzzled to death. Pretty soon he begun to speak, and I see straight off he pronounced *like* an Englishman—not the king's way, though the king's *was* pretty dang good for an imitation. I can't give the old gent's words, nor I can't imitate him; but he turned around to the crowd, and says, about like this:

"This is a surprise to me which I wasn't looking for; and I'll acknowledge, candid and frank, I ain't very well fixed to meet it and answer it; for my brother and me has had misfortunes; he's broke his arm, and our baggage got put off at a town above here last night in the night by a mistake. I am Peter Wilks's brother Harvey, and this is his brother William, which can't hear nor speak—and can't even make signs to amount to much, now't he's only got one hand to work them with. We are who we say we are; and in a day or two, when I get the baggage, I can prove it. But up till then I won't say nothing more, but go to the hotel and wait."

So him and the new dummy started off; and the king he laughs, and blethers out:

"Broke his arm—*very* likely *ain't* it? —and very convenient, too, for a fraud that's got to make signs, and ain't learnt how. Lost their baggage! That's *mighty* good!—and mighty ingenious—under the *circumstances!*"

So he laughed again; and so did everybody else, except three or four, or maybe half a dozen. One of these was that doctor; another one was a sharp-looking gentleman, with a carpet-bag of the old-fashioned kind made out of carpet-stuff, that had just come off of the steamboat and was talking to him in a low voice, and glancing towards the king now and then and nodding their heads—it was Levi Bell, the lawyer that was gone up to Louisville; and another one was a big rough husky that come along and listened to all the old gentlemen said, and was listening to the king now. And when the king got done this husky up and says:

"Say, looky here; if you are Harvey Wilks, when'd you come to this town?"

"The day before the funeral, friend," says the king.

"But what time o' day?"

"In the evenin'—'bout an hour er two before sundown."

"How'd you come?"

"I come down on the *Susan Powell* from Cincinnati."

"Well, then, how'd you come to be up at the Pint in the *mornin'*—in a canoe?"

"I warn't up at the Pint in the mornin'."

"It's a lie."

Several of them jumped for him and begged him not to talk that way to an old man and a preacher.

"Preacher be damned, he's a fraud and a liar. He was up at the Pint that mornin'. I live up there, don't I? Well, I was up there, and he was up there. I see him there. He come in a canoe, along with Tim Collins and a boy."

I started to slink out of there, but it was too late. The doctor made a grab for my arm and hauled me up before the husky. He says:

"Would you know the boy again if you was to see him, Hines?"

"Why, I reckon that's him," says Hines. "I know him perfectly easy, bein' as you don't see a boy as downright *ugly* as that very often."

Well, that give the crowd a laugh, and I says, "Mr.

Hines, you better damn well watch out, if you know what's good for you." I'd a said it out loud, except the doctor cut right in. He says:

"Neighbors, I don't know whether the new couple is frauds or not; but if *these* two ain't frauds, I am an idiot, that's all. I think it's our duty to see that they don't get away from here till we've looked into this thing. Come along, Hines; come along, the rest of you. We'll take these fellows to the tavern and affront them with t'other couple, and I reckon we'll find out *something* before we get through.

It was nuts for the crowd, though maybe not for the king's friends; so we all started. It was about sundown. The doctor he led me along by the hand, and was plenty kind enough, but he never let *go* my damn hand.

We all got in a big room in the hotel, and lit up some candles, and fetched in the new couple. First, the doctor says:

"I don't wish to be too hard on these two men, but *I* think they're frauds, and they may have complices that we don't know nothing about. If they have, won't the complices get away with that bag of gold Peter Wilks left? It ain't unlikely. If these men arn't frauds, they won't object to sending for that money and letting us keep it till they prove they're all right — ain't that so?"

Everybody agreed to that. So I judged they had our gang in a pretty darn tight place right at the out-start. I was skairt, that I know, and my innards begun to churn, but the king he only looked sorrowful, and says:

"Gentlemen, I wish the money was there, for I ain't got no disposition to throw anything in the way

of a fair, open, out-and-out investigation o' this mis-
able business; but, alas, the money ain't there; you
k'n send and see, if you want to."

"Where is it, then?"

"Well, when my dear niece give it to me to keep
for her I took and hid it inside o' the straw tick o' my
bed, not wishin' to bank it for the few days we'd be
here, and considerin' the bed a safe place, we not
bein' used to niggers, and suppos'n' 'em honest, like
servants in England. The niggers stole it the very
next mornin' after I had went down-stairs to give
comfort to the girls; and when I sold 'em I hadn't
missed the money yit, bein' so trustful and all, so
they got clean away with it. My valley here k'n tell
you 'bout it, gentlemen."

The doctor and several said "Shucks!" and I see
nobody didn't altogether believe him, which was
funny, because the king *was* telling the truth now, as
least as far as *he* knew. One man asked me if I see
the niggers steal it. I said no, but I see them sneaking
out of the room and hustling away, and I never
thought nothing, only I reckoned they was afraid they
had waked up my master and was trying to get away
before he made trouble with them. That was all they
asked me. Then the doctor whirls on me and says:

"Are *you* English, too?"

I says yes; and him and some others laughed, and
said "Stuff!" Hines says "Bullshit!" and lets rip with
a horse-laugh, for which I didn't admire him none the
more.

Well, the king butt in then, and says it was time to
put away all pretextions, and come out with the
truth, no matter where the chips landed. He said that
I *warn't* English, and that old Hines *had* seen him

and me in a canoe, only not with anybody named Collins, but his dear brother, William. He said his money
and baggage had been stole in Cairo, and that he had
been put off the steamboat somewhere below there,
and that this boy had come along in his canoe and
had kindly offered to paddle them to where they was
going, on credit so to speak, and that he had decided
to adopt him, who was an orphan, as his valley. He
said he was ashamed to come before his dear relations a temporary bankrupt, though he had plenty
left in England, so he had tried to conceal his shame
by pretending to come on the boat all the way with
the little money he had left in his pockets, and he was
sorry now that he had done it, because the man who
was rich in his friends need not worry about an empty
purse. And when he said it, he give the words a
mouthy sound like it was from Scripture, which I'm
sure it warn't, but it didn't make no difference because you could see he had already taken that trick,
and the crowd—most of them, leastwise—was on his
side again. Old Hines he grumbled that he thought he
knew the difference between Tim Collins and a
dummy, but somebody said *he* didn't rightly know
there *was* any, and everybody laughed except Hines,
who got mad and shoved himself out of the crowd.

Well, the doctor he persisted, even though the
crowd had its mind near made up, so they sailed in on
the genral investigation anyways, and there we had it,
up and down, and nobody never said a word about
supper, nor ever seemed to think about it—and
so they kept it up, and kept it up; and it *was* the
damnedest mixed-up thing you ever see. They made
the king tell his yarn, and they made the old gentleman tell his'n; and anybody but a lot of prejudiced

chuckleheads would a *seen* that the old gentleman was spinning truth and t'other one lies. And by and by they had me up to tell what I knowed. The king he give me a lefthanded look out of the corner of his eye, and so I knowed enough to talk on the right side, but I didn't get pretty fur till the doctor begun to laugh; and Levi Bell, the lawyer, says:

"Set down, my boy: I wouldn't strain myself if I was you. I reckon you ain't used to lying, it don't seem to come in handy; what you want is practice. You do it pretty awkward."

I didn't care nothing for the compliment, but I was glad to be let off, anyway. The doctor he started to say something, and turns and says:

"If you had been in town at first, Levi Bell—"

The king broke in and reached out his hand, and says:

"Why, is this my poor dead brother's old friend that he's wrote so often about?"

The lawyer stood there, looking at the king's hand; he never took it, but you could see he was doing some thinking, and then he reached down and picked up his carpet-bag which he opened. He says:

"I reckon we can get this cleared up mighty fast."

Well, the king kinder drooped his hand, and then lay it on the table and leaned on it, as if that was what he meant to do all along, and I could see he was trying hard not to be bothered by what Levi Bell was taking out of his bag, which was a packet of letters.

The lawyer says to him:

"These here is some letters which Peter Wilks's brothers wrote from England, and if you are who you say you are, it's easy proved."

The king looked sold and damn foolish, I tell you,

when he see how it was him that dealt the lawyer
sech a hand, but he went and took the pen and paper
which they give him and set down and twisted his
head to one side, and chawed his tongue, and
scrawled off something which he handed the lawyer
with a smile which anybody could see warn't what he
wanted it to be; and then they give the pen to the
duke, who was looking mighty sick. But he took the
pen and wrote, and give it back to the lawyer, who
turns to the new old gentleman and says:

"You and your brother please write a line or two
and sign your names.

The old gentleman wrote, but nobody couldn't read
it. The lawyer looked powerful damned astonished,
and says:

"Well, it beats me. Anybody can see that the
writing on Harvey's letters don't match *this*"
(meaning the king's and the duke's) "and here's *this*
old gentleman's handwriting, and anybody can tell,
easy enough, *he* didn't write them—fact is, the
scratches he makes ain't properly *writing* at all.
Now here's some letters from—"

The new old gentleman says:

"If you please, let me explain. Nobody can read
my hand but my menuensis, who makes copies for
me. It's *his* hand you've got there, not mine."

"*Well!*" says the lawyer, "this *is* a state of things.
I've got some of William's letters, too; so if you'll get
him to write a line or so we can com—"

"He *can't* write with his left hand," says the old
gentleman. "If he could use his right hand, you
would see that he wrote his own letters, but it's
broke, as I have told you."

"Yas, *broke*!" says the king. "Convenient, hain't

it? *Very*." He drew himself up and looked around, as if that proved everything in his favor. He says:

"Well, the menstruensis tale is int'restin', but it so happens that most people in England uses one. *I* use one, an' my dear brother William here uses one. All our fren's uses menstruensises, and so do all o' *their* fren's. It's the style in England, and I'm surprised that folks in a town as fashionable and modern as this 'un don't use 'em too. It saves a heap o' time."

And so he warmed up and went warbling right along till he was actuly beginning to believe all that crap he was saying *himself*; but pretty soon the new gentleman broke in, and says:

"I've thought of something. Is there anybody here that helped to lay out my br—helped to lay out the late Peter Wilks for burying?"

"Yes," says somebody, "me and Ab Turner done it. We're both here."

"Perhaps this gentleman can tell me what was tattooed on his breast?"

Damned if the king didn't have to brace up mighty quick, or he'd a squshed down like a bluff bank that the river had cut under, it took him so sudden; and, mind you, it was a thing that was calculated to make most *anybody* sqush to get fetched such a solid one as that without any notice, because how was *he* going to know what was tattooed on the man? He whitened a little; he couldn't help it; and it was mighty still in there, and everybody bending a little forrards and gazing at him. Says I to myself, *Now* he'll throw up the sponge—there ain't no more use. Well, did he? A body can't hardly believe it, but he didn't. I reckon he thought he'd keep the thing up till he tired them people out, so they'd thin out, and him and the duke could break loose and get away. Anyway, he set there, and pretty soon he begun to smile, and says:

"Mf! It's a *very* tough question, *ain't* it ! That is if there *was* a tattoo on my dear brother, Peter, which there warn't, so far as I ever knowed. And I must say, that is a pretty old trick, Mr 'Harvey Wilks,' since that's what you calls yourself."

Well, *I* never see anything like that damn old blister for clean out-and-out cheek.

The new old gentleman turns brisk towards Ab Turner and his pard, and his eye lights up like he judged he'd got the king *this* time, and says. "There — you've heard what he said! Now, did you not see on his breast a small dim P, and a B (which is an initial he dropped when he was young), and a W, and dashes between them, so: P—B—W" — and he marked them that way on a piece of paper. "Come, ain't that what you saw?"

Both of them spoke up at once, and says:

"No, we *didn't*. We never see any marks at all."

Well, you should a seen the king spread out at that one, and even the duke begun to perk up a little. Everybody was whooping at once, and there was a rattling powwow, but the lawyer he jumps on the table and yells, and says:

"Gentlemen—gentle*men*! Hear me just a word — just a *single* word — if you PLEASE!"

It took a while, but between him and the doctor they got the crowd calmed down somewhat, though the new old gentleman and his partner got considerable shoved around in the meantime, and there was a large number that was for riding them out of town on a rail right then and there.

The lawyer says:

"It does look bad for these strangers, but for justice to be done, we must go and dig up the corpse and look. It's the only fair way, and the people of Riverton have always been fair and square with every man and give him every chance to prove himself innocent."

That took them.

"Hooray!" they all shouted, and was starting right off; but the lawyer and the doctor sung out:

"Hold on, hold on! Collar all these four men and the boy, and fetch *them* along, too!"

"We'll do it!" somebody shouted; "and whoever's been lying, we'll give 'em a fair trial before we lynch 'em!"

The king tried to object to anybody's messing around with the remainders of the dearly departed, but the uproar was so great you could hardly hear him, and the duke sidled up and give him a punch in the ribs and an eye, and I knew he was saying, Shet up you old fool—our best chance is to run for it as soon as we can. I could see that he was scared, and *I* was scared, too, I tell you. My guts was in an uproar, and I wanted nothing more than to find a place and let go, but there warn't no getting away, you know. They gripped us all, and marched us right along, straight for the graveyard, which was a mile and a half down the river, and the whole town at our heels, for we made noise enough, and it was only nine in the evening.

As we went by our house I wished I hadn't sent Mary Jane out of town; because now if I could tip her the wink she'd light out and save me, and blow on our dead-beats.

Well, we swarmed along down the river road, just

carrying on like wildcats; and to make it more scary the sky was darking up, and the lightning beginning to wink and flitter, and the wind to shiver amongst the leaves. This was the most awful damn trouble and most dangersome I ever was in; and I was kinder stunned; everything was going so different from what I had allowed for; stead of being fixed so I could take my own time if I wanted to, and see all the fun, and have Mary Jane at my back to save me and set me free when the close-fit come, here was nothing in the world betwixt me and sudden death but just them tattoo-marks. If they *did* find them, I was a goner, sure as shit.

I couldn't bear to think about it; and yet, somehow, I couldn't think about nothing else, and the whole time my innards was getting worse and worse, and I knew that if I didn't do something soon, I would have to let go right in my damn britches. It got darker and darker, and it was a beautiful time to give the crowd the slip; but that big husky had me by the wrist—Hines—and a body might as well try to give Goliar the slip. He dragged me right along, he was so damn excited, and I had to run to keep up.

When they got there they swarmed into the grave-yard and washed over it like an overflow. And when they got to the grave they found they had about a hundred times as many shovels as they wanted, but nobody hadn't thought to fetch a lantern. But they sailed into digging anyway by the flicker of the lightning, and sent a man to the nearest house, a half a mile off, to borrow one.

So they dug and dug like everything; and it got awful dark, and the rain started, and the wind swished and swushed along, and the lightning come brisker and brisker, and the thunder boomed out reglar ball-busters; but them people never took no notice of it, they was so full of this business; and one minute you could see everything and every face in that big crowd, and the shovelfuls of dirt sailing up out of the grave, and the next second the dark wiped it all out, and you couldn't see nothing at all.

At last they got out the coffin and begun to unscrew the lid, and then such another damn crowding and shouldering and shoving as there was, to scrouge in and get a sight, you never see; and in the dark, that way, it was hell. Hines he hurt my wrist dreadful pulling and tugging so, and I reckon he clean forgot I was in the world, he was so excited and panting, and my innards was griping me so, I most wished I *warn't.*

All of a sudden the lightning let go a rip-snorting white glare, and somebody sings out;

"By the living Christ, here's the bag of gold on his breast!"

Hines let out a whoop, like everybody else, and dropped my wrist and give a big surge to bust his way in and get a look, and the way I lit out and shinned for the road in the dark there ain't nobody can tell.

I had the road all to myself, and I fairly flew—leastways, I had it all to myself except for the solid dark, and the now-and-then glares, and the buzzing of the rain, and the thrashing of the wind, and the splitting of the thunder; and sure as you are born did I clip it along! I only stopped when I had put a good half mile between me and the graveyard, and then only to duck into the trees and yank my britches down and let go of that goddamn load of agony I had been carrying around since that new old gentleman showed up.

When I struck the town I see there warn't nobody out in the storm, so I never hunted for no back streets, but humped it straight through the main one; and when I begun to get towards our house I aimed my eye and set it. No light there; the house all dark — which made me feel sorry and disappointed, I didn't know why, and then the house and all was behind me in the dark, and warn't ever going to be before me no more in this world. She *was* the best girl I ever see, and had the most sand.

The minute I was far enough above the town to see I could make the towhead, I begun to look sharp for a boat to borrow, and the first time the lightning showed me one that warn't chained I snatched it and shoved. It was a canoe, and warn't fastened with nothing but a rope. The towhead was a rattling big distance off, away out there in the middle of the river, but I didn't lose no time; and when I struck the raft at last I was so damned fagged I would a just laid down to blow and gasp if I could afforded it. But I didn't. As I sprung aboard I sung out:

"Out with you, Jim, and set her loose! Glory be, we're shut of them!"

Jim lit out, and was a-coming for me with both arms spread, he was so full of joy; but when I glimpsed him in the lightning my heart shot up in my mouth and I went overboard backwards; for I forgot he was old King Lear and a sick A-rab all in one, and it most scared the piss out of me. But Jim fished me out, and was going to hug me and bless me, and so on, he was so glad I was back and we was shut of the king and the duke, but I says:

"Not now; have it for breakfast, have it for breakfast! Cut loose and let her slide!"

So in two seconds away we went a-sliding down the river, and it *did* seem so good to be free again and all by ourselves on the big river, and nobody to bother us. I had to skip around a bit, and jump up and crack my heels a few times—I couldn't help it; but about the third crack I noticed a sound that I knowed mighty damn well, and held my breath and listened and waited; and sure enough, when the next flash busted out over the water, here they come!— and just a-laying to their oars and making their skiff hum! It was the king and duke.

So I wilted right down onto the planks then, and give up; and it was all I could do to keep from crying.

XXIX

The gold saves the thieves

When they got aboard the king went for me, and shook me by the collar, and says: "Tryin' to give us the slip, was ye, you damned pup! Tired of our company, hey?"

I says:

"No, your majesty, we warn't — *please* don't, your majesty!"

"Quick, then, and tell us what *was* your idee, or I'll shake the insides out o' you!"

"Honest, I'll tell you everything just as it happened, your majesty. The man that had a-holt of me was very good to me, and kep' saying he had a boy about as big as me that died last year, and he was sorry to see a boy in such a dangerous fix; and when they was all took by surprise by finding the gold, and made a rush for the coffin, he lets go of me and whispers, 'heel it now, or they'll hang ye, sure!' and I lit out. It didn't seem no good for *me* to stay — *I* couldn't do nothing, and I didn't want to be hung if I could get away. So I never stopped running till I found a canoe;

and when I got here I told Jim to hurry, or they'd catch me and hang me yet, and said I was afeared you and the duke warn't alive, now, and was awful sorry, and so was Jim, and was awful damn glad when we see you coming; you may ask Jim if I didn't."

Jim said it was so; and the king told him to shut up, and said, "Oh, yes, it's *mighty* damn likely!" and shook me up again, and said he reckoned he'd drownd me. But the duke says:

"Leggo the boy, you goddamned old idiot! Would *you* a done any different? Did you inquire around for *him* when you got loose? *I* don't remember it."

So the king let go of me, and begun to cuss that town and everybody in it. But the duke says:

"You better a damn sight give *yourself* a good cussing, for you're the one that's entitled to it most. You hain't done a thing from the start that had any frigging sense in it, except coming out lucky on that tattoo-mark, and if them two jakes had been given eyes made out of something besides glass, even that wouldn't a helped none. They'd a jailed us till them goddamn Englishmen's baggage come—and then—the penitentiary, you bet! But that bit o' luck took 'em to the graveyard, and the gold done us a still bigger kindness; for if the excited fools hadn't let go all holts and made that rush to get a look we'd a slept in our cravats tonight—cravats warranted to *wear*, too—longer than *we'd* need 'em."

They was still a minute—thinking; then the king says, kind of absent-minded like:

"Mf! And we reckoned the *niggers* stole it!"

That made me squirm!

"Yes," says the duke, kinder slow and deliberate and sarcastic, "*we* did."

After about a half a minute the king drawls out:
"Leastways, *I* did."
The duke says, the same way:
"On the contrary, *I* did."
The king kind of ruffles up, and says:
"Looky here, Bilgewater, what'n hell 'r you referrin' to?" The duke says, pretty brisk:
"When it comes to that, maybe you'll let me ask what was *you* referring to?"
"Shit!" says the king, very sarcastic; "but *I* don't know—maybe you was asleep, and didn't know what you was about."
The duke bristles up now, and says:
"Oh, for Chrissakes, let *up* on this bullshit; do you take me for a damn fool? Don't you reckon *I* know who hid that money in that coffin?"
"*Yes*, sir! I know you *do* know, because you done it yourself!"
"It's a goddamned lie!"—and the duke went for him. The king sings out:
"Take y'r damn hands off!—leggo my throat!—I take it all back!"
The duke says:
"Well, you just own up, first, that you *did* hide that money there, intending to give me the slip one of these days, and come back and dig it up, and have it all to yourself."
"Wait jest a minute, duke—answer me this one question, honest and fair; if you didn't put the money there, say it, and I'll b'lieve you, and take back everything I said."
"You damned old scoundrel, I didn't, and you know damn well I didn't."
"Well, then, I b'lieve you. But answer me only jest

this one more—now *don't* git mad; didn't you have it in your *mind* to hook the gold and hide it?"

The duke never said nothing for a little bit; then he says:

"Well, I don't care if I *did*, I didn't *do* it, anyway. But you not only had it in mind to do it, b᷎ ᷎ you *done* it."

"I wisht I never die if I done it, duke, and that's the honest-to-Christ truth. I won't say I warn't *goin'* to do it, because I *was*; but you—I mean somebody—got in ahead o' me."

"It's a damn lie! You done it, you old son-of-a-bitch, and you got to *say* you done it, or—"

The king began to gurgle and claw at the duke's hands. It was an awful moment, and I was sure he was about to get killed, but then he gasps out:

" 'Nough!—I *own up*!"

I was awful goddamn glad to hear him say that; it made me feel much more easier than what I was feeling before. So the duke took his hands off and says:

"If you ever deny it again I'll drown you. It's *well* for you to set there and blubber like a baby—it's fitten for you, after the way you've acted, you tunnel-bellied old sewer. I never see such a goddamn old ostrich for wanting to gobble everything—and I a-trusting you all the time, like you was my own father. You ought to been ashamed of yourself to stand by and hear it saddled on to a lot of poor nig-gers, and you never say a word for 'em. It makes me feel ridiculous to think I was soft enough to *believe* that frigging rubbage. Damn you, I can see now why you was so anxious to make up the deffisit—you wanted to get what money I'd got out of the 'Shame' and one thing or another, and scoop it *all*!"

The king says, timid, and still a-snuffling:

"Why duke, it was you that said make up the deffersit; it warn't me."

"Dry up, you old snot-rag! I don't want to hear no more *out* of you!" says the duke. "And *now* you see what you *got* by it. They've got all their own money back, and all of *ourn* but a shekel or two *besides*. G'long to bed, you old fart, and don't you deffersit *me* no more deffersits, long's you *live*."

So the king sneaked into the wigwam and took to his bottle for comfort, and before long the duke tackled his bottle; and so in about a half an hour they was as thick as thieves again, and the tighter they got the lovinger they got, and went off a-snoring in each other's arms. They both got powerful mellow, but I noticed the king didn't get mellow enough to forget to remember to not deny about hiding the money-bag again. That made me feel easy and darn well satisfied. Of course when they got to snoring we had a long gabble, and I told Jim everything.

XXX

You can't pray a lie

W e dasn't stop again at any town for days and days; kept right along down the river. We was down south in the warm weather now, and a mighty long ways from home. We begun to come to trees with Spanish moss on them, hanging down from the limbs like long, gray beards. It was the first I ever see it growing, and it made the woods look solemn and dismal. So now the frauds reckoned they was out of danger, and they begun to work the villages again.

First they done a lecture on temprance, but they didn't make enough for them both to get drunk on. Then in another village they started a dancing-school; but they didn't know no more how to dance than a dang kangaroo; so the first prance they made the genral public jumped in and pranced them out of town. Another time they tried to go at yellocution; but they didn't yellocute long till the audience got up and give them a solid good cussing, and made them skip out and leave the take behind. They tackled missionarying, and mesmerizing, and doctoring, and telling fortunes, and a little of everything; but they couldn't seem to have no damn luck. So at last they got just about dead broke, and laid around the raft as she floated along, thinking and thinking, and never saying nothing, by the half a day at a time, and dreadful blue and desperate.

And at last they took a change and begun to lay their heads together in the wigwam and talk low and confidential two or three hours at a time. Jim and me got damned uneasy. We didn't like the look of it. We judged they was studying up some kind of worse deviltry then ever. We turned it over and over, and at last we made up our minds they was going to break into somebody's house or store, or was going into the counterfeit-money business, or something. So then we was pretty goddamn scared, and made up an agreement that we wouldn't have nothing in the world to do with such actions, and if we ever got the least show we would give them the cold shake and clear out and leave them behind. I had seen enough of that king to know his threats wouldn't hold no more water than a blame sieve, and the duke wouldn't harm us none anyway. Besides, the river was so big down there, and there was a jillion dang creeks and swamps and places to hide for months at a time, that I knew they'd never find us once we cut out.

Well, early one morning we hid the raft in a good, safe place about two mile below a little bit of a shabby Lousiana village, and the king he went ashore and told us all to stay hid whilst he went up to town and smelt around to see if anybody had got wind of the "Burning Shame" there yet. ("House to rob, you mean," says I to myself.) And he said he would be sure to be back by midday with the news, good or bad.

So we stayed where we was. The duke he fretted
and sweated around, and was in a mighty sour way.
He scolded us for everything, and we couldn't seem
to do nothing right; he found fault with every little
thing. Something was a-brewing, sure as hell. When
noon come, and no king, I thought sure he would take
me up to town with him, and that would be the chance
I needed to break and run for it whilst he was looking
for the king, but no, he sent me on up alone to find
out what had happened.

Well, I found the village and hunted around there
for the king, and by and by I found him in the back
room of a little low doggery very tight, and a lot of
loafers bullyragging him for sport, and he a-cussing
and a-threatening with all his might, telling them
they better give him his money back, or *else*, but he
was so drunk he couldn't walk, and couldn't do
nothing to them. He didn't see me, and I didn't want
him to. I lit out of there and ran on down the river
road, but I hadn't gone more'n half a mile before I
met the duke, coming around a bend. He was carrying his own carpet-bag and the king's, and seemed
tolerable surprised to see me. He asked where the
king was, and I told him, and he whitened up and
grabbed a-holt of my shirt.

"Drunk, is he? And what about the money?"
I says:

"Well, I didn't know he *had* any money, but when
I was there he was accusing everybody of taking it
from him."

The duke he groaned and turned me loose. He
headed toward town without paying me any more
heed, and I took off down the road like a deer, for I
see our chance; and I made up my mind that it would

be a damn long day before they ever see me and Jim
again, even if we had to let go of the raft and take to
the canoe. They could have all our truck; it was
just a burden, anyhow.

But then, another mile on, I met some boys about
my own age, coming up the road, so I slowed down
not to let on I was in a hurry, but I couldn't keep
from panting a little, and I was all red and sweaty
anyhow. There was one boy ahead of the others, and
he waved to me and says:

"No sense in runnin'; it's all over anyways."
Well, I stopped and he stopped, and I says:
"*What's* all over?"

He had on a old straw hat and was considerable
freckled. The sun come down through the holes in
the brim and added so to the genral confusion you
couldn't hardly find his face. I guess he had a nose
and the rest, but it was like a rabbit laying low in the
brush — you had to take it on faith. He says:

"Why, they caught a runaway nigger! Didn't you
hear?"

I don't exactly remember what I said just then. I
felt awful, *knowing* it was Jim they had got, but not
wanting to know it. Maybe I didn't say anything. By
then they was all around me, everybody talking
at once:

"They drug him to Silas Phelps's place, down-
river!"

"But it warn't easy, no sir!"

"I never see a nigger with so much danged fight
in him!"

"It took a heap o' doing to git the chains on him!"

"They was five men a-setting on him — "

"And three others was knocked silly!"

Freckle-face says:

"He run off f'm down South, som'ers, an' fought like the very devil to keep f'm gettin' tuk back!"

Then they all looked at me to say something. I says, very weak:

"It's a good job they got him."

"Well, I *reckon*!" says freckle-face. "There's two hundr'd dollars reward on him."

That was it; they didn't have to tell me no more. But they did. They told me how an old man come up to town and said he and his friend was just passing through, and this nigger had jumped out at them and tried to rob them, but they hadn't even got steamboat fare. They recognized him from a bill they'd picked up in Orleans, and let on they was Ab'lition preachers from Cincinnati, and they would help him get free as soon as they got in touch with a man they knew in town who was with the Underground Railway, and so one of them—the young one—stayed behind with the nigger while the old one went into town to get help. He sold out their chance in the nigger for forty dollars to Phelps, because he said they got to go on up the river and couldn't wait. He said he warn't interested in the money so much as he was in seeing the rightful owner get his nigger back. He said that was always his way.

"Think o' that now!" says Freckle-face. "You bet *I'd* wait, if it was seven year."

"That's me, every time," I says. "But maybe his chance ain't worth no more than that, if he'll sell it so cheap. Maybe there's something ain't straight about it."

"But it *is*, though—straight as a string. I see the handbill myself, It tells all about him, to a dot—

paints him like a picture, and tells the plantation he's frum, below Newr*leans*. Nosiree-*bob*, they ain't no trouble 'bout *that* speculation, you bet you. Say, gimme me a chaw tobacker, won't ye?"

I said I didn't have none, and begun to get uneasy, because I could *feel* him staring at me out of all them freckles. Then he says:

"You from these parts? *I* hain't never seed you before."

I told them I was from someplace up-river, and was visiting my aunt here in town. I started to tell them more, but they was in a powerful hurry to get back to town with the news, and couldn't stop to listen, so they went one way and me another. As soon as I could I cut into the trees and lay down and cried. It was weak of me, but I couldn't help it. Them two sons-a-bitches had sold Jim out, after we had done everything they said, and stuck by them, and *all*. It was too much to bear, and I cried till I was dry.

Then the thought come to me that those skunks would be coming back to the raft as soon as the king could stay on his feet, so I got moving again. But when I got back to the raft I see there warn't no sense in hurrying—they had cleaned the place out. All our traps was thrown around and scattered and they had even busted open the ticks, hoping maybe to find more money. They had left the pots and pans and the clothes, such like truck, but all the money was gone, every cent. Well, after doing such an ornery thing as that, I didn't believe they'd ever come back, but there was no telling what them pricks would do. They was solid brass, from top to bottom. So I shoved off out of there right away and didn't rest easy till I come to a little woody island where I could lay low.

If they did come after me, they wouldn't take time to search around every towhead or island on the way, but would go a-booming down the river and count on finding me drifting along like the last time.

After I had got things shipshape again and covered with branches, I crept into the wigwam for a smoke and a think. But I couldn't come to nothing. I thought till I wore my head sore, but I couldn't see no way out of the trouble. After all this long journey, and after all we'd done for the goddamn cocksuckers, here it was all come to nothing, everything all busted up and ruined, because they could have the heart to serve Jim such a low-down mean trick as that, and make him a slave again all his life, and amongst strangers, too, for forty dirty dollars. I didn't care about the money they took; I'd a gave it to them if they'd asked.

Once I said to myself it would be a thousand times better for Jim to be a slave at home where his family was, as long as he'd *got* to be a slave, and so I'd better write a letter to Tom Sawyer and tell him to tell the widow where he was. But I soon give up that notion for two things: she'd be mad and disgusted at his rascality and ungratefulness for leaving her, and so she'd sell him straight down the river again; and if she didn't, everybody naturally despises an ungrateful nigger, and they'd make Jim feel it all the time, and so he'd feel ornery and disgraced. And then think of *me*! It would get all around that Huck Finn helped a nigger to get his freedom; and if I was ever to see anybody from that town again I'd be ready to get down and lick his boots for shame. That's just the way: a person does a low-down thing, and then he don't want to take no consequences of it. Thinks as long as he can hide, it ain't no disgrace. That was my fix exactly. The more I studied about this the more my damn conscience went to grinding me, and the more wicked and low-down and ornery I got to feeling. And at last, when it hit me all of a sudden that here was the plain hand of Providence slapping me in the face and letting me know my wickedness was being watched all the time, whilst I was stealing a poor old widow's nigger that hadn't ever done me no harm, and now was showing me there's One that's always on the lookout, and ain't a-going to allow no such miserable doings to go only just so fur and no further, I most dropped in my tracks I was so goddamn scared.

Well, I tried the best I could to kinder soften it up somehow for myself by saying I was brung up wicked, and so I warn't so much to blame; but something inside of me kept saying, "You know better; you knowed all along that people that acts the way you've been acting about that nigger goes to everlasing Hell-fire."

It made me shiver. And I about made up my mind to pray, and see if I couldn't try to quit being the kind of boy I was and be better. So I kneeled down. But the words wouldn't come. Why wouldn't they? It warn't no use to try and hide it from Him. Nor from *me*, neither. I knowed very well why they wouldn't come. It was because my heart warn't right; it was because I warn't square; it was because I was playing double. I was letting *on* to give up sin, but away inside of me I was holding on to the biggest one of all. I was trying to make my mouth *say* I would do the right thing and the clean thing, and go and write to that nigger's owner and tell where he was;

but deep down in me I knowed it was a damned lie, and He knowed it. You can't pray a lie—I found that out.

So I was full of trouble, full as I could be; and didn't know what to do. At last I had an idea; and I says, I'll go and write the letter—and *then* see if I can pray. Why, it was astonishing, the way I felt as light as a danged feather straight off, and my troubles all gone. So I got a piece of paper and a pencil, all glad and excited, and set down and wrote:

> Dear Widow Douglas, your runaway nigger Jim is down here two mile below Pikesville, and Mr Phelps has got him and he will give him up for the reward if you send.
> Yours truly, Huck Finn.

I felt good and all washed clean of sin for the first time I had ever felt so in my life, and I knowed I could pray now. But I didn't do it straight off, but laid the paper down and set there thinking—thinking how good it was all this happened so, and how near I come to being lost and going to hell. And went on thinking. And got to thinking over our trip down the river; and I see Jim before me all the time: in the day and in the night-time, sometimes moonlight, sometimes storms, and us a-floating along, talking and singing and laughing. But somehow I couldn't seem to strike no places to harden me against him, but only the other kind. I'd see him standing my watch on top of his'n, 'stead of calling me, so I could go on sleeping; and see how glad he was when I come back out of the fog; and when I come to him again in the swamp, up there where the feud was; and such-like times; and I think how he would always call me honey, and pet me, and do everything he could think of for me, and how good he always was;

and at last I struck the time I saved him by telling the men we had small-pox aboard, and he was so grateful, and said I was the best friend old Jim ever had in the world, and the *only* one he's got now; and then I happened to look around and see that damned paper.

It was a close place. I took it up, and held it in my hand. I was a-trembling, because I'd got to decide, forever, betwixt two things, and I knowed it. I studied a minute, sort of holding my breath, and then says to myself:

"All right, then, I'll *go* to hell" — and tore it up.

It was awful thoughts and awful words, but they was said. And I let them stay said; and never thought no more about reforming. I shoved the whole thing out of my head, and said I would take up wickedness again, which was in my line, being brung up to it, and the other warn't. And for a starter I would go to work and steal Jim out of slavery again; and if I could think up anything worse, I would do that, too; because as long as I was in, and in for good, I might as well go the whole hog.

XXXI

What happened at the saw mill

Well, I slept like a dead man that night, and woke up after the birds did. The sky was heavy and grayish, and even that early the air was so warm that your skin got prickly with sweat if you budged. The sun was trying hard to break through, but all it could manage was a sickly chalky streak along the East, low down, and the rest of the sky was a washed-out lead color, like old flannel. It pressed on you, and even the damn birds felt it, and seemed to chirp no more than they had to, and then without much heart for it. A day like that meant trouble or tornadoes, pap used to say, and it was best to stay in a hole till it was over. But time was a-wasting, so I crawled out and rummaged up something for breakfast. Then I squatted on the downstream end of the raft to take a dump and figure what to do next.

From where the raft was tied I got a good view of the Louisiana side, for maybe a mile or so down the next bend. There was this little steam-sawmill on the bank there, where they had wood stacked and a landing. That seemed a likely spot to start soundings for the place where they had got Jim locked up. I didn't have no real plan. I reckoned one would come along when I needed it.

So I put on my store clothes, and tied up a few traps in a bundle, and took the canoe and cleared for the mill. There warn't nobody about, but it didn't matter none, because painted right across the front was "Phelps Wood Yard," so as to let the steamboats see it, and I knowed I was somewheres near the farm where they had Jim. About a half mile further down there was a clump of cottonwoods running out into the easy water, and I figured to run in there and hide the canoe whilst I poked around a bit. But I hadn't no more'n cleared the mill before there come a power of whooping and hollering from the shore, gun-shots and dogs barking to beat hell. I dug out for the channel, not wanting anybody to see me using around there just then. But that was a mistake.

Because when I was already a hundred yards out somebody come a-crashing through the willow thickets—and I see it was Jim! He was all bloody and his clothes was tore up awful. They had been pushing him hard, and he was all weighted down with chains, too. He took one wild look around and seen me out in the river. He didn't say a word, he didn't even wave, he just charged ahead like he was a-going to run all the way, right off the cut bank. It was more'n fifteen feet high there, a reglar bluff, and he went down like a goddamn stone. I thought he was a goner, sure, but I turned the canoe around anyway and come a-booming back in; I hadn't gone very far when a crowd of men and dogs come busting out of the thicket, everybody yelling and howling at once, making powwow enough for a million. It was just like a bear-hunt, only Jim was the bear.

"There he goes!" somebody yelled, and I thought they meant me, only sure enough, there was Jim a-coming on as best he could with all them chains on. A couple of men begun to fire and load, only it's hard to hit a mark in the water, and the bullets didn't come nowheres near to Jim, but went a-whizzing past me with a funny little whispery sound that once you hear it you damn well don't ever forget.

But then a big-assed man with a broadbrim straw and a red goatee held up his hand and hollered: "Hold your fire, goddamn it! That nigger hain't wuth a Continental, dead!"

I figured the man was Mr. Phelps, because that's the way it always is. The people most anxious to shoot a nigger that ain't done just right is always the ones which ain't got any money tied up in him, whilst the man who's got an interest in that nigger, why he's more careful about the nigger's health than his own.

All this time poor Jim kept on a-humping through the water towards me, with only his head showing on account of the chains. He had that worried look a dog gets in the water, and I knew he was having trouble with all that iron on him. But I had to let up paddling because them rips on the bank seemed particularly anxious to shoot somebody, it didn't much matter who.

"You, boy!" Phelps shouted. "Stop that nigger!" He begun to jog along the top of the bank so as to keep up with me and Jim, but warn't having an easy time of it because of the brush growing there. Him and most of the others was fairly awash with sweat, and their clothes was black and limp. Some had throwed themselves down on the bank and was passing a jug around, watching another man who was running around trying to get the dogs together. But they was having such a good time scampering back and forth barking at the place where Jim had jumped off that they paid him no heed. You could see it made him mad, and when the men with the jug begun to poke fun at him and laugh, he got so riled up he hauled back and kicked one of his own hounds right off the bank into the water. It was an ornery thing to do. There ain't no harm in a hound, only sometimes they get so excited they can't hear nothing but their own barking and howling.

I says to Phelps, polite as pie:

"I'd like to help you sir, but I'm only a boy, and that nigger is a full-grown man."

"Well, bring that goddamn canoe in here and *I'll* stop him!"

"There ain't no place," I says, and that was the plain truth. The bank was so high along there that you couldn't a beached a danged scow, let alone a canoe. Just then Phelps run whack into a clump of willows and knocked off his hat. I seen then he was bald as an egg, except where there was a little turf around his ears and the back of his head. It was black, like his eyebrows, which was thick and bushy and run in a straight line across, which is always a sign of meanness, you know.

All above that line was bone white, and below was red as a turkey where he had been sun-burnt. He was glistening so with sweat it looked as though somebody had varnished him.

He says:

"Listen, boy. You see that cave-in about fifty yards down?"

A body would a had to been blind not to, so I said I did.

"Well, you head right for it, and I'll cut around and meet you there."

There warn't anything else I could do that I could see, so I said I would, and he and his men cut back from the bank, where there was less brush. Jim was getting close now, and I could hear him groan whenever he could get his head up to take in air. The rest of the time all you could see was his wool and his eyes, which was all bloody whites, bobbing back and forth. He was having to use most his strength just staying afloat. It was awful to see, but I give him as good a smile as I could work up, the sort of weakly thing you put on when somebody is in their last sickness, and you knowed it and they knowed it, but nobody will let on anybody knowed it.

I looked ahead to the caved-in place, which was getting closer all the time, and I see that the cottonwoods on that little point of land was just a bit further down, and that if Jim and me could get past that point, we'd be clear, because nobody on the bank would be able to see us through them trees.

So now I had a plan, or leastwise half a plan, and the other half come to me in a flash. It was for all the world like one of those puzzles, where all you got to do is figure out where one piece goes and all the rest simply finds their own way.

Phelps and his crew come out of the thickets just then, and I swung the bow round as if to make a run in. The old man he begun to clamber down towards

the water, half-sliding in the greasy muck. He had
his gun with him, and was holding it out with one
hand, so there was only the other free to help himself with, and being so fat and all when he was about
half-way down he fell right on his ass and slid to the
waters edge, a-cussing to beat hell as he went.

I got up and moved towards the stern end of the
canoe, like I was about to get the forrard end high
so's to beach it. But then I made as if to stumble,
letting go the paddle so it would fall in the river down-
stream and out of reach. Phelps seen it all.

"Jesus H. Christ! What did you do that fer?"

I begun to rip and carry on, and told him I couldn't
swim and would drown for sure and it was all his
fault.

"Hain't you got but one friggin' paddle?"

I shook my head, but that was a lie. The other paddle was snuggled down under the front seat, and all
the time we was getting closer to the cottonwoods.

The drift was keeping Jim in line with the canoe,
but I see he was pretty much played out. He warn't
pulling ahead any more, just struggling to keep his
head out of the water. But if he could only keep afloat
a while longer, everything would be all right. Even if
I couldn't pull him in, he could grab a-holt of the
stern, and I could clear for the Mississippi side. It
was wide down there, more'n a mile across, and there
was considerable hiding places—creeks and back-
waters and such. They wouldn't ever find us. Once it
come on dark we would strike out for the island
where the raft was hid, cut her loose, and be fifty
miles downstream before daylight. Then I could hunt
up a hammer and cold chisel somewheres, and we'd
get Jim out of them damn chains for good and all.

Old Phelps was still down in the cave-in, having one hell of a time trying to get back up on the bank, like a red ant caught in a doodle-bug hole. One of his men crept down to give him a hand, but when Phelps took holt of it, he give such a tug that the man come a-tumbling down with him. Somebody had fetched along a rope, like they always do when they go nigger hunting, and next they got it around Phelps and begun to haul him out. He warn't no lightweight, and it took considerable hauling. About the time he was reaching out for the top of the bank, some of the men noticed a steamboat coming up the channel and let out a holler, which the rest joined in with, firing off their guns and jumping up and down, making a power of noise so as to get the pilot's attention. That left only one man on the rope, so down Phelps went to the bottom, leaving the man cussing and spitting on his burned hands.

Well, the pilot seen them, and even give a couple blasts with his whistle, but he kept on a-chunking upstream, most likely figuring they was a bunch of drunks and rowdies, wanting to get on board at the sawmill landing.

By now I was nearly to the cottonwoods, but I had been spending so much time looking back that I only then see what I should a seen before, that them trees was on a sandspit built up by the water from a big creek that emptied in right there, and if I didn't buckle to my paddle right away, the current would take me where I didn't want to go. I fairly bent that paddle, and got through the wash and in towards the easy water by the bank, but when I turned around and looked for Jim, he was already fifty yeards out. Well, I'd druther not have old Phelps see me pull Jim into the canoe whilst we still had less than a gunshot betwixt us, but I didn't have any choice. Besides, the way the current come a-booming out of that creek mouth, there was a good chance we'd be pretty far out before I caught up with Jim.

Well, I laid into the paddle again, and went shooting out into the river. It warn't a minute before a ball went whizzing past and then I heard a pop from the shore, and then two or three more whistled by, and there came a popping like it was Fourth of July. The creek was still carrying me, so I just lay down in the bottom of the canoe, knowing my only chance was to stay low. A couple of bullets thunked into the wood, but it was two-inch thick cypress and I couldn't a been safer if I'd been behind a stone wall.

I could feel the canoe swing this way and that, till she worked free of the cross-currents, and then she swung south and held steady. The shooting had stopped, so I poked my head up and looked around. Phelps's sawmill was out of sight now, behind the spit with the cottonwoods, so I sat up and looked for Jim. I couldn't see him nowheres, and my heart flopped up into my mouth. Next I stood up, bracing myself with the paddle I was a-shaking so, but it warn't no use. There was nothing on that whole broad river but me, and I knowed then there warn't no sense looking further for Jim, because he was somewhere deep down under, weighted by them goddamn heavy chains.

Well, I knowed it wouldn't do no good to cry, because all the crying in the world won't bring a dead man alive, but I couldn't help blubbering a little anyhow. For Jim *was* the best cretur, and he was the only true friend I had, even though he was a nigger, and a runaway, too. I guess I didn't rightly know how much he meant to me till he was gone, and I remembered all the good times we'd had on the river, and how fine everything had been up to when them two thieving sons-a-bitches come along and ruined it all.

But now he was gone, just as if he hadn't ever been alive, not even leaving something behind to bury or mourn over, which is a nigger's worst fear, because then he's sure to come back and ha'nt the places where he was happiest, and groan and carry on so because he can't come back, never, except as a ghost, and then only at midnight when everybody is gone or asleep. If I'd knowed where Jim had sank, I would a fetched one of them nigger preachers out to pray over his remainders, but it warn't no use, because the current would carry him somewheres else, downstream, till he caught on a snag maybe. There warn't no use in doing anything, because cannon wouldn't bring him up, nor quicksilver in bread, nor prayer, nor cussing, nor crying. Jim was gone forever, down deep in that old muddy river.

I had left off crying for a spell, and was just lying in the bottom of the canoe thinking these thoughts, when blump! she runs into some willows hanging down from a bank, and a little shower of tiny leaves come tickling down over me. I sat up then and pulled the canoe in under the willows where there was a kind of cave, cool and dark, and I laid back down and tried to think of what I should do next, but it warn't no good. Nothing would come.

It warn't only that I felt low-down and miserable because Jim was dead, that warn't the half of it. Because my conscience begun to work on me, and told me it was all my fault that Jim was dead, and if I had only listened to it before, and done what it said to do, he'd still be alive. It warn't no good blaming the King and the Duke, because they was sent by Providence to trouble us so we'd do right, along with the snakeskin, and the fog, and the rest. For that's always His way, to toss evil in a man's path so he'll do good, and if a body don't pay heed to a little nudge, why Providence'll kick him ass over teakettle next trip around. It's His way, every time.

First He sets your conscience a-picking at you, and if that don't do it, He'll send you a little misery, like a blister, maybe, or a hole in your pocket so you lose something you're particular fond of, or snarl your trot-lines, and if you still don't mend your ways, He'll knock you all kersmash. A body can put up with a talky conscience, but once Providence has it in for him, goodbye! After that, you ain't got no show at all, and only a mullet-head like me will try his luck and stay in the game for another hand. Providence was in it from the very start, and there warn't a damned thing we could a done about it. I suppose I should a been grateful to Him for drownding poor Jim instead of me, but I warn't. It was ornery and wicked, and I knowed it, but I didn't even try. That's how bad I felt, right down to the soles of my feet.

All around it was still and Sunday-like, with everything hot and gray. Gray sky, gray water, everything seemed to have had the color squoze right out of it. The air was full of them kind of faint dronings of bugs and flies that make it seem so lonesome and like everybody's dead and gone, like the sound a spinning-wheel makes, wailing along up and sinking along down again; and that *is* the lonesomest sound in the whole world. When a breeze would come along and quiver the willow leaves it made me feel mournful, because it was like spirits whispering — spirits that's been dead ever so many years, or them that's just died. It made me wish I was dead too, and done with it all, and pretty soon I started in blubbering again, and I kept it up off and on until I fell asleep.

Next thing I knowed I woke up with a start, and there was a boom-booming outside on the river like they had got cannon out to raise Jim, but it warn't, it was the storm coming on. The wind swished through the willows something fierce, and I pulled back in as far as I could go. The river was all whitecaps in a flash, foam a-blowing in a line straight as any ruler could make, and then there come a monstrous clap of thunder overhead, and another, and the lighting split everything wide open. The rain come then. It beat down like hailstones, and steam rose up from the river so you couldn't see a thing, just a solid damn sheet of white. The water come trickling through the willows, so I unrolled my blanket and covered up, lying there and listening to the thunder and the swoosh of the rain until I went asleep again. I dreamt then, bad dreams, but I won't tell you what they was about. I already told you.

XXXII

Nothing more to write

When I waked up again it was dark night, and the rain had stopped. Leastwise it had stopped outside, but it kept a-dripping down around me through the willows. My blanket was soaked, and my clothes, and the skeeters had sat down on me for dinner, so I figured I might as well get moving once again, and pushed out from under the willows. It took me an hour or two, but I found the little island where I had the raft hid, and clumb aboard. I didn't stay long. I tossed what I wanted into a sack and put it and the gun into the canoe, and the rest I left for anybody that wanted it. Just before I shoved off, I took a last look around to make sure I hadn't forgot anything, and the sight of that lonely raft, all shadows and emptiness, sent a dern lump into my throat like somebody had hit me there. I got into the canoe and never once looked back.

I scrummaged a meal out of some scraps and then I lay down in the canoe with my pipe and thought over what I was to do next. Money warn't no problem, because I still had that yaller boy left in my pocket, and the canoe was worth ten dollars any day. I thought maybe I would go on down to Orleans and ship as a cabin boy on one of the big riverboats. Or maybe head out for the Territory all by myself. I didn't give much of a damn either way. When there's nothing you want to do, or got to do, why you can do anything, but there ain't much joy in it.

Tom Sawyer, now, I knew he'd give his right arm to be me, and to be able to come back to St. Petersburg from the dead, and have Aunt Polly and Becky Thatcher a-weeping over him and maybe have a big parade up to the jail and then a showy trial before they took him out with a brass band to hang him for helping a nigger escape instead of being killed by that nigger and properly dead. Oh, Tom could do it up bully, but somehow I didn't much cotton to the idea. Besides, most likely pap would get a-holt of me again, or even worse the widow, who'd start in sivilizing me all over again, and I couldn't a stood it. I been there before.

It was monstrous quiet out on the river that time of night, and somewheres far off there was a church bell ringing, but you couldn't hear all the strikes, only a slow *bung . . . bung . . .* and then the next one would drift away before it was finished and there would be nothing for what should been a couple of strikes, and then you could hear *bung . . . bung,* again, and then nothing. At that time of night all the sounds are late sounds, and the air has a late feel, and a late smell, too. All around you can hear the river, sighing and gurgling and groaning like a hundred drownding men, and laying there in that awful dark, I could hear the river terrible clear, and it seemed to me like I was floating in a damn grave yard.

Being out there all alone at that time of night is the lonesomest a body can be. The stars seem miles and miles away, like the lights of houses in a valley when somebody stops on a hill to look back before going on down the road, leaving them all behind forever; and my soul sucked up whatever spark of brashness and gayness I had managed to strike up since that afternoon, and then all the miserableness come back, worse than ever before. But dark as it was and lonesome as it was, I didn't have no wish for daylight to come. In fact, I didn't much care if the goddamn sun never come up again.

THE END